THE CRITIC JULIE MOFFETT!

A DOUBLE-EDGED BLADE

"Ms. Moffett has written an enjoyable tale of treachery, betrayal, mystery and passion....*A Double-Edged Blade* is an adventurous read."

—*Romantic Times*

"An amazing tale of time travel, history and romance emerges from the pages of this captivating and exceptional novel."

—*Rendezvous*

"Author Julie Moffett has mixed a sharp-tongued, strong-willed, love-hungry heroine with a dynamic, sympathetic, humorous, and physically attractive hero to create a spellbinding romantic adventure."

—*Gothic Journal*

THE THORN & THE THISTLE

"Ms. Moffett's lyrical prose can almost be heard by the reader. Few authors can use dialect so skillfully in their stories while retaining the smooth flow of the writing of the story. Ms. Moffett accomplishes both in a tension-filled, heartfelt romance of honor and betrayal."

—*Romantic Times*

FLEETING SPLENDOR

"Julie Moffett writes spirited, well-crafted historical romances that truly satisfy the reader."

—*Romantic Times*

A TOUCH OF FIRE

"A very enjoyable read! The well-paced book dwells with a different time frame and place in European history not covered by the majority of romances. A definite keeper."

—*The Paperback Forum*

A PROMISE TO KEEP

"You don't know the first thing about me."

Ian straightened, crossing his thick arms casually against his chest. "Aye, but sometimes it takes but a moment for two people to know they are right for each other."

Fiona flushed bright red and hated herself for it. "You bloody well flatter yourself, Scotsman, if you are referring to me and you. I don't even like you."

"Ye dinna like me? Then mayhap those weren't your verra soft lips brushing my cheek. And certainly those weren't your arms winding their way around my neck."

"Maybe I was thinking about strangling you."

He laughed, his teeth flashing white. "Or mayhap ye canna resist my Scots' charm."

"God save me from arrogant men," Fiona snapped, rolling her eyes. Lifting her skirts haughtily, she started up the embankment away from him. Without warning, he grabbed her arm from behind. With one hard pull, he drew her to him, holding her tight against his chest.

"Ye were right when ye said I dinna know much abut ye, Fiona Chancellor," he said, his face inches from hers. "But when we finally are together, 'twill be on my terms, no' yours."

Fiona clenched her teeth together. "There won't be any 'together.' I'm here to help my cousin and that's all, Mister Maclaren."

"The name's Ian," he said with an infuriatingly calm smile. "And we will be together, lass, ye can mark my words on it."

Fiona's pulse skyrocketed. His words held a promise that she knew he would keep—and God help her, she *wanted* him to keep.

Other books by Julie Moffett:
A DOUBLE-EDGED BLADE
THE THORN & THE THISTLE
FLEETING SPLENDOR
A TOUCH OF FIRE

Across a
Moonswept
Moor

Julie Moffett
Across a
Moonswept
Moor

Montlake
Romance

Text copyright © 2001 by Julie Moffett

Published by Montlake Romance
P.O. Box 400818
Las Vegas, NV 89140

ISBN-13: 9781477841501
ISBN-10: 1477841504

This book is for you, ladies....

Kit Greening
Cathy Vida
Martha Tarpenning Yates
Merrie Margolin Kippur
Maria Kieslich
Laura Demas Petrosian
Jolka Karbarz
Diane Bennett

Because some friends come and go,
and others stay in your heart forever.
Sisters, for always.

Separation between past, present and future is only an illusion, however tenacious.

—Albert Einstein

Chapter One

County Tyrone
Northern Ireland
September 1997

A good Irish storm was brewing.

Wind blew deceptively soft across the autumn-bare hedgerows when the sky abruptly darkened and the wind began to howl like a banshee freed from a lifetime of confinement.

Glancing up at the clouds worriedly, Fiona Chancellor slid her petite form out of the rented sports car, slamming the door behind her. Her stylish tan raincoat whipped about bare legs as she held tight to a silk scarf that repeatedly threatened to fly from her dark head.

She stared ahead to a quaint old cottage painted white with blue shutters and sheltered by several ancient trees in the front yard. To one side, a small fenced garden lay fallow and the windowsill flower boxes were empty.

Digging into her pocketbook with a free hand, Fiona pulled out a fluttering scrap of paper, comparing the address on it to a small hand-painted wooden sign swinging wildly back and forth on a lamppost.

ANTIQUITIES AND CURIOSITIES, it read.

Still hanging on tightly to her scarf, she stuffed the paper back into her bag and scurried to the front door. She lifted the heavy brass knocker and brought it down several times on the weather-beaten wood.

When no answer was forthcoming, she grasped the doorknob and turned it. The door swung open with a loud creak.

"Hallo?" Fiona called out, cautiously stepping into the entranceway. "Is anyone here?"

The shop itself was dark, with just a little light filtering in through the windows. She peered into the dimness, seeing shadowed and cluttered silhouettes of what appeared to be numerous pieces of furniture.

"Are you open?" she called again, walking farther into the room. A gust of wind from the open door blew the scarf off her head, but she managed to catch it by one corner.

"Blast this horrid weather," she muttered, shaking out the scarf and stuffing it into her coat pocket.

The door banged shut behind her unexpectedly, causing her to start. Feeling foolish, Fiona turned around to reach for the knob when she felt a tap on her back. She shrieked in surprise, whirling around. In the dim light, she could make out the figure of a short, stumpy man.

"Och, I didn't mean to frighten ye, lass," the man

said in a thick Irish brogue. " 'Tis just that I didn't expect any customers on a blustery day like this."

Fiona took a deep breath, urging her heart to return to a more normal cadence. "The door was open," she said, her voice trembling slightly. "And I thought since it's only half past three, there would be someone here." She was babbling now and forced herself to stop.

There was a marked silence, and then she heard his shuffling footsteps. After a moment, she saw the soft glow of a lantern coming from a nearby table. He seated himself and said quietly, "Ye are English."

It wasn't a question, but a statement. Fiona cleared her throat uncomfortably. "Well, yes."

"What brings the English to Gogarty's Antiques?"

"Are you the owner?"

"I'm Seamus Gogarty. What can I do for ye?"

Fiona moved toward the table and looked at him closely in the light. Her first impression of his size had been correct—he was a dwarf, aged somewhere from fifty to seventy-five years old. He was dressed in a thick wool fisherman's sweater and sat upon a small wooden stool, his short, stocky legs dangling several inches from the floor.

He had pure white hair and a matching goatee, which Fiona thought quite strange but somehow fitting to him. His face had chiseled and distinguished features, and his eyes were curious and intelligent.

"Well, lass?" he prompted again. His small hands cupped the base of the lantern, and she blinked when he angled it toward her face. "What would you like to see?"

"It's more what I want *you* to see," Fiona replied, reaching into her pocketbook and pulling out a cloth-

Julie Moffett

wrapped object. Setting it on the table, she carefully unwound the material from it. Gingerly, she held up an antique dagger, the light of the lantern glinting off its double-edged blade.

"Have you ever seen anything like this before?" she asked him, holding out the dagger.

The dwarf gasped in surprise, reaching out to take it. "Where did ye get this?" he asked, turning it over in his hands.

"It belonged to my cousin. Do you know what it is?"

"I think so. But I've only seen it in pictures."

Fiona exhaled the breath she had been holding in one big rush. "I'll be damned. It appears those bloody expensive experts I consulted were right after all."

"Experts?" Seamus inquired, raising his head to look at her.

"Yes, I consulted several experts about the origin of this dagger. All of them placed it here in Northern Ireland, in this county. I've been to every antique shop within fifty kilometers of here. I'd almost given up hope, you know. Your shop was the last place I was going to try before returning home to London."

He looked mildly surprised. "The dagger was in London, ye say?"

"Yes. My cousin was a collector with a fondness for antique weaponry. But she...ah...disappeared more than a year ago. I thought perhaps this dagger might hold some clues to her whereabouts."

"Hmmm," the dwarf murmured noncommittally.

Fiona sighed. "Look, is this dagger supposed to be evil or something? I'd appreciate knowing that up front."

He smiled, and Fiona noticed how perfectly white

and straight his teeth were. "I didn't know the *Sassen-ach* were a superstitious lot."

Fiona leaned forward on the table and lowered her voice even though there were no other people in the store. "Normally I'm not. But there is something odd about this dagger. Before my cousin disappeared, she showed it to me. There was an inscription on the blade that was unreadable—we both agreed on that. But about a year after my cousin disappeared, I happened to come upon the dagger again. This time I could read the inscription. And it was a message familiar to me."

The last words came out in a rush, and Fiona held her breath, waiting for the laughter, the snicker or general look of disbelief she was sure would come. But Seamus didn't laugh or shake his head as the others had done. Instead, he sat quietly, staring at the dagger. Fiona felt an enormous sweep of relief. For once, as outlandish as her story was, at least someone was giving it a chance and not showing her to the door.

She paused, clearing her throat. "If you would bear with me, I would like to elaborate a bit further. The inscription that appeared on the blade after my cousin disappeared is part of a phrase the two of us used to recite to each other as children. Yet the antiques experts I consulted in London unanimously agreed that the inscription was carved in the seventeenth century. Do you think it might be an elaborate hoax of some kind?"

Fiona felt the heat rush to her cheeks in embarrassment. It sounded absurd even to her own ears. Why in the world would someone go to such bizarre lengths to play a hoax on her? She was a nobody.

Seamus said nothing at first, gazing at her pensively before speaking. "The experts are certain the inscription can be dated to the seventeenth century?" he finally asked.

Fiona nodded. "They each independently confirmed it. I truly don't know how it's possible, but it seems to be the consensus. I know they thought I was some kind of loon, insisting the phrase was familiar to me. Frankly, I don't blame them. It does sound insane."

Seamus looked down at the dagger and angled the blade toward the light.

"*Sisters*," he murmured, reading the inscription and then turning the dagger over. "*For always*. This is the saying?"

Fiona nodded. "Actually, it's part of a poem we recited to each other."

> "My sister for always,
> Naught can us part.
> My sister forever,
> One bond to one heart."

Seamus frowned and thoughtfully set aside the dagger. Grasping the lantern by the handle, he hopped to the floor and made his way around several pieces of furniture until he came to a large bookshelf. Fiona watched with interest as he searched for a particular volume and then heard him grunt when he found it and lifted it down.

Making his way back to the table, he placed a large leather-bound book on the table with a thump. A cloud of dust rose from the volume and Fiona coughed, turning her head.

"Sorry," Seamus mumbled, opening the book and flipping through the pages. "Pull up a chair, lass," he said. "It may be a while."

Moving off a few feet, Fiona groped in the dim light for a chair, finally locating one and pulling it over to the table. She removed her raincoat and placed it neatly over the back before she sat down.

It had started to rain heavily. The wind howled ferociously, water slashing angrily against the outside walls of the house.

Folding her hands in her lap, Fiona studied the queer little man as he diligently turned the pages of the large book and murmured to himself. She hoped he knew what he was talking about and wasn't just leading her down another blind path. She didn't know if her heart could take much more disappointment.

Fiona had done everything in her power to discover what had happened to her cousin, but she had precious little information to go on. Other than the dagger, which was likely leading her on a wild-goose chase, Fiona knew only that her cousin Faith had disappeared while on a top-secret mission for the British government in Northern Ireland. The investigation—which lasted about a year—had turned up nothing. Officially, Faith was presumed dead.

But unwilling to give up, Fiona had followed the dagger here, to this godforsaken town in rural Northern Ireland, where she was now conversing with an odd antiques dealer who apparently didn't pay his electricity bill.

She crossed her legs and smoothed down her skirt, willing herself not to despair. Maybe this man would give her a lead, reveal a clue, revitalize a search that for two months had gone absolutely nowhere. He was her last, best hope.

Suddenly Seamus let out a small cry and abruptly pushed the book across the table toward her.

Startled, Fiona looked down at the page and gasped aloud. On the yellowed, fragile page was a near perfect drawing of the double-edged dagger in her possession.

"That's it," she exclaimed excitedly. "Other than the missing jewels in the hilt and the strange bend at the tip of the blade, this appears to be the exact same dagger."

Seamus nodded. "Aye, 'tis as I suspected. But this dagger hasn't been seen for centuries. There's quite a legend surrounding it."

Fiona looked at him with interest. "Legend? Not a curse, I hope."

He chuckled. "No curse that I know of. But see this small flaw on the blade, near the hilt?" he commented, sliding the lantern closer to her.

Fiona picked up the dagger and held it up to the light. "Yes, my cousin pointed that out to me as well. She said it was what made the dagger unique."

"She was right. 'Twas only one double-edged dagger made in this style that had such a flaw. The O'Bruaidar dagger."

"The O'Bruaidar dagger?" Fiona said, puzzled.

"The O'Bruaidars were a noble Irish family that lived in this region for centuries. In fact, my family served them for many years. As I remember the legend, the double-edged dagger belonged to the women of the family and was passed down among them for several generations. The dagger is said to be enchanted."

"Enchanted?" Fiona repeated in surprise, looking doubtfully at the dagger. "This old piece of metal?"

Seamus stroked his white goatee, his eyes taking on a dreamy, faraway look. "Aye. The legend has been told many a time in my family. It all began when Isabel, the youngest daughter of the king of the fey folk, fell in love with Kieran O'Bruaidar. Now, Isabel happened to come upon Kieran one fine summer day when he was swimming in the lough. She thought him so handsome, so magnificent, that she fell in love with him at once. And because her love was so great, she forsook her magic heritage to become mortal and live with him."

"Ha," Fiona muttered bitterly. "Why is it always the woman who has to give up something for the man?"

"Pardon?"

Fiona sighed. "Never mind. Please continue."

Seamus leaned forward, resting his elbows on the table. "Understandably, the fey folk, and especially the king, were greatly sorrowed by their loss," he resumed. "So the fairies decided to fashion a blade offering her a wee bit o' magic for defense, now that she was mortal. To make it unique and instantly recognizable, they made the small flaw in the blade. The magic is said to have been passed down to all the O'Bruaidar women who owned it."

Fiona shifted restlessly in her chair. "Well, Mr. Gogarty, that's a delightful tale, quite romantic actually, but what does that have to do with the inscription on the blade and the disappearance of my cousin?"

Seamus leaned over the book, running a stubby finger along the blade in the drawing. "The dagger disappeared when the O'Bruaidar family line ended. The last living male heir, Miles O'Bruaidar, was beheaded at the city of Cavan, along with eleven other Irish rebels during the invasion of Englishman Oliver Cromwell in the mid-seventeenth century. He left no children and had no siblings."

Fiona shuddered. "How dreadful."

"Aye, 'twas a great tragedy. The heritage of a noble Irish family ended with the stroke of a sword. Castle Dun na Moor, the O'Bruaidar residence, was burned to the ground. Today the site is naught more than grazing land for sheep. The dagger was presumed destroyed or looted by the English."

"I suppose that could explain the dagger's appearance in England," Fiona replied. "But when you said the dagger was enchanted, what exactly did you mean?"

"According to the legend, the dagger is presumed to have magical powers."

"What kind of magical powers are we talking about?"

Seamus shrugged. "I canno' say exactly. But I do know that the magic is supposedly enhanced when in the presence of a holy site at midnight."

"Holy site? You mean like a church?"

"I mean Druid holy ground."

Fiona blinked. "Stonehenge or something like that?"

"Aye, something like that."

Fiona rubbed her fingers between her brow. "Well, magic or no, I still don't understand how this inscription, dated to the seventeenth century, appeared on this blade. I'm certain it wasn't there the first time I looked at it."

"At your cousin's flat in London?"

"Yes. She was very proud of the dagger and spent a great deal of time explaining every detail about it to me. There was no readable inscription on that dagger just one year ago. I'm positive."

"Ye say your cousin disappeared here in Ireland?"

"I think so," Fiona said uncertainly.

"Ye don't know for certain?"

Fiona scowled. "Unfortunately, no. She...ah... worked for the government, and they refused to give me many details about her whereabouts the night of her disappearance. You know, protecting national security and other such rubbish."

Seamus nodded in sympathy, and Fiona pressed her lips together tightly. The government's secrecy rankled her no end. She simply could not understand why they couldn't be more forthcoming with information. After all, Faith had been missing for more than a year. For God's sake, her cousin was a British citizen, risking life and limb for queen and country, and this was how she was repaid—with apathy and inaction?

Seamus slid the dagger across the table toward her. "I'm sorry, lass, but I can't help ye further. That's all I know about the dagger. But there is a small library in the town of Omagh that might have more information on the O'Bruaidars. Mayhap that would help ye in your quest. They are open 'til half past five today."

Fiona picked up the dagger and began rolling it in the cloth. "I just may do that. But I'll confess that I'm about out of hope. Despite learning more about this mysterious dagger, I feel no closer to discovering what really happened to my cousin."

Seamus reached out and patted her gently on the hand. "Just remember, lass, since ye now own the dagger, if there is any enchantment to it, mayhap it will work for ye."

Fiona put the dagger in her pocketbook. "I truly appreciate you taking the time to talk with me, Mr. Gogarty. I really don't know what I expected to hear. All this talk of magic and legends has me feeling a bit foolish."

She pulled out a collapsible umbrella. By the sound of the rain, it was still pouring. Seamus gallantly held up her raincoat, and Fiona bent down so that he could help her slip it on.

"By the way," she said, reaching for her scarf and tying it firmly under her chin, "you mentioned earlier that the O'Bruaidar castle is now a sheep pasture. Weather permitting, I thought I might drive by and take a look at the area. Can you tell me where the castle was once located?"

Seamus nodded. "Of course. The O'Bruaidar castle once sat proudly atop the small rise just beyond the Beaghmore Stone Circles. 'Tis no' far from here."

"Beaghmore Stone Circles?"

"Aye, one of our most popular tourist sites."

Fiona started in surprise. "Stone circles—as in Druid stone circles?"

He smiled slightly, a strange twinkle in his eye. "Aye. But I thought ye considered Druid magic and legends naught more than foolishness."

She shrugged. "Oh, I suppose it wouldn't hurt to take a quick look at those circles as well. I've already planned to stay in Cookstown for the night and have nothing else planned for the rest of the day. Thank you again, Mr. Gogarty. You've been very helpful."

Seamus took her hand, shaking it firmly. "May the luck o' the Irish be with ye, lass."

Fiona nodded wryly. "Believe me, I need all the luck I can get."

Chapter Two

Ireland
September 1649

Ian Maclaren hated traveling in the rain.

Especially an Irish rain. The rain was cold and hard, and it slashed in relentless torrents against his large frame and unprotected face, blurring his vision and rendering him thoroughly wet and irritable.

Rain in his native Scotland was much more agreeable and of a softer, sweeter nature. Even in its fury, it was far more tolerable to a man.

But choice was a luxury no longer available to him—neither in regard to his presence in Ireland nor this sudden journey to the castle of his best friend, Irish rebel leader Miles O'Bruaidar.

It was a most difficult time in Ireland. The British troops under the command of Englishman Oliver

Cromwell had been ravaging and plundering Ireland for more than a year. Ian had come to Ireland to aid the Irish resistance once the Scots had failed in their own battle against Cromwell's army.

"Curse the English that they have brought us to this," he muttered under his breath, taking a swipe at his dripping brow. He was tired and hungry, having been on a horse for most of the day and now into the wee hours of the night. He still had at least an hour or more until he reached the castle, and his pace had slowed because of the weather, the darkness, and his traveling companion.

Ian turned around on his horse, carefully lifting the covered lantern he held in one hand, and prayed that the rain would not penetrate the cover and extinguish their only light.

"Father Michael," he called over his shoulder. "Are ye all right back there?"

"Bless my soul, I'm drenched yet still alive," came the weak reply. "Keep on, Ian, for I know we must make haste."

Ian nodded, pushing back a lock of his dripping hair from his brow and urging his horse forward. It was a dangerous trek they were undertaking—riding to the O'Bruaidar castle in the dead of night. If British soldiers caught them, it was unlikely that a Scotsman and a Catholic priest would be dealt much mercy.

But Ian had to go. Miles was in trouble and he needed help. More than that, Ireland needed help. Miles wasn't just a friend; he was the legendary Irish Lion—his true identity a secret to all but a few—and one of the primary leaders of the Irish resistance to Cromwell.

Besides, Ian was partly to blame for Miles being in

trouble in the first place. The two had been close since childhood, their families bound together by politics, religion and friendship. Both the Maclarens and O'Bruaidars had long belonged to a secret Catholic organization committed to keeping the English out of Scotland and Ireland. When Cromwell began his war with Scotland, Ian had been personally sent to Ireland to enlist Miles's aid in the fight.

But now that Cromwell had dealt a punishing defeat to the Scots and was well on his way to conquering Ireland, Miles's death would be a horrible blow to the resistance. And it was something Ian would do his damnedest to prevent.

Ian frowned, remembering the message sent by Miles's wife, Faith, and relayed by the priest.

The English have captured Miles. We believe he's still alive, but he'll certainly be executed soon. Help us, please.

Ian had quickly gathered provisions and dragged the poor priest back out for another day's journey. He knew that Faith had sent the priest because she trusted him, and trust was a precious commodity these days. In times of war, a misplaced comment or a single word could cost a man his life. One could not be too be careful.

Ian peered ahead in concentration as he guided his horse across some particularly rocky terrain. Thankfully the rain had eased to a steady drizzle, but the path was still treacherous. He tried to keep an even pace so as not to tire the priest too much, but he was impatient to get to the castle. He knew full well that as each minute passed, so lessened the hope for a successful rescue mission.

It was nearly two hours later that the impressive profile of Castle Dun na Moor came into view. Sitting on top of a small hill, the stone walls of the enormous castle loomed steeply. Two formidable towers stretched to the darkened sky and beckoning lights flickered in several of the windows.

Heartened by the familiar sight, Ian urged his mount to a gallop and raced into the courtyard. He was met by a young stable boy. Quickly, Ian tossed him the reins and dismounted. He strode toward the castle, entering the structure just as the priest rode into the courtyard behind him.

"Ian, bless the saints that ye are here," he heard a voice cry and saw Patrick O'Farrell, Miles's young cousin, come running toward him.

The youth flung himself into his arms, and Ian affectionately patted the boy's fair head. It was a difficult time for the lad. Patrick was just fourteen; no longer a boy, yet not quite a man. Ian knew that in Miles's absence, Patrick had been forced to shoulder more responsibilities than were fair for a lad his age.

"Where's Faith?" Ian asked, removing his sodden cape and handing it to the boy.

"She's waiting for ye in the library," Patrick replied anxiously. "Make haste, for I fear she's made herself ill wi' worry."

Ian pushed past the boy, striding down the corridor until he reached a large oak door. It was ajar, so he knocked softly.

"Ian, by God, is that you?"

The clipped feminine English accent made Ian wonder, as it had a hundred times before, how ironic fate was to have matched a passionate Irish rebel with a woman from enemy territory. Miles had at first believed her to be an English spy. But instead, Faith had turned out to be Miles's strongest ally and eventually his wife.

She was a remarkable woman—strong, intelligent, and beautiful. Christ, how many times had he told himself that he would have gladly wed her himself had Miles not found her first?

Yet he had never before seen a couple so in love and so perfectly matched for each other. He hated to admit it to himself, a man who had avoided marriage as long as he, but he was truly envious of what they shared.

Sighing, Ian pushed open the door and crossed the threshold. He had little time for such reflection. Better to face the bad news now and determine what, if anything, he could do to help.

"Ian, thank God you are here," Faith said softly when she saw him.

She stood alone near the hearth, a white woolen shawl draped across her shoulders. Her pale hair hung loosely about her shoulders and her normally bright blue eyes were tinged red and swollen. She had been weeping.

He walked across the room and took her hands into his own, squeezing gently. They were freezing cold.

"Ye are unwell," he observed.

"Just tired and worried," she replied, her voice trembling slightly. "Thank you for coming."

"Ye knew I would," he answered simply.

"Yes, I knew," she said, managing a grateful smile. Ian felt a twinge of admiration at the way she refused to collapse under the weight of her concern.

"Come," she said, leading him to a chair near the fire. "You are drenched, exhausted, and most certainly famished. Sit down and warm yourself by the fire. I'll see that Molly prepares you something to eat."

Ian nodded, lowering his large frame into the chair and holding out his hands to the fire. Faith disappeared for a few minutes, and by the time she returned, Ian felt almost human again.

"We must talk, Faith," Ian said quietly. "We dinna have much time. What do ye know o' Miles's capture?"

Faith clasped her hands together in front of her. "Only what Furlong told me."

"Furlong?" Ian exclaimed in surprise, imagining the weathered face of Miles's trusted scout and friend. "He was no' captured wi' the others?"

"He was no'," came a reply from the doorway.

Ian quickly shifted around in the chair. "Furlong!" he exclaimed when he saw the hawk-nosed man standing in the doorway. A thick sling cradled the stocky man's right arm, and he was sporting several bruises on his face, including two rather nasty black eyes.

"Blessed Christ," Ian said in concern, rising from his chair. "What happened to ye?"

"The English," Furlong replied simply. "Miles got orders to come to the aid o' the town o' Dundrum. We kept the Roundheads out for three days. But the bastards got reinforcements. Broke through our defense three nights ago and took the town."

"Miles was captured?"

"Aye," Furlong said flatly. "Along wi' most o' our men. I managed to escape with two others, although I was badly beaten first. We made our way back here two nights ago."

"Do ye think Miles is still in Dundrum?" Ian asked.

Furlong shook his head, tugging uneasily on the

greasy cap that sat upon his head. "I doubt it. The town was destroyed and the troops were readying to move on. But I canno' say where they might have taken him."

Father Michael walked into the room and Faith strode across to grasp his hands gratefully. "Thank you, Father," she said softly.

The priest dipped his head slightly. "We came as quickly as we could."

Ian exhaled a deep breath, raking his fingers through his damp hair. "A pox on the English. God only knows where they will have taken Miles by now."

"We have to find him," Faith interjected fiercely. "We can't give up."

Furlong shifted uneasily on his feet. " 'Twill be a near impossible task. Even if Miles still lives, he could be anywhere in Ireland by now. And I promise ye, he'll no' live for long, or at least he will no' want to, after what the English will do to him."

Ian frowned, knowing exactly to what he was referring. Torture. Brutal, horrible torture. Certainly made worse if the English ever discovered he was the legendary Irish rebel leader.

"But they wouldn't kill him outright," Faith argued. "Even if they don't uncover his true identity—just the fact that he was the leader of the resistance in Dundrum makes him too valuable a prisoner to kill immediately. He'd have information they would want."

Furlong stiffened. "He'd tell them naught."

"Of course not," Faith replied. "But they'll certainly try to get him to tell. And that would take time. Time we can use."

"To do what?" Furlong asked.

"Rescue him."

"Rescue him?" the men exclaimed in surprised unison.

"How can we rescue him if we don't even know where to begin looking for him?" Father Michael asked.

"We'll have to figure out something," Faith replied firmly. "Speculate on his location, if we must. But I will not just sit here and do nothing. Will you help us, Ian?"

Ian rubbed his bearded jaw thoughtfully. "As futile as it may be, ye know that I will do all I can. But 'twill be a very dangerous undertaking, indeed."

"I will help, Ian," Father Michael declared bravely.

"As will I," Furlong added.

Faith stepped forward, putting her hand lightly on his shoulder. "You'll have all the resources of Castle Dun na Moor at your disposal," she said, her jaw set determinedly. "We are going to find him and bring him home safely."

Ian stood, nodding grimly. "Either that or we shall die trying. Well, now that's been decided, let's put our heads together and figure out where to start looking for him."

Chapter Three

Beaghmore Stone Circles
Northern Ireland

Fiona had no idea what she was doing, creeping around old, damp stones in the middle of the night, armed with nothing more than a pocketbook and her torch.

This was not like her at all. She abhorred adventure, disliked getting dirty, despaired when she broke a nail, and absolutely hated having wet feet. So what in the bloody hell was she doing out here on a night like this?

Pulling her jacket tighter around her shoulders, she wondered if she truly had lost the last vestiges of her sanity. After talking with the odd antiques dealer, she had spent the rest of the afternoon huddled in the small library at Omagh, reading about the history of the O'Bruaidar family. Then, as dusk fell, she wandered about the sheep pasture, curiously looking for remnants of the family's long-destroyed castle. Later, she tried to indulge herself with a hot bath and a glass of excellent Irish wine in her room at the cozy bed-and-breakfast in nearby Cookstown. But her thoughts kept returning to Seamus Gogarty and his mysterious tale about the double-edged dagger.

"According to legend, the dagger is presumed to have magical powers. This magic is supposedly enhanced when

in the presence of a holy site near midnight."

Suddenly Fiona Chancellor, the most sensible woman in all of England, was seized by some bizarre impulse to investigate the Beaghmore Stone Circles in the dead of night.

Daft, indeed.

Well, here she was now, so she'd better get on with it. At least it was no longer raining.

She flicked on the torch, shining its beam across the stones. Carefully, she took a step forward, groaning when her boots sank into the mud, the brown gunk reaching all the way up to the cuffs of her expensive jeans. She distastefully shook one leg, grimacing as a chunk of mud flew off, landing a few feet away.

"Disgusting," she muttered. She'd need at least an hour in a scalding hot bath and a fresh pedicure after this misbegotten excursion.

Fiona paused, leaning against one of the thigh-high stones to take better stock of her surroundings. Despite her initial tendency to discount such things as druids and fairies, she had to admit, it was a rather supernatural sight heightened by the sweep of her torch.

A tiny pathway led from the carpark up to the

Beaghmore Stone Circles in a straight east-southeast line. The configuration itself consisted of seven stone circles in all, six of them situated in pairs, with diameters ranging from thirty to seventy-five feet.

The seventh circle clearly stood apart from the others, and Fiona recognized it immediately as the "Dragon's Teeth" configuration. She had read about it earlier in the library and been intrigued by the nickname.

She swept the beam over the stones and shivered, seeing how the cluster had come by the description. It certainly looked like the teeth of a dragon with its mouth wide open. Sharp, jagged rocks were stabbed into the ground within the circle and pointed upward to the sky.

Crikey, she could almost hear it growling. Or snarling. Or whatever noise it was dragons were supposed to make.

She shuddered, unzipping her pocketbook and pulling out a bar of chocolate. Quickly she unwrapped it and took a huge bite. She immediately felt her anxiety lessen.

"My name is Fiona Chancellor and I'm a chocoholic," she murmured between chews. "Damn, I'm so bloody witty, I slay myself." She took another bite for luck and then stuffed what was left into her bag. Then, taking a deep breath, she stepped into the Dragon's Teeth. Holding the torch under her chin, she lifted the double-edged dagger from her bag and slowly unwound the cloth from it.

Her hand trembled as she examined it under the beam of the torch. It looked the same as it always had—the blade glinting dully in the dim light. She turned it over and sighed in disappointment when she

saw no evidence of enchantment, magic, or anything
even remotely extraordinary.

"You're absolutely loony, Fiona," she chided herself
aloud, winding the cloth about the dagger and sticking it back in her purse. "Mad as a hatter. A boil-
brained twit. It's time to be a good girl and go home."

As she turned to head back to the carpark, she heard
an odd crackling noise from behind her.

Gasping, she whirled around, holding the torch in
front of her as if it were some kind of weapon. The
artificial light illuminated nothing, but the crackling
sound continued and seemed to be getting louder.
Fiona imagined the sound to be like a static electricity
charge, and it seemed to be all around her now.

"What the devil?" she murmured half in curiosity,
half in mounting terror.

A faint humming noise filled the air. "Who's there?"
Fiona cried out, swinging the torch about wildly. She
saw nothing out of the ordinary, but nevertheless
thought it only prudent to get the bloody hell out of
the place.

She took a step backward, brushing her leg against
one of the Dragon Teeth stone markers. She screamed
in surprise as a searing, burning pain shot through her
leg. Leaping aside, she swung the beam at the offend-
ing marker. Her mouth dropped open in shock when
she saw that the marker, as well as those around it,
were now glowing red.

Letting out a frightened cry, she dropped the torch
and it went out, leaving her surrounded only by the
eerie red lights. Terrified, she stumbled backward and
slipped in the mud. As she went down on one knee,
her pocketbook slid from her shoulder and fell open,
spilling its contents onto the ground. Whimpering in

fear, Fiona frantically began groping about the muck for her car keys.

Just as her fingers closed around something hard, she felt a wave of nausea slam into her. She gagged and then began crawling on all fours, sobbing openly now. She lifted her head just as a bright flash of light exploded in front of her. Screaming, she pitched forward, expecting to land face-first into the muddy ground. Instead, she felt as if she were falling from a great height, her body spinning downward and out of control.

A loud, horrible humming noise buzzed in her ears, and she could feel the wind rushing past at great speed. Her voice seemed locked in her throat and her eyes were squeezed tightly shut.

Then, as abruptly as it had begun, the motion stopped. Her stomach lurched crazily as she hung motionless in some sort of bizarre suspension. She could neither see nor hear but sensed impending doom pressing down upon her.

"Noooooo," she managed to scream before the ground rushed up to meet her and the whole world went black.

Ireland, 1649

Ian paced restlessly back and forth in front of a blazing fire in the library. Although barefoot, he hardly noticed the cold stone flooring. Having removed his wet plaid from the journey, he now wore only a long white tunic that reached down to his knees. His sword lay propped against the side of the hearth next to his boots, and his stockings were drying over the back of a nearby chair. His hair hung loose about his shoulders, freed from the confinement of the thong that normally secured it at the nape of his neck.

Frustrated, Ian turned to stare into the fire. His mind raced through a hundred possible scenarios to locate Miles and bring him home alive—if he even still lived. None of the plans offered much chance of success, and not a single one had the remotest chance of succeeding unless they could find where the Roundheads had taken Miles. Going to Dundrum was the most logical course of action. The townsfolk might know where the English had taken the prisoners. But the trip would be exceedingly difficult and dangerous.

Grimacing, he rubbed the back of his neck, methodically working out the kinks in his muscles. Dundrum was at least a two-day ride, and the English controlled the town now. Once there, he knew that no matter how much discretion he used, anyone inquiring about the location of the Irish prisoners would immediately be suspect.

"Ian?"

He lifted his gaze from the fire and looked over his shoulder to see Faith standing in the doorway.

"I'm sorry to intrude on your thoughts," she said. "Did you eat?"

A faint smile touched his lips. "Och, Molly saw to it that I won't go hungry for a week. There's no finer cook in Ireland, I say."

Faith smiled back, and he thought it almost touched her eyes. "For you alone, Ian Maclaren, she'd cook a feast. She is completely besotted with you. For that matter, you could probably charm the stockings off of any woman, age notwithstanding."

"Well, I never got a chance wi' ye," he teased gently.

"But ye know, ye never did tell me whether or no' ye have a sister."

Faith laughed outright. "Only a cousin. And believe me, you're not her type."

"Type?"

"I mean, she rather prefers a man who dresses elegantly, has excellent social skills, moves in exclusive circles, and is well-spoken and polished. Not that you couldn't be that kind of man if you wanted, Ian, but frankly I would consider that to be a rather confining representation of you. Besides, my cousin can be a bit stuffy. She hates getting dirty or wet, doesn't care much for animals, and always keeps to an exact schedule. It's a miracle we ever got along as children and adults." Faith smiled at the memory. "But she is the most loyal person I've ever known. She is kind and friendly, and I miss her terribly."

"London is no' so far away," he said softly.

"It's farther away than you can possibly imagine," she replied, the smile fading from her face. "A lot farther."

"Well, 'twas nice to see ye smile, even if for just a moment."

She sighed. "I'm worried, Ian. We'll need a miracle to find Miles. Furlong was right; he could be anywhere in Ireland by now. It will be like searching for a needle in a haystack."

He put a hand on her shoulder reassuringly. "We'll find him, Faith. I'm leaving on the morn for Dundrum. Mayhap someone there will know where the prisoners have been taken."

"I'm going with you."

Ian blinked in surprise. "Och, Faith, dinna even talk such nonsense. 'Twill be a long, hard ride as it is.

There are English patrols everywhere. 'Tis far too dangerous for ye to be riding about the countryside."

Faith put her hands stubbornly on her hips. "You need me. As an Englishwoman, I'll be better able to get us past sentries and into locations you wouldn't have a chance at entering without me."

"Do ye think me daft?" Ian growled. "I'll no' even consider it."

Faith softened her voice. "Please, let's not waste time arguing. We must do everything we can to save Miles. You know that I can help you. I realize travel now is dangerous, even life-threatening. But if something happens to Miles, I don't even care to live. Please, I beg you not to fight me on this."

He opened his mouth to answer when a stocky dwarf dashed into the room, skidding to a stop beside Faith. His vest of green and gold brocade flapped open against a long-sleeved white shirt that was tucked into a pair of black pantaloons. A small hat with a plume feather slid down across one eye.

"Milady," he said in a breathless rush, pushing the hat back on his head. "Ian. Forgive the intrusion."

"It's all right, Shaun," Ian said, putting a concerned hand on his shoulder. "What happened?"

The dwarf took a deep breath, pressing a hand to his heaving chest. "A routine patrol about the grounds has revealed a body in the forest. Two o' our men stumbled across it in the dark."

"A body?" Faith gasped.

"A lad, I'd venture to say. He's still alive. We've brought him to the courtyard."

"My God," Faith breathed. "He's likely been harmed by one of the English patrols. Have the men bring him into the castle at once, and ask Molly to prepare a room upstairs."

"Aye, milady," Shaun said, scooting off in his gold-buckled shoes.

Faith exhaled, turning back to Ian. "The atrocities become worse every day," she said. "Even children are not spared."

"War is no' as noble a venture as some would like to believe."

"Yes," Faith agreed. "I'm afraid you are all too right. Come, let's see if there is anything we can do for him."

Ian followed her out of the library and up the stairs, where he could hear people talking excitedly. A young serving boy was lighting a fire in the hearth as Molly spread sheets and blankets on the bed. Another man held the limp form of the boy in his arms.

"All right, now, lay him down on the bed gently," Molly instructed the man.

The man complied, setting the boy on top of the blankets. Molly leaned over the form, smoothing back the strands of hair that concealed his face.

"Mary Mother o' God!" she exclaimed. " 'Tis no' a lad we have here, but a lass."

Ian stepped forward, picking up a lit candle from a nearby table and holding it close to the bed. Faith came up beside him, placing a hand on his arm and leaning over their unconscious charge. She inhaled a sharp breath, and Ian glanced at her just as the color drained from her face.

"Oh my God," she breathed. "It can't be." She staggered, bumping into Ian and nearly causing him to drop the candle. He quickly grabbed her elbow, steadying her as she swayed.

"What's wrong?" he asked worriedly. "Do you know who she is?"

She nodded, her eyes wide as saucers. Her entire body had begun to tremble.

"Faith, for Christ's sake, who is she?" Ian asked again, his concern growing.

She pressed her shaking hand against her breast, as if willing air to enter her lungs. "Her name is Fiona Chancellor," she said softly. "She's my cousin."

Chapter Four

Fiona's first conscious thought was that she had been struck by lightning. Her ears rang, her stomach churned, and some sadistic dwarf pounded away in her head. Such a blinding episode would also explain why she was having a hell of a time opening her eyes.

Employing a supreme effort, she finally forced them open, blinking several times as the initially blurry view came into focus.

The surroundings astounded her. No longer was she in the muddy field among stone configurations. Instead she lay on her side in a dry but rather lumpy bed, curled up in a fetal position with her left arm tucked under her head. From the feel of it, her jeans were gone, and she was dressed in a warm but scratchy nightgown of some kind. Candlelight lit the room and shadows danced on the wall from a flickering fire.

Curious, she pushed herself up on her elbows and immediately wished she hadn't. The clang of a dozen hammers against steel exploded inside her head. Gritting her teeth, she wiggled the rest of the way to a sitting position, resting back against the headboard. She closed her eyes and took several deep breaths.

When she opened them again she saw someone else was in the room. Fast asleep in a chair near the bed was the most gorgeous man she had ever seen. She blinked rapidly, thinking surely he must be a figment of her imagination and would likely disappear. When that failed to occur, she realized that he indeed was a real person. Then who was he and what the hell was he doing here? For that matter, what was *she* doing here?

Suspicion mingled with curiosity as she stared at him. The chair barely held this enormous man. The thick biceps of his arms were crossed against his chest and rose and fell with every breath he took. Tousled, sandy blond hair hung loose to his shoulders and curled slightly below the collar of his shirt. He was oddly dressed, in some sort of long white tunic and what appeared to be a thick Scottish plaid. Even stranger, his muscled shins were encased in dark hose that molded to every curve of his calves, although he wore no shoes on his very large feet.

Bizarre clothing aside, he was the most magnificent male specimen Fiona had ever seen.

An amusing thought struck her—perhaps she was dead and in heaven. This man might be her angel. A dreamy smile broached her lips. Not a bad start to eternity, if he stuck around awhile.

Fiona opened her mouth to speak to him, but only a croak came out.

Nonetheless, the man snapped open his eyes and leapt to his feet with surprising grace. "By all the saints, ye're finally awake," he said worriedly. "Are ye feeling all right, lass?"

He had a heavy Scottish accent to go with the strange clothes. His warm brown eyes were filled with concern, and the soft burr in his voice was both musical and seductive. Fiona felt a warm tingle of attraction start in the bottom of her stomach and spread outward.

"Water," she whispered, reaching up to touch her throat.

"Thirsty, are ye?" He reached over and picked up a bowl that sat atop a small table near the bed. "Here, let me aid ye."

He pressed a large hand to her back, holding her up firmly. With his other hand, he gave her the bowl, their fingers touching lightly. Her flesh prickled at his touch and she was keenly aware of the strength and power in it. He radiated heat, and his warmth had a drugging, languorous affect on her. She sighed with pleasure, thinking she just might stay like this forever, propped cozily between his two large, capable hands.

"What is it, lass?" he finally asked. "Can ye no' drink?"

Fiona looked at him dreamily. "Drink?" she repeated.

"Ye said ye were thirsty."

"I did?"

"Here now, drink up," he urged, holding the edge of the bowl to her lips.

Fiona could feel the raw strength in his hand and suddenly had an unbidden image of those hot hands on her body. She smiled and put her lips on the bowl.

"There now," he murmured, rolling his *R*s in his peculiar Scottish way.

It was curious that her angel would be Scottish, Fiona thought. She had never once dated a Scotsman. They were not among her exclusive circle of friends in London and, of course, they had that funny way of speaking. Still, if most Scotsmen were like the one in front of her, she had definitely been missing out on something.

Dutifully, she took a sip. She took another and then grabbed the bowl and began to drink greedily. The water was sweet and refreshing, her body apparently parched. When she was done, he took the bowl and sat back down in the chair.

"Do ye feel better?" he asked, studying her intently.

"Not yet," she replied with a sigh. "Kiss me."

He made a funny choking noise in his throat. "What did ye say?"

"Kiss me," she repeated, slightly annoyed that he had not immediately leapt to her bidding. When he stood there dumbly, she lifted her hands in exasperation. "What? Don't tell me that kissing is forbidden here."

He looked at her oddly for a long moment and then stood. Slowly, he walked over to the bed. The muscles in his arms rippled beneath his white tunic as he moved, quickening Fiona's breath.

He possessed a perfect male form, his body a combination of sensual grace and compelling virility. He sat beside her, the mattress sagging under his weight. Slowly, he lifted one hand and slipped his fingers under the hair at the nape of her neck. Gently, he tilted her head back until she was gazing directly at him.

His eyes were beautiful—brown, intriguing, and

covered by long black eyelashes. He leaned forward, brushing her lips with a feather-light kiss.

As she waited expectantly, his mouth descended again, this time his tongue lightly tracing the fullness of her mouth. With a sigh, Fiona tangled her fingers in his hair, closed her eyes, and lifted her mouth to him again.

She felt him start in surprise, but without hesitation he deepened the kiss, covering her lips and moving his tongue inside to conduct the most sensual devouring of her mouth she had ever experienced. She shivered with pleasure and heard him make a small noise in the back of his throat as her hands tightened in his hair. Fiona melted against him, leaning into the contours of his hard body, uttering a small moan of her own.

Abruptly, he stopped the kiss, pulling away. Fiona gave a whimper of disappointment as her angel stood and looked down at her, his eyes glowing with an undefined light.

"I should no' have done that," he said, but Fiona thought he sounded uncertain. "Ye are unwell."

"Of course I'm unwell," she snapped, wishing he would shut up and kiss her again. "I'm dead, aren't I?"
"Dead?" he exclaimed.

Fiona looked at him in shock. "You mean I'm not dead?"

He laughed, a deep-throated sexy sound. "A lass who kisses like ye? 'Tis no' likely, I say."

Fiona looked around the room in surprise. It looked all dark and mysterious, just like she thought heaven might be. Several candles and a flickering fire lit the room, casting a shadowy glow. She could see the faint outline of several pieces of large furniture, and oddly, it seemed as if the walls were made of stone. If she weren't mistaken, she was in a castle of some sort.

"You mean this isn't heaven? You aren't my angel?"

He laughed again. "I've been called many things in my lifetime, but I assure ye, 'tis the first time anyone has mistaken me for an angel."

Fiona flushed with mortification. "You mean I just kissed you with wild abandon and you aren't my angel?"

" 'Twould be my honor to serve as your angel, milady, if ye think it would speed your recovery."

Fiona looked closely at him and was certain she detected laughter in his eyes. Her mortification deepened. "Oh, bloody brilliant. This is just my luck of late. I do apologize, Mister..."

"Maclaren. Ian Maclaren, at your service."

"Well, Mr. Maclaren, I do hope you'll let me start over. I don't normally throw myself like that at men who rescue me. I do presume it was you who rescued me from my foolhardy late-night adventure at the Beaghmore Stone Circles. I must have slipped and hit my head. Harder than I thought, as I appear to have completely lost my senses. I want to thank you."

He chuckled. "I think ye just did. Altho' 'tisn't me whom ye should thank, lass. A patrol stumbled across ye lying amid the stones and brought you here."

"Patrol?"

"Aye, fortunate for ye, we've increased the number of patrols lately. Those damn Roundhead scouts are everywhere. One can't be too careful of the English these days. Och, begging your pardon, lass."

Fiona's eyes widened. "Sorry. I thought you said Roundhead."

"Aye, and I must say, t'wasn't verra wise of ye to travel here alone even in disguise. 'Tis dangerous these days."

"I see," Fiona said slowly, although she hadn't a clue what he was talking about. If she wasn't dead after all, her situation suddenly seemed quite precarious. This man was either delusional or psychotic; and neither prospect bode well for her at this particular moment, especially since she had just thrown herself at him with unrestrained passion.

"Would you mind telling me where I am?" she asked, amazed that her voice sounded remarkably calm.

"Ye are in Ireland, o' course."

"In Northern Ireland?"

"To the north o' what?"

"Of... of..." she stammered. "I mean, how far are we from the Beaghmore Stone Circles?"

He now looked at her oddly, as if she were the one who had lost her marbles. "Not far. The circles are part of O'Bruaidar land."

"O'Bruaidar land?" she exclaimed. "Are you saying this is the O'Bruaidar castle? It wasn't destroyed after all?"

"Destroyed? O' course not."

Alarm bells rang in her head, and a sense of growing panic was making it hard for her to think clearly. "Where are my clothes?"

He shrugged. "I dinna know. Molly likely disposed o' them somewhere."

"Molly? You mean you weren't the one who dressed me in this nightie?"

He grinned. "As much as 'twould have been my pleasure, 'twasn't me who dressed ye in that bedgown. I'm only here wi' ye now because your cousin asked me to watch o'er ye while she attends to some things about the castle. She was verra insistent that only a few o' us be permitted to tend to ye."

Fiona looked up sharply. "My cousin?"

"Aye. I fear 'twas a bit o' a shock for her to see ye. She said your arrival here was most unexpected."

"How did you know I was looking for my cousin?" Fiona stammered, her heart hammering fast.

"Your name is Fiona, is it no'?"

Fiona gasped in surprise. "Yes, it is. But how did you know that?"

"Faith told me."

"My cousin Faith?"

"Well, now, how many cousins named Faith do ye have?"

Fiona looked at him in stunned amazement. "My God. I've found Faith? She's really here?"

"Aye, she was here for some time while ye were sleeping. I finally insisted she get some rest o' her own. I was under strict orders to fetch her as soon as ye awoke. 'Tis a rather difficult time for us all right now, and your cousin is quite distressed o'er her husband."

"Husband?" Fiona choked.

He looked surprised. "Ye know naught o' their wedding? Well, I'm certain Faith will explain everything to ye." He stood and headed for the door.

"Wait," she called, and he paused in the doorway. "You are a friend of Faith's?"

"That I am."

"May I ask you a question, then? Why are you dressed like that? Isn't it a bit cold for such an outfit?"

He shrugged. "It serves me well enough."

"No offense, but it's rather…eccentric."

"No more peculiar than the way ye were clad when we found ye."

"The way I was clad?" she repeated in disbelief. This whole exchange had started to be rather surreal. Perhaps she was dreaming after all. She could almost believe that, except her stomach was doing painful flips and her heart was racing so hard she was having trouble breathing.

"There is also the matter o' your hair," he added.

Fiona reached up and touched her dark bob. "My hair?"

"Why, 'tis cut like a man's. It doesn't suit ye."

Fiona gasped. "I'll have you know this is a French bob. It's the rage across Europe, and frankly, it cost me a small fortune, Mr. Maclaren."

"Call me Ian. And 'tis really o' no consequence. Ye are pretty enough even wi' that ridiculous hair."

Fiona opened her mouth to reply but wasn't certain if she should be insulted or pacified by his comment. "Look," she finally said irritably, "let's clear this up once and for all. Something is just not right here. Am I dead or not?"

Ian laughed, his baritone rich and warm. "I assure ye, ye are verra much alive. Short hair and odd manners notwithstanding, ye are a vibrant bit o' goods beneath that bedgown."

"B-beneath my bedgown?" she spluttered as he stepped out of the room. "How do you know what I look like beneath my—"

"No need to thank me for watching o'er ye," he smoothly interrupted. "I assure ye, 'twas *all* my pleasure."

Fiona gaped as he winked at her. For a moment her

body relived the velvet warmth of his incredibly sensual kiss and she tingled pleasurably. Scowling, she looked down at her nightgown and then back at the door as it closed with a thud.

"I'll be damned," she said, narrowing her eyes. "I'd bet a pound, Ian Maclaren, that you were the one who changed me into this nightie after all."

After the sexy but strange Scotsman left, Fiona pushed aside the bedcovers and stood up, steadying herself against the side of the bed for a moment. Could it be true that she had found her cousin at long last?

Her headache was rapidly subsiding, but her sense of uneasiness was growing. Just what exactly had happened to her at the stone circles? She clearly remembered the sound of static electricity, burning her leg against one of the stones that had weirdly started to glow red, and then falling into the mud. She remembered nothing else.

Carefully, she lifted the nightgown and examined her bandaged thigh. The injury was real, so her memory of what had happened must be at least partially intact.

But why was she here? Was the Scotsman telling the truth when he said she was in the O'Bruaidar castle? She found his claim barely credible as she had stood in the sheep pasture where the castle had purportedly once stood and seen nothing. She supposed it might have been rebuilt nearby, but then why hadn't she come across that fact while researching the family history?

No answers readily came to mind, so she rubbed her temples and walked toward the hearth. The cold stone floor chilled her bare feet and she shivered.

"Fiona?"

She turned around quickly, her eyes widening. For a moment she could only stare in shock. Her cousin Faith stood in the doorway, as beautiful and ethereal as a ghost.

"Is that… is that really you?" Fiona croaked, forcing the words from her throat.

Faith shot across the room and into her arms. "Oh my God, Fiona. I've missed you so much," she cried.

Fiona flung her arms around Faith and hugged hard, relieved to feel solid flesh and bone. "You're alive! I can't believe it."

Faith squeezed her back fiercely. "Yes, pet, I'm really here and I'm fine."

Fiona pulled back slightly and studied her cousin's face. The delicately carved cheekbones, full mouth, and short, straight nose of her cousin's face were definitely familiar. As was the small scar on her chin that Fiona herself had put there when they were both six. Faith's pale blond hair was considerably longer and fuller than it had been a year ago, but her skin was unhealthily pale and her light blue eyes were red-rimmed and heavily shadowed.

"You don't look fine to me. Are you ill?" Fiona asked worriedly.

Faith shook her head, wiping the tears with a corner of her sleeve. "No. I'm just worried. Things are very difficult for me right now."

"Difficult for *you?*" Fiona said, stepping back from Faith. "Do you have any idea how bloody worried I've been about you? Where have you been for the past year? Why didn't you contact me?"

Faith let out a deep sigh, leading Fiona back to the

bed. "Sit down, pet. It's a long story and one I'm not certain you're in any condition to hear."

"The hell with my condition. I'll hear it and I'll hear it *now*. You're not leaving my sight until I find out what is going on around here. You can't imagine what I've been through to find you. I don't know whether I'm relieved or furious with you right now." She impulsively reached out and touched Faith's hand. "Don't you *ever* leave me again."

Faith squeezed her hand back. "Oh, Fiona, I've missed you more than you can imagine."

Fiona pulled her hand away. "Then why didn't you come home? And don't give me some super-secret cock-and-bull story. You could have contacted me somehow, you know. And what is this I hear about a husband?"

Faith sighed. "I clearly have a lot to tell you. I'm not certain where to begin. Why don't you start by telling me how you got here."

Fiona crawled back under the covers and pulled them up to her chin. "Frankly, I don't think I've ever had a more bizarre day in my life. First, I spend the morning driving all over Tyrone County visiting antiques shops. Finally I find the shop I'm looking for but have to sit in the dark, listening to a man spout a load of local codswallop about fey folk and enchanted druid sites. Then I traverse a wet sheep pasture searching for the remains of some old castle, and later, while away the afternoon in a godforsaken provincial library. Then, because apparently I hadn't enough excitement for the day, I impulsively decide to spend the evening traipsing about some old druid circles. I think lightning or something hit me. When I awake, I discover I'm being watched over by the most gorgeous man I've ever seen. Just between you and me, I thought I'd died and gone to heaven and he had been appointed my angel. I throw myself at him only to discover I'm not dead, but have miraculously found my long-lost cousin. Voila—you appear. Blast it, Faith, that's more excitement than I've had in my entire life-time." She paused, running her fingers through her disheveled hair. "I am ready for an entire box of truf-fles, a manicure, and a foot massage. Pronto."

Faith rose from the bed. "Well, I'm afraid you don't yet know the half of it."

"I suppose I don't," she said, squinting her eyes. She suddenly realized Faith wore a long-fashioned gown with a lace décolletage. "What in God's name are you wearing?" she gasped in horror. "Has everyone in this place completely lost their sense of fashion?"

Faith blew out a deep breath. "Yes, I knew you'd be curious about that. But first, tell me why you came to Ireland in the first place. The south of France is much more your style for a holiday. And incidentally, I didn't know you were all that interested in antiques."

"It's all your fault, really."

"My fault?"

"Yes. When MI5 said they couldn't find you and presumed you were dead, I was devastated."

Faith's face crumpled. "I'm sorry, pet. I wish there had been a way to contact you personally."

"Well, I wish you would have. It would have spared me a lot of trouble. I'd postponed the wedding, you know."

"Wedding?" Faith gasped. "You mean you married Edward Hawthorne?"

Fiona grimaced. "I came bloody close. I caught him in bed with some trollop a week before the wedding.

I suppose it was better that way, discovering his true nature before we got married."

"Oh, Fiona," Faith said sadly. "I'm sorry."

"Don't be. He was a twit. A rich twit, but a wanker just the same. I should have been able to see it."

"It's just a bit of bad luck."

"More like a streak. Less than a week later, I got dumped from my job."

"At the Prestwick Advertising agency? Oh, no, really?"

"Really. Downsizing, they said. And there you have it—my life as I knew it, literally down the loo."

Faith frowned. "Hardly. You're a vibrant, intelligent woman—you'll bounce back. But none of this yet explains why you are in Ireland."

"Well, a few weeks earlier I went to your townhouse to clear out your things and sell the place."

"Sell my place?" Faith replied in surprise.

"The officials at MI5 told me you were dead. I didn't know what else to do."

Faith leaned forward, putting her hand on her cousin's arm. "It's all right. It doesn't really matter anymore."

"Well, that's when I found the dagger. The one with the double-edged blade."

Faith inhaled a quick breath. "You found it?" she asked in a hushed voice. "Did you see the inscription?"

Fiona nodded. "Yes, and I knew that somehow you had written it because it was our special saying. I knew full well that it hadn't been there when we looked at it before. But all the experts I consulted dated the inscription to the seventeenth century. It was so strange."

"Yes," Faith murmured.

"The experts also said the dagger was Irish in origin and placed it somewhere in County Tyrone in Ulster."

"So, it *was* the dagger that led you here."

Fiona nodded. "I must have visited over fifty antiques shops in the area before I finally found one that could tell me something about it."

Faith sighed. "Oh, pet. I didn't mean to lead you on a merry goose chase. I wanted simply to let you know that I was all right and not to worry about me."

Fiona shrugged. "What did I have to lose? I'd been betrayed by my fiancé and lost my job all in the same week. I decided to put my energy and some of dear old Papa's money to good use. It seems like I got a good return on my investment."

Faith smiled softly, patting her cousin's hand. "I'm so glad to see you. But how did you get here, Fiona? No, let me guess. You paid a visit to the Beaghmore Stone Circles."

Fiona looked at her cousin strangely. "How did you know?"

Faith exhaled a deep breath. "Again, it's a long story. Why did you go to the stones?"

"Well, it all started when I visited this small antiques shop. The owner, a Sean... no, Seamus Gogarty, was the first person in the area who had any knowledge of the dagger."

"Gogarty?" Faith said in a strangled voice. "He wasn't by any chance a dwarf, was he?"

Fiona blinked. "Why, yes. Did you meet him, too?"

"In a manner of speaking. Please continue."

"Well, he told me the dagger belonged to a noble Irish family by the name of O'Bruaidar. I tracked down the family's records in the small town library and discovered that they had once owned a castle near here. It was called Castle on the Moor or something like that."

"Castle Dun na Moor," Faith breathed.

"I went to the location of where the castle should have been, but I found only a sheep pasture. Records indicated that the castle had been destroyed in the seventeenth century during the invasion of Oliver Cromwell and had never been rebuilt."

Faith closed her eyes. "My God," she whispered.

"Are you all right?" Fiona asked, looking at her cousin in concern. "You don't look so well yourself."

"No, I'm all right. Please, go on."

"Well, this Mr. Gogarty had told me something about the dagger being magic, and a legend saying how this magic could be enhanced at midnight at a druid holy site. So, I got this brilliant idea that I would check it out using the nearest druid ruins I could find—the Beaghmore Stone Circles, of course. You should have seen me, Faith. There I was, a person who positively loathes dirt and grime, wandering about these muddy stones in the dead of night. I swear, I was convinced I had gone completely mad. Then I heard a strange crackling noise, like a discharge of static electricity or something, coming from amid the stones. I stepped back and burned my thigh on one of the damned markers. Somehow the bloody things were glowing and had become searing hot. Horrified, I slipped and dropped my pocketbook. While I was groping about in the mud for my car keys, I must have passed out. I woke to find myself in this bed."

Faith squeezed Fiona's hand. "I'm so glad you're here, but you couldn't have picked a worse or more dangerous time to look for me. There are many things going on right now, the most important of which involves a man whom I love dearly. I have a lot of things to tell you, but first of all, I need to ask you something. It's very important. During your research about the O'Bruaidar family, do you remember anything about a man named Miles?"

Fiona ran her fingers through her short bob. "Actually, I do. I remember him in particular because it struck me as odd that this Miles had an English wife named Faith. Quite an eerie coincidence, wouldn't you say?"

The color drained from Faith's face. "Do you remember what happened to him?" she asked softly.

"He was allegedly some kind of rebel, I think, during Cromwell's campaign on the island. He was captured during a skirmish and executed along with twelve other men in the city of Cavan. A pity, I guess, because he left no heir. He was the last in the family line of the O'Bruaidars. I suppose that would explain why the castle was never rebuilt."

Faith closed her eyes. "Cavan. He's at Cavan. My God, we may have a chance to save him."

Fiona looked at her in bewilderment. "Save who? Why are you so interested in all of this history? And when are you going to tell me where you've been for the past year and a half?"

"I'm not certain you really want to hear what I have to say. It's going to be quite a shock, I'm afraid."

"Damn it, Faith, I'm not a child. I think you owe me a simple explanation, at the very least."

Faith nodded. "I agree you are entitled to an explanation. But I'm not promising it's simple. I just want you to keep an open mind as I tell you what has happened to me."

She stood up from the bed and began walking slowly back in front of the fireplace. Fiona's heart began to thump in nervous anticipation. She didn't like the way Faith kept wringing her hands together as she paced. For as long as Fiona could remember, Faith had always had nerves of steel. It had served her cousin well in her profession, as well as her turbulent private life. No matter what troubles came her way, Faith had always managed to maintain an outer aura of calm and composure. But now Fiona could almost feel the waves of tension rolling off her. That loss of control, more than anything, began to frighten her deeply.

Faith stopped pacing and looked at Fiona. "There is no easy way to say this, so I'm just going to come directly to the point. There appears to be a time portal—a rip in time, if you will—at the Beaghmore Stone Circles that somehow transports those who step into it back to the past. It happened to me by accident. I was on a mission for the government, tracking a man called Padriac 'Paddy' O'Rourke, an assassin for the IRA. We had cornered him near his ancestral home not far from here, and I drew the Beaghmore Stone Circles as my stakeout location. O'Rourke unexpectedly confronted me at the stones, and during the struggle, we both fell into the time portal."

"Sorry, did you say...time portal?" Fiona stuttered in disbelief.

"Yes. Give me a chance to explain. It didn't take either of us too long to discover what had happened," she continued quickly. "We realized that somehow we had traveled back in time and were existing in seventeenth-century Ireland—the year sixteen hundred and forty-eight, to be exact. But while all I wanted to do was get back to my own time, Paddy decided to capitalize on the situation by doing what he did best—assassinate public figures."

Fiona tried to say something, but her mouth opened and shut wordlessly, as if she were a fish on a hook.

"He decided to kill Oliver Cromwell before his march on Ireland and change the future," Faith explained, starting to pace again. "Of course I had to stop him. Not because I was particularly fond of the policies of Cromwell, but because I feared that if he changed history, it would create a massive time paradox—the results too catastrophic to contemplate."

Fiona swallowed hard, forcing the words from her mouth. "Yes, I distinctly heard the words 'time portal.' "

"I know it sounds bizarre, pet, but stay with me. Have you followed my story so far in regard to Padriac O'Rourke?"

"I d-don't know," Fiona answered in a shaky voice, wondering why she was even participating in this bizarre conversation. "There was something about an O'Rourke chap who was a member of the IRA?"

"Yes, you are following me. I managed to stop O'Rourke, thanks to Miles. When Miles and I first met, he was convinced I was a British spy. After all, I was a proverbial fish out of water here in the middle of rural Ireland in the seventeenth century. Miles is a well-loved rebel here called the Irish Lion, leading the fight against Oliver Cromwell. Despite my heritage, he finally began to trust me. He married me ostensibly to save my life—however, we had fallen deeply in love." She paused, her voice breaking slightly. "I have to save him, Fiona. He is my soulmate. I couldn't bear life without him."

Fiona suddenly straightened, myriad pieces of information snapping together and making a sudden picture.

"Wait just a bloody minute. Are you saying that *you* are the Faith I read about in the library? That *you* are the English wife of Miles O'Bruaidar?"

"That's what I'm saying," Faith replied softly.

Fiona began to laugh. "By our lady, Faith, you almost had me there. Time portals, dashing Irish rebels... well, it was a damn good try. If this is just some new-fangled way of protecting national security, than just bloody say so. Mum is the word, I promise."

Faith walked over to the bed and sat down on a corner. She took Fiona's hands and squeezed them hard. The chill of Faith's skin shocked Fiona.

"It's not a fairy tale or a matter of national security," Faith said steadily. "As odd as it sounds, it's the truth."

Fiona laughed again, but this time it was more a nervous release of energy. "Come on, Faith, lighten up. This is your cousin, Fiona, here. You don't have to play these ridiculous games with me."

Slowly Faith unclenched the fist Fiona had unconsciously made, and then pressed her own palm flat against Fiona's in a solemn gesture they had made since childhood.

"*Lies shall not part, one bond to one heart*" Faith recited softly. "I'm telling the truth, Fiona. I swear it."

Fiona searched her cousin's eyes but saw no hint of deception or untruth. "You...you really mean it?"

"I really mean it."

"And that's why you are so interested in all this

history? This Miles—he is really your husband and some kind of famous Irish rebel? You are saying that he has been captured by Cromwell's forces—as in Oliver Cromwell of the seventeenth century—but hasn't yet been executed? And you want to try and save him."

Faith nodded, tears filling her eyes. "I'm not going to let him die, Fiona."

Fiona withdrew her palm and realized she was trembling. "All right. Just give me another ruddy minute to think about all of this. Let's assume that I'm not delusional and you aren't either. So, you are convinced we are now living in the past. What year is it?"

"Sixteen hundred and forty-nine."

Fiona swallowed hard and then continued. "Well, let's say, then, that I accept this bizarre theory of having stepped through a time portal. What if you save Miles and he was supposed to die in Cavan? What will happen to the future as we know it?"

"I don't know," Faith replied quietly. "And quite frankly, at this moment, I don't care. I only pray that the paradox is so small it won't have any noticeable impact on the time line as we know it. After all, it seems that other than the message on the dagger and a small mention of me in an old history book, my presence in this time has done little to change events in the future."

"But Miles is a rather famous figure, is he not? Won't his survival have a greater impact on the future?"

"Presumably, yes."

"But you still intend to try to save him, despite the possible consequences?"

"I know it is selfish, but yes."

63

Fiona sighed. "But I still don't understand all of this. Why does this time portal lead to the past and not to the future?"

Faith shook her head, her blond hair tumbling around her shoulders. "I don't know. But I do remember once reading a theory regarding the two regions of space and time and how, when connected by a combination of exotic matter and certain conditions, it could act as a time machine to the past. Einstein even speculated on the possibility of time-travel when he wrote—"

"Enough," Fiona said sharply, holding up a hand. "Now I remember why I hated physics in school. Look, I'm not a complete idiot. I've seen the film *Back to the Future*. I get the general idea."

A slight smile touched Faith's lips. "Good."

"The real question is, can I ever go home?"

Faith let out a deep breath. "Honestly, I don't know. I believe the key is creating the same exotic conditions under which the portal opens. Right now, the circles are missing several stones. I tried to return a year later on the same day and time I arrived, but it didn't work. Apparently these stones together somehow act as a catalyst for the time-travel. Without them, I'm not certain we'll ever be able to return."

"But you can't believe that this is something that has happened just to us. I mean, certainly other people have stumbled across the portal—like that IRA assassin you were talking about."

"That's probably true. But perhaps not as many as we think. It appears that time is another condition under which the portal opens. I came through at midnight, and judging from when we found you, so did you. Perhaps there aren't many odd people like ourselves who choose to wander about the stones in the dead of night."

"Rubbish," Fiona countered. "It would be the perfect spot for a group of young teenagers out for a night of drinking, or a young couple looking for an unusual site for a romantic interlude."

"I won't disagree with you, and for all I know, they come through by the dozens. Perhaps some of them were executed or persecuted for witchcraft. Given that, how fast do you think they learned to keep their mouths shut and assimilate like I did?"

Fiona studied her cousin closely. "Does Miles know about you—that you came from the future?"

"Yes, I told him. But I was terrified, and it took me a long time to summon the courage to do so. And it took him even longer to believe me. But we managed to get through it."

"Does anyone else know?"

"No. And you must be very careful, Fiona. People of this time are very suspicious of anything they do not understand."

Fiona crossed her arms against her chest. "So, the bottom line is that I'm not going back home any time soon."

"I'm sorry, pet. I don't know what else to say."

"How about pinching me so I can wake up from this nightmare?"

"It's not so bad, really."

"Where are my clothes?"

Faith stood and walked over to a wooden trunk that had been pushed against the wall. Removing a small key from a tiny leather pouch around her waist, she knelt down and opened the trunk. She lifted something in her hand and dangled it in front of Fiona.

Julie Moffett

Fiona gasped, swinging her legs over the side and hopping off the bed. "The keys to my auto," she exclaimed, walking over to Faith and taking them.

"You must have had them clutched in your hand when you came through the portal."

"What else of mine do you have in that trunk?"

"Your jeans, blouse, jacket, underclothes, and boots. Not items I want to leave lying around in the open for all to goggle at. It seems that nothing else of yours made it through the portal."

"The dagger," Fiona whispered. "The double-edged dagger was in my purse."

Faith's eyes widened. "Now there was a possible paradox. I have the original dagger in my bedchamber. Who knows what would have happened if you had brought the dagger through the portal with you?"

"What objects did you have when you came through?" Fiona asked curiously.

"My torch, some tissues, a few breath mints, and my shoes. Paddy O'Rourke had a gun with a silencer. They're in here, too. But that's the total sum of my twentieth-century existence."

Fiona leaned against the stone wall. "My God, how will I ever survive here?"

Faith gently touched her cousin's shoulder. "I'm so sorry, Fiona. I didn't mean for this to happen to you. But you'll do just fine and I'll help you. For now, though, you'll have to be on your own for several days. I'm leaving at daylight for the city of Cavan. I must try to save Miles."

Fiona looked up sharply. "Oh no, you don't. You're not leaving me alone here. I'm coming with you."

Faith shook her head. "You've been through a lot.

66

You need time to rest and get adjusted mentally to what has happened to you."

Fiona straightened. "I'm fine."

"For God's sake, Fiona, let me explain something to you. It's an extremely dangerous, not to mention difficult, ride to Cavan. There are no buses or autos to take us there in comfort. I'm talking about riding a horse for ten to twelve hours at a time and sleeping on the hard ground at night. There are no tents, baths, air mattresses, or sleeping bags. It will be cold and damp, and we'll be in profound danger the entire time. Then there's the risk that we could be set upon at any time by bandits, thieves, or other assorted rabble, not to mention the horrible chance we run of being raped, killed, or both. Besides, if anyone discovers we are trying to free Miles, we could be executed on the spot—English subjects notwithstanding."

"I don't care," Fiona replied stubbornly. "I'll manage."

"Fiona, don't be ridiculous. You get carsick, airsick, and seasick. You're allergic to cats, dogs, and probably horses as well. And look at your fingernails, for God's sake."

Fiona looked down at her fingernails. "What about them?"

"You'll break every one of them. Trust me."

Fiona paled. "I don't care," she repeated firmly. "You're not leaving me alone in this castle with a bunch of people I don't know, and that's final. If you do, I swear, I'll... I'll make all kinds of trouble and get myself hanged as a witch. Imagine the guilt you'd have to live with. You have no other choice than to take me with you. Besides, two Englishwomen traveling together would be less suspicious than one."

"What do you know about traveling in this century?"

"Enough to know that I can do it. Don't underestimate me. You need me."

Faith frowned and set her mouth in a determined line. "Listen very carefully to me, Fiona: Life in this century is very, very unyielding. Now, be the sensible woman I know you are and agree to wait here in relative comfort for me. I don't want to get you back just to lose you again."

"We've always stuck together since we were children," Fiona replied quietly. "And you should know that I'm not going to abandon you in your hour of need. I'll adjust to the discomfort and I promise I'll do my best not to slow you down. Now, let's end this pointless arguing and start planning our rescue of your husband."

"Our rescue?"

Fiona managed a smile. "Lest you forget, I once worked in advertising. If there is one thing I learned, it's that people are vulnerable to suggestion and manipulation. I presume that goes for any century. So, if we intend to avoid bloodshed, including our own, I suggest we figure out a way to use our feminine wiles that will permit us to waltz into Cavan and waltz back out with your husband. And then figure out how to get me home."

"Fiona, I—"

"I'm serious, damn it," Fiona snapped. "Let's bloody well get to it. I'm not going to back down on this."

Fiona was gratified to see a measure of shock and respect on Faith's face. "I never knew you could be so unyielding."

"I'm a lot tougher than you think," Fiona answered firmly. "Now let's get to work."

Faith nodded slowly. "All right. Just what do you have in mind?"

Chapter Five

"*Nay!*" Ian fumed, stalking back and forth across the library floor. His boots thudded in an angry cadence across the stones. "I'll no' even consider such madness. Need I remind ye ladies that this is a rescue, not a bloody pleasure outing?"

"I know the request seems odd, Ian, but it is necessary," Faith said quietly. "Fiona can help us."

"Help us?" Ian snorted, furious that he had even agreed to participate in this conversation. "Look at her. She's a mere slip o' a lass, likely to break in two at the slightest bit o' adventure."

"I certainly will not, and I'll bloody well thank you to speak directly to me when I'm present," Fiona snapped, stepping up beside Faith. "I'm not a ruddy ghost and I'm fully able to speak for myself."

Ian noticed she was a good head shorter than her cousin and quite small-boned, but still she drew herself up haughtily. She didn't seem bothered in the least that she stood before him half-clad in naught more than a long white bedgown and a dressing robe. For some reason, the sight of her naked toes suddenly conjured visions of what the rest of her body might look like without any garments. Ian swallowed and shifted uncomfortably on his feet, annoyed at himself for losing his train of thought.

"Then I'll tell ye directly that ye are no' going wi' us," he said to her sternly. "Do ye sincerely wish to die so soon, lass? For that is what ye are proposing wi' your wish to accompany us."

"Well, I'm sorry to disappoint you, Mr. Maclaren, but I have no intention of dying just yet," she retorted, eyes blazing. "Why does everybody think I'm such a bloody delicate creature? I made it here in one piece, didn't I?"

She was beautiful, but a stubborn bit o' goods, Ian thought, and foolish if she really thought he would permit her to accompany them on this arduous journey. Better she understood that now.

Donning his fiercest look, he placed his hands on his hips and stared at her in his most intimidating manner. If she wanted his attention, he'd damn well give it to her.

He was surprised when she didn't even flinch. She was either remarkably foolish or uncharacteristically brave.

"Fiona…" Faith warned.

"No. I've been through enough today, and I'm not going to let this overbearing, kilt-clad barbarian talk to me like this." Fiona stubbornly crossed her arms against her chest. "He hasn't even bothered to listen to what we have to say."

Ian marveled at the sight of her even as his impatience grew. Christ's wounds, she was lovely when she was angry. Her ridiculously short dark hair was all tousled and wild, her cheeks flushed red, and that generous mouth had curved into a magnificent scowl. When he remembered how sweet that mouth tasted, his heart thumped erratically.

Ian steeled himself, forcing his mind back to the matter at hand. "I dinna care what ye say because 'twill make no difference," he replied, planting his legs on the floor and folding his arms across his chest. "I'm no' going to change my mind."

Faith sighed, throwing up her hands. "Instead of this stubborn bickering we should be spending our energy planning the rescue. Ian, listen to me. Fiona knows where Miles is being held."

He blinked in surprise. "She knows where Miles is? How does she know?"

"She...ah...overheard some English soldiers talking about him on her journey here. He's at Cavan."

"Cavan?" he echoed. It made sense in many ways as the English had held the town for some time now and had a large number of troops deployed in the area. But how could Fiona have figured this out in such a short time? Unless she was something more than just Faith's cousin.

"How do ye know she is telling the truth?" he asked Faith, narrowing his eyes suspiciously. "She didn't even know that Miles was your husband."

"You have to trust me. If Fiona says he's at Cavan, then that's where he is."

Ian looked slowly between Faith and Fiona. He'd known women long enough to recognize there was a lot more here than was being said. They both looked as guilty as a fox that had just swallowed a chicken whole.

"I dinna like any o' this," he said finally, fixing his gaze on Fiona. "Just how exactly did ye get here? Ye certainly dinna travel here from London alone, yet we found neither your mount nor an escort. And for what purpose were ye dressed in a lad's guise? For that matter, what were ye doing in the company o' English soldiers in the first place?"

Faith put her arm protectively around Fiona's shoulders. "It doesn't matter how she got here, Ian. I trust her, and you should, too."

"There is something verra important ye aren't telling me about your cousin, Faith."

She avoided his gaze, and Ian felt a twinge of worry. Her directness and honesty had always reassured him. Her evasiveness at this moment deeply troubled him. Whatever secret she hid about her cousin, it was likely monumental and, even more certainly, dangerous.

"I'm sorry, Ian," she said softly. "I know it is unfair of me to ask you to risk your life while at the same time not giving you all the answers to your questions. But Fiona's presence here is so uncommonly complicated that to even begin such an explanation would take valuable time away from rescuing Miles. I assure you that she is here to help in the effort, not jeopardize it. Please, you must believe me. I promise you all the answers you seek... in time. But now isn't the time for that discussion."

"Besides," Fiona interjected eagerly, "we have a plan to save Miles."

He turned his gaze back on her, annoyed that she didn't yet seem the least bit deterred from accompanying them. Did she really think this was going to be some kind of bloody adventure?

"A plan?" Ian repeated warily, wondering with no little trepidation what in God's name the two women were plotting.

"Yes, and a damn good one, if I do say so myself," Fiona said.

Ian hardened his voice, deciding it was time to get forcefully blunt with the two of them. "Plan or no plan, the journey to Cavan will be at least a two-day ride directly into territory now held by the English. The going will be verra difficult, as we must take routes other than the main roads. If by some chance the Roundheads come across us, 'twill be a fight to the death for the other men and me, but ye lassies will have a much worse fate. Your being English will likely no' even save ye. These are lonely, hardened men— many o' them outright criminals—who haven't had the luxury of being wi' a woman for awhile—certainly no' wi' lassies as pretty as ye two. They willna kill ye, but keep ye alive for purposes so base and immoral, ye would have wished ye were dead. Do ye understand what I am saying?"

To her credit, Ian saw Fiona blanch but then set her mouth firmly. "Nonetheless, I intend to take my chances, Mr. Maclaren. My cousin needs me, and I'll be of no help to her here at the castle."

Ian scowled and looked to Faith for help. "Faith, ye know better than anyone the danger your cousin will be facing. Think about what ye are asking her to do."

Faith was silent for a few moments. "Ian's right, Fiona," she said quietly. "It's not too late to change your mind. We don't even know if we will be able to free Miles once we get to Cavan. It's not fair of me to ask you to risk your life for one man. I want you to stay here where you will be safe."

Fiona took Faith's hand. "You didn't ask me to come. May I remind you how I insisted? Besides, Miles is not just one man—he's your husband, and an important historical figure to boot. I understand the danger, and while I might not be thrilled about the possible consequences, I'm still in. I might remember something critical that will help us save him. You're family, Faith, the only family I have left in the world. We are sticking together on this one."

Ian let out a frustrated breath. "Christ's wounds! Listen to me, women. If we don't die on the journey, Miles will kill me himself for putting his wife and her cousin in such danger just to save his neck from the noose. Faith, ye know I speak the truth. Honestly, I dinna want either one o' ye to come. Let me handle this myself."

"You can't stop us," Fiona retorted, blue eyes blazing. "If you won't help us, we will undertake our own rescue effort, thank you very much."

"Your own rescue effort?" Ian roared. "Are ye truly mad?"

Faith put a restraining hand on Fiona's arm. "The truth of the matter is that we have the best chance at saving Miles if we work together. Now that we know where Miles is, we at least have a decent chance at rescuing him. Fiona and I have come up with an idea that might just free him. Ian, if we intend to help the rebels in Ireland, then at least listen to our plan and tell us what you think."

Ian threw up his hands. "God save me from the two most stubborn lassies in all o' Ireland. Do either o' ye ever listen to reason?"

"We're only asking you to listen," Faith said quietly. "To give our plan a chance."

Ian clenched his jaw angrily. "I'll listen, but my mind is made up."

"God help us, are all Scotsmen so bloody hardheaded?" Fiona said, running her fingers through her short hair.

"I'm not being hardheaded," Ian thundered. "I'm being reasonable. Verra reasonable."

"Then at least have an open mind," Fiona challenged.

"I said I'll listen," Ian replied, a dark scowl on his face. " 'Tis as open as I'll be. But ye two should know that my mind is already made up, and a Scotsman rarely ever changes his mind."

"We'll see about that," Fiona countered.

"Aye, we will, lass. Indeed, we will."

Ian changed his mind.

It hadn't been easy, but he had finally been convinced that their plan had a decent chance of success. Fiona had to give him credit for doing as he promised. He listened patiently and attentively as they laid out their strategy. When they finished, he asked thoughtful, intelligent questions. He immediately grasped the advantage of their plan. But his male chauvinistic mind-set took a lot longer to change. Eventually he came around, but only when Faith shamelessly appealed to his desire to help Ireland and defeat Cromwell.

Yet even after the discussion was over, Fiona didn't feel all that victorious. Especially now, as she sat in the castle courtyard astride a bloody enormous horse.

She hadn't appreciated how far away the ground would seem while sitting upon one.

She leaned over slightly to the left and stared down at the earth. Her stomach turned over and she clutched the mane of the horse, straightening herself.

"No' used to riding such a fine Irish horse, are ye?" someone asked, jolting her from her thoughts and causing her to grip the saddle as her horse moved a step.

Fiona looked up to see a bearded, dark-haired man expertly maneuver his horse from behind the castle water trough and next to hers. He was dressed in a long-sleeved white shirt with a vest of gold and green brocade. A black hat with a plume feather sat jauntily on his head. His short, stocky legs barely reached over the sides of the horse, and Fiona realized with surprise that he was a dwarf.

"Seamus Gogarty from the antiques shop," she breathed. "That's who you remind me of."

"Did ye say Gogarty?" He smiled broadly. "So ye have heard o' me."

She lifted an eyebrow. "In a manner of speaking."

" 'Tis quite intriguing. I don't believe we've met."

"No, we haven't. I'm Faith's cousin, Fiona Chancellor."

"So I've heard. Quite a bonny lass, ye are."

She managed a smile. "How kind of you to say so. I certainly don't feel that way right now."

"Ye are fearful o' the horse, then," he stated gravely. " 'Tis naught to be ashamed o'."

"I'm not afraid," she lied bravely, trying to look at ease on the smelly beast. "Why would you think that?"

77

Julie Moffett

"Well, ye are a wee pale. And your knuckles are white from gripping the horse."

She looked down at her knuckles. They were indeed bloodless.

Well, all right, maybe she was a bit pale. If the truth were known, she also felt sick to her stomach. Wasn't she entitled to feel that way? If Faith was right about this being the seventeenth century, then Fiona was now likely talking to the great-great ancestor of the antiques store owner she'd just met a little over twenty-four hours ago. That damn well entitled her to be pale.

She glanced at him with morbid curiosity. He cocked his head at her.

"What is it, lass?" he asked. "Ye look as if ye have seen a ghost."

She supposed in a way he was a ghost, if you looked at it from her perspective. Taking a deep breath, she tried to calm her jittery nerves.

"I'm just a bit overwhelmed at the moment. But I'm not afraid. After all, I have ridden before." Of course, she'd been ten and the horse a pony, but who wanted to get into details about that now? She straightened in the saddle and raised her chin determinedly. How difficult could riding a horse be? She just had to stay on, that was all.

He clucked sympathetically. "Ye know, I've always wondered what Faith's cousin would look like. Faith speaks o' ye often. Ye two don't look much alike, but ye do share that odd way o' speaking and, o' course, the same color o' blue eyes. A bonny blue, exactly the color o' Lough Emy on a warm summer day."

Fiona smiled. "Thank you. You're quite the charmer, aren't you?"

78

He leaned toward her conspiratorially and gave her a wink. "They say the Irish have a smooth tongue and tender hands wi' the lassies. Now the Scots, on the other hand..." He let the sentence trail off as he looked pointedly at Ian, who sat on his prancing stallion, a thundering scowl on his face. "The Scots are said to have a sharp tongue and heavy hands wi' their women. 'Tis a shame, is it no'?"

Fiona followed the dwarf's gaze to Ian. He cut an impressive figure sitting astride his horse, his sword hanging from his side and the first rays of the morning sun glinting off his shoulder-length blond hair. He had changed out of that ridiculous Scottish outfit and now wore tan-colored breeches, boots, and a dark cloak. He looked unbelievably sexy.

Her gaze lowered to the hands that lightly held his horse's reins. Those hands definitely didn't look like they would be heavy on a woman. Instead, they appeared quite capable, sensuous, and very well versed in just how to touch a woman in all the right places. God help her, if he handled a woman as well as he kissed her, it would be an incredible encounter indeed.

A delicious shiver raced up her spine. Irritated by her wanton thoughts, Fiona pursed her lips and looked away. This was hardly the time or place for hormone-driven fantasies. As it stood, she was still having a hard time coming to grips with everything Faith had told her. Part of her clung to the rational belief that this was just a bizarre dream. Any time now she would wake up and have a ruddy good laugh at her overactive imagination. Time-travel, mysterious portals, a charming dwarf, and a hot-blooded Scotsman. God help her, maybe she just needed a holiday more than she thought.

Or at least a visit to the nearest psychiatric ward.

Except it didn't feel as if she were dreaming. The horse felt quite real beneath her and the smell... well, she didn't think she'd imagine such an overpowering scent if this were just a dream. Besides, if this were a dream, she'd certainly have picked more comfortable and attractive clothing than what she was currently wearing.

She looked down at herself and couldn't help but grimace. Faith had insisted she put on a long, uncomfortable dove-gray gown with a high waist and a thick, full skirt. With her jeans and blouse locked tight in Faith's wooden chest, it wasn't as if she had much choice. But it was clear that she wouldn't be making any kind of fashion statement today.

It was shameful enough that the dress was such a drab color, but to make matters worse, the sleeves were puffed wide and had turned-back cuffs that were edged with frilly lace. The neckline was square and unflattering, and the waist cinched impossibly tight. The only bright side was that the horrid thing was currently hidden beneath a heavy cloak of muted brown. Unfortunately, the cloak couldn't hide the ghastly white lawn cap that sat on her head, decorated with a wide band and tied firmly under her chin. She looked like a gormless idiot.

Fiona had balked at wearing the outfit at first glance, but it was the only gown Molly could find on short notice and had been able to expertly shorten to her height. Molly, whom Faith had affectionately referred to as a second mother and the castle matron, had been patient but insistent that Fiona dress in the garments she had chosen. In the end, Fiona had had

80

little choice; either she wear the horrid gown or stay behind.

She sighed, glancing at Ian again. She couldn't seem to help herself. She'd just met him and yet he seemed to have some sort of compelling power over her. The only logical explanation was that he intrigued her. He had an astonishing self-confident presence—a man used to getting his own way. She imagined her refusal to stay safely at the castle bothered him a lot more than he let show. Although, at this particular moment, he let a lot show—his square jaw was visibly tensed and a scowl marred his handsome face as he unexpectedly looked up, capturing her gaze.

Fiona flushed, realizing he'd caught her staring. But he didn't seem to mind. Instead, he gave her a look so hot and intense, she thought she might melt on the spot.

Her flush deepened and she averted her eyes. There was a tingling in the pit of her stomach, and her pulse was pounding. Sheer insanity was the only way to explain why she felt attracted to such a man. Typically she preferred educated, urbane, and cultured men. Men who respected her intellect and shared her taste for the civilized things in life. Not strangely dressed, overbearing men who ordered her about as if she were some kind of bloody soldier.

Fiona's horse suddenly took a small step sideways on the courtyard stones, almost causing her to slide out of the saddle. She clenched her legs together and held tight to the horse's mane before managing to right herself. Ian's scowl deepened, and he nudged his horse near hers. Again her horse shied a step or two, and Fiona's stomach lurched crazily as she fought to keep her balance.

"Ye carina ride," he stated matter-of-factly.

"I can too," Fiona insisted, clutching the reins. "I'm still up here, aren't I?"

He turned his horse around to face the castle. "Your cousin canna ride," he called out to Faith just as she exited the castle with a cloth bundle in her hands.

"He's exaggerating," Fiona protested, shifting her weight back and forth while the horse pranced from one foot to the other. "My mount and I are just getting to know each other a bit. It's completely natural that he'd be a little shy of me at first."

Ian snorted. "Ye are riding a mare, lass. He's a she."

Fiona darted a quick glance toward the horse's underbelly. "I am? I mean, of course I am. I knew that."

Faith dropped the bundle and walked over to Fiona. With one hand, she held the reins of the horse, while lightly stroking the mare's nose with the other. "You told me you'd ridden before," she said, looking up at her cousin.

"I have ridden before," Fiona insisted. "Granted it was some time ago—"

"How long ago?" Faith asked.

"Well, I suppose I was much younger then—"

"How much younger?" Ian suddenly thundered, his voice causing her mare to shy again.

Fiona clutched the reins in terror. "Oh, bloody hell, I was ten, all right. Are you satisfied?"

Faith exhaled a deep breath. "This does complicate things a bit."

"A bit, I'd say," growled Ian. "I told ye the journey we're about to undertake is no' for the weak and delicate."

"Well, I'll be certain to pass that on to the weak and

delicate as soon as I return from this journey and see some of them," Fiona snapped angrily.

Ian frowned at her but remained silent. After some time had passed, he sighed. " 'Tisn't the best solution, but I suppose she can ride wi' the Father, if hell agree to it."

"The Father?" Fiona repeated in surprise. She twisted in the saddle and saw a middle-aged man with ruddy cheeks, thinning reddish brown hair, and sparkling blue-gray eyes hurrying on foot toward them. Clearly a man of God, he was dressed in a black woolen robe with a simple wooden cross hanging around his neck. His expression was open and friendly, and Fiona sensed genuine warmth in his smile as he looked up at her curiously.

"What have ye need o', Ian?" the priest asked.

"We need ye to ride wi' the lass here," he answered. "Fiona, meet Father Michael."

"It's a pleasure to make your acquaintance," Fiona said. "Faith has told me all about you."

"Leaving out all o' my many wayward faults, I hope."

"I can't recall even a one," she replied with a smile, deciding she liked this priest already.

"Well, are we going to jabber all day or get on wi' it?" Ian asked, jolting Fiona from her thoughts. "We are all here."

Fiona looked around and counted silently to herself. Ian, Faith, Shaun, Father Michael, a hawk-nosed man named Furlong, and herself—six people. All at once, the plan for Miles's rescue seemed a little outlandish. Could the six of them—a rather motley group to say the least—really spirit Miles and his men out of the English-held garrison safely?

Either that or they'd die trying, Fiona thought with a shiver of dread. God in heaven, what had she gotten herself into?

Father Michael and Faith hurried to their horses and began securing their belongings to their saddles. When Fiona didn't move, Ian looked over at her and slowly raised a golden eyebrow.

"Well?" he asked questioningly.

Fiona looked over one side of the horse and then back at Ian. This whole rescue thing was going to be a lot harder than she'd thought.

"Oh, hell," she said irritably. "Can someone please get me off this bloody animal?"

Chapter Six

Riding a horse was grueling work, Fiona decided, even if all you did was try to stay upright on one. Worse yet, Ian didn't follow any kind of road or path, but took treacherous routes through dense patches of forest and over uneven and rocky hills.

Still, Fiona could not help but marvel at the countryside they passed. This was Ireland as she had never seen it. Cool autumn wind swept across the moors, rustling the grass and leaves on the trees. The sun shone warm for September and the heavily wooded slopes and woodland burns sparkled a magnificent emerald green in the brilliant light.

Fiona breathed deeply, the perfume of the forest filling her nostrils. They had spent a lot of time picking their way among the trees, but the last hour or so they had followed a small stony path leading up a hillside and across a large meadow. Carefully, Ian led the horses around moss-green boulders, through deep grass, and into shadowy ravines.

Fiona's fair cheeks and nose had long ago become sunburned and every muscle in her body ached. Even her teeth hurt from being constantly rattled together. She was alternately hot and cold, and had had to pee for about the last hour. However, she held her tongue, afraid to insist on a stop and be accused of slowing down the group.

Ian finally called a halt in what appeared to be the early afternoon. Without a watch it was difficult to judge the amount of time that had passed, but Fiona thought they'd been traveling for at least four hours. Maybe five. It felt like a lifetime. Her head pounded and her nerves were wired from the unspoken tension that thrummed in the air among the small group.

They took refuge in a small grove of ancient oak trees near the edge of a natural clearing. On one side of the grove, a rocky hill led down into a bush-covered ravine. The other side contained a cheerful, bubbling creek. Fiona had never seen a spot so beautiful, though she suspected Ian had chosen this location not for its beauty but because it offered water for the horses and cover from any unexpected passersby.

Father Michael helped her dismount and then led the horse to the nearby water for a drink. Fiona rubbed her lower back and watched crankily as Ian dismounted in a fluid, graceful motion. He didn't spare her a glance, instead following Father Michael to the creek with his mount. Damn him, but the bloody man didn't seem bothered whatsoever by the ride. At least Faith had the decency to groan and stretch her arms above her head.

Trying to maintain some dignity, Fiona hobbled

away from the group and into the trees until she found a tall clump of bushes. She needed desperately to take care of business, but it wasn't a simple matter with the heavy gown and cloak. Cursing, she lifted and bunched the voluminous material until she finally prevailed, thinking it amazing what one could accomplish when hastened by a full bladder.

After she finished, she straightened, every muscle screaming. She wondered with no little trepidation how she'd ever get back in the saddle without shrieking endlessly in pain. Father Michael had been a wonderful companion, and she'd appreciated his endearing efforts to distract her from the discomfort of the ride. But the truth was that thirst, exhaustion, and hunger threatened to tumble her straightaway from the horse. Moreover, her legs and back ached something fierce, and her bum... well, that was another matter altogether.

She looked around and, seeing that no one had followed her, surreptitiously slid her hands up under her skirts and began rubbing her sore bottom. It was unbelievable, the bloody indignity of it all. Faith had been right; she wasn't well suited to a century like this one. She'd been born a twentieth-century woman, and by God, there was good reason for it. She'd never again complain about an auto, no matter how horrid its color or cramped its interior. Hell, she'd take a bicycle right about now.

Relishing her moments of privacy, Fiona wandered among the huge trees toward the edge of a hill where the ground sloped sharply to the bottom of a bush-covered ravine. She had to admit it was exceedingly beautiful scenery, if a bit on the rugged side. It had been ages since she had gone on any kind of outing outdoors. This wasn't exactly the kind of outing she might have envisioned—wine, cheese, and a checkered blanket beneath a tree in Hyde Park was more her style. Nonetheless, fresh air and a bit of sun did quite invigorate the senses.

If only Ian weren't leading the group, it would be a lot easier, she thought with a scowl. She felt as though he was watching her, waiting for the slightest sign of weakness so he could humiliate her in front of the others and insist that she was mucking up the entire operation. Well, she was a lot stronger than he thought. Her job at the Prestwick Advertising agency had given her ample opportunity to face down men a lot more intelligent and sophisticated than Ian. She could handle him.

For heaven's sake, just because she found him attractive, it didn't mean she would let him lord it over her like a king over a peasant. It didn't even mean she had to like him. She just had to tolerate his presence until they rescued Miles and returned to Castle Dun na Moor. Then she could concentrate on getting back to the twentieth century where she belonged.

Thinking she'd probably been away from the others too long, Fiona turned to head back when she heard Ian's voice behind her in a hushed but urgent whisper. Mortified that he might have seen her rubbing her bum in what she thought was a moment of personal privacy, she whipped her hands out from beneath her skirts and whirled to face him. Before she could speak, he launched himself at her, crashing into her with a thud and sending them rolling down the rocky embankment.

Startled, Fiona could only gasp as they tumbled

down the bank in a tangle of arms and legs, rolling to a stop in a grove of thick bushes.

"Are you bloody insane?" she spluttered indignantly when they came to a stop. "Throwing yourself at me like some kind of sex-starved—"

Before she could say another word he rudely clamped a hand over her mouth. He now lay directly atop her, one hand still clamped on her shoulder.

"Shhh," he mouthed when she started to squirm beneath him. "Roundheads."

Fiona immediately stilled and heard what Ian must have already detected—the faint sound of breaking branches, men's voices, and horses' snorting. Frightened, she stared at Ian, who shook his head slightly in warning. Fiona wondered with growing alarm where the others were and whether they had been alerted in time to hide.

Clearly it was too late to do anything about it now. The voices above them grew louder. Ian carefully lifted his hand from her mouth and lowered his head down against her shoulder. Fiona trembled, hoping they were concealed enough to avoid detection by the English soldiers.

Ian seemed concerned as well. Fiona could feel his body taut and tense against her. The hand he lifted from her mouth slowly curled around the hilt of the shortsword that was attached to his belt and now pressed against her left thigh. His mouth almost touched her neck and his breath tickled her throat every time he exhaled. He was heavy, but Fiona, who couldn't help but be conscious of his slightest movement, knew he tried to distribute his weight so as not to make it unbearably uncomfortable for her.

Fiona tried to keep her breath shallow, but her pulse

pounded uncomfortably. She wasn't sure whether it was from fear of being discovered by the soldiers or from being pinned beneath one of the most sexy, if annoying, men she had ever met.

Her breath caught in her throat as one of Ian's knees slipped between her legs. Her pulse skyrocketed. Oh, God, it was definitely the latter. Now she was certain she had lost her mind. Perhaps only moments away from receiving grievous bodily harm from a group of raucous English soldiers, and all she could think about was Ian's hard muscular body pressed against her.

Ever so carefully, she inhaled a breath. She had to think about something other than the fact that she was trapped beneath Ian. Unfortunately, it wasn't so easy. Her skirts were tangled about her thighs, her cloak half wrapped around her neck. She dared not move even a millimeter to adjust them for fear of alerting the soldiers to their location.

The sounds of the voices were louder now, above them near the ledge where she had stood just moments earlier. Fiona closed her eyes. Her heart hammered so loudly, she was certain they would hear it and be on them at once.

Ian must have sensed her fear because he placed his lips against her ear and murmured something soothing in Gaelic. She relaxed and her fingers, which were curled in a death grip on his scratchy cloak, loosened slightly. She breathed deeply through her nose, reveling in.Ian's pleasant scent of earth, pine, wool, and male.

"You have to take a piss again?"

Fiona flinched as she heard a male voice directly above them on the ledge. "I'll be telling the captain, no more bloody ale for the sorry likes of you."

"Oh, sod off," came the irritated reply. "I didn't have that much to drink."

Coarse laughter floated down. "Like hell you didn't. You were squiffed blind. If the captain knew you'd been drinking while on duty, you'd have your arse kicked from here to Dublin."

"And who would tell him?"

"I would, you hairy git, unless you hurry and finish your business. And quit your moaning. I'm hungry and tired and looking for a soft bit of totty to work off some of my tension."

Fiona stiffened and felt Ian tense as well. Then she heard the sound of the man relieving himself, and then the two of them moving back into the trees. She held her breath until she could hear no more sounds and then let it out in a big rush.

She squirmed a little as a signal for Ian to get off, but he didn't move.

"Not yet," he murmured, his breath hot against her cheek. "We have to make certain 'tis safe."

"If you say so," she murmured back, shifting slightly beneath him.

"Dinna move, lass," Ian ground out between clenched teeth. "Please."

Fiona could feel his breath coming faster now against her throat in heated, tickling puffs, although he remained rigidly motionless atop her. All the same, she knew he wanted her; she could feel his arousal pressed hard against her leg. Of course, just about any man lying prone on top of a woman would be moved to such a physical reaction. But a part of her hoped that it was more than just that. It seemed only fair that she should drive him as crazy as he drove her.

Except that right now she really, really wanted to

kiss him. And why shouldn't she? He had the most amazing body. He was hard and muscular in all the right places. It wasn't a body sculpted by plastic surgeons or hours at the gym but by good, old-fashioned exercise and exertion. Who knew it could be such a turn-on?

Her legs twitched involuntarily and she heard Ian draw a ragged breath.

"Sorry," he whispered, even though it was she who had moved.

"My fault," she whispered back, surprised when she felt a drip of perspiration from his forehead slide onto her temple. It would take so little to start something here, she thought. One expert shift of her body or a slight turn of her lips into his. Yet she paused, unsure of his reaction.

Certainly in the seventeenth century men lived by a different code. It was just her luck that this man would be more honorable when it came to sexual encounters—certainly compared to modern men, in her experience. Instinct told her that even if Ian lived in her century, he wouldn't be the type who she would meet in a bar and take home to her flat only to wake up alone the next morning. Most of those men would never ring her, and they'd likely not meet again, except perhaps during a brief and awkward encounter at the same bar some weeks later.

Fiona blew out an exasperated breath. Oh God, why had she kissed him back at the castle? Of course, she'd just been through the most frightening experience of her life and thought she was dead, but that didn't explain everything.

The truth of the matter was that the moment she had set eyes on Ian, she'd wanted to kiss him. Some-

how she'd known instinctively that it would be an incredible experience. And indeed, it had been the most
dreamy, sensual kiss she'd ever had. His mouth had
been both persuasive and delicious, coaxing her into
wanting...no, *needing* more. No wonder she couldn't
seem to think of anything else these days.

To hell with it, Fiona thought in annoyance. Maybe
if they kissed again, it would relieve some of this un-
bearable tension. After all, she had just been in serious
harm's way and was entitled to a little release. It
wouldn't be a completely selfish act, either, she
thought. She'd do it for Ian, too. Perhaps it would sa-
tiate them long enough so they could concentrate on
other more important things, like rescuing Miles and
staying alive.

It was settled, then. Ever so slowly, Fiona turned her
head, her lips brushing against Ian's earlobe and
cheek. Her hands crept tentatively around his neck
when Ian all but leapt off her.

"I think they are gone now, lassie," he said abruptly,
turning his back to her and adjusting his sword and
kilt. " 'Tis safe now."

For a moment she simply stared at him incredulously. Then she pushed herself up into a sitting position. Humiliation and disappointment swept
through her. The rat knew full well what she had just
about done.

Her cheeks flaming, she ignored his offer to help her
up and staggered to her feet. Her left leg was asleep
and she hopped around on it the best she could, wincing as the pins-and-needles sensation bloomed across
her foot.

"I suppose I should thank you for your timely actions," she said stiffly. "I hadn't heard a thing. Are the others safe?"

"I didna have time to warn them," he replied, picking some bramble from his hair. "But Shaun likely heard. He has the ears o' a rabbit, he does. And Furlong has the nose o' a hawk—he's legendary in these parts and an excellent scout. I, on the other hand, was too busy chasing after ye. Why did ye stray so far from us?"

Fiona felt her ire rise. "Stray? I didn't stray. I moved a discreet distance away to have a bit of privacy."

"Ye are straying if it takes ye more than a stone's throw from the rest o' us. Dinna do it again."

"That's ridiculous. It's not like I was running away or anything. I simply needed a place where I could conduct a bit of nature's business in private."

"Well, from now on ye stay within my sight," he said, brushing the dirt off a very well-muscled thigh. "No more straying."

Fiona raised her gaze to glare directly at him. "Frankly, I don't care how much danger we are in. I'm not peeing in front of you."

He glanced up at her in surprise and then laughed. "Aye, but ye will. And I'm enough o' a gentleman to turn my back when ye need a moment by yourself."

"A gentleman does not even begin to describe you," Fiona snapped, her pride still stinging. "A true gentleman would never be so domineering."

"A real lady would no' be so disobedient."

"I never claimed to be a lady."

He raised an eyebrow. "Have ye always been so willful?"

She brushed off her skirts. "Why shouldn't I be? I'm used to taking care of myself."

"I dinna believe that for a moment, princess."

"Princess?" she spluttered.

"Aye. It seems to me that ye are a pampered sort. Ye want people to take care o' ye, and yet ye like to have things done your way. Except for Faith, I'd venture to say that the people ye surround yourself wi' are o' a certain kind—golden-tongued, polished, and cultured."

Fiona's mouth dropped open in outrage. "Are you implying that I'm a snob?"

"I dinna know what a 'snob' is, but I imagine 'tis something close to what I mean."

"You don't know the first thing about me."

He shrugged. "I consider myself a good judge o' character. 'Tis a gift, ye see. My da had it, as did his da before him. 'Tis a birthright o' any good laird."

"Laird, my arse," she snapped, gratified when he looked taken aback at her language. "Titles don't mean a thing here. You're not even in Scotland. Besides, this whole conversation is absurd. I haven't even known you for an entire day."

He straightened, crossing his thick arms casually against his chest. "Aye, but sometimes it takes but a moment for two people to know they are right for each other."

Fiona flushed bright red and hated herself for it. "You bloody well flatter yourself, Scotsman, if you are referring to me and you. I don't even like you."

"Ye dinna like me? Then mayhap those weren't your verra soft lips brushing my cheek. And certainly those weren't your arms winding their way around my neck."

"Maybe I was thinking about strangling you."

He laughed, his teeth flashing white. "Or mayhap ye carina resist my Scots' charm."

"God save me from arrogant men," Fiona snapped, rolling her eyes. "And particularly from Scottish ones. You know something? You can't hold a candle to a true English gentleman."

Lifting her skirts haughtily, she started up the rocky embankment away from him. Without warning, he abruptly grabbed her arm from behind. With one hard pull, he drew her to him, holding her tight against his chest.

"Ye were right when ye said I dinna know much about ye, Fiona Chancellor," he said, his face inches from hers. " 'Tis something verra interesting at work here between the two o' us. That I canna deny. But I dinna like the way ye look at me, down that royal little nose o' yours. Mayhap I'm no' as cultured as the other men ye know, but ye'd better understand that I'm no' one to be trifled wi'. Ye canna bend me to your will, nor expect to have your way wi' me. When we finally are together, 'twill be on my terms, no' yours."

Fiona clenched her teeth together. "There won't be any 'together.' I'm here to help my cousin and that's all, Mr. Maclaren."

"The name is Ian," he said with an infuriatingly calm smile. "And I think that after our tumble down the hill, we can be a wee more personal, dinna ye? And we will be together, lass, ye can mark my words on it."

Fiona's pulse skyrocketed. His words held a promise that she knew he would keep—and God help her, she *wanted* him to keep it. Even now she fought an irrepressible need to wind her fingers in his hair and pull his mouth down on hers. Her body practically hummed at the thought.

"We have to work together to save Miles," Fiona answered, deliberately squelching any hint of desire. "It doesn't mean we have to like each other."

He laughed, a deep sexy baritone sound. "See, there ye go again, looking down your nose at me. Ye know what I think, princess? I think ye do like me. In fact, I think ye've even discovered ye might enjoy a man who is a wee bit unrefined."

Fiona turned her head away. "I don't know what you're talking about."

He took her chin and turned it back to him so that he could stare directly into her eyes. He had the most beautiful brown eyes she had ever seen. Now they smoldered, as if he barely kept a hidden fire banked beneath them.

"Oh, aye, ye do know what I mean. Has anyone ever told ye that ye are a rotten liar?" He whispered the words, his breath hot against her cheek.

A shudder of need shook her body, and she knew he felt it, understood it.

"Never," she said, keeping her chin up defiantly.

He gazed at her for a long moment. "Then I'm honored to have been the first. I may know ye better than ye think. Come now, the others are probably worried sick about us."

He released her, and Fiona scrambled away. Her entire body felt on fire. She refused his assistance up the ravine when he offered it, bloody determined she'd never touch him again after her humiliating performance. In fact, the only good thing about this whole incident was that she had lost the ghastly lawn cap and had no intention of going back to look for it.

Silently, Fiona followed him through the trees, nearly stumbling into the back of him when he abruptly stopped. Before she could move, he surprised her by turning and brushing his lips across her temple. The heat of his mouth against her skin sent her stomach in a crazy whirl.

"I meant what I said, Fiona," he murmured. " 'Tis no' finished between the two o' us. But the time is no' quite right, *mo gradhach.*"

Taken aback by the tender note in his voice, Fiona stared at him speechless until his mouth curved into a grin.

"Ye know, if we had the time, I'd show ye how a Scotsman eases the pain o' a sore bum," he said. "But 'tis our misfortune that now is neither the time nor place for such delicate instruction. Ye'll have to manage on your own."

Fiona's eyes narrowed. "You're bloody well right that I'll manage on my own."

He crooked a finger and put it under her chin, nudging it up until she looked directly at him. "Good, because we've another several hours to go before our next stop. Still glad ye came along?"

"I wouldn't have missed it for the world," Fiona said firmly, ignoring the stab of pain in her bum that flared up at just the mention of further travel. "And I am a lot stronger than you think."

"Spoken like a true princess," he said with an infuriating grin. "Then get yourself ready, lass. From now on, ye ride wi' me."

Chapter Seven

"I think it's going to rain soon," Fiona observed, shifting in her saddle. The sun warmed her shoulders through her cloak, but the distant shadows in the sky were in clear dissent with the pleasant warmth seeping through her body. "We should probably find shelter for the night," she added hopefully.

"If ye are tired o' riding, then just say so, princess," Ian said from behind her, a trace of amusement in his voice. "I thought ye said ye had a much tougher bum than that."

"I'll thank you to keep your concerns about my bum to yourself," Fiona snapped haughtily. "And for your information, it's just fine."

"Aye, a fine bum 'tis, indeed," he agreed.

She pressed her lips together in annoyance. "Very amusing. I suggested we stop primarily because I'm thinking of the others. I mean, everyone looks about ready to drop from the saddle."

That, at least, was the truth. Everyone looked as tired as she felt. "Besides, we don't want anyone to get soaked and catch a death of cold out here," Fiona added for good measure.

In an unexpectedly affectionate gesture, Ian reached up and brushed a strand of hair from her cheek. "Fiona, lass, we have a lot more to fear out here than just a chill. The English are everywhere. I sent Furlong on ahead some time ago to look for a spot for us to camp for the night. We must wait for him to return."

Fiona shivered as a deep rumble came from the northern sky. Dark, heavy clouds rolled above them, temporarily blotting out the sun and casting long, grotesque shadows across the countryside.

"Well, I hope he comes back soon or else we'll be drenched," she said grumpily.

"Dinna fash yourself, princess," he said with a smile in his voice. "I'll keep ye warm."

He let go of the reins with one hand and slid his arm around her waist, pulling her back closer against him. Fiona stiffened but soon relaxed against him when his hand did not move farther and she realized he had no other agenda. Right now he felt unbelievably warm and solid, and she was so very tired and sore.

To hell with pride, she thought wearily. To hell with self-respect. In a matter of just two days, her entire life had turned into a modern re-telling of *Alice in Wonderland.*

What in the hell was she doing here? At this very moment she wanted nothing more than a steaming bubble bath, a decent bed, and a wickedly strong vodka martini. She sighed just thinking about it.

"Chin up, lass," Ian murmured, resting his cheek against her head. " Twill no' be much longer."

Fiona sighed again, looking up at the sky. The hairs on her arms prickled as if in anticipation of the storm. Angry black and purple storm clouds continued to mushroom and swell across the sky. She jumped as a bolt of lightning lashed toward the ground like the tongue of a serpent.

"Jesus, did you see that?" Fiona exclaimed as another roll of thunder boomed. "How close do you think it was?"

"Close enough, I'd wager," Ian replied.

Fiona snuggled deeper into the safety of his arm. Energy snapped and crackled around her, raising the hairs on her arms and neck. As bizarre as it seemed, she also felt unexpectedly aroused by the ferocity of the approaching storm, coupled with the warmth and strength of Ian's body. She had never felt such a strong physical attraction toward anyone before.

"What are we going to do?" she asked softly, knowing exactly what her body wanted to do.

"Well..." Ian murmured, his hand tightening around her waist. Fiona inhaled a quick breath, wondering if he too could feel the sensual pull of the storm.

"Ian?" someone called out unexpectedly, and Fiona yelped in surprise as a dark shape on a horse materialized out of the forest directly in front of them.

Ian had already withdrawn his shortsword and had it pointed at the shape.

"Furlong, what took ye so blasted long?" he asked irritably, resheathing his sword. Fiona wondered if he had been as distracted as she by the coming storm.

The hawk-nosed man rubbed his chin thoughtfully. "Took longer than I expected. The English are everywhere. Wi' the storm coming, I knew we'd need a bit different kind o' shelter. I found a small cave just ahead, no' far from the tiny village o' Drumasladdy that should keep the rain off o' us. 'twill be a squeeze, but we should be protected there."

Ian nodded. "Good. Then let's make haste, for I fear the storm is nearly upon us."

"Ian," Furlong said, moving his horse closer to him. His mouth was drawn thin, his thick brows nearly meeting over his nose. " 'Tis something else ye should know. The English have already been through Drumasladdy. They burned the village."

Ian swore fiercely under his breath. "How long ago?"

"Two, mayhap three days ago at most."

"Any survivors?"

"Some."

Ian clenched his jaw. "Well, 'tis little we can do now wi' the storm nearly upon us and two women in our care. In the morn', we'll see if there is something we can do to help."

Furlong nodded in agreement and turned his horse around. Ian motioned with one hand for the others to follow.

Fiona fell quiet, sobered by her first close-up encounter with the ravages of war. Quickly they made their way through the forest to their stopping point.

Thunder boomed as Ian slid off the horse, reaching up to help Fiona down. She shivered as the wind rose up about them, leaves swirling and the treetops bending over from the force of the gale. She took a few steps and nearly collapsed, leaning heavily against a tree for support. Faith stumbled over beside her, rubbing her backside and then stretching her arms over her head.

"This is some blow, isn't it?" Faith shouted to Fiona over the wind, putting an arm around her shoulders and squeezing hard. "You've ridden bloody well for a woman who hasn't been on a horse since she was ten."

"Tell me that again later when I can feel my bum and legs," Fiona groaned.

She shivered as the first drops of rain began to spatter around them. The men were busy securing and sheltering the horses the best they could and untying their supplies from the saddles.

"Furlong," Ian shouted over the wind, "get the women to the cave. We'll be there shortly."

Furlong nodded, motioning for Faith and Fiona to follow him. They ducked beneath several branches until they came to a small cave.

"Ye'll find some blankets in the pack," Furlong said, dropping a bundle at their feet. Fiona gasped in surprise as he carefully uncovered a small lit lantern held in his other hand. The soft glow gently lit the interior of the cave, casting strange and dancing shadows on the walls.

"I'll go help the others now," he said shortly. With a quick dip of his head, he disappeared outside.

"Doesn't say much, does he?" Fiona commented, watching the squat man buffeted by the wind as he made his way through the trees.

"No, he doesn't. But he has a warm heart and is a good and loyal friend to both Miles and me."

Loyalty seemed to be a common trait among these people, Fiona thought as she turned to survey the cave

103

more closely. It appeared to be no more than three or four meters deep, with a low, sloping ceiling. She could stand straight up, but Faith, who was several centimeters taller, hunched slightly. Fiona could only imagine how uncomfortable it would be for Ian in this tiny space.

In one dim corner of the cave Fiona saw a nest of brown grass and leaves. Some animal or animals had obviously once made their home here. Fiona only prayed that whatever they were, they were long gone. Just in case, she warily backed up against the earthen wall.

Faith knelt and unfastened the bag Furlong had left, pulling out a roll of blankets. She started to spread them out, and Fiona swallowed her fears and knelt down to help her.

"How are you doing, pet?" Faith asked her. "I know all of this has been enormously difficult for you."

"Actually, I'm doing better than I expected," Fiona answered honestly. "Still, I rue the day that I ever longed for adventure."

Faith laughed, smoothing out a corner of the rough-hewn blanket. "I've never been so proud of you or loved you more. I can't tell you how much I've missed you and how glad I am you're here with me. I know this all seems very strange to you. It took me a very long time to adjust to the fact that I was living in seventeenth-century Ireland."

Fiona reached out and squeezed her cousin's hand. "You didn't have anyone to explain to you what had happened. At least I have you."

Faith smiled. "And Ian seems to have taken a liking to you as well."

"You mean he bloody well enjoys commanding me around."

Faith chuckled. "It means he likes you. He's just being protective. He's a good man, Fiona."

Fiona took a corner of the blanket and pulled it tight. "I'm sure you're right. It's just that at this particular time in my life, I need to be attracted to him as much as I need an extra thumb. Although, on second thought, with everything that has been happening to me lately, perhaps it could only help."

"So you do fancy him," Faith exclaimed. "I knew it!"

Fiona snorted. "What's the surprise? Do you think I'm blind to the fact that the man is bloody gorgeous? I may be a bit delusional lately, but I'm not dead. Still, I'd like him better if he were...well, a bit more accommodating."

Faith smiled affectionately. "He's not like any man you've ever dated, Fiona. He's not going to be so easy to bend to your will."

"Bend to my will? I do not try to bend men to my will. And I have no bloody intention of dating him."

"Sorry, pet, that came out badly. It's just that you have a set idea of the kind of man you think you want," Faith explained. "When they don't exactly fit that mold... well, sometimes you try to help them along."

"I do not," Fiona huffed, and then stiffened when Faith reached out and touched her arm.

"Fiona, it's not criticism. I too wish some people had more of the traits that I admire. It's just that sometimes we have to accept people for who they are. Ian has a good sense of himself. He's not a man who would easily change for anyone."

They both looked up in surprise as Father Michael stepped into the cave, followed closely by Shaun. Both were soaking wet.

"I'm afraid it's a deluge out there," Father Michael said, wiping his dripping face with the back of his hand. "Any more rain and we'll need to build an ark."

"Aye, 'tis as wicked a storm as I've seen in some time," Shaun agreed.

"Well, come in and dry yourselves," Faith said, immediately taking charge. Fiona could not help but admire the way Faith always seemed so sure of herself and in control of the events around her. As she watched, Faith deftly helped the priest remove his cloak from his shoulders.

Fiona took her cue and moved to help Shaun shrug out of his cloak. Surprised, she realized the cloak was damp but hardly soaking.

"How is it that your cloak is barely wet?" she asked the dwarf in astonishment, turning the garment around in her hands as if it were magic.

Faith looked over her shoulder and smiled. "It's made of pure wool, Fiona. The natural oils in the garment repel the water."

"Fascinating," Fiona murmured, already imagining herself in a deep burgundy cloak of wool with a hood and oversized gold buttons. One would hardly need an umbrella with such a coat, and it would be warm enough to wear during an evening stroll down London's many streets. It would be gorgeous and likely to set off a fashion storm in all of the city's exclusive social circles. And she, Fiona Chancellor, would model the very first one off the line.

"Where are the others?" Faith suddenly asked Father Michael, snapping Fiona out of her pleasant reverie. Remembering she was in a cold, dank cave and not on a well-lit fashion runway, she sighed in disappointment.

"Right here," came the answer as Furlong and Ian stepped into the cave.

Ian's large frame barely fit in the cave even though he bent over completely at the waist. In order to remedy the situation, he quickly sat down near the entrance to the cave, stretching his long legs across the opening. Who knew one man could be so large?

"Don't you want to get out of your clothes... I mean, cloak?" Fiona asked, flushing hotly. What the hell was wrong with her?

Ian pushed back a lock of wet hair from his forehead and grinned at her. "Ye wish me to remove my garments for ye, lass? For ye, I'd do anything."

Fiona felt heat suffuse her body at the suggestion in his voice. "You can forget it. I was just trying to be bloody helpful."

Ian laughed. "Aye, and right helpful ye are. Nay, but I'm fine as I am, lass. Dinna be angry wi' me. Come now and sit. We all deserve a wee bit o' rest."

Furlong sat down opposite Ian, effectively blocking the cave entrance. He crossed his arms against his chest, pulled his hat over his head, and said nothing more.

Shaun plopped down next to him, followed closely by a weary Father Michael. With a tired groan, Faith collapsed next to the priest.

The only space left was next to Ian. Fiona looked around at the group, suspecting that their placement was not as casual and random as they were pretending.

Ian looked up at her and patted the ground next to

Julie Moffett

him. "Well, are ye going to stand there all night, lass? 'Twould be a mite uncomfortable, I'd say."

Letting out a tired sigh, Fiona sank down on the blanket next to him, wrapping her skirts around her legs.

"Can't we have a fire?" Fiona asked, her teeth starting to chatter. The rain poured furiously outside, slashing relentlessly against the ground.

" 'Tis too dangerous, as it might attract unwelcome attention," Ian commented. "We'll have to make do without one. Come sit near me and I'll help keep ye warm, Fiona."

He held out an arm, but Fiona shook her head. "I'm fine, thank you," she said stiffly.

Father Michael leaned back against the cave wall and let out a deep breath. "Don't worry, lass. I'm certain that in no time the cave will be cozy warm wi' all o' us here in such a small space. Right, Shaun?"

"Right," agreed the dwarf. He removed his plumed hat, and Fiona noticed that in the flickering lantern light he was a dead ringer for the antiques shop owner. Again, Fiona felt a dizzying sweep of déjà vu.

"Shaun, lad," Ian said, his voice sounding remarkably cheery, "how about telling us one o' your infamous tales to make us sleepy?"

"My tales do no' make people sleepy," he protested indignantly. " 'Tis impossible."

"Oh, please," encouraged Faith. "Let's hear one, Shaun."

The others murmured in agreement until the dwarf sat cross-legged on the blanket and puffed out his chest.

"Well, 'twas the time that I single-handedly fought off four English soldiers during a skirmish," he began.

" 'Twas only my lightning skill wi' the rapier that fended them off and sent them running back to England wi' their tails 'tween their legs."

Fiona listened in rapt attention as Shaun wove the most preposterous yet entertaining tale she'd ever heard. The others chuckled, and even she could not help but smile at the dwarf's animated storytelling.

Yet she found her thoughts often straying toward Ian, her gaze drawn to his generous mouth and square jaw, now covered with a day's beard. She felt herself increasingly attracted to him, but for reasons far more complex than just his pleasing appearance. How that was possible with a man she'd barely met—she didn't know. But he seemed to radiate certain qualities, both annoying and appealing, that intrigued her. Perhaps if they got out of this adventure alive, she might even try to figure it all out before she returned to her own time. She would have to get back somehow. There was no way in hell that she would stay in this barbaric time without autos, hotels, chocolate truffles, or foot massages. Gorgeous Scotsmen notwithstanding.

After some time Fiona realized that the others were dropping off to sleep. Shaun finished his story and leaned back against the wall, closing his eyes. Faith was already asleep, propped up against Father Michael, her head resting on his shoulder. The priest snored happily, his arm wrapped companionably around Faith's shoulders. Furlong looked like a stone statue, and Fiona was certain he hadn't moved a muscle since he sat down. Ian also sat completely still, his legs still stretched out in front of him, his eyes closed.

Fiona rubbed the back of her neck wearily. The ground felt hard beneath her and she was still cold, although it had warmed up considerably in the cave.

Her legs and back were incredibly stiff, and she felt periodic cramps in her calves. Worse than that, she felt completely exhausted and wanted to cry in self-pity.

"Come here, lass," came a soft whisper.

Fiona looked up sharply. Ian was awake and held open his arms again.

"Let me rub your back a wee bit," he said quietly. " 'Twill help ye rest and will make it bearable for the ride on the morrow."

Fiona stared at him questioningly. He looked so warm and inviting. Even worse, his eyes held none of the amusement or challenge she often saw in them. Tonight she saw only concern, and something else, perhaps a hint of gentle affection.

Wordlessly, she snuggled up against him, and he began kneading the muscles in her back. She bit her lower lip to keep from crying out in pain, but after a few minutes of his gentle ministrations, she began to feel warm and sleepy.

" 'Twas a long journey, Fiona, lass," he murmured, his mouth against her ear. "Ye did yourself proud. A true princess."

Fiona didn't trust herself to talk, so she didn't. Instead she simply leaned against him, soaking up his warmth and reveling in the way he made her feel safe and wanted.

He kept up the steady kneading on her back until the pain disappeared and she felt only a languid, drowsy peace. Her eyelids drooped shut and her head fell back against his chest.

"Sleep well, princess," she heard him whisper as she drifted off to sleep.

For the first time in her life Fiona dreamed of a man on a white horse who swept her off her feet and carried her away to his kingdom. He was a man of imposing height with golden hair and lips as soft and gentle as the night sky. His kisses... they were the stuff made of dreams.

Her dreams.

Chapter Eight

Drumasladdy, Ireland
September 1649

Lianna Devlin was only a child, but at eight years of age she had seen enough of the wretchedness of the world to make her old.

Abandoned in infancy by a mysterious woman who passed through the tiny village of Drumasladdy on a chilly winter night, Lianna knew nothing of her parentage or from whence she came.

She knew that at first no one in the village wanted to take her in. When they unwrapped her from the tiny woolen blanket, they discovered to their horror that she was marked. Red hair and two strangely deformed hands indicated that she was either the outcast offspring of the fey folk or worse—borne of the unholy womb of the devil himself.

Although frightened, they were too afraid to abandon the child completely. The villagers instead persuaded old widow Mary Devlin to take in the child. But while the widow had provided for Lianna's basic needs, she had showed little warmth or affection. When the old woman passed on six years later, Lianna again found herself alone, with no one willing to step forward to help her.

The villagers held council to decide what to do with Lianna next. Finally they agreed she could live in the small cattle shed that housed the villagers' few livestock.

Lianna soon came to love her little home. Although small, it was warm and all her own. It also had the advantage of being near the cottage of her one and only friend in the whole world, twelve-year-old Colleen O'Reilly. Colleen often brought Lianna food and clothing, but more importantly, she talked with her.

It was from Colleen that Lianna learned the important fact that she was a witch. According to Colleen, witches had red hair and special marks upon their bodies—just as Lianna had unmistakably fire-colored hair and missing index fingers on both hands.

"Hair the color o' blood and fire is a warning to god-fearing folk that a witch is among them," Colleen explained. "Yet 'tis the marks on the body, like your missing fingers, that are signals to other witches that ye are truly one o' them."

Lianna shivered. "Do ye really think I'm a witch?"

Colleen shrugged. "Mayhap. But I think ye are a good witch. Bad witches can fly thro' the air, make themselves invisible, and destroy their enemies by breathing fire from their mouths. I don't think ye can do any o' that now, can ye, Lianna *gra?*"

Lianna could neither fly nor breathe fire, so either she was a good witch or a very inept bad witch. She hoped fervently she was a good witch and that good witches went to heaven. Colleen told her all about heaven and that it was a safe, warm place.

So, for the past year, Lianna had lived in relative peace in her little shelter until a whispering began in the village about the arrival of the English.

At first, Lianna thought a visit by the English would be an exciting adventure. After all, these fierce warriors lived far across the sea, wore fine leather boots, and had tall, shiny hats on their heads. In fact, Colleen had told her many of the villagers call the men "Roundheads" after their special hats.

It sounded quite thrilling until Lianna heard Kevin O'Malley say that the Roundheads were coming to kill every Irish man, woman, and child. But Tom Garry told Kevin he was an old fool and said the Roundheads wanted to keep the Irish alive to force them into slavery and conquer the land.

Lianna didn't understand why the English would want Ireland so badly. In Drumasladdy, at least, it was wet and cool in the summer, rainy all spring, and blistering cold in the winter. Still, it made her curious about these strangers. Colleen informed her that for centuries, the English had swept across Ireland, ravaging, looting, but never managing to snuff out the Irish spirit. And although Lianna waited eagerly to meet these exotic people, months passed and they never arrived. Finally, even casual talk about these Roundheads ceased.

Until two nights earlier when Colleen awoke her from a deep sleep in her cozy loft bed.

"Lianna, rouse yourself, lass," Colleen urged, shaking her shoulders hard. "The Roundheads have come."

Lianna awoke at once, startled by the sounds of shouting and scurrying. She ran outside with Colleen and saw fires burning on the darkened horizon.

"Stay here in the shed," Colleen advised. "I must help Mama. Papa left hours ago to meet the English on the outskirts o' the village. We'll be safe here. Certainly the English will no' hurt women and children."

"But Kevin O'Malley said..." Lianna started before Colleen impatiently cut her off.

"Och, Kevin O'Malley has a mouth as big as a horse and no' a shred o' sense in his head. Just stay here, Lianna, *mo gra.* You'll be safe."

"Stay with me, please," Lianna begged, but Colleen gave her a quick hug and returned to the cottage.

For an hour, Lianna sat outside the shed, listening to the anxious snorting and rustling of the animals and watching the glowing horizon. She clutched her hands together in her lap, leaning back against the shed wall, her anxiety growing as the screams and shouts came closer. A visit from the Roundheads didn't seem like an exciting adventure after all.

Eventually Lianna returned to her loft bed, curled up under her blanket, and waited.

She must have dozed, for she awoke with a start to the sound of a horrible cry. She sat straight up, clutching the blanket, her heart frozen in terror. When the cry came again, Lianna forced her limbs into action.

She wrapped a blanket around her shoulders for warmth and climbed down the loft. Carefully, she crept to the door of the shed, opening it a crack and peeking out.

The village was on fire. Flames crackled and roared

into the sky, brightening the darkened sky with showers of sparks and grotesque flickering shadows. Screams and shouts came from all over, but another shriek, this one much closer, at once captured her attention.

Horrified, she glanced at Colleen's cottage. Two horses had been tethered to a nearby tree, and the door stood open. She could hear the sounds of breaking wood and Colleen's mother frantically shouting something.

Lianna opened the shed door a bit wider to slip outside as a tall, unfamiliar shadow of a man abruptly appeared in the lighted cottage doorway. She froze in place, her tiny bare foot exposed across the shed threshold. Her body remained in the shed and she held herself as still as she could. For a long, agonizing moment, the man stared directly at her as if his eyes could peel away the darkness and expose her standing there alone.

Lianna held her breath, not even daring to inhale lest she give the man the slightest reason to come investigate. At last he turned away, stepping back into the cottage and closing the door behind him.

The shouting within the cottage abruptly ceased, and after a moment, Lianna darted from the shed into the forest. Taking cover behind a tree, she sank to the ground, breathing hard before she burst into tears. For the first time in her life she wished she were a bad witch. She'd breathe fire or cast a horrible spell that would whisk the strangers away from Colleen's cottage.

"Lianna, ye've never amounted to anything in your whole life," she said fiercely, clasping her small hands together. "Ye've got to do something."

First she had to stop crying like a baby and think. She was eight years of age now, old enough to do something to help. Yet how could someone as small as she draw out the men who had gone inside the cottage?

The screams started again, and Lianna resisted the urge to simply run to the house and throw open the door and shriek at the men to go away. Colleen said the English wouldn't hurt them, but something terrible was happening inside the cottage. Mayhap she could create a diversion that would cause the men to come out of the cottage.

Summoning every ounce of courage she possessed, Lianna quickly formed a plan. Frantically, she groped around on the ground for some large stones. When she found three suitable ones, she cradled them against her stomach and crept along the cottage wall toward the front door. She intended to throw them at the door, causing a racket and drawing out at least one of the strangers.

She was nearly at the front when the door abruptly opened. Swallowing a frightened gasp, Lianna pressed herself back against the cottage wall and sank into the shadows.

She held her breath as two men exited the cottage, neither of them glancing her way. When their backs were turned, she darted behind the house, leaning heavily against the wall. When she dared to peek around the corner, she saw the men standing at their horses, talking softly. She exhaled a deep rush of breath, certain she hadn't been spotted.

Lianna stiffened as one of the men left his horse and disappeared into the shed. After a few minutes, he came out again and spoke to the other man. Then he walked over to his horse and pulled out several objects from a saddlebag. While Lianna watched in horror, he knelt on one knee and scraped a flint against a stone until a small spark shot out, catching fire to a cloth he'd laid nearby on the ground. Once it was lit, the man deftly wound the cloth around a stick and stood.

He lifted the torch until it touched the thatched roof of the shed. Lianna recoiled in shock when she saw the strange tattoo of a black hawk on the top of his right hand, clearly illuminated by the torch. When he moved his hand, it almost looked as though the hawk might fly off his hand in search of prey. Lianna felt herself shake in terror, and then forced herself to take deep breaths to calm herself.

When the roof burst into flame, the tattooed man turned and returned to the cottage, lighting a comer of the roof and tossing the torch against the wall. Then, without another word, the men mounted their horses and rode away.

For a moment, Lianna could only stare in shock and terror at the burning buildings. Then she darted from her hiding place and through the open cottage door. Through a thin veil of smoke, she saw Colleen lying near the door, naked from the waist down, her skirts wound around her neck. Her head lay at an odd angle and her eyes were open and still.

"Colleen!" she screamed, kneeling beside the girl and shaking her arm. "Wake up."

When Colleen didn't move, Lianna stood, tears streaming down her face from fear and smoke. She ran to the corner where Colleen's mother lay facedown. Coughing and gagging on the smoke, Lianna rolled her over, but her arms and legs were limp and her eyes as open and unmoving as Colleen's.

"Nay," Lianna shrieked and then jumped up as part of the cottage wall collapsed.

Barely able to see, Lianna staggered out the door. Just a few feet away on the grass her legs buckled beneath her and she fell to the ground, retching and sobbing. As she choked and gagged on her own refuse, the cottage collapsed completely, the fire roaring and crackling in some kind of morbid glee.

Gulping air, Lianna wiped her streaming eyes with the back of her hand and watched what was left of Colleen's cottage and the shed that had been her home burn to the ground.

Finally she pushed herself to her feet, her heart empty and cold. She pressed her fists against her eyes, burning the images of this night into her memory and promising Colleen never to forget.

"I curse all ye English," she whispered. "Wi' every bone in my body, I promise that ye will pay for what ye have done."

Rage such as she had never known churned and roiled inside her. It burned in her veins and seared the blood in her temples before it settled like a hard, cold knot in the pit of her stomach.

At that very moment, deep in her eight-year-old heart, Lianna Devlin had but one thought about the English.

Revenge.

Chapter Nine

Ian awoke with a start, surprised to find his arms were still wrapped firmly around Fiona. She sat sideways in his lap, her dark head resting against his chest. He smiled when he saw that her mouth had parted and she breathed deeply and evenly. She was warm, soft, and inviting in that mysterious womanly way. He felt a stirring in his chest but quickly pushed it away. Better that he not get too attached to her. She clearly had no intention of settling for a man like him, and he had no desire to let it even get that far. Besides, the relationship would be much more entertaining if he kept the attraction between them lighthearted and amusing.

Still, it had been years since he'd spent the entire night with a woman, he mused. In fact, he couldn't ever remember holding one all night. Especially one he hadn't had the pleasure of knowing in the most intimate way. He shook his head, fully aware of the irony that he had just done so with an Englishwoman. Fate certainly had a twisted sense of humor.

He yawned and rubbed the back of his neck, working out the kinks. A quick glance out of the cave indicated that it was nearly morning. The rain had stopped and the sky was streaked pink and gold. A quiet mist danced above the ground as a cool breeze, heavy with the scent of fresh pine, lifted and whirled it among the trees.

Feeling uncharacteristically lighthearted this morning, he tightened his arms around Fiona and buried his face in her short, mussed hair. He'd be damned, but even after a day long ride in the hot sun and a night in a small, dank cave, she smelled good. He could detect a faint flowery scent that reminded him of a field of fresh apples. He grazed his lips against her temple and was rewarded when she smiled in her sleep, snuggling closer.

"Och, Fiona, lass," he murmured, brushing his lips across her cheek. "Ye make a man wish he could lie abed wi' ye, instead o' tend to his duties."

Regretfully, he unfastened his cloak and slipped her off his lap. In one quick motion, he set her down, slipping the cloak beneath her head like a pillow. She mumbled something and then rolled over, burying her face in the soft folds. Ian ran his fingers lightly across her cheek and stood.

As if on cue, Furlong lifted his cap from his face and stood. He nodded a simple greeting.

"And a top o' the mornin' to ye, too, Furlong," Ian said cheerfully after they stepped out of the cave.

Furlong raised one craggy eyebrow and gave the slightest hint of a smile but said nothing.

Julie Moffett

Ian paused a few steps from the entrance and looked around. In just the few minutes it had taken him to exit the cave, the morning mist had begun to lift from the grass, spiraling up toward the sky in magnificent silver streaks. The cool autumn wind whistled through the trees, rustling the leaves and ruffling the purple heather in the nearby meadow.

As the perfume of the forest rose to his nostrils, Ian inhaled the rich aroma of wet black soil, moss, and fertile, marshy ground. The distant cry of a curlew sounded, and he exchanged a questioning glance with Furlong. The hawk-nosed man listened and then nodded slowly.

" 'Tis still secure," he said simply.

Ian nodded and without another word led the way to their horses. The two stopped only to splash water on their faces at the cold stream and take care of personal business before untethering the animals and climbing on.

Slapping the reins lightly, Furlong quickly led the way to the tiny village of Drumasladdy.

Or what was left of it.

Ian felt a tightening in his gut as they approached the village. A dead dog lay ominously to one side of the path and the acrid smell of smoke and burnt thatch hung heavy in the air, like an oppressive, smothering weight.

As the village came into view, Ian saw the charred remains of several small cottages, some of them still smoldering. Pieces of clothing and furniture littered the area, and the place seemed suffocated by an odd and unnatural stillness.

Ian clucked softly to his horse, urging it in the direction of the only structure left standing. The stone

122

village well—once the home and heart of the people— had now become their only refuge. Young children and a few women slept huddled near the base of the well. A boy who appeared to be no more than twelve abruptly jumped up from the ground, brandishing a dirk when he saw them coming. The others sat up, clutching their blankets and young children to their chests.

"Put your sword down, lad," Furlong said in Gaelic, bringing his mount to a halt. "We are no' your enemy."

At the sound of his native tongue, the boy lowered the sword but looked warily at them. "Who are ye?" he asked.

"I am Furlong and this is Ian. We hail from Castle Dun na Moor, about a day's ride to the north. How many o' ye have survived?"

"Why do ye wish to know?" the boy asked suspiciously, narrowing his eyes.

A young woman with a threadbare blanket wrapped around her shoulders stood, placing a hand lightly on the boy's shoulder. A baby behind her began to squeal.

"I am Nuala," she said softly, her eyes lined and weary. "There are four and twenty o' us left in Drumasladdy. Those with enough strength have gone to Rockcorry for food and supplies. The rest o' us stayed here." She swept out her hand, and Ian's jaw clenched with anger as he surveyed the tiny group. Only women and children were left—and all were desolate, hungry, and clearly terrified.

Ian took another glance around the village. No need for repairs here; only a complete rebuilding would suffice.

He exhaled a deep breath. "Furlong, tell the villagers that Rockcorry is probably already held by the English. They must make their way north to Castle Dun na Moor. Molly will feed and shelter them 'til the time comes when we can rebuild the village."

Furlong quickly translated Ian's words, and for the first time he saw a flicker of hope in the villagers' eyes as they began to murmur among themselves.

"There's naught more we can do here," Ian said quietly to Furlong. "Let's make haste back to the others. Daybreak is nigh and we've a long day yet ahead o' us."

The two rode in silence back to the cave. Ian felt deeply disturbed by the bleakness and desolation evident in the villagers' eyes. He had seen it before, less than a year earlier, in his own country. The English had waged a bloody civil war on their own soil and beheaded their king. Cromwell had then ordered his soldiers to march through Scotland, rampaging, looting, and murdering, all in the name of religion and peace. Now Cromwell was doing it all over again here in Ireland, curse his bloody black soul.

"Ian," Furlong warned in a low voice. "Halt!"

Ian looked up quickly. He hadn't been paying attention to where they were going and realized they were nearing the cave. He pulled back on the reins, bringing his horse to an immediate stop.

"What is it?" he asked softly, staring attentively at Furlong. The man was legendary for his scouting abilities, and Ian trusted Furlong's instincts completely.

The stout man lifted a finger to his lips and slid off the horse. He knelt to the ground, examining the soil. Ian's concern deepened.

"I think we've got trouble," Furlong replied quietly.

"What kind o' trouble?"

Furlong stood, sniffed the air with his hawk-beaked nose, and then closed his eyes.

"The English kind," he said simply.

Fiona awoke with a jolt, not certain what had caused an end to her marvelous dream of languishing beneath the expert hands of a handsome Swiss masseur. Or had he been Scots?

Groggily, she sat up, rubbing her eyes until the fog of sleep lifted and she remembered the events of the previous day. A quick glance around the cave showed her that Ian and Furlong were missing, but the rest of the group slept on peacefully.

Faith still leaned against the priest, her pale blond hair spread about her shoulders, her cheeks pink from the long exposure to the sun. Fiona had never seen her look so beautiful. Faith had always been the one who abhorred fashion, avoided makeup, and cursed her lack of curves and breasts. She'd been too tall, too skinny, and too brainy. So much of an introvert, in fact, that Fiona often had to drag her out of her flat on occasion for fun.

Fiona, on the other hand, loved being petite and curvaceous. She was born to shop, enjoyed facials, manicures, and expensive salons, and delighted in every aspect of her femininity. Friends, parties, and fashion were her life.

But while Fiona had spent the last year indulging in these pleasures, it was Faith who had truly blossomed. If she understood everything her cousin had told her, Faith had fallen in love with a man who understood her, respected her, and helped her become the woman she had always wanted to be. Fiona felt a twinge of envy and wondered how it would feel to receive that kind of love from a man. Would she blossom as Faith had?

Sighing, she stretched her arms over her head, wincing when the muscles in her lower back protested. She stood awkwardly and slipped outside. She looked around for Ian but didn't see him.

Her stomach growled angrily and she remembered that her last meal had been some stale bread and cheese that she had gnawed on shortly before they stopped for the night.

"Oh, God, what I wouldn't do for a caffe latte and a chocolate scone," Fiona murmured. "Or two."

When they didn't magically appear, she shrugged and headed off into the bushes to relieve herself. Before lifting her skirts, she checked around carefully to make certain Ian wasn't spying on her. She'd sworn she wouldn't pee in front of him, and by God, she meant it.

She had just finished and begun rearranging her skirts when she heard a crackling sound behind her. Yelping, she whirled around.

A small girl with flaming red hair peeked out of the bushes at her. Her wary eyes were an unusually deep green and freckles liberally spotted her nose and cheeks.

"You scared the bloody hell out of me," Fiona said, pressing her hand to her chest and willing her heart to cease its thundering gallop. "But it looks like I frightened you as well. Come here, sweetheart. I won't hurt you."

The little girl stiffened when she heard Fiona's words and her green eyes narrowed. For a moment, Fiona thought they flashed with open hostility and anger. But then the girl gave her a shy, innocent smile and batted her eyelashes in a darling fashion.

"Come on, now," Fiona said encouragingly, holding out a hand. The girl took a step forward, and Fiona gasped when she saw the child was clad in a threadbare dress with no shoes. Leaves and twigs were matted in her hair, dirt smudged her cheeks, and she looked gaunt with hunger.

"Where is your mum, dear?" Fiona asked. "Is she nearby?"

The girl took another step closer and then stood silently in front of Fiona, her gaze downcast.

Fiona knelt down to be eye-to-eye with the child. "You don't speak English, do you?" she said. "That's all right. If you've lost your mum, perhaps I can help you find her."

The girl's upper lip trembled and she nodded. Then, with a strangled cry, she abruptly hurled herself at Fiona, knocking them both backward onto the ground.

Fiona managed to get her arm up in front of her face just as the girl whipped a small dirk from the folds of her skirt and thrust it at Fiona's face.

"Hey!" Fiona yelled in surprise as the dirk slid across the top of her arm.

Clawing and cursing frantically, Fiona managed to get one hand around the wrist that held the dirk and the other pushed up against her face.

"Get off me, you little hellcat," Fiona screeched, rolling over and pinning the girl beneath her. "What do you think you're doing?"

The girl struggled ferociously, and Fiona narrowly avoided having her wrist bit. But as petite as Fiona was, she weighed at least three times as much as the girl, and right now felt damned outraged.

Squeezing hard, Fiona lifted the girl's wrist and slammed it against the ground until she dropped the dirk. The girl struggled some more and then stilled, looking up at Fiona with hate-filled eyes.

"Well, it's bloody nice to meet you, too," Fiona said, breathing hard. A quick glance at her arm showed that the girl had indeed scored a hit. Her sleeve had been slashed and blood trickled out. Cautiously, Fiona flexed her wrist, relieved when she felt only a slight burning. Luckily, the wound wasn't deep. Still, the gown was now thoroughly ruined, and Fiona felt her ire rise.

"For your information," she said to the girl, "I'm not a morning person in the slightest. Add to that, I haven't had coffee in two days or anything resembling real food. My bum hurts like hell and I slept on the ground last night. Right now, I'm the crankiest woman on the planet. You picked the bloody wrong person to confront this morning."

The girl said nothing, but stared angrily.

Ruefully, Fiona sat, pulling the child up with her. She struggled angrily, but Fiona held her arms behind her back gently but firmly. The girl yelped and ceased all movement.

"I'm afraid I'm going to have to take you back to the others," Fiona said, standing and bringing the girl with her. "Can't have you jumping from the bushes again, brandishing a knife and screeching like a banshee. It's a good thing I'd just finished my morning business or I might have wet myself." She smiled wryly when the girl narrowed her eyes and clenched her teeth.

They took two steps before walking directly into a broad chest.

Yelping in surprise, Fiona stepped back. An enormous man stood silently in front of her, dressed in a large doublet, breeches of dark green wool, and tall black leather boots. A dark red sash hung across his body from his right shoulder to his left hip, with a sheathed sword dangling from it. A helmet with a rounded crown, a flat peak in front, and two curved bars of metal sat on his head. He looked at her appraisingly and without the slightest bit of friendliness in his eyes.

Opening her mouth in shock, Fiona tried to say something but found her voice locked in her throat. Instinctively, she took another step back, releasing the girl. The child darted off to the right but screamed as another soldier stepped out of the bushes, scooping her up and depositing her unceremoniously at Fiona's feet. The girl scrambled up, backing into Fiona's arms.

"Now, what do we have 'ere?" the solider asked, tapping a finger thoughtfully on the chin strap of his helmet. "A little girl and her mum, taking a peaceful walk in the forest. How quaint, methinks." He glanced curiously at her arm. "Except you are bleeding. How did you do that? Scratch yourself on a branch?"

Fiona looked down at her arm and then quickly drew her wits about her. "Ah, it was just an unfortunate accident. Anyway, I'll thank you to let us pass peacefully. We are causing no harm here."

The two men stared at her dumbfounded for a minute, and then the enormous one in front of her began to laugh heartily. The other one joined in, and Fiona looked at them warily.

"What's so funny?" she asked.

The large soldier wiped an eye. "You are, luv.

Where 'ave you been? We've been expecting you in Rockcorry for two days now."

"You have?" Fiona asked in surprise.

"Aye, we 'ave. Where are the others?"

"Others?" Fiona repeated dumbly.

The other soldier stepped closer. "This one's a bit dense," he said, staring at her closely. "And kind of unsightly, too. What happened to her hair?" Fiona got a whiff of stale body odor and sweat and turned her head away to keep from gagging.

The enormous soldier shrugged. "I don't care how she thinks or what she looks like. Only how wide she spreads 'er legs."

Fiona choked on a breath in revulsion. "I beg your pardon?"

The soldier crossed his arms against his chest. "Don't play shy with me, luv. Where are the others? Surely they didn't send just the two of you to whore for our entire detail."

Fiona felt the bile rise in her throat and swallowed hard to keep it down. "Wh-whore? Us? Are you bloody insane or just morally deranged? I'm certainly not a whore, and this child isn't even ten years old. You've clearly mistaken us for someone else."

The man crossed his considerable arms against his chest. "And why would a nice English girl be 'ere in the middle of Ireland if not to service the loyal soldiers of the Crown?"

Fiona felt her palms dampen with sweat. "I'm...I'm here in Ireland on holiday, and this child is my...my niece. Yes, that's it. And we were just having a pleasant walk in the woods when we...ah...came across you gentlemen."

She took the girl by the shoulders, maneuvering her

around the big soldier. "Now that this foolish misunderstanding has been cleared up, we'll just be on
our way."

The big man shot out a beefy hand and clamped it
hard on Fiona's shoulder. "Having second thoughts
about your profession now, are you, luv? Most unfortunate timing, especially when I've been needing a
woman for some time now."

"You can't do this," Fiona warned. "I'm an English
citizen. I have rights."

He laughed. "I 'ave me rights, too, and I'm in need
of a reward. Come on now, luv. Don't be shy. We
found you first, so we get the first sample of what you
'ave to offer."

Fiona wrenched away from him angrily. "Get your
bloody disgusting hands off me, you revolting pig. If
you lay one finger on me or the girl, I swear you'll be
sorry."

The other soldier laughed. "I like 'em a bit feisty.
This one will ride me hard. Let me 'ave her first."

The big man shook his head, removing his helmet.
"She's mine. Looks like she needs a strong hand. You
take the girl. We can switch later."

Fiona took a step back, holding the girl tightly in
her arms. The girl didn't resist, only pressed herself
against Fiona as if she knew what was about to happen.

Left with only one option, Fiona opened her mouth
and screamed bloody murder. It was risky, as it would
likely bring more English soldiers to investigate, but
she couldn't let anything happen to the girl, and
frankly speaking, she wasn't crazy about the way
things looked for herself either.

With an angry grunt, the large soldier slapped her

hard across the face. Fiona gasped in shock at the violence of his action. Furiously, he wrenched the girl from her arms, throwing her hard to the ground. When Fiona stepped forward with a cry of protest, he grabbed her arm and snapped her head back with one hand fisted in her hair.

"Shut up, wench," he growled against her cheek, unfastening the front of his breeches with one hand and pressing her down to the ground with his considerable weight. Fiona kicked and scratched at him, still screaming at the top of her lungs.

"Get the girl," he shouted to the other soldier as the child leapt to her feet and darted off.

From the corner of her eye, Fiona saw the girl scramble across some branches and trip in her haste. The soldier fell on top of her and she screamed. It was an eerie, unnatural sound, and Fiona felt her blood chill.

"You bloody bastard!" she screamed, twisting and scratching. "Leave her alone. She's only a child."

Suddenly, the soldier on top of her let out an angry bellow and slid sideways. "I've been shot in me shoulder," he screeched at the other soldier.

Before Fiona could move, the soldier dragged her up, clutching her to his chest. Abruptly she felt the cold chill of steel against her neck.

"Come any closer and I'll slit her throat," he warned.

Fiona blinked and saw Shaun standing next to a tree, a bow in his hands and an arrow cocked and aimed at the soldier who held her. She'd never seen a more welcome sight, and tears formed in her eyes.

"Let the lassies go," Shaun said, "or this next arrow will hit ye in the heart."

"He means it—he's a master marksman," Fiona offered, and then quieted when the soldier drew blood from her neck.

"I can slit her throat faster than any arrow can reach me," the soldier replied, gripping her so tightly that Fiona began to have trouble breathing. "I'll do it. Now get out of 'ere. What's happening 'ere is none of your concern. The trollops are only doing what they came 'ere to do, service the loyal servants of the English Crown."

"I said let them go," Shaun insisted, his aim never wavering.

"And I say drop the bow or you'll have a blade in your pitiful Irish back," came a voice from behind Shaun.

Fiona felt her heart sink as Shaun slowly lowered the bow and took a step forward. Another English soldier emerged from the forest, holding a sword to the dwarf's back. Matters had now gone from terrible to completely horrid, and Fiona felt a lump rise in her throat. Would this nightmare never end?

"Oh, hallo, George," the soldier holding Fiona boomed, lowering his knife from her neck. "Good thing you came along when you did. We were just trying to 'ave a sample of the whores 'ere when we were interrupted. That blasted dwarf shot me."

George looked at Fiona curiously. "What 'appened to her hair?"

"Who cares?" he answered, shrugging, and Fiona resisted the urge to punch him.

"Why are there only two whores? Where are the others?"

"We don't know. That's what we are trying to find out," the soldier holding the young girl spoke up.

133

Fiona saw with relief that it appeared the girl had not yet been violated.

"What do we do with 'im?" George asked, nicking Shaun in the back with the tip of his sword. "Shall I run him through?"

The big soldier shrugged. "As you wish. We'll take the whores back to camp before we sample any more of their charm. There may be others like 'im about."

"Wait!" Fiona shouted as George lifted his sword. The soldier paused in midstroke, surprised by her outburst.

"Don't hurt him," she said hurriedly. "He's only been doing his job. He's my pimp."

The three soldiers stared at her dumbfounded. "Your what?" George asked.

"I mean, my... ah, guardian. You were right. He was paid handsomely in London to deliver me to Rockcorry and watch over me until I was safely delivered to the...ah...captain. The girl, she's just his daughter, an Irish girl and certainly not a whore. Now you can't blame poor Shaun here for doing his job."

"But he's Irish," George protested.

"Of course he's Irish, you thick-headed idiot," Fiona snapped. "Who better to know Ireland? He's an excellent guide and has protected me well—up until this moment. Now, why don't you just release us and we'll all be on our way to Rockcorry to meet your captain."

She smiled encouragingly at Shaun and then grimaced when she saw he was staring at her with the same dumbfounded expression as the soldiers.

The big man holding her blinked and then frowned. "We'll take you to Rockcorry, but only when I say so," he said. He jerked his head at Shaun. "Kill him," he ordered.

"Not so fast," came a voice from the forest, and Fiona nearly wept for joy when Ian stepped into the clearing. Her relief was short-lived, however, as the enormous soldier pulled her to his chest again, placing the knife against her throat.

"This ceased being fun a bloody long time ago," Fiona snapped, and then choked for air when the soldier squeezed her throat hard.

The three English soldiers came together, each of them holding a hostage. Fiona glanced worriedly at Ian, wondering where Furlong and the others were. She was amazed that he didn't look the slightest bit nervous. Instead he appeared mightily annoyed. Probably with her, she thought in dismay, for endangering everyone by going out for a private pee again. Oh, God, if she lived through this, she'd likely never ever be able to relieve herself in private.

"Well, now, isn't this interestin'," the big soldier observed. "First I find meself an English whore protected by an Irish dwarf. Then along comes a Scotsman ready to meddle in me affairs. I'll give you one warning, sheep-shearer: Leave now. This is none of your concern."

"Och, but 'tis my concern when you have a friend o' mine in your grasp," Ian replied in his thick Scottish burr, pointing at Shaun. "Let me have him and ye are free to go about your business wi' the women."

Fiona's eyes widened in shock. "Wh-what did you say?" she gasped.

The big soldier ignored her. "And why should we let you 'ave what you want? There is one of you and three of us."

"Because I'll kill all of you," Ian said simply, and

Fiona shivered at the certainty in his voice. "So, let the dwarf go. Now."

Surprised, Fiona felt the blade against her neck loosen. "You 'ave no interest in the women?" he asked.

Ian shrugged. "Why should I? They're English, are they no'? 'Tis none o' my concern what ye do wi' your womenfolk."

Fiona gasped in outrage, struggling against the soldier. "Why, you bloody, arrogant…" she fumed at Ian, and then gasped as the big soldier tossed her to the ground like a sack of potatoes.

"Watch her," he said to George and grabbed Shaun's arm, hauling the dwarf like a shield in front of him.

"You want the dwarf, Scots, then come and get him," the soldier said with a grin. "I'm in need of a little sport."

Ian nodded and took a step forward. Fiona saw him glance her way for a fraction of a second, and in that brief moment tip his head ever so slightly toward the girl.

Curious, Fiona turned her head and saw that George had released her and moved slightly behind the big soldier. The girl stood transfixed, clearly terrified by her ordeal. The three English soldiers now stood grouped closely together, ringed around Shaun, but still within a footstep of herself and the girl.

Wondering what Ian had up his sleeve, Fiona reached out a hand and pulled the girl into her lap. She didn't resist, instead turning her head into Fiona's breast and shuddering.

"So, who is the dwarf to you?" the big soldier asked with a smile, clearly enjoying the moment. "A friend?

A brother, or just an arse to put your stick in?" He snickered, and the other soldiers chortled noisily.

Ian took another casual step forward, and Fiona wondered with growing concern why he hadn't yet drawn his sword.

" 'Twas my solemn promise to his da on his death-bed that I'd look out for him," Ian said conversation-ally. "And I always keep my promises."

"I'm afraid your time for keeping promises is at an end," George said and laughed.

"Is that so?" Ian asked, lifting an eyebrow. "And I thought 'twas just the time to show ye how I keep them."

The big soldier stepped forward, leaving Shaun in the care of the other men. He tossed his dirk from one hand to the other, and Fiona shivered when she imag-ined that sharp steel blade slicing into Ian. Why in the bloody hell hadn't the idiotic man yet drawn his sword?

"Fiona, *mo gradhach,* dinna scream any more, all right?" Ian suddenly said, and Fiona started in sur-prise.

"S-scream?" she stuttered. "M-more? Why would I scream more?"

Faster than she could blink, Ian whipped a dirk from a sheath on his waist and sent it sailing directly between the eyes of the big soldier. The soldier took one step in astonishment and then fell to the ground with a thump.

At the same time, Shaun whipped a dirk from his boot and slid it between George's ribs. Shrieking a wild banshee cry, Furlong dropped from a tree on top of the third soldier, finishing him off with a slash of his sword across the neck. The injured soldier took one step toward her and the girl and then fell face-first in a bloody heap at her feet.

Fiona looked in shock at the three fallen English soldiers and then back at Ian.

He calmly wiped the blade of his dirk on the grass and then resheathed it. "Ye did well, princess," he said. "But let's get out o' here. Wi' all the screaming ye've been doing, we're likely to bring the entire English army down on us."

Fiona blinked and opened her mouth to speak. "I... I can't."

Ian lifted one eyebrow in surprise. "Ye carina get up?"

Fiona shook her head. "No, I... I can't go right yet. I have to be sick first," she managed before turning her head to the side and throwing up in a most unprincesslike fashion.

Chapter Ten

"We carina take her wi' us," Ian said, standing beneath the trees and tying his pack to the saddle. "She's naught more than a bairn."

"I'm fully aware of the fact that she's a child," Fiona snapped back. Her stomach still churned from the bloody exhibition in the forest, and she felt dizzy and lightheaded. "Which means we can't simply abandon her. We have to figure out where she came from."

"Isn't there a village nearby?" Faith interjected. "Certainly she must have come from there."

Ian exchanged a knowing glance with Furlong, who was untethering his horse from a tree. "If she hails from Drumasladdy, then we may have a wee bit o' a problem." Sighing, he turned to Father Michael.

"Father, try to talk to her again."

The priest knelt before the girl and spoke to her softly in Gaelic. The girl pressed her lips together and did not answer. He spoke again, this time in both English and French, but she simply turned her head away and remained silent.

Father Michael stood. "I'm afraid we'll get no help from her."

"Why is it a problem if she comes from this Drumasladdy place?" Fiona asked. "Can't we just take her back?"

Ian shook his head. "The village has been destroyed by the English. Burnt to the ground."

Fiona gasped. "No wonder she tried to kill me. When she heard me speak English, she must have assumed that I was with the soldiers. But surely there are some survivors."

"Aye, there are," Ian answered. "But I instructed the villagers to go north to Castle Dun na Moor until we can help them rebuild the village. 'Tis likely they've already gone."

"Maybe we can catch up with them," Fiona suggested.

"We dinna have time for this discussion," Ian said impatiently. "Miles waits at Cavan, and the English likely have more men in this area. Most, if no' all o' them, heard ye screaming at the top o' your lungs. They'll hunt us, since we've killed three o' their men. We have to go *now*. Father Michael, the girl will ride with ye until we reach the next village. We'll leave her there."

Shaun cleared his throat. "Ian, I know this isn't a good time to bring this up, but we'll no' be leaving her anywhere. 'Tisn't a village in all o' Ireland that'll willingly take this lass."

"Why not?" Fiona asked.

"Well, first o' all, because o' this," the dwarf answered, lifting a strand of the girl's hair. The girl snatched it away from Shaun and glared at him.

Fiona stared at him uncomprehendingly. "Her hair? What does her hair have to do with any of this?"

"It's red," Faith answered quietly, stepping up beside Fiona. "It's considered the mark of the devil."

Fiona blinked in surprise. "You've got to be bloody joking. They're going to brand her simply because of her hair?"

"Yes," Faith answered softly. "It's a real and tangible fear among most villagers in Ireland."

"You can't hold the child accountable because of her hair color," Fiona argued back.

"You know I agree with you, but our opinions are not going to sway the entire nation of Ireland at this particular moment," Faith said in a low, warning voice. "Got it?"

Fiona took a deep breath, reminding herself that this was seventeenth-century Ireland. "Right. Still, it's so bloody unfair."

"There's also the matter o' this," Shaun interrupted, taking the girl's hand and holding it up. "She's missing the pointing finger on both hands."

Fiona heard a sharp intake of breath and turned around, astonished to see that even Furlong had paled slightly. Father Michael quickly made the sign of the cross.

"You mean the English cut off her fingers?" Fiona exclaimed in horror.

Shaun shook his head. "Nay, she was born without them. Look, ye can see there is no' even a space for them. And 'tis most significant which fingers are missing," he explained further, releasing the hand and stepping carefully away from the girl. "She'll have difficulty casting a spell without her pointing finger. But it may simply be an indication that a far greater power lies within."

Fiona rolled her eyes in disbelief. "You've got to be joking. Can't you see she's just a destitute child who has likely seen her entire life destroyed? We have to take her with us."

"Fiona is right." Ian spoke up after listening to the exchange. "We carina leave her alone. She'll go wi' us until we can decide what to do wi' her. Father Michael, she'll ride wi' ye. If she truly is wi' the devil's powers, then ye'll be the best protected among us."

Fiona stared at Ian in surprise. "Surely you don't believe that nonsense."

"Fiona," Faith warned, "leave it alone. We have to Go."

Ian mounted his horse and stretched out a hand to her. "Come on, lass, ye'll ride wi' me."

Fiona hesitated for a moment but then took his hand when she saw the girl did not resist getting on the horse with Father Michael.

"It's bloody unfair," she muttered. Now, more than any other moment since she had arrived in this century, she longed for a return to her own more civilized time. Seventeenth century or not, considering a child dangerous because of her hair color and an unfortunate deformity was simple barbarism.

Ian gently snapped the reins, and the horse began moving. Fiona sat straight-backed until Ian gently pulled her against his chest.

"Ye protect the child like a lion wi' a she cub. Ye'd make a good mother, ye know."

Fiona shuddered. "Oh, please, don't even say that. I'm just trying to be the single voice of reason here."

"Nonetheless, ye like her, dinna ye?"

"I wouldn't go that far. Normally I don't get on with children. They are dirty, noisy, and unpredictable. Besides, need I remind you that she tried to kill me at our first encounter? Not a great start on motherhood, I'd say."

Ian chuckled. "Well, ye are a bit prickly at first. She just needs to know ye a bit better."

"She wasn't interested in knowing me at all. She tried to skewer me like a pig. And she completely ruined my gown."

"Ye still protected her."

"She was about to be ravished by a group of English soldiers."

"So were ye. Ye had one on top o' ye, yet ye screamed at them to get off the girl."

"It was a moment of temporary insanity. Or terror, for that matter."

"Nay, ye simply have the natural instincts o' a mother, Fiona Chancellor. Admit it."

Fiona sighed. "This is just brilliant. I'm stuck with a Scotsman who thinks I have a natural propensity with children just because I didn't let some soldiers ravish the wild child from hell."

He laughed. "Ye are the most unusual lass I've ever met. So unusual, in fact, I didna even understand what ye are saying most o' the time. But ye make me laugh."

"Unusual and amusing? That's how you'd best describe me? Ugh. Frankly, all things considered, my epitaph is likely to say, 'Her life went down the loo.' "

"Loo?"

"No!" Fiona exclaimed, emphatically shaking her head. "Don't even go there. I will not discuss with you again the issue of relieving oneself. This is not a normal topic of conversation."

"And I was beginning to think ye English were obsessed wi' it."

Fiona heard the amusement in his voice and grimaced. "This could only happen to me. Here I am, riding into the sun with one of the most gorgeous men in the world, and the main topic of discussion is children and the removal of bodily waste. It bloody well figures with my luck."

"Ye think I'm gorgeous?"

"Don't let it go to your head, Scotsman," Fiona warned. "You've got a lot more things stacked against you."

He brushed his mouth against her cheek, and she felt a warm coil of heat spring up in her stomach. "Ye haven't even seen my best side yet," he murmured.

She sighed. "That's what I'm afraid of. But a woman can't live on adventure alone. I suppose it's too much to hope that we could stop and have breakfast anytime soon."

He chuckled again. "A lass who thinks wi' her stomach. I like that. As soon as we get a fair distance away from Drumasladdy, we'll have something to eat."

"Coffee and scones, I presume?"

"Oatcakes and ale."

"Figures."

Ian's arms tightened around her. "What's coffee?" he asked.

"A bitter-tasting black drink that numerous people are addicted to because it has marvelous eye-opening properties," she replied with a sigh, her mouth watering at the mere thought of it. "It's hard to start the day without a steaming mug of it. And I've been without it for two days now. No wonder I'm cranky."

"The way ye say that makes me jealous."

It was Fiona's turn to chuckle. "Just keep your eyes and mind on the trail, please. I'd like to get to Cavan in one piece. So far it hasn't been looking that good for me."

Ian harrumphed. "Didna I save ye back there in the forest?"

She twisted around in the saddle. "That reminds me—what took you so bloody long? And what exactly did you mean by saying you didn't care what those soldiers did with their womenfolk?"

Ian grinned. "I knew Shaun had a dirk in his boot and could take care of himself. But I needed that knife removed from your pretty little neck. I had to make him think I didna care about ye and the girl."

"Well, you could have been a bit more diplomatic about it."

Ian tightened his arms around her. "Ye doubted me, lass? Ye know I'd never let anything happen to ye."

She leaned back against his muscled chest and closed her eyes. "You have an odd way of showing it, Ian Maclaren."

"Ye just dinna know me well enough...yet."

Fiona smiled. The way he said it made her feel all warm and tingly inside. But more than that, it made her feel safe.

Lianna observed the two Englishwomen through narrowed eyes as she rode on the horse with the priest. She had no idea why the women were in Ireland, nor why an enormous man with a strange accent rode with them. Also accompanying them was the tiniest man she had ever seen, with a beard and a funny hat, a man with a big hook nose who rarely talked, and, of course, the priest with whom she rode. She didn't understand what they were saying, although occasionally she heard the priest and the little man exchange words with each other in her own native tongue.

Still, it was the pretty Englishwoman with the short dark hair that fascinated Lianna the most. She'd heard the others call her by the name of Fiona. Fiona was English, yet she was the one who had tried to protect her from the soldiers. Fiona had also been attacked herself, so she clearly wasn't in league with them. Yet it was puzzling that she'd risked her own life to try to save a girl who moments earlier had tried to kill her.

Lianna squinted her eyes and stared at the back of Fiona's head. She seemed quite familiar with the big man. He had to be the leader of the group. The man seemed protective of her and held his arm tightly around her waist while they rode his horse, even when Lianna was certain it wasn't necessary. She didn't understand what they were saying to each other when she could overhear them, but sometimes Fiona seemed angry with him, while at other times she laughed and gave him a pretty smile.

The woman with the blond hair spoke very little but was so beautiful and sad, Lianna felt a strange tug in her chest each time their eyes met.

Overall, she didn't trust a single one of them, but it was such a relief to have food in her stomach that she didn't really care. From the snatches of conversation in Gaelic that she'd heard between the priest and the little man, she determined they were headed for the nearby town of Cavan, which was now occupied by the English.

That fit her plans just fine.

She'd accompany them right into the town. Then, when no one was looking, she'd slip away and find the man with the black hawk tattooed on the top of his right hand. But this time, care would have to be taken. Her emotions would be held tightly under control. She'd bide her time, watch his every movement. Then, when he was alone and vulnerable, she'd kill him. He would pay for what he had done to Colleen and her family.

Fiona had never ached so much in her entire life. The journey became more difficult as they neared Cavan and the English presence increased. They were nearly discovered by English patrols on three separate occasions, but Ian somehow managed to elude them. By the third encounter, Fiona's nerves were jangling, and her body was so sore that she felt certain a nervous breakdown was imminent. Thankfully, it was at that precise moment that Ian called a halt for the evening.

They were in a cluster of trees near a small embankment that led down to a bubbling stream. The men went off to brush and water the horses, while Faith and Fiona spread blankets beneath a thick canopy of branches. The girl sat nearby, warily watching the two of them work. She had yet to speak to any of them.

"Do you think she's mute?" Fiona asked Faith, pulling a corner of the blanket tight.

Faith shrugged. "I don't know. Sometimes traumatic experiences can render people unable to speak. It's more likely that she simply doesn't understand English. But that wouldn't explain why she won't talk to Shaun or Father Michael in her own tongue."

"She probably doesn't trust them. After all, they are cavorting with two Englishwomen. That likely makes them suspect in her eyes."

"I suppose you are right," Faith said, sitting down on the blanket and arranging her skirts around her legs. "Pretty astute observation from a woman who has always claimed she didn't get on with kids."

Fiona joined her on the blanket and motioned for the girl to join them. She shook her head and stayed where she was.

"You were always the one who had the magic touch with kids," Fiona said with a sigh. "Haven't you and Miles discussed having any?"

"It's not like we're using birth control. It's just that we've been together more than a year and nothing has happened."

Fiona felt a trickle of alarm skitter up her back. She knew how much Faith wanted children. "A year? That's nothing. Give it time."

"Oh, we will, of course. But I have this strange feeling that it just isn't going to happen. Maybe something happened to me when I came through time that made me barren. Or maybe I've been barren all along."

"That's balderdash! You're not barren. For all you know, the problem could be on his end. It's not like you can go to a lab and find out."

Faith smiled. "No need to be so defensive on my behalf. I'm not interested in assigning blame. It doesn't really matter who has the problem; it only means that Miles and I may have to face the fact that we may not be able to have children of our own."

Fiona reached over to take her cousin's hand. "It could still happen, you know. People sometimes try for years before being able to conceive. You shouldn't give up."

"We won't. I just hope we make it to Cavan in time. I can't bear the thought that we might be too late."

"Don't worry. We are going to get there in time and save him. Then you two will have all the time in the world to do something about enlarging your family."

Faith exhaled a deep breath. "Cromwell is in the process of invading Ireland. My husband is an important rebel leader. How much time will we really have?"

"You'll make the most of what time you have. You are the most resourceful and intelligent woman I've ever known. Miles is damn lucky to have you for a wife."

"You have changed, Fiona. Not a single word about my fashion style or lack thereof."

"Yes, well, I have to say being back in the seventeenth century certainly does change the focus of one's priorities. But I meant what I said, and I've always thought that."

"That means a lot to me," Faith said softly. "Just having you here is helping me in more ways than you can imagine."

They both fell silent before Faith spoke up again. "What about you?" she suddenly asked. "Have you ever given thought to having children of your own?"

Fiona blinked, taken by surprise at the question. "Me? Children? No, not really. I always thought it would be more appropriate to find a decent bloke first. Besides, I never really had much of a knack with little ones. They either cried or peed on me." She jerked her head toward the young girl who sat nearby, with her arms wrapped around her legs and her chin on her knees. "A better case in point is sitting over there. She's the first one in some time that I've actually had some interaction with, and she tried to kill me. Not a promising start."

"But you did a lot of work for children's charities," Faith protested.

"Of course I did. That's because they are somebody else's kids."

"You have a good heart, Fiona."

"Sometimes, perhaps. It's just that I've always thought of myself as a career woman. Of course, getting unceremoniously dumped from the Prestwick Agency, losing Edward, and finding myself in the seventeenth century in the period of just a few months has had me rethinking my position."

"Really?"

"Really. Perhaps I should look at it in a good way."

"You aren't worried about money, are you?"

Fiona laughed. "Heavens, no. Papa left me a fortune and the name of a good accountant when he died. I didn't squander it while you were gone. And frankly, I rather lost the pleasure in spending it after he died."

"I'm so sorry—"

"It's not that important," Fiona interrupted with a wave of her hand. "You know, maybe I've just gone mental. All of this—you, Ian, the girl, discussions of children—perhaps I've simply had a breakdown of some kind, and all of this is really just some kind of subconscious exploration of my inner demons."

To her surprise, Faith nodded vigorously in agreement. "I understand completely. I had those exact same sentiments for the first several months after I discovered that somehow I was living in the seventeenth century. Then I decided to get on with my life."

"Do you miss it, Faith? I mean, think about everything you left behind. You were on the fast track to the top. You were one of the first female undercover operatives for MI5 with a specialty in Ireland and counter-terrorism. A real Jane Bond. You were really making something of your life."

"It all seems so long ago—another lifetime ago," Faith said. "Yes, it was an exciting life. But it was an empty one. I was dreadfully lonely, Fiona. I can't explain exactly what it means to meet your soulmate— a person who makes you whole. It's like discovering a part of you that you never even knew existed. Miles is my life now, and I wouldn't give him up for all the money or career advancements in the world."

Fiona looked down at her hands. "If I'm honest with myself, I'll admit that I never felt that way with Edward, or any other man for that matter. I suppose it was lucky I didn't get married after all."

"You'll meet the right man, Fiona. A man with whom you can share your life."

"I don't need a man to make my life complete."

"No, you don't," Faith agreed, her blue eyes serious. "But if a relationship is right, it can be a magical thing. I understand how being here in this time seems so surreal and even unbelievable. It caused me to completely reevaluate my life, too. Living in this century and knowing what we do about events to come—not to mention technological and political developments— is mind-boggling. Life is exceedingly more difficult and much more primitive here than we ever imagined. But it's wonderful, too. It really didn't take me that long to adjust."

Fiona blew out a deep breath. "Perhaps. But I'm not certain I could ever get used to this. I'm two days without a bath, coffee, chocolate or toothpaste. Honestly, those are my basic requirements for survival. I don't know how much longer I can go without and still maintain whatever vestiges of my sanity I have left. That isn't even to mention other important items like toilet paper, mascara, nail scissors, and hairspray."

"Now that's the Fiona I remember. You will adjust, I promise. Life is full of compromises. These are just a bit different than the ones you may have always expected."

"I've spent my entire life with a nonnegotiable label on those things."

"You'll find replacements."

"I'd rather find a way home. I don't belong in this time and we both know it. I'm not like you. You are intelligent and adaptable. You even had survival training."

"This is quite different than what I trained for."

Fiona pushed her bangs off her forehead in frustration.

"It's just that everything in this century is so... physically demanding."

Faith chuckled. "Now you're just feeling sorry for yourself."

"Damn right I am. I'm in a pitiful state. I suppose now would be an opportune time to blame my wretched childhood."

Faith's smile slowly faded. "Life hasn't been easy for either of us, has it, pet?"

"No, it hasn't." Fiona paused, reflecting for a moment. "You know, I have so many regrets in my life, but the biggest one is not being there more for you, Faith. You've never really talked to me about it, but I

152

know your father blamed you for your mum's death. That must have been a terribly difficult burden to shoulder alone."

Faith pressed her lips together tightly, her face turning a shade paler. "It was difficult, but made worse by the fact that he was partly right. If I hadn't disobeyed him and gone to play at the lake, Mum wouldn't have lost her life trying to save me."

"Bugger that," Fiona snapped, heatedly. "You were eight years old, Faith. A child."

"I know. But I still feel responsible. Perhaps because of that, I desperately needed Father to love me...and to forgive me."

"So, that's why you became so determined to follow in his footsteps."

"Yes."

"Except you not only imitated his career as an agent, you far surpassed it."

"I thought it would make him proud," Faith whispered.

"Instead it infuriated him."

"He never thought women were suited to such work. It only widened the gulf between us. And then he died. I'm still trying to make peace with him... and with myself."

Fiona was quiet for a moment. "I'm sorry we never spoke of this before."

"You had problems of your own."

"I did," Fiona acknowledged with a deep sigh. "I made quite the reputation for myself, didn't I? Money made it all respectable, of course, not that it ever did me any good with Father."

"Your father was a very influential and busy

man..." Faith started, but Fiona cut her off with a curt wave of her hand.

"Please, don't bother to defend him. It won't help. The brutal truth is that he had no interest in me. He wouldn't have noticed if I went ten bloody years without contacting him. As it was, after Mum died, there was virtually no contact between us except for a weekly cheque sent to the boarding school. But while you sought your father's attention by emulating him— I sought mine by getting into trouble, spending his money as fast as I could, dating playboys, and engaging in high-profile affairs. I know you heard all about it, but you never once said a word, bless your heart. Did you know you were the only person who ever loved me for me?"

Faith's lower lip trembled. "Oh God, Fiona. I never knew you felt that way. If the truth be known... I actually envied you. You stood up to your father and did as you pleased. I thought you had a perfect life— exciting and adventurous. I should have known better. I could have helped you."

"You did help. You are my family, Faith. My only family. Trying to take care of you, drag you out to social events; it gave my life purpose. You are closer than a sister to me. That's why I never gave up looking for you. I damn well followed you through time just to make certain you were all right."

"And that's why I left the message for you on the double-edged blade of the dagger," Faith replied quietly. "I couldn't bear the thought that you'd never know what happened to me. You were all I had...in my other life."

A quick stab of hurt pierced Fiona. She was happy Faith had finally found the family and love she deserved, but she couldn't help but be envious that she was no longer really an integral part of it.

Faith must have seen the expression on her face, because she put a hand gently on Fiona's arm.

"You will always be a part of my family, pet. It doesn't matter where I am or *when* I am, for that matter. You'll always be in my heart. Sisters forever. Remember?"

Fiona managed a smile. "I remember. It's just that you have a new family now. A wonderful family that people like you and me only dream of having. I admit I'm envious when I see the look in your eyes when you talk about Miles. I'm downright jealous of the way Father Michael, Shaun and the others are so protective of you. That is part of the reason I insisted on going along on this journey. If someone is threatening to take that away from you—well, they'll have to get through me first."

Faith hugged her. "I swear, I feel better already."

"Me too. Do you realize that for the past ten minutes I totally forgot that I am in acute, not to mention possibly life-altering, pain from all this bloody horseback riding?"

Faith laughed. "Well, get some rest. If I know Ian, he'll want to get started well before daybreak."

Fiona awoke with a start, and for a moment believed she was safe in bed in her comfortable London flat. Then a muscle in her calf twisted in pain, and with a low moan, she realized she lay flat on her back on the cold, hard ground, sharing a blanket with Faith and a little girl who had tried to kill her.

She pushed aside her cloak and sat up, a shaft of pain shooting directly from her neck to her bum.

"First things first," she muttered, reaching down and kneading her calf until the cramp eased.

Exhaling a breath of relief, she looked around. The moon shone brightly, casting spears of gold through the tiny openings of the heavy tree branches. Ian slept sitting up at the base of a nearby tree, his cloak wrapped tightly around him and his sword in his lap. Shaun and Father Michael shared another blanket nearby, and Fiona could hear the dwarf snoring noisily. Furlong slept on his cloak a short distance away.

Groaning inwardly, Fiona stood up, careful not to wake the others. She glanced once more at Ian, but he hadn't moved. Stiffly, she slipped into the trees to take care of personal business. Her lower back and legs ached and her bum felt as if it were on fire. She felt an intense longing for the comfort and familiarity of home and leaned back against a nearby tree, covering her face in her hands.

"I want to go home," she whispered.

"Fiona?" a deep voice inquired.

Fiona glanced up, somehow not surprised to see it was Ian. He had probably known the second she'd awakened. She was grateful that he had at least given her a few minutes of privacy.

"I'm here, Ian," she said softly.

"Are ye all right?"

"I suppose," she replied wearily. "Other than the fact that everything hurts."

"For a lass who hasna had much experience on a horse, ye've done a fine job. I've ridden ye hard." He walked over until he was close enough to brace one hand against the tree and lean next to her.

"Thanks, I guess."

He reached out and pushed a strand of hair from her cheek. "Ye seem sad, lass."

"I suppose I am a bit homesick."

"Ye miss your family? Your mum and da?"

She shook her head. "No, Faith is my only family. My mother died when I was nine and my father passed on a few years ago. I suppose a conversation I had with Faith this evening about our rather wretched family lives has made me reflective."

"Ye had a difficult childhood?"

She looked at Ian in the moonlight. His eyes were gentle and compassionate. It was strange, but she really wanted to open up to him, to talk about her life and feelings. She had never spoken about her family with any other person besides Faith. Now after just two days of knowing Ian, she felt a peculiar urge to bare her darkest secrets to him.

"I... well, yes and no. My father made a bloody lot of money and invested it well. I never lacked for any material things. But love and affection... well, that was another matter. Neither my mum nor my father did much in that department. But I shouldn't complain; I know a lot of people had it much worse."

"Still, growing up in a family scarce o' love can be verra difficult," he said softly.

"How do you know?" she asked, looking at him curiously. "Did it happen to you?"

He smiled, and Fiona unconsciously moved a little closer to him. "Nay. I consider myself verra lucky. My da and mum cared well for my brothers and me. But I've seen the harm a lack o' love can cause to others, especially to those who are deeply caring people."

She laughed wryly. "You think I'm a deeply caring person? You just don't know me well enough."

He stroked her cheek in a remarkably tender gesture. "Ye are here on a verra dangerous journey, risking your life for your cousin's husband who ye haven't even met."

"But he's family," she protested. "That's different. Besides, you're here, too, and Miles isn't even part of your family."

"Och, Fiona, it seems ye and I are no' so different, are we?"

She stared at him for a moment and then laughed, shaking her head. "You're bloody amazing, Ian. How can you possibly know all the right things to say? You can't possibly be real."

"I'm real, I assure ye."

Fiona gazed at him in amazement. He looked so handsome in the moonlight, leaning casually against the oak tree. His dark cloak billowed around his large frame, the moonlight glinting off his sword. She felt extremely conscious of his virility and found herself as mesmerized and breathless as if she were a girl of eighteen. Even more fascinating was the slender thread of trust and respect that had begun to build between them. She realized with a start that she had not only an intense physical attraction to him but that she also liked and admired him. The insight was unsettling, yet instantly wrapped around her like a warm blanket.

"This is insane," she said, lifting her hands in exasperation and arguing aloud with herself. "I don't even know the first thing about him... you." She looked up at him. "I mean, I don't even know how old you are."

He grinned. "I'm four and thirty. I was born on the twenty-seventh day of April."

"Taurus the bull," she said wryly. "Why am I not surprised? So, why haven't you ever married?" Then a horrid thought hit her. "Or perhaps you *are* married."

His eyes softened and she flushed, realizing her openly stricken expression told him a lot more about her feelings than she had intended.

"I'm no' wed, lass, and ne'er have been. I ne'er seemed to have the time, and there wasna ever a lass wi' whom I felt the need to stay. Besides, as a third son, there wasna much need for me to wed right away. Then the war came, and any such thoughts were put away. I dinna know who would have me now that the English have taken our land and holdings."

"Why, I'm certain any woman in her right mind would have you," she said indignantly. "I mean, who gives a bloody whit about land and such when you have so much else to offer." As soon as the words slipped from her mouth, she paused, staring at him in mortification. What in the hell was she saying?

He grinned, looking down at her with such warmth, she felt the blood surge from her fingertips to her toes. "I like a lass who speaks her mind," he said softly.

Tenderly, he traced the line of her cheekbone and jaw before sliding his finger sensuously down to the bare skin at her neck. The smoldering flame she saw in his eyes both startled and thrilled her.

"Ian," she whispered breathlessly. At the base of her throat her pulse beat and swelled as though her heart had risen from its usual place.

Gently, his large hands cupped her face and held it still. He made no attempt to hide the fact that he wanted her, and her heart hammered painfully in response. He was so close now, she could smell his musky scent, and his breath was warm against her cheek.

"Ye are so lovely," he murmured, his lips brushing against hers as he spoke.

Standing on tiptoe, Fiona lifted her mouth to his, winding her arms around his neck and pulling him closer.

He hesitated for the barest of seconds before his mouth descended, devouring hers hungrily and leaving her lips burning. Any doubts she might have had about him were shattered forever by the sheer need and intensity behind his kiss.

In a dim part of her brain she was shocked by her eager response to his kiss and the depth of her desire for him. Her legs weakened and she slumped against him, her breasts tingling against the linen of her shift.

"Och, lass, I've wanted to kiss ye again since I first had a taste o' ye back at the castle," he murmured as his lips left her mouth to nibble at an earlobe.

Fiona tried to snatch a breath. "And I've wanted you to kiss me again," she admitted. "Why didn't you do it sooner? You could have, you know."

He chuckled against her neck, and Fiona felt a shiver of desire race through her as his tongue discovered the soft indentation behind her ear.

"Because the time wasna right."

"And the time is right now?"

He kissed her chin. "What do ye think?"

She wound her fingers in his hair. She had a burning, aching need for another kiss. "Why do men always want to hear that they're right?"

He laughed, pulling her roughly, almost violently, to him. He lowered his mouth until it almost touched hers. Fiona breathed in sharply, the blood coursing through her veins like an awakened river.

"Because I intend to be careful wi' ye, *mo gradhach,*" he said, his Scottish burr deepening. "I said it before and I'll say it again. 'Tis something verra particular happening 'tween the two o' us. I'll be honest wi' ye and say I've never felt this way toward another woman before. I canno' seem to stop thinking o' ye."

She knew exactly what he meant. Some kind of extraordinary bond had formed, tangling them in a web of attraction, fascination, respect, and driving physical need.

"You called me *mo gradhach* again," she said softly. "You've called me that several times. What does it mean?"

He smiled. " 'Tis the Gaelic for 'my love.' "

"My love?" she repeated with a strange tug at her heart. She knew it was just an endearment and that he didn't really love her, but she was moved nonetheless. "It's beautiful," she whispered.

"Nay, ye are beautiful," he said, kissing her again, his tongue tracing the fullness of her lips. This time the kiss was slower and more thoughtful, a gentle promise of what was to come. She quivered at the tenderness of his mouth, losing herself in the dreamy intimacy of their sensual embrace. His hands slipped beneath her cloak, exploring the hollows of her back. In response, she molded her curves to the contours of his hard body, her thigh pressing against his arousal. Then, abruptly, he pulled away, pressing a kiss to her forehead.

Fiona looked up at him in disappointment. "What's wrong?"

He sighed. "I'm on watch, lass. I dinna think 'twill

bode well wi' the others if I have my mind on things other than their protection."

So, he hadn't been asleep as she'd thought. He had likely witnessed her every move but had been generous enough to give her a few precious minutes of privacy. For that, she was grateful.

"I..." she started to say when she heard a slight crackling noise in the forest. Instantly, Ian drew his sword and pushed her behind him.

"Ian?"

Ian resheathed the blade, cursing softly under his breath. "Furlong?"

The hawk-nosed man stepped into sight. "I didna see ye at the clearing and thought perhaps something had..." He let the sentence trail off when he suddenly noticed Fiona standing there.

Ian put an arm around her protectively, pulling her against him. "I was just seeing to the lass here," he said.

Furlong nodded, as if it was the most natural thing in the world to see them together. "Aye, well, if ye'd like, I'll take the watch now."

Ian exhaled wearily. "Aye, 'twould be a good thing. Come, lass, and I'll take ye back to the camp."

They held hands, hers pitifully small in his. As they approached the blanket where Faith and Lianna slept, Fiona stopped, shivering.

Ian drew her close. " 'Tis a bitterly cold night," he said softly against her ear.

She leaned into him, marveling that his body managed to radiate so much heat despite the cool weather. "Yes, it is. Would it disturb your rest too much if I kept close for warmth?"

He kissed the top of her head. "Ye can stay wi' me always," he murmured. " 'Twould be my pleasure."

Chapter Eleven

Ian awoke, instantly realizing that he had slept propped up against the trunk of a tree with Fiona in his arms. Pink streaks of light were peeking though the canopy of trees and he realized dawn was nigh.

Fiona stirred, and he rubbed his bearded chin against the top of her head. He was getting used to this, he thought. In just a few short days he had become completely besotted with her. She both intrigued and challenged him, and to his surprise, he found he liked that in a woman. Capable and independent, she sometimes showed a vulnerable side that made him want to hold her and protect her from the world.

This was dangerous territory for him—a man used to living his life alone. He'd never felt the urge to wed or settle down until he'd met Fiona. 'Twas just his luck that it would happen now, at a most inconvenient and inopportune time.

He sighed in resignation. When, and if, they got back to Castle Dun na Moor, he would sit her down and insist on a civilized talk about their future together—if she'd even agree to any kind of future with him. Frankly, he wasn't at all certain she'd be the slightest bit interested in such a thing with him. He was a man without a country, a home, an income. What could he offer her?

As if she knew he thought of her, Fiona murmured something and snuggled closer. Ian brushed a kiss across her temple. He had no right to think of her now. Not when so many lives were in danger. He had to put thoughts of her—of them—aside and concentrate on rescuing Miles. Somehow, if Miles was indeed still alive and at Cavan, he had to spirit him out of the clutches of the English. It would not be an easy task.

They had known all along they wouldn't be able to use force to free Miles—not with just three men, two women, a priest, and now a child, too. They would have to rely on their wits. The English would not be expecting a rescue attempt, so they had to use that to their advantage. They were close enough to Cavan that he could put the first part of the plan into action this morning. The sooner they got their plan under way, the better the chance they had of saving Miles.

"Ian?"

He started, realizing that Fiona had awakened. Her blue eyes were half-closed and heavy with sleep, her mouth warm and inviting. His heart skipped a beat. She was beautiful. Brave, bossy, and spirited.

Mine, he thought, tightening his arms about her. *All mine.*

"How long have you been awake?" she murmured.

"No' long."

She gazed up at him, and he saw the drowsiness slip from her eyes. "You're worried."

He brushed her hair from her cheek and nodded. "Aye, a bit."

"It will be all right," she said and his heart warmed at the confidence in her voice. She truly believed he could do this.

"Fiona, I need to ask ye again: Are ye certain Miles is in Cavan?"

She sat up, leaning her head against his shoulder. "Yes, as far as I know."

He fell silent, and she reached up and touched his cheek. Her fingers were cool and soft against his skin.

"You've never asked me how I know that, and I appreciate it," she said softly. "Someday, when this is all over, I promise I'll tell you. But for now, you'll just have to trust me."

"I do," he said simply.

"Then what are we going to do?"

He rubbed his chin with one hand. "Shaun and I will slip into town and mingle with the other townsfolk. Hopefully, someone will be able to tell us exactly where the prisoners are being held."

"It will be dangerous asking that question."

"We'll be discreet. The rest o' ye must wait here. Ye all must be verra careful not to be discovered. We are close to Cavan and the English soldiers. At night we are relatively safe, but during the day, your position here will be vulnerable to passing patrols."

"I know. But I'll be more worried about you."

"Dinna worry about me. I have the easy part. Furlong has the hard task of keeping an eye on a priest, two independent-thinking women, and a mute bairn. Now *that* is what I call dangerous."

165

She cupped his cheek with her hand. "Ian, kiss me, please."

She smiled at him, her mouth softening with tenderness and passion. He slipped his hands slowly up her arms to the base of her neck, where his thumb stroked her skin. He heard her sharp intake of breath and watched her eyelashes flutter over remarkable blue eyes that had suddenly turned dreamy and languorous.

He lowered his head, pressing his lips against hers and then gently covering her mouth. He kissed her slowly and thoroughly, teetering between the fierce need to please her and his own powerful desire to possess her completely. She responded by winding her arms around his neck and kissing him back with abandon, her velvet-soft mouth creating a host of feverish sensations that left him near dizzy.

Regretfully, he pulled away, pressing a kiss to her forehead. " 'Twill be another time for this, *mo gradhach*," he said softly.

He heard her exhale in disappointment just as a slight movement caught his eye. The girl was awake, lying belly down on the ground, her head resting on her elbows. She watched him openly and curiously.

"We've got an audience," Ian said in amusement.

Fiona lifted her head from Ian's chest and glanced over at the girl. "Can't we tell her to go back to sleep?" she asked irritably.

Ian chuckled while disengaging himself from Fiona and standing. "Ye are a wanton woman, ye know. But I fear 'tis already too late. The others are stirring as well."

He stretched out a hand to help her up. She came to her feet, grimacing and rubbing her lower back.

"It's bloody official," she said, groaning. "I'm too old for adventure."

He grinned and gave her a swat on the rump. "Ye haven't even had a taste o' real adventure yet."

He started to move away and she grabbed his arm. "Ian, be careful today. I mean it."

He ran a finger tenderly along her jawbone. "I've got unfinished business wi' ye, Fiona. Ye can count on me coming back."

Fiona paced back and forth across the forest floor, wearing a path in the grass. Furlong watched her calmly from beneath a tree, his sword in his lap and a piece of grass in his mouth. Faith and Father Michael spoke softly nearby, and the girl sat as far away as she possibly could while still managing to keep them in sight.

After another few minutes of pacing, Fiona stopped and put her hands on her hips. "Isn't anyone the slightest bit concerned that Ian and Shaun have been gone for most of the day and we haven't seen or heard a thing from them?" she asked in annoyance, splaying out her hands. "How can you people be so calm about this?"

Father Michael looked up and patted the ground next to him. "Come, sit down, lass. Ye are worrying enough for all o' us."

Fiona released a deep breath and plopped down on the grass next to the priest. She examined her nails and wished she hadn't. Half were broken, the other half chewed to the quick. At least they were clean. She'd spent part of the morning under the discreet but watchful eyes of Furlong, washing herself in a nearby creek as best she could with her clothes still on.

Julie Moffett

She sighed again. Father Michael took her hand and patted it. "Ian and Shaun must be very careful about how they enter the town. They must not raise suspicion. After that, they'll need to mingle a bit to get a feel for whom they can trust. Only then are they likely to get the information they seek."

Faith nodded in agreement. "If it helps any, I'm not calm in the slightest. I'm trying not to think about it. After all, Ian and Shaun could come back with the news that... that we are too late." She paled, clasping her hands in her lap. Fiona felt a stab of guilt that she had been so worried about Ian, she'd forgotten all about the danger Miles and the other men were in.

"Oh, pet," Fiona sighed. "I'm sorry. We're not too late. I just know he is still alive and everything will work out all right. I just feel so bloody helpless sitting here and doing nothing."

"Mayhap now might be a prudent time to give ye one o' these and show ye how to use it," Father Michael said, rummaging in his pack and pulling out a small dagger with a curved handle. He turned the blade to himself and held the weapon—handle out— to Fiona.

She took it, marveling at how heavy it felt. "No synthetic materials here," she murmured.

Father Michael stood, pulling Fiona up with him. "Make certain your hand is firmly gripping the handle," he instructed, demonstrating with his hand. "That way, if ye have to stick it in someone, ye can easily pull it back out."

Fiona looked at the priest with something between horror and fascination. "That's some kind of catechism they teach in Ireland these days."

He smiled benignly but offered no rebuttal. "How-

168

ever, if ye intend to throw it, make certain your hand wraps around the outside o' the handle. Keep your arm straight and worry about aim instead o' speed." He pointed to a nearby oak. "Here, let me show ye."

He took the dagger and in one fluid motion threw it straight at the tree. The blade hit the bark about halfway up the trunk and slid in nice and easy, the blade thrumming.

Fiona looked at him in astonishment. "That was amazing. Remind me to never make you mad."

"Now you try," the priest encouraged, his mild and friendly expression at complete odds with what he had just done.

Fiona took the dagger and slid her hand around the handle. She took a deep breath, closed one eye to make her aim straighter, and threw the dagger. The blade hit the tree and bounced off, falling harmlessly to the ground. "No fair, you made it look easy," she complained.

She tried several more times with no success. Still, it was better than pacing, so she kept at it until her arm tired. Frustrated, she sank to the ground even though Father Michael encouraged her to keep trying.

"I know. I know," she said wryly. "Practice makes perfect." She rubbed her arm and then looked up in surprise when she saw the girl hesitantly approach her, holding out a hand.

Fiona shook her head. "Oh, no. You almost killed me with one of these."

The girl leaned over and took Fiona's hand, trying to pull her to her feet. Fiona stood, wondering what the girl was trying to tell her.

She angled Fiona's body in the direction of the tree and then went behind her, taking the arm with the dagger. For a moment she flexed Fiona's arm, and then she held it out straight—tracing her fingers from her elbow to her thumb. When she got to Fiona's thumb, she put her head down on the appendage and peered at the tree as if she were looking through a scope.

"I get it," Fiona exclaimed. "She's trying to tell me to use my thumb to guide the dagger to the target. I have to keep it straight when I throw."

The girl looked up at her expectantly and stepped back. Fiona lined up the tree using her thumb as a guide and threw it, keeping her thumb straight. The dagger hit the tree a bit skewed, but the blade stuck in the trunk and held fast.

"I did it!" Fiona enthused. "Thank you."

She retrieved the dagger from the trunk and the girl held out her hand. Fiona sighed. "All right, but don't try any funny stuff."

The girl took the dagger in her deformed hand and turned to the tree. With a fierce cry emitting from her throat, she threw it hard. The blade hit the trunk at exactly center spot and smoothly slid all the way in to the hilt. Everyone looked at the girl in shock.

"Well, I'm bloody glad you are on my side now," Fiona said a bit shakily as the girl calmly returned to her spot under a tree and watched them with unblinking eyes.

Fiona thought she saw a smile dart across the girl's mouth. Then the girl did something that surprised everyone. Looking directly at Fiona, she lightly touched her hand to her chest.

"Lianna...me," she said simply.

★ ★ ★

"What took you so bloody long?" Fiona cried when Ian and Shaun finally returned. Dusk had long fallen, Lianna had been put to bed hours earlier, and Fiona had worried herself sick.

" 'Twas more difficult than we thought to get information," Ian said wearily. "The townsfolk were naturally cautious. But thanks to Shaun and a half dozen pints of ale, we got what we came for. Then we had to have a look for ourselves at where the prisoners are being held."

The dwarf collapsed on the ground and Furlong brought him a chunk of bread and a flask. Shaun began to eat hungrily.

Faith put a hand on Ian's arm. "Is Miles alive?" she asked, her voice barely a whisper.

Ian nodded, and Fiona could see the weary strain around his eyes. " 'Tis most likely. Eleven prisoners in all—reportedly captured at Dundrum. Fiona was right; they are here at Cavan."

Fiona exhaled the breath she hadn't even known she was holding and Faith took a shaky step back, her eyes filling with tears. Fiona put her arms around her cousin, comforting her.

"I told you we wouldn't be too late," Fiona said.

"He's alive." Faith sobbed against her shoulder. "Oh, God, Fiona, he's still alive."

Ian sank to the ground next to Shaun and took some food from Furlong. The others gathered in a tight group. Fiona kept her arm around Faith's shoulders.

"They are being held at O'Reilly Castle on the outskirts of town," Ian continued after a sip from his flask. "The English are using the castle as a temporary garrison headquarters. The men are in the dungeon. I

171

dinna know how well they have fared, but the word is that none have yet expired."

Fiona straightened. "Well, now it's time to put the second part of the plan into action. Faith and I will be ready in the morning to do our part."

Ian held up a hand. "Nay, 'twill no' be so easy. Faith canna go wi' ye, Fiona."

Faith looked at Ian in surprise. "Why not?"

Ian exchanged a long glance with Furlong. The hawk-nosed man had hardly said two words all day. But he seemed to know what Ian would say, even before he said it, for he rubbed his nose thoughtfully and then frowned.

"Bradford," he said simply.

"What?" Fiona exclaimed.

"Nicholas Bradford is the garrison commander," Shaun piped up, his mouth full. " 'Tis a bad omen, that is."

Faith and Father Michael gasped in shock, leaving Fiona to stare at them in bewilderment.

"Who in the bloody hell is Nicholas Bradford?" she demanded.

"Oh, God help us," Faith whispered. "There is no telling in what condition Miles will be if he has been this long in the hands of Bradford."

"He's alive," Ian reminded her. "And if I know Miles, it has likely only stiffened his resolve. Bradford will no' have had so easy a time o' it either."

"Pardon me," Fiona interrupted, "but have I bloody disappeared off the face of the earth? Who is Nicholas Bradford?"

Faith sighed. "He is Miles's nemesis. Two years ago Bradford invited Miles and several other Irish noblemen to a meeting, presumably to discuss peace. Instead, it was a ruse. Bradford and his men killed two of the noblemen outright, and Miles and the others barely escaped with their lives. He is a cold, ruthless man, utterly without honor. He tried to kill Miles some time later, using me as bait. Thank God Ian intervened, saving me just in the nick of time. There is no way I can confront Bradford. He'll know exactly why I'm here."

Fiona thought for a moment. "Then it's settled: The next part of the plan is up to me. I'll just have to do it alone."

Ian rubbed his bearded chin thoughtfully. "Nay, no completely alone. I have another idea."

Chapter Twelve

Lianna dreamed of her mother. At least she thought it was her mother. She could smell her unique scent—flowers, freshly cut herbs kissed with radiant sunshine. A wisp of golden brown hair touched the woman's cheek and she brushed it back with a dazzling smile as she held open her arms to her daughter.

Lianna ran into her arms and her mother whirled around until they fell laughing into the grass. Her mother's eyes were as blue and as beautiful as the deepest lough she had ever seen, filled with love and happiness. Lianna had never felt so loved and safe.

She sighed, wishing her dream would go on forever. She was old enough to know this wasn't really how her mother looked. But somewhere in Lianna's mind lay the seed of a memory that for years she had carefully tended and nurtured. Now it had grown into a comforting reverie, one Lianna always sought when she was alone and frightened.

Still safe in her dream, Lianna buried her head in her mother's breast, listening to her steady heartbeat, feeling the soothing strokes of her mother's hand on her hair. Her mother was warm, soft, and beautiful. And today, Lianna realized something else.

The image of her mother had changed slightly so it now resembled the brown-haired Englishwoman named Fiona.

Fiona was certain she had just fallen asleep when Ian woke her, nibbling on her earlobe.

"Fiona, *mo gradhach,*" he murmured in her ear. "The others are asleep. Come with me. I need to talk wi' ye."

Fiona yawned as Ian helped her up. Lianna stirred in her sleep nearby, mumbling something unintelligible and tossing fretfully. Fiona bent to cover her with the blanket, taking a moment to smooth the child's hair back from her face.

Ian smiled at her and took her hand, leading her a little distance away beneath another tree. The moon was full and it made silver pools of light on the forest ground where it was able to penetrate the heavy canopy of leaves.

Ian spread his cloak, put his sword nearby, and motioned for Fiona to sit. She did and then opened her cloak to him so they could both snuggle beneath it. She wiggled up against his broad chest, wrapped her arms around his waist, and listened to the steady thump of his heart. His arms slid around her and he pressed a kiss on the top of her hair.

"She spoke today," Fiona said, stifling another yawn.

"Who?"

"The girl. She told us her name is Lianna."

Ian was silent for a moment. "Did she say anything else?"

"No. But she seemed friendlier. I don't know, it's almost as if she's beginning to trust us."

"We canna keep her," Ian said, fingering a tendril of her hair.

"And if no one else will take her?" Fiona asked, looking up at him.

He sighed. "We'll worry about that when we have to. Right now I have ample else to be concerned with."

Fiona nodded. "I know. Don't worry about me, Ian. I can take care of myself."

"Mayhap. But ye need to be verra careful around Bradford," he said softly. "He can seem charming and polished, but underneath he is a cold and dangerous man."

"So everyone says," Fiona said sleepily. "Look, we've discussed the plan to death and you've warned me a hundred times. I promise to be careful, Ian. Believe me, I have no desire to expose myself to any kind of grievous bodily harm."

"There is something else. I want ye to have this," Ian said, fumbling with something at his waist. Curious, Fiona sat up just as he took her hand and pressed something cold and heavy into it.

"What is it?" she asked, holding it up to the moonlight. She gasped when she saw it. It was a man's ring made of solid silver. The center of the ring was an ancient Celtic cross surrounded by a gold circle. At the center glowed a dazzling emerald in the same vibrant hues of the Irish countryside.

"It's beautiful," Fiona gasped.

" 'Twas a gift to my father from an Irish nobleman he once aided. I want ye to wear it on a string around your neck. There is a place along the north wall of O'Reilly castle where a mortar stone is missing. 'Tis a large enough space permit us to talk, but not to see each other. Ye can put your hand through it, though, and when 'tis time for us to meet there, I want ye to slip the ring on your finger if all bodes well. If ye do no' wear it, then I know ye are either in trouble or being coerced. No one else need know about it."

"I can't take this. What if I lose it? It looks extremely valuable. Are you certain you want to risk it by using it as some kind of signal?"

"I want ye to have it for always, Fiona," he said and then paused for a moment. "In case something happens to me."

Fiona looked up sharply. "Nothing is going to happen to you, Ian. I absolutely forbid it."

"Then take the ring, Fiona. Ye can return it to me later, if ye insist."

She slid the ring on her thumb and wound her arms around his waist. "Oh, Ian, I couldn't bear it if something happened to you."

Ian laughed softly. "Why, now, princess, are ye admitting that mayhap ye do care for me just a wee bit?"

"Of course I care for you," Fiona said, lifting her head indignantly. "But I never know what to expect from you. That, I suppose, is part of the attraction. But I do know one thing—over these past few days you've made me feel more like the woman I've always wanted to be than any other man I've ever known."

He nuzzled her neck. "I'm glad," he breathed against her skin.

Fiona sighed, tilting her head back and giving him free access to her neck. "It's quite puzzling, really. I've always sought after the wrong kind of man. Subconsciously I think I was attracted to men like my father, even though I didn't get on with him. No wonder none of those relationships ever lasted. I didn't even know the character traits I really wanted were the ones I would find in you, Ian. You're everything I have ever needed in a man."

He lifted his head from her neck and looked at her with a smile touching his lips. "Fiona, *mo gradhach,* I already know all o' this. Now shut your gob and kiss me."

She laughed and flung her arms around his neck, shamelessly opening her mouth and tasting him. His hands slid sensuously down her back and he returned her kiss with a fierce and thorough possession.

She clung to him while he eased her down onto the cloak, his mouth never leaving hers. Fiona's emotions whirled and skidded as he slipped one hand beneath her bodice and caressed her breast, running his thumb across her nipple. The mere feel of his hot, callused fingers against her cool skin electrified her, awakening needs she'd never even imagined.

With surprising ease, he slid the gown off her shoulders, pushing it down to her waist until her breasts were fully exposed. She shuddered as the breeze caressed her skin, but she was not cold. She could feel the heat emanating from his body course down the entire length of hers. Slowly, he kissed a path down the hollow of her neck to the tip of her sensitive, swollen nipples.

"Oh," she gasped as his tongue circled and teased, her thoughts scattering in a hundred different directions. Anxious to feel him, she slid her hands up beneath his shirt, kneading the thick muscles in his shoulders and then slipping lower to his abdomen. She was rewarded with a heady groan, and he grasped her hips, pulling her against him. Her gown was now tangled about her waist and she shifted anxiously in an attempt to get free of it completely.

Ian stopped her struggle by putting a hand under her chin, tilting up her head. His eyes were dark and probing, his breathing unsteady and raspy.

"Fiona, lass, ye know where this is headed, do ye no'?" he asked gently. "For 'twill come a point where I'll be neither able nor willing to stop."

"I know what I'm doing, Ian."

He raised an eyebrow in surprise. "Ye do?"

Fiona flushed. "I'm sorry. I should have told you earlier. I was young and stupid when I lost my... ah...virtue. But what we are about to do isn't wrong. I want to be with you, Ian."

He was quiet for so long that Fiona feared he no longer desired her. She flushed deeper, feeling ridiculously close to tears. She tried to turn her head away, but he wouldn't let her.

"I've no' treated ye fairly either," he said gently. "Ye are a passionate woman, Fiona. 'Tis wrong o' me to ask ye to join wi' me in a moment o' danger. So I want ye to think hard. I dinna want to ruin ye for another, if..." He hesitated and then swallowed hard. "... if ye will no' want me after all this is over."

Fiona cupped his face with her hands, marveling at how handsome he looked with the moon illuminating his warm brown eyes, bearded chin, and strong, angular face. "You've already ruined me for all men, Ian Maclaren. How could any of them possibly live up to you?"

A grin spread across his face before it slipped away and was replaced by regret. "Ye dinna know much about me, Fiona. I'm no' a man with a lot to offer. I'm a third son with no' much income. The English have now confiscated what little property would have been mine in Scotland. My father is dead, and I am a sympathizer to King Charles. Ye should know there is a bounty on my head, so travel to England and Scotland is verra dangerous for me. Here in Ireland I am little more than a soldier, aiding the rebels in their fight against the English—a fight we Scots have already lost. Simply put, I am man without holdings or means."

Fiona felt her eyes fill with tears. Before she met Ian, had any other man said this to her, he would have been history. God help her, had she really been that shallow? Ian didn't have a single worldly thing to give her except his love and his loyalty. And for the first time in her life, Fiona realized that that was enough— more than enough. She would be truly blessed to receive this man's love and loyalty.

"Ian, there is a lot you don't know about me either," she confessed, feeling foolish that her voice was shaky with emotion. "You don't know how I came to be here in Ireland or a thing about my past. You may change your mind about me when I tell you the entire story. But now isn't the time for such long-winded tales. Now is the time for us to share what we feel for each other. My whole life has been turned upside down in just a matter of days, and I'm finding that it has all been for the better."

"Then I shall love ye now, Fiona."

She slid into his embrace, his hands moving down her shoulders and arms, touching every hidden crevice and caressing them. Fiona shuddered with pleasure, and he slid her gown the rest of the way off, his lips following the same path his hands had made.

Wanting to feel the heat of his nakedness against her, Fiona reached for the front of his breeches and untied them. She pushed them down his hips and then rubbed provocatively against him. He made a guttural sound deep in his throat and abruptly stood, kicking off his boots and removing his breeches and stockings. He remained clad only in his tunic. Fiona stood and lifted it over his head while raining kisses across his chest and abdomen.

When they were both naked, she molded herself to his form, winding her arms around his neck, pulling his mouth down on hers. Their kisses were more urgent now, needy and hungry.

Ian moved his hands downward, skimming either side of her body until he reached her buttocks, pressing her firmly against his arousal. They stood kissing like that for what seemed like an eternity, two silhouettes in the moonlight.

Then, holding her by the hips, he lifted her up as if she were weightless. Fiona quickly wrapped her legs around his waist and his arms locked beneath her buttocks. As he intensified their kiss, he gently rocked her back and forth. A gasp of ecstasy slipped past Fiona's lips. She had never engaged in such an incredibly sensuous experience. Her skin literally burned from his touch, heightening her erotic pleasure.

Her body arched toward him in need when he lifted his mouth from hers to ravage her neck and earlobes.

"Oh, Ian," she murmured. "This feels unbelievably good."

He replied by showering smoldering kisses on her collarbone and jaw.

"Please," she begged him, her breath coming in long, surrendering gasps. "I want you now."

"Aye, and I want ye," he said, his burr deep and husky. "But no' quite yet."

Still holding her, Ian sank down to one knee and laid her carefully on the cloak. Tormentingly slow, his tongue forged a languorous path down her neck and breasts to her stomach, searching and finding all of her pleasure points. The heat of his tongue was intoxicating, and she burned and twisted, amazed by the strength of his restraint. He was the only man who had ever really made her feel like a princess and, more importantly, like a woman deserving of love.

Her eyes filled with tears, and he seemed to instinctively know what she was thinking.

"Ye've no' been loved like this, have ye?" he whispered, pausing to stroke the inside of her thigh. Each movement of his fingers sent jolts of pleasure through her.

"No," she whispered back. "Never. Please don't stop, Ian."

"I won't, *mo gradhach*," he said, lifting his head and kissing the tip of her nose.

His hands moved magically over her breasts, but now his touch was gentle and tender. His kisses were softer, his tongue lovingly tracing the fullness of her lips. Fiona was hypnotized by his caress, knowing that with each kiss he drained away all her doubts and fears.

"Let me touch you, too," she murmured as her

hands explored the hard contours of his chest and shoulders. She trailed her fingers down his stomach toward his manhood and smiled as she heard his tormented groan.

He moved his body to partially cover hers, their legs tangling. His arousal pressed hard against her stomach, and she quivered with both delicious anticipation and expectation. Her breasts tingled against his hair-roughened chest and her body vibrated with need. She could feel a tremor beginning deep between her heated thighs.

"Ian, now," she whispered.

With one knee he pushed open her legs and poised himself above her. She arched up to meet him, desperate for the feel of him inside her. With one thrust he pushed inside her, and she cried out in a burst of passionate sensations, welcoming him into her body. Love spurted within her like warm honey, exploding in a downpour of fiery sensations.

As he moved within her again and again, Fiona felt her world spin and careen on its axis. With each thrust he claimed a piece of her soul until he owned her completely. A deep feeling of peace entered her even as she strained to reach her sexual fulfillment. An ache inside her began to build.

"Ian," she gasped, her nails digging into his back. "Yes."

"Ye are mine," Ian said in a rush of breath and hard Scottish syllables. "Mine forever."

With those words still echoing in her ears, she soared to an awesome, shuddering ecstasy. She could feel Ian reach his peak at the same moment, and he clutched her so forcefully, his passion seemed to arc through her all the way to her toes.

With a groan, he collapsed on top of her, breathing unsteadily, his heartbeat roaring against her ear.

"Stay wi' me, *mo gradhach*," he murmured, his breath warm and moist against her skin.

For the first time in her life Fiona was filled with a staggering sense of completeness. She wrapped her arms about his neck, squeezing him as tightly as she could. Her body hummed in the aftermath of his fire, possession, and tenderness. And as they lay pressed together with their limbs intertwined she had both a terrifying and a breathtaking revelation.

She had met her soul mate at last.

Chapter Thirteen

Fiona pinned up her hair with two unwieldy wooden hairpins, hoping its short length wouldn't attract too much unwanted attention. Who would have guessed that a French bob could cause her such trouble? It was just her luck that the cut had cost her a fortune, too.

Taking a deep, steadying breath, she patted her hair into place. She wanted desperately to appear dignified and calm even though her nerves were jangling. What she was about to do was probably the most important thing she had ever done in her life, and at the very least she wanted to look presentable while she was doing it.

It had taken her longer than usual to get dressed in one of the two black gowns Ian had carried all the way from Castle Dun na Moor. Her hands shook the entire time she dressed, and at one point, Ian was so dismayed, he tried to talk her out of the plan.

But she persevered, convincing him with all the right arguments that she could pull this off. Surprisingly, the weight of his ring, nestled between her breasts, gave her comfort and courage. She could do this. *She had to do this.*

Fiona smoothed clown her gown and looked over at Ian. The bright autumn sun made his dark blond hair look golden. He was pacing back and forth in exactly the same spot she had done yesterday. She smiled. They were more alike than she cared to admit.

He must have felt her gaze upon him for he stopped his pacing and came to her.

"Ye look bonny in black, ye know," he said, putting his hands gently on her shoulders. "No' many women do."

Fiona smiled at him. She hadn't had a decent bath in days, had rinsed her hair in creek water without a drop of shampoo, and had brushed her teeth with no toothpaste and a horrid wooden toothbrush made with horsehair. Still, Ian made her feel beautiful and desirable. God, she loved him for that.

"You are an amazing man," she said, placing a kiss on the tip of his nose. "And you are worrying too much. The plan is a sound one."

"I dinna want any heroics from ye, Fiona," he said, his voice unusually gruff. "Get as much information as ye can—and then get out. If ye feel as if ye are in danger or trouble, ye know what ye need to do to get a message to us."

Fiona touched his arm. "We went over this a hundred times last night. I know exactly what I'm supposed to do. I promise you, I have no intention of deviating from the plan. Don't worry, Ian, I'll hardly even see Bradford. I'm certain that, as garrison commander, he'll be much too busy to have time for the likes of me."

She smiled again, hoping she sounded more confident than she felt. When she and Faith had come up with this plan, she'd expected to let Faith do all the talking. But now she would have to take charge and step into a far larger role than she felt prepared for. But there was no one else, and no more time.

And everybody, including Ian, knew it.

"I suppose now isn't the time to ask what the English did with the O'Reilly family when the soldiers confiscated their castle," she said with morbid interest.

"I assure ye, ye dinna want to know."

"That's what I thought," she said and fell silent.

Ian sighed and then pulled her into his arms. "I'm liking this plan less and less. Do ye have the ring?"

She reached around her neck and pulled it out from beneath her bodice. "Right here."

"And the dagger?"

"Still tied uncomfortably to the outside of my thigh, exactly where you put it ten minutes ago. For God's sake, Ian, you are treating me like an infant. Stop worrying."

"I should be the one going in with you."

"You said Bradford might recognize you."

"He might," Ian admitted.

She blew out a breath in exasperation. "Then why risk it? Nothing is going to happen to me. Besides, I won't be alone; Father Michael will be with me. And as I told you, I'm sticking to the plan. No heroics."

He bent his head and kissed her hard on the mouth. For a moment his lips lingered on hers, and then he pulled away. "Be good, lass," he said softly.

"The best."

Julie Moffett

He touched her cheek softly and then walked over to speak in low tones with Furlong, Shaun, and Father Michael. Faith and Lianna sat on the ground not far away. When Faith saw Ian leave, she stood and walked to Fiona.

"What's going on with you two?" Faith asked, cocking her head at Ian.

Fiona sighed. "I'm completely over the moon for him."

"That's wonderful!" Faith exclaimed earnestly. "He's a good man, Fiona."

"I know. It's just that this is happening so fast. I've barely had time to consider what it all means."

"He doesn't know, does he? I mean about you being from the future?"

Fiona shook her head. "Not yet. I don't know how I'm supposed to break the news to him. How did Miles take it when you told him?"

Faith looked at the ground. "Horribly. It took a lot of faith and trust on his part to believe me. I imagine it will be the same for Ian. But love can conquer a lot of things."

"I didn't say anything about love," Fiona protested.

"You didn't have to," Faith replied with a smile. "I know you too well."

Fiona glanced at Ian. He spoke animatedly with the others, towering at least two heads over Father Michael and Furlong. He was incredibly handsome, with a broad chest, powerful shoulders, and a commanding air of self-confidence.

There was no sense in hiding how she felt about Ian from the people she loved. All the same, it was disconcerting to know she wore her heart on her sleeve when it came to him.

188

"You're right," Fiona admitted. "I do love him. But I need more time to sort it out. Truthfully, I'm not certain what to do about it yet, and I fear telling him the truth about me."

"You'll talk it out when you're ready," Faith assured her.

"Well, it certainly isn't going to be now," Fiona said, rubbing her temples with her fingertips. "I think we are all too bloody stressed out as it is at the moment."

"Fiona, how can I ever thank you for what you are doing?" Faith said, her voice quavering slightly.

"You'd do the same for me and you know it," Fiona replied. "Besides, it's not that big a deal. I'm only doing what you James Bond types would call reconnaissance."

"It's dangerous all the same."

"So everyone keeps telling me. I intend to speak very little and I'll rely on Father Michael to politely extricate me if I commit any major faux pas. I'll blame any lapses of judgment on stress and grief. Everything will be fine."

"Just stick to the cover story and try not to fabricate any more than is absolutely necessary. It's hard to keep track of all the details when you're nervous and under pressure. Bradford is especially astute about such things."

"Did they teach you all that in spy school?"

"That and a bit more," Faith replied with a smile.

"To tell you the truth, I expect I'll hardly see Bradford at all. I mean, it's not like I'm going to have dinner with him or anything. He'll likely assign some poor, lowly subordinate to take care of my needs. Then everyone will have had their knickers in a twist for nothing."

189

"That's what we're counting on."

Faith hugged her and, over her shoulder, Fiona saw Lianna rise to her feet and shuffle about uncomfortably. Her red hair was matted, her face filthy. She refused to let either Fiona or Faith wash her and chose not to do so herself.

"Poor thing," Fiona said softly. "She knows something is going on but probably doesn't have a clue what it is. Has she said anything more?"

"No," Faith said, turning to look at the girl. "I had Shaun explain to her in Gaelic that you and Father Michael would be leaving temporarily but would be back soon. I think she understands that we are in a very dangerous situation. She's been extraordinarily quiet and has stayed close to us. But whether or not she understands exactly what Shaun told her, I don't know. She just gave us the same expression she's always given—wary and slightly hostile.

Fiona smiled encouragingly at Lianna. "Come here, sweetheart," she said, stretching out a hand.

The girl shook her head and Fiona sighed. "Lianna, it's all right. I'll be back. You stay here with Faith and the others. You'll be safe. Okay?"

Lianna blinked and hesitantly took a step forward, ready to bolt at any sudden movement. When she finally moved closer, Fiona took her hand, squeezing it gently. Quickly the girl withdrew it, but a shy smile appeared on her lips.

"My Fiona," she said softly, and pressed the flat of her hand across her heart.

For Fiona, the most terrifying part of the plan was riding the horse to the castle, all the while having to look as if she knew what she was doing. Luckily, her mount was either unaware of her ineptness or had taken pity on her and plodded along slowly and steadily. Thankfully, Father Michael led the way, so she at least didn't have to worry about where they were going.

Earlier Ian had told her that they could avoid riding into Cavan altogether since O'Reilly Castle was on the outskirts. They would have to pass through a small village, but Fiona had assured him that she could do it.

Now, as they came upon the village, Fiona looked about in amazement. Small thatched huts lined a path toward the castle and a number of campfires blazed in between them. People moved briskly between the huts and the fires, dressed in garments that were little more than rags. They seemed happy enough, and Fiona could hear their lilting chatter in Gaelic. Dogs, cats, chickens, and sheep roamed about freely, and the villagers showed no apparent concern about the huge, foul-smelling piles of animal excrement lying about.

The full reality of seventeenth-century Ireland hit her like a fist in the stomach. Up until now, all her impressions of this time had been disjointed and fleeting. The sight of the village and people all in one place was like putting the final pieces of a puzzle together. She had really traveled back in time—no dream could be this realistic. For a moment she could only stare, speechless.

Father Michael turned to look at her over his shoulder and then stopped his horse. He waited until she trotted up beside him, somehow managing to stop.

"Chin up, lass," he said encouragingly, misunderstanding her expression. "O'Reilly Castle is just ahead."

"I know, but I'm worried about you. Are you certain it's safe to expose yourself in this manner? Didn't... I mean, *isn't* Cromwell making it his life's goal to try to eradicate Catholics entirely from Ireland?"

Father Michael nodded grimly. "Aye, he is, lass, But there are many in the Church who have sworn loyalty to him just the same. Cromwell needs spies both in and out of the Church in Ireland, and he has granted amnesty to far more priests than I care to acknowledge. They may have received a temporary reprieve, but they've sold their eternal souls to get it. I would no' care to count myself among them. But I shall play the part now in order to save Miles and the other prisoners. And to answer your question, lass, nay, I am no' afraid. I am under God's protection."

Just then the villagers began to come out of their huts, looking curiously at them. When they saw Father Michael wearing his black wool cloak and heavy wooden cross, they ran toward him, calling out.

"They're likely going to warn me away from the castle," he said in a low voice. "When I tell them I intend to enter anyway, they'll assume I'm in league wi' the English. It pains me, but 'tis necessary."

He rode on slightly ahead of her and then dismounted, speaking with the villagers who, without further comment, quickly returned to their huts. Once back on his horse, the priest motioned for her to follow. Fiona clucked softly, amazed when her horse started moving again. Maybe she was starting to get the hang of this horseback-riding thing after all.

She saw the castle as soon as they cleared a rise leaving the village. It loomed on a small hill, its steep stone walls huge and seemingly impenetrable. Two impressive turrets on opposite ends of the building jutted proudly toward the sky, and a large wooden gate stood open, guarded by at least a half dozen soldiers. Two carts loaded with hay and supplies were being examined, and several peasants milled about while the soldiers conducted their inspection.

Father Michael turned in his saddle. "Are ye ready, lass?"

She took a deep breath and nodded. "Let's get this over with."

They rode toward the gate, stopping when a young soldier held out a hand in warning. He was dressed in the same outfit as the men who had accosted her and Lianna in the forest, including the ridiculous round helmet. She shuddered involuntarily.

"State your business," he said curtly in a clipped English voice that Fiona placed as slightly north of London.

"My name is Fiona Phillips," she said, using her most haughty English tone. If this soldier knew anything, he would place her accent squarely in the royal part of London, among society's most exclusive circles.

"My husband, Captain John Phillips, was recently killed in Enniskillen," she continued. "His commanding officer, Major Edward Carruthers, sent me here as the first stop on my journey to Drogheda. I'm to leave there on an English passenger vessel for home sometime next week." She fumbled with the pouch around her waist and pulled out a rolled parchment. Shaun and Father Michael had worked several hours last night making it.

"Here," she said, handing it to him. "This is my introduction. It is to be given to the garrison commander." She held her breath, praying he would think it authentic.

The soldier unrolled the parchment and looked at it for a long moment. When he said nothing, Fiona suddenly realized it was probably because he couldn't read. She wasn't certain if that was a good or bad development.

Finally he squinted up at her. "Where is your escort?"

Fiona looked over her shoulder. "We parted ways in the village. The men needed to get back to their duty at Enniskillen. I was told I would be given a fresh escort here to take me to Drogheda."

The soldier pushed his helmet back and scratched his head. "Why is he with you?" he asked, jerking his head toward Father Michael. The tone of his voice suggested that he was asking about a rodent instead of a priest.

"The priest is loyal to the Lord Protector, and was the only person available to escort me all the way to Drogheda," Fiona explained. "He served in my husband's household. He's harmless enough."

The soldier narrowed his eyes at Father Michael. "I don't know. The commander don't like no popish clerics."

Fiona drew herself up on the horse. "Frankly, I don't care what he likes or doesn't like. I am recently widowed and beside myself with exhaustion and grief. All I care about right now is having a decent meal and a warm bed. Your orders are spelled out in that document, so I suggest you follow them and show me to a place I can rest."

"I wasn't told you was coming," the soldier said uncertainly.

"My husband's death was quite unexpected. Do I need to report that you were uncooperative with me, soldier? What is your name?"

The young man swallowed hard and then handed the parchment back to Fiona. He waved them toward the gate.

"I don't need me no trouble. You may enter," he said. "Leave your horses at the stable and present your letter to Corporal Windham. He'll take care of you."

Fiona nodded, tucking the parchment back in her pouch. So far, things weren't going all that badly.

"Thank you," she said, raising her chin and dismissing him.

She clucked at her horse softly, but the beast did not move. She kicked her heels in his side, but the animal simply whinnied softly. Just as she was about to panic, Father Michael rode on ahead of her, and her horse miraculously followed.

Fiona sighed with relief, not daring to look back over her shoulder at the soldier. Whether he noticed her lack of riding skill or not, he did not stop them.

They left their horses where they had been instructed and walked through an enormous courtyard covered with cobblestones. Father Michael carried her small bag, which contained another black gown, two extra shifts, a brush, and a few other assorted sundries. Ian had assured her that it was just the right amount of items a grieved and widowed woman might carry with her as she traveled in haste across dangerous and arduous territory to get home.

The sheer number of people bustling about the courtyard surprised Fiona. Maidservants ran back and forth carrying water and bags of flour, while the men formed a human chain to unload several heavy crates of supplies. To her great relief, no one paid them any attention.

Staying close to Father Michael, she followed him into the castle. She stopped, letting her eyes adjust to the dim light, and then moved forward, abruptly bumping into a man.

"Oh, pardon me," she said, taking a step back.

"The fault was all mine," a cool English voice replied.

As he turned to face her, Fiona realized the voice belonged to a tall blond man with a finely trimmed mustache and a thin, angular face. He stood in the doorway, sunshine from the courtyard spilling in behind him, giving his silhouette a golden halo. Impeccably dressed, he wore a flowing white shirt and a pair of dark-colored breeches that ended just above his knees. His feet were encased in a long pair of sleek dark boots, and a light cloak was fastened loosely around his neck with a glittering brooch.

She couldn't see his eyes clearly, but she could feel his intense perusal of her face and gown before they shifted to Father Michael, who stood silently.

His gaze returned to her face, and Fiona felt a strange shiver run up her spine.

"You are English," he said, crossing his arms against his chest.

Fiona nodded. "Yes. My name is Fiona Phillips. My husband, Captain John Phillips, was recently killed at Enniskillen. Major Carruthers, my husband's commanding officer, sent me here, saying the commander of the garrison would provide me with food and shelter for the night. I am on my way to Drogheda to board a ship for home."

The man said nothing, but his gaze never left her

face. Fiona felt her anxiety rise and fought to keep from fidgeting on her feet.

"Your accent is strange," he finally said, taking a step toward her. "Where in London do you live?"

"On Rutherford Street," she answered without missing a beat. "But my mother was French, and I grew up partly in France."

"And that accounts for the unusual rhythm and nature of your speech?"

Fiona shrugged. "Perhaps. Why? Do you doubt I am English?"

He stared at her for a moment and then laughed. "No, I most certainly do not."

Fiona didn't see what was particularly funny, and her ire began to rise. "May I be so bold as to ask just who you are?"

He took a step toward her, his eyes raking over her. "Just a soldier in the loyal service of our Lord Protector, Oliver Cromwell. Have you the documentation from Captain Carruthers?"

"I was expecting to give it to Corporal Windham."

"He is indisposed at the moment. I shall see that he is informed of your arrival."

"Thank you," Fiona said, reaching into the pouch and handing him the parchment. "Does this mean I am permitted to stay the night?"

"Of course. Please have a seat in the drawing room and I will see that someone prepares a chamber for you."

Fiona glanced at Father Michael. "And one for him as well?"

The man's gaze flickered to the priest, and Fiona was shocked to see unconcealed revulsion and hostility in his eyes. "He travels with you?"

"He served in my husband's household and was permitted to minister to the Irish prisoners and villagers. He agreed to serve as one of my escorts to Drogheda. He is loyal to the Lord Protector."

He raised an eyebrow. "Surely you did not come all this way with just a priest to protect you?"

"Of course not. I parted ways at the village with the three soldiers who accompanied me. They were ordered to return to Enniskillen at once. As you will see from my documentation, I was told the garrison commander here would see that I had another escort to take me on to Drogheda."

He looked down at the parchment but did not open it. Instead he drummed it restlessly against his thigh. "I see," he said. "Well, Madame Phillips, it has been a pleasure making your acquaintance. I am sorry for your loss."

"Thank you. But what about the Father?"

The man clicked his boots together as he turned away, his cloak whirling around him in a dramatic motion.

"The priest can stay in the stables," he said over his shoulder. When Fiona opened her mouth to protest, he added coolly, "Be glad, madame, that I do not kill him."

Fiona only had a few minutes to speak with Father Michael in the drawing room before a maidservant arrived to tell her that a room had been readied for her. The priest seemed satisfied with the arrangement, feeling that they would have a better chance of discovering more about the location and condition of the prisoners if they were separated. Fiona, having seen the way the English looked at him, was concerned for his personal safety. But again he reassured her, saying that he put his faith in God to protect him.

Reluctantly she left him, following the maidservant up a steep staircase and down a long, dim hall. Torches lined the hallway, casting eerie shadows on the ceiling and walls. The young woman stopped in front of a room and opened the door, ushering Fiona inside.

"I hope this will suit ye, milady," she said shyly with a deep Irish brogue, careful not to look Fiona directly in the eye.

Fiona glanced about the chamber. A fire crackled and sparked in the hearth, slowly starting to warm the room. A huge four-poster bed with curtains, a wooden wardrobe, and a small table with a bowl of water were the only other pieces of furniture. It was rather small compared to the chambers she had seen briefly at Castle Dun na Moor, but after sleeping for days on the cold, hard ground, the room looked heavenly.

"It will be fine," Fiona said kindly to the young girl. "After I freshen up I would like to take a stroll about the grounds. Could you answer a few questions for me about the layout of the castle so I don't get lost?"

The girl happily obliged, and after ten minutes, Fiona had a pretty good idea of where most everything was located, including the dungeon. She had more questions but decided to wait until later so that she didn't raise the girl's suspicions.

"Would it be possible to get something to eat?" Fiona asked before the girl left.

The girl drew in a horrified gasp and then blushed a deep red. "Oh, milady, I almost forgot to tell ye. The garrison commander has requested your presence for late supper this evening. But I'll send ye up something to tide ye over until then."

She scurried out of the room, probably fearing she would be berated for nearly forgetting to relay her message.

Fiona watched her go, still reeling from the news of the surprise summons. Well, that was certainly something she hadn't expected. Nicholas Bradford wished to dine with her.

She could plead illness or exhaustion and refuse his request. She didn't think it would raise his suspicions. After all, she had just arrived from a long and exhausting journey and was understandably weary and grief-stricken. Add that to the fact that Miles and Faith had warned her in no uncertain terms to stay as far away from Bradford as possible.

But who better to inform her on what was happening at the garrison? Certainly Bradford did not intend to eat dinner with her alone. Besides, how dangerous could it really be to spend one hour in his company?

There, it was settled. She'd eat whatever the servant girl sent up and go have a look about the grounds. Most importantly, she needed to locate the rendezvous point with Ian while she still had daylight, and she also wanted to get a feel for the number of soldiers who were milling about inside the castle walls.

She felt a rush of confidence. So far everything had gone just according to plan. Getting in the castle had been a piece of cake. Supping with Nicholas Bradford would simply be the icing on the cake.

Chapter Fourteen

Fiona spent a productive morning and afternoon roaming about the castle, chatting innocuously with servants and soldiers, and learning everything about the layout of the castle as she possibly could. She had purposefully gone past the stables to see how Father Michael was doing, but he was not around. She presumed he was scouting as well, but just the same, she would have felt better seeing for herself that he was all right.

Now she readied herself for supper. She stripped naked, washed her hair in a bowl, and gave herself a sponge bath. Then she dried out on the thick wool rug that had been placed in front of the hearth. Earlier she had shaken out her gown and laid it on the bed, trying to smooth out the wrinkles. For the hundredth time, she went over her cover story, reassuring herself that she wouldn't mix up any of the details. Several times she caught herself fingering the ring Ian had given her, missing him and wishing he were here.

She was ready when there was a knock at the door and a middle-aged maidservant appeared. Fiona followed the plump woman down the stairs, surprised when she stopped in front of the entrance to the castle's great hall and motioned for Fiona to enter.

Puzzled, Fiona took a step into the enormous dark room and looked around. A half dozen long wooden tables lined the room, surely able to seat two hundred persons or more. At the end of one of the tables, closest to the only fireplace lit in the chamber, a single man sat. When she moved toward him, he stood.

"Madame Phillips," he said in a deep voice. "How kind of you to join me for supper."

"It's you!" Fiona exclaimed when she saw the same blond-haired man she'd met at the castle entrance this morning. "You are Nicholas Bradford, the garrison commander. Why didn't you tell me?"

He smiled. "I do sometimes enjoy being a man of mystery," he said, moving around the table to greet her. "Please, do have a seat."

Fiona approached the table, realizing with a sinking feeling that only two places were set. Even worse, the atmosphere was all wrong—quiet, cozy, and intimate. She felt her confidence flee. Perhaps this had been a mistake after all.

When she hesitated, he took her by the elbow, motioning for her to sit. "Please, do make yourself comfortable," he insisted. Seeing no other way out, she complied.

He walked to the hearth, picked up a poker, and stirred the fire. The kindling broke at his touch, hurling red sparks and ashes into the air.

"This wasn't necessary, commander," Fiona said, watching the shadows dance across the room. "I would have been content to eat in my chamber and then retire early."

He set the poker aside and sat down across from her. He picked up a flask and poured some dark red liquid into two silver goblets, holding one out to her.

"It isn't often that I have the opportunity to dine with a lovely and spirited English lady. And please, call me Nicholas."

Something in the tone of his voice immediately put Fiona on her guard. "I'm afraid I'm not very good company," she said, lifting her goblet and taking a sip. It was wine—dark, rich, and superb. And certainly the oldest year she'd ever had the privilege of drinking. "My husband's death came as quite a shock."

He lifted his own goblet, openly and frankly assessing her. He looked quite handsome in a fresh shirt open at the neck and dark-colored breeches. His gaze was warm upon her—quite compelling, and if she was honest with herself, somewhat magnetic. There was some weird attraction going on here, but it unsettled more than excited her.

"Widow's clothes suit you," he commented, taking a sip of his wine. Fiona started when she remembered Ian's similar words to her. Who knew that black was her color?

She shook her head, trying to clear it. This conversation was becoming increasingly strange. "That is kind of you to say," she said demurely, looking down at her lap.

He sipped some more. "If I were to be utterly honest, I would admit that I think you quite a stunning and intriguing woman."

Oh, bollocks, she thought; this evening was definitely not progressing in the right direction. Figuring she was better off not responding to that whatsoever, Fiona glanced about the hall. Firelight danced across the smoke-stained stone walls in their little corner of the enormous room. The scents of tallow and smoke hung heavy in the air, and Fiona thought it not unpleasant. But even though she sat near the hearth, she felt oddly cold and vulnerable.

So intent was she on not meeting Bradford's eyes that she nearly jumped out of her skin when he suddenly snapped his fingers. A manservant who had been standing near the door hastened to his side.

"Bring us the food," Bradford ordered briskly.

The servant, a middle-aged man who was tall and balding, nodded without a word and scurried out.

As he brushed past her, Fiona thought she glimpsed him throwing her a hostile look, but he was gone so quickly, she wondered if she might have imagined the entire thing. Her nerves really were stretched taut.

"So, how was it that you decided to leave the comfort of your home in London to accompany your husband on such a dangerous mission here in Ireland?" Bradford suddenly asked, causing her to start again.

God, she had to get a grip and settle down if she were to remain in control here.

"I loved my husband dearly," she started, giving her well-rehearsed answer. "My father was a physician in London and I had some experience in treating illness and binding simple wounds. Colonel Brooks himself personally approved my request to accompany John. Actually, there were a handful of other women there, so I wasn't lonely."

"That's a touching story."

"You are just being kind." Fiona smiled brightly and took a rather large gulp of her wine. It had sounded better when she practiced it in the forest with Faith and Ian.

Bradford turned his goblet around in his hand, studying it intently. "I presume you were friends with Colonel Brooks's wife?" he asked casually, his long fingers caressing the silver stem.

Fiona looked up sharply. "His wife did not accompany him, sir," she said, praying that Shaun's information had been correct. They were on dangerous ground now. This was the extent of her knowledge about the people at Enniskillen, and she could sense Bradford was testing her.

His leg brushed against hers under the table in a gesture that could have been casual but wasn't. Fiona fought to keep from leaping out of her seat. God help her, if this man didn't keep his wanger in his trousers, she was going to be in bigger trouble than she thought.

He smiled. "Yes, of course. How foolish of me to forget." He took another drink and then added, "And I do think I asked you to call me Nicholas." It was not a request or a simple reminder—it was a command, crisply delivered and clearly expected to be obeyed. She shivered involuntarily.

Thankfully, the manservant chose that precise moment to enter the chamber, carrying a large tray of meats. Two maids accompanied him, holding a huge platter of bread and cheese.

"Here ye are, sir," the servant said deferentially in a deep Irish brogue, but Fiona could practically feel the hostility rolling off him in waves.

If Bradford noticed his resentment, he didn't show

205

it. He simply dismissed the man with a flip of his hand. The servants filed out quietly, and Fiona noticed that this time all of them avoided looking at her.

Bradford offered her the platter of meats, and Fiona speared a piece with a knife and put it on her plate. Apparently regular utensils had yet to be introduced.

"Have you been here at Cavan long?" she asked, taking the momentary lull in conversation to steer it in a direction with which she was more comfortable.

"Only a couple of weeks," he replied, heaping meat and bread on his plate. "Actually, I'm based in Drogheda and my presence here in Cavan is only temporary."

"How temporary?" Fiona asked, taking a bite of the meat. It was venison, tender and marinated in some kind of sweet brown sauce. It was delicious, but she felt a twinge of guilt as she ate, wondering what Ian, Faith, and the others were supping on this evening.

"Quite temporary," he said, cutting a piece of cheese with his fork. "In fact, I think I might soon terminate the reason I'm here and accompany you myself back to Drogheda."

Fiona choked on the piece of meat she was eating. Eyes watering, she reached for her goblet of wine. Bradford stood and patted her several times hard on the back until she could breathe normally.

"Thank you," she gasped, drinking large swallows of wine. "I must have swallowed too big a piece."

He took the opportunity to sit down next to her on the bench, his hand still resting lightly on her shoulder. She resisted the urge to shrug it off and smiled at him instead.

"I wouldn't want to interfere with your business here at the garrison," she said earnestly.

He smiled, his hand beginning to knead the muscles in her shoulder. His fingers were cold and she could feel them, even through the thick material of her gown.

"Truthfully, my business here at Cavan has come to an end," he said. "I had already decided to finish it before you arrived." He leaned closer, his breath warming her cheek.

She felt like screaming but instead turned into him. "When you say you intend to conclude your business here soon—how soon is that? I only ask because I must ensure that I have enough time to reach Drogheda before my vessel leaves for England."

He reached out a finger and trailed it along her cheekbone. "Two days hence, my dear. That would mean spending at least two more nights here at the garrison with me."

She didn't like the way he'd emphasized *with me*.

"I guess that will just have to do then," she said with a sigh. "I don't suppose I could be so bold as to ask you again for your hospitality once we are in Drogheda. Perhaps your wife might welcome a brief visit from a fellow Londoner."

Faith and Ian had told her that Bradford's wife lived at Drogheda, and she hoped her barb might throw a wrench in his little seduction plan.

But instead of being deterred, Fiona saw he was amused. Nonetheless, he stood and returned to his place at the table.

"You seem to have me at a disadvantage," he said, breaking off a piece of bread and popping it in his mouth. "You know more about me than I know about you."

"Major Carruthers was kind enough to ease my

mind about coming here and told me all about you," she said brightly. Her appetite had fled completely, leaving her no other option than to push the food around on her plate with her knife.

"What else did Major Carruthers tell you about me?" he asked.

Fiona finished off her wine, and Bradford smoothly refilled her goblet. She realized she was drinking too much, too fast, and the wine was far more potent than she was used to. She had to be careful.

"He said you were likely to be far too busy to have any time to entertain me," she answered. "He said you had to take care of some Irish prisoners or something. Luckily for me, it appears as if he was wrong. I haven't seen any of the heathen about."

Nicholas refilled his own goblet and took another sip. "He wasn't wrong about the prisoners; they are being held safely in the dungeon. But the major was wrong to think I wouldn't be able to find time to comfort a distressed widow whose husband was killed in service to the Crown."

Fiona nodded, letting her lips quiver. "It has been a very difficult time for me."

He reached across the table and took her hand. His fingers were smooth and cold and she couldn't stop the shudder that raced up her spine at his touch.

He apparently misunderstood her reaction. "Widows are entitled to comfort—wherever they might seek it," he said softly.

She carefully withdrew her hand. "You have been far too kind to me, Nicholas. I thank you for that. But are you certain I'll be safe here with heathen prisoners being held right below?"

He studied her across his goblet, and Fiona sensed

he was trying to figure out whether she was playing hard to get or simply wasn't interested. She hoped like hell he got the latter vibe.

"I assure you, madame, that the prisoners are well guarded. Your safety is not at risk. And their termination will be completed two days hence, so their presence will no longer be a concern for you."

"Oh," Fiona gasped in horror.

Bradford sighed. "I apologize for discussing such base and unpleasant matters at supper. Let's put all such talk aside and simply enjoy ourselves, shall we?"

Fiona nodded and then, in a moment of inspiration, lifted her goblet. "To England," she declared.

He smiled, holding up his goblet and clinking it lightly against hers.

"To England," he agreed, adding with a mysterious smile, "and to us, of course."

Ian waited impatiently beneath a heavy canopy of trees, glancing frequently at the long stone wall that protected the castle. Furlong sat beside him, his back up against the trunk of a tree, polishing his sword with an old cloth. Ian resisted the urge to pace and forced himself to sit quietly and listen for any sounds that indicated that Fiona was on the other side.

"She's late," he finally said, not able to stand the silence any longer. "What's taking her so long?"

"Could be any number o' things," Furlong commented practically. "We may have to wait all night. The lass will get here when she can. Dinna worry, Ian, she's a strong one."

"Have ye forgotten that it is Bradford who is in there wi' her? That cold bastard nearly killed ye."

Furlong didn't cease his methodical strokes across

209

his sword, but his voice deepened slightly. "I haven't forgotten."

Ian blew out an exasperated breath. He had a nagging feeling that something wasn't right. To make matters worse, the wind had begun to pick up, blowing through the trees and stirring up dust and leaves. Earlier, Shaun had warned him that it was no ordinary fall wind. A storm was approaching—rising cold from the east and slowly gathering speed as it approached them.

Even now, Ian could feel the cold chill of the breeze lifting the hair on his arms and the back of his neck. Dark clouds were settling above them. In the distance, he could see the occasional flickering of lightning.

"Come to me, Fiona," he whispered to the wind, crossing his thick arms against his chest. "Come to me."

It was well after midnight and long past Fiona's arranged time for a rendezvous with Ian when she finally felt it safe to slip from her room. She had managed with great difficulty to ditch Bradford an hour earlier, although he had made a rather impressive attempt at seduction. A few months ago, it might have worked on her, but not anymore. She was a changed woman. Demurely pleading grief and fatigue, she had retired to her chamber, leaving him alone in the Great Hall and clearly irate.

She knew Ian would wait all night for her, and while she felt guilty that he was likely worried sick about her safety, she had one more thing to do before she met him.

She quietly closed the door to her chamber and pressed herself against the cold stone wall, listening.

Torchlight shone brightly, casting dancing, grotesque shadows across the walls. A strong breeze swept though the hallway, lifting tapestries and causing the torches to flicker wildly.

"I've heard of drafty castles, but this is ridiculous," Fiona murmured, clutching her cloak tighter about her.

Walking carefully, she left the hallway and padded down the stone staircase. The castle was eerily quiet, and she could hear no one moving about. She peeked warily into the Great Hall, but it was dark and empty. The dishes from supper had long been cleared away and the fire banked. She breathed a sigh of relief and passed the hall, moving toward the great arched entrance leading into what she hoped was the kitchen.

She stood in the corridor for some time, listening for sounds, but heard none. Cautiously, she took a step into the kitchen, marveling at what she saw.

The enormous room was silent except for the crackle of a blazing fire in a giant hearth. Obviously, cooking continued throughout the night. A huge black kettle hung on one side of the hearth, and something inside it bubbled merrily, sending a delicious smell through the chamber. On the other side of the fireplace was a spit, clearly for roasting meat, that was currently unused.

On the mantel above the hearth sat copper pots and pans, and several trestle tables were placed strategically throughout the room, many of them containing jars and large heavy rocks that she assumed were for pounding grains and meat.

Fascinating as it was, she didn't dare tarry. She needed to quickly get the information she'd come for. She crept all the way through the kitchen until she

211

reached a dark stairway she was certain led down into the dungeon.

She thought it interesting that the dungeon wasn't guarded at the top of the staircase. She didn't know if this was true during the day, so she'd have to find out. She'd concoct some excuse to pass this way in the morning.

The stairway down was brightly lit by torches on the wall, and she noted a second door at the bottom of the stairs that was closed. She wanted to count the steps and see if she could hear any sound of activity on the other side of that door.

Warily, she had begun to descend the stairs when a muscular arm wrapped firmly around her neck and a hand clamped over her mouth.

Her surprised scream came out as nothing more than a muffled groan, and she felt herself being dragged back into the kitchen. She squirmed and kicked her legs furiously, but her attacker was surprisingly strong. When they reached the giant hearth she could hear a voice with a heavy Irish accent urging her to be quiet.

She stilled immediately and he released her. She whirled around, her mouth falling open in surprise.

"You!" she exclaimed when she saw the balding servant who had brought her supper with Nicholas. "What in bloody hell do you think you are doing?"

"I could ask the same of ye, milady," he said, looking at her intently. "Either way, I suggest ye keep your voice down." She could see none of the hostility in his eyes that she had noted earlier, only wariness and caution. "Do ye know where ye were headed?"

She shook her head, feigning ignorance. "I thought it was the wine cellar. I could use something to drink, and I didn't want to wake anyone at this late hour."

"And that is why ye are clad in a heavy cloak?"

She looked down at herself, realizing that her excuse sounded quite lame. "The castle is drafty," she said defensively, her heart still thundering in her chest. "And I don't have to explain myself to you." She pulled herself up haughtily and turned away, intending to pass him by.

She stopped when she felt his hand on her arm. It was a bold servant indeed who would dare to touch her. Either that or he was incredibly desperate. But desperate for what?

" 'Tis no' a wine cellar down there, milady," he said in a low tone. " 'Tis the dungeon. And ye should know there are valuable prisoners being held there. It is heavily guarded, even at night, and I didn't want ye to have the misfortune o' running into any o' the guards at this late hour."

There was something in the man's voice that made Fiona take a second, closer look at him. She'd be damned, but she felt certain he was trying to convey something. But she couldn't figure out what in the world she'd have in common with this household servant. Except perhaps for one thing.

"I see," she replied equally careful. "And how many of those guards might there be, just in case I do run into any of them as a result of my sheer ignorance and misfortune?"

He stared at her for a long moment, and Fiona got the distinct impression he was weighing whether or not to trust her.

"Why do you travel with a Catholic priest?" he suddenly asked, his Irish burr deep and thick.

"Come again?" Fiona said, blinking in surprise.

"You are traveling with a Catholic priest. I would ask for his name."

Fiona stared puzzled at the servant. "You want to know the name of the priest that accompanied me here?"

The servant nodded just as the fire flared up in the hearth behind him. Streaks of yellow light shot across the stone walls in a crazy, morbid dance. She had to be damn careful with him. He might be on their side, but on the other hand, Bradford could have paid him to find out more about her. Then she remembered the servant's hostile glances at Bradford during dinner and sincerely doubted it. But one could never be too prudent, especially when lives were at stake.

"His name is Father Michael," Fiona answered, shrugging. She offered no new information here. "He served in my husband's household in Enniskillen and was a good and loyal..."

"Ach, don't waste your time jabbering that bit o' nonsense wi' me," the servant broke in impatiently. "Ye speak the truth when ye say the priest's name is Father Michael. I've seen him before. But he is no' from Enniskillen."

Fiona drew in a sharp breath. Did she deny or confirm this? Better to play it safe.

"I'm afraid you must have mistaken him for someone else. Father Michael is indeed from Enniskillen as I have just come from there myself and can vouch for him."

The servant stroked his chin thoughtfully as he looked at her. "I saw ye talking to him earlier on your arrival. I can see he cares for ye."

"Of course he does. He was a member of my household and has counseled me in my grief. I appreciate his words of comfort."

" 'Tis more than that, I think."

"You think a bloody lot for a servant," Fiona snapped, her patience wearing thin. If he had something to say to her, let him come out and say it. She was already late to meet Ian.

"There are three," he said suddenly.

"Excuse me?"

"There are three guards in the dungeon. One sits by the door at the bottom of the stairs. Two others stay in a small room across from the cells. They are not very alert in their duties—especially after they have indulged in too much wine."

Fiona exhaled a breath, regarding him closely. "Why are you telling me this?"

"Ye asked; did ye no?"

Fiona nodded, trying to steady her nerves. "Yes, I suppose I did. Um... do the guards indulge in wine every night?"

"Aye, and they are drinking more o' late, preparing themselves for the executions on Friday."

"Then it is true," she exclaimed. "The commander told me he intended to execute them in two days hence."

"The prisoners' fate concerns ye, then?"

She paused, not certain what to answer. She had the strangest sensation of being in some kind of weird dance with this man. One step forward, one step back—neither wanting to lead and neither trusting the other.

"I'll admit to being curious about their fate," she said neutrally. "Do you know what time the executions are scheduled?"

"Sometime in the early afternoon. I don't think the commander has yet received all the information he needs from the prisoners. One o' them in particular has raised his ire, and he has spent quite a bit o' time... ah...talking wi' him."

Torture was more like it, Fiona thought, assuming the servant was referring to Miles. This news was not good; it meant Bradford would likely spend most of the next two days intensifying his torture of Miles— perhaps to death. She prayed he could last another day. This meant they would have to make their move tomorrow night under the cover of darkness. But they had little time to plan—and she didn't have any idea how they could get the men out with the dungeon was so well guarded.

She'd have to get this news to Ian immediately. With a determined breath, she decided to abandon all pretense with this man and bet her own life on the hope that she had been reading this exchange correctly.

"Who are you?" she asked bluntly.

"My name is Tom O'Connor. My family have been loyal servants to the O'Reilly family for centuries."

"You know why I'm here, then?"

He gazed at her fixedly, the firelight reflecting off his bald head. "I'm no' certain. Ye are English, are ye no'? Yet there is something different about ye both in the way ye act and speak."

"Not bloody surprising since I'm under a great deal of stress right now. But yes, you are right. I am different. I need to know what else you can tell me about the condition and location of the prisoners."

Tom pressed his lips together, a look of relief crossing his face. "Then, 'tis as I hoped. The big man they have in the dungeon—he is Miles O'Bruaidar. He

216

sits in a cell alone and has taken the brunt o' the punishment here. He is one o' Ireland's finest sons."

"So I've heard," Fiona breathed. "Do you know how he fares?"

"His spirit is no' broken, but he has been badly beaten. I saw him walking in his cell yesterday, so at least he is no' a cripple."

"Thank God for that. But, if I understand what you are telling me, he and the rest of the prisoners will be dead by Friday afternoon."

"Aye, if the English get their way." He paused, rubbing his chin thoughtfully. "But there might be a way to save them, if ye are interested."

Fiona raised an eyebrow at him. The moment of truth had arrived. "I'm interested," she replied grimly.

"There is a secret tunnel leading out from the dungeon. The English do no' know about it. The exit is on the south side o' the castle, beneath a large oak tree with a gnarled branch sticking up at an odd angle toward the sky. 'Tis called the Angry Tree, for 'tis as if the tree is clenching a fist at God."

"Oh," Fiona breathed, staggered by the implication of what he had just told her.

"The tunnel has no' been used for years. The door beneath the tree is likely to be overgrown. And there is still the matter o' the guards. 'twill take at least three strong men to surprise them and bring them down." He looked at her curiously. "Ye do have help, do ye no'?"

"I do." She wrapped her cloak more tightly about her neck. "How did you know to trust me?"

" 'Twas simple. I've seen Father Michael before and know he lives at Castle Dun na Moor—the home o' Miles O'Bruaidar. There is but one reason the priest would come here to O'Reilly Castle—in search of Miles. I wanted to approach him, but didn't dare as the English are watching him carefully. All the same, he seemed to genuinely like and trust ye. So, I turned my attention to ye. Ye were truly a puzzle—all friendly wi' Bradford and dining in private wi' him. Yet, 'twas something about your manner that spoke o' a distaste for him. Tonight when ye slipped from your room, I followed. As soon as I saw ye sniffing about the dungeon, I decided to approach ye. I knew ye were either a blessing or a curse, so I took a leap o' faith that ye were here to help. Time is running out for Ireland."

Fiona nodded. "Thank you for helping me."

" 'Tis no' for ye, milady. 'Tis for Ireland."

"Then Ireland thanks you, Tom O'Connor," Fiona said sincerely. He straightened, a proud look crossing his face, and Fiona added softly, "God bless your soul."

He dipped his head and then turned away, melting into the darkness. "And your soul as well, milady," she heard him whisper. "For if Bradford catches wind o' this, we'll both be dead."

Chapter Fifteen

Ian had long ago abandoned all pretense of waiting patiently and paced furiously beneath the canopy of trees. Hours had passed and Fiona still had not shown up at the rendezvous.

"I'm going in after her," Ian warned Furlong, who still sat calmly beneath a tree.

"I'd no' advise it, Ian."

"No one asked ye," Ian growled.

Furlong didn't reply, but sat with his hat pulled low over his brow, his sword resting on his lap. He appeared the image of leisure, but Ian knew he was listening intently and would be on his feet quicker than a blink if they were unexpectedly attacked.

Ian looked up at the dark sky through a small opening in the branches. The storm clouds were heavier and swollen now, obscuring what little light the moon had once provided. Ian had a small covered lantern with him, but he dared not light it so close to the castle for fear of alerting the guards to their presence.

A rumble of thunder sounded in the distance, and Ian suspected that within an hour the storm would be on top of them.

"Where is she?" he breathed, resuming his pacing. "I knew I should never have gone along wi' this foolish plan."

" 'Tis little foolish about it," Furlong offered from beneath his hat. " 'Tis a sound plan and ye know it."

" 'Tis all madness," Ian argued. "I shouldn't have allowed her within sight o' Bradford. What was I thinking?"

"Ye are letting your feeling for the lass interfere wi' your judgment. All will be well."

"How can all be well if she isn't here yet? Mayhap something happened to her. Mayhap Bradford tried to harm her. God's wounds, if he's laid a finger on her, I swear I'll kill the bastard wi' my own—"

"Ian?"

Without even checking to see if the clearing was empty, Ian darted out from beneath the trees and pressed himself tightly against the stone wall of the castle. Through a small chink in the wall, he saw Fiona stick out her hand, complete with his ring on her thumb.

"Fiona," he breathed, grasping her hand and placing fervent kisses on her fingers. "Are ye all right, lass?"

"I'm fine," she said, but he could hear that her voice was tense and strained. "Please, you must listen carefully. The prisoners are scheduled to be executed on Friday."

Ian drew in a sharp breath and felt Fiona squeeze

his fingers in support. "But I've discovered a way we may be able to save them."

"Tell me," he ordered.

"I have it on good authority that there is a hidden tunnel that leads to and from the dungeon. Bradford doesn't know about it. The entrance to the tunnel lies beneath a large oak tree on the south side of the castle wall. It is likely covered with dirt and grass, so you'll have to dig to find it. You can't miss the tree, as it has a gnarled branch that looks like it's an arm shaking a fist at the heavens."

"God's wounds, Fiona, how did ye find all this out?"

"It's a long story and we don't have time to go into it now. Anyway, there are three guards in the dungeon. One is guarding the door at the bottom of the stairs that lead to the dungeon from the kitchen. The other two are said to be in a small room across from the cell. All the prisoners are in the same cell except for Miles. He is by himself. Bradford has been torturing him, and I'm afraid he intends to accelerate that torture. Miles has reportedly been beaten badly, but as of today can still walk. I don't know about the condition of the other prisoners."

"Dinna worry, *mo gradhach*. We'll no' be able to concern ourselves about that now."

"Another thing—the guards have been drinking heavily these past few days. That should work to our advantage. But Ian, I don't know where this tunnel comes out inside the dungeon. It could lead you directly into the guards' waiting arms. Moreover, the castle grounds are filled with English soldiers milling about. Fortunately for us, they are cocky and inattentive. As it was, I didn't see a single sentry about the

221

grounds as I came here tonight to meet you. I'm certain they do not suspect anyone of trying to rescue the prisoners."

He pressed her hand against his cheek. "Just the same, ye be careful, lass. There may be some about ye haven't seen." Yet, as he said the words, he knew her suspicions to be true. His own observations of the castle grounds today had confirmed as much.

"Ye've done well, Fiona. Does Father Michael know any o' this?"

"Not yet. We've been separated, but that's another story. I'll try to find him first thing in the morning and fill him in. By then, I hope we will have been able to put the next part of the plan into action."

" 'Tis becoming increasingly more dangerous for ye. I want ye and Father Michael out by dusk tomorrow. No matter what. Promise me, lass."

"I promise. Believe me, I have no desire to stay here a moment longer than necessary. We'll meet you at the scheduled rendezvous point. Ian, I miss you."

"I miss ye, too, lass."

She squeezed his hand hard. "Please be careful in the dungeon. I have at long last found the man of my dreams and I have no intention of losing him. Do you hear me?"

He rubbed his thumb against the palm of her hand. "I hear ye."

"I'm so worried," she said, her voice choking up. "I wish you could hold me right now."

Ian felt his heart twist in his chest. God's wounds, he sudddenly realized how much he loved her—like he had never loved another. Yet he didn't trust himself to speak of his love for fear he would leap over the castle wall, drag her to safety, and be damned with

222

everyone else. He heard her draw in her breath as thunder rumbled overhead.

"We have much to talk about, ye and I," he finally managed to say. "Dinna fash yourself, Fiona; all will be well. But a storm is coming, so ye'd best go. Take care."

With a final squeeze, her hand slipped from his. Ian waited pressed against the wall until he could no longer hear her footsteps. He felt an emptiness fill him as he darted back beneath the trees to where Furlong waited, sword in hand.

"Did she get the information we needed?" he asked.

Ian looked back over his shoulder at the castle wall and the small opening, now empty. "Aye, that she did, Furlong. Now the question is, what shall we do wi' it?"

Fiona didn't quite make it back into the castle before the rain began to fall. She threw up the hood of her cloak, but rain pelted her head and face anyway.

She found the servant's side door from which she had exited the castle and slipped inside. She crept down the corridor and headed up the main stairs toward her room.

Opening the latch, she stepped inside, glad to see the fire still glowed. She unfastened her damp cloak and let it drop to the floor, holding her hands out to the warmth.

"Not a very pleasant evening for a stroll."

Fiona yelped in terror, whirling around as a dark figure rose from her bed. He had been sitting so still, she hadn't even noticed him when she entered the room.

"Nicholas!" she exclaimed, her breath coming in

short, horrified gasps. "What are you doing here? You nearly frightened me to death."

He stood by her bed, not moving, his face hidden in the shadows. Outside, thunder boomed so loudly that it seemed to shake the castle walls.

"What are you doing here?" she asked again, her knees wobbling.

He took a step forward, and she gasped when the firelight touched his face. He had the same slender build, finely trimmed blond mustache, and thin, angular face as Nicholas Bradford. But he had an unusual scar near his right eye, and when he lifted his hand, she saw a dreadful tattoo of a large-winged black bird on the back of his hand.

She took a wary step backward. "You are not Nicholas Bradford," she said, stating the obvious.

He laughed and moved toward her, effectively standing between her and the exit. "So, it's Nicholas to you, is it? No, madame, it is to my great misfortune that I am not my elder brother. My name is Andrew. I presume Nicholas did not tell you about me."

"Brother?" she exclaimed, backing toward the hearth, her hand behind her, frantically searching for the poker iron. "No, he didn't mention he had a brother."

Andrew laughed. "I'm not surprised. I'm rather what you would call the black sheep of the family," he said, his words slurring.

Fiona realized with a spurt of fresh terror that he was drunk. God help her, if this man was the black sheep in a family that had Nicholas Bradford in it, she was in serious trouble.

"What are you doing in my room?" she asked, her fingers circling around the poker. She pressed it into the folds of her skirts. If that failed, she always had the dagger Ian had so thoughtfully strapped to her thigh.

"I heard that my brother was entertaining a lovely English lady tonight. Sadly, I was not invited to the intimate gathering, and I wanted to get a glimpse of you. It was to my great amusement that you were able to resist my brother's considerable charm."

Fiona gasped in mock outrage. "How dare you suggest such a thing of Nicholas. He was a perfect gentleman."

Andrew laughed. "And you, my lady, are a fine actress. I thought you retired early because you were unwell and exhausted."

Fiona drew herself up tall. "I was unwell and exhausted. So much so that I couldn't sleep. I thought some fresh air and a brisk walk would help me rest better."

"A two-hour walk in such blustery weather?" he asked, raising an eyebrow.

"How dare you lie in wait for me in my chamber," she said, hoping she looked properly scandalized. "You had no right to spy on me."

He walked up close, standing directly in front of her. Fiona's grasp on the poker tightened.

"Just what are you up to, my dear? You are so very mysterious," he murmured, running a finger down her jawbone and nudging her chin up until she was looking directly at him. His blue eyes were flat and cold and Fiona shivered, horrified by the sheer emptiness in them.

"No answer for me? Well, it is most fortunate for you that I like mysterious women," he whispered. He stood so close that she could smell the wine on his breath. She backed up against the stone wall of the hearth, realizing she had nowhere else to go.

"Your sudden presence here is quite fortuitous, you know," he continued. "Times are hard and trying. A beautiful woman is a welcome distraction. No wonder my brother is attracted to you."

Fiona swallowed, her voice all but dying in her throat. "Sir, need I remind you that I am recently wid-owed?" she managed to say. "This is most improper."

He smiled, and Fiona felt strangely hypnotized, like a rabbit in the thrall of a wolf.

"No one need know I am here," he said softly. "I could help you forget all about your recent misfor-tunes. I could make you blind with pleasure and make you beg for more. Come, lady, let me unlock the pas-sion I feel simmering just beneath your skin. I will show you what it is like to be taken by a master."

Fiona could sense something darkly sensual about him, like his brother. Both had an unfathomable, po-tent magnetism that promised astonishing sexual ful-fillment, but in a sinister, tainted, and depraved sort of way. Jolly good fun, if one liked that sort of thing.

"I want you to leave now," she whispered, her heart pounding fiercely. "Or I shall tell Nicholas that you came here tonight."

She wasn't certain what made her invoke Nicholas's name, but it seemed to have an effect. It was as if Andrew snapped out of a trance, and he stepped back from her.

"We are not finished yet, my lady," he said, finger-ing the top of his shirt in a way that made it look as if his bizarre bird tattoo was ready to fly off his hand.

"We are for tonight," Fiona said, more firmly than she felt. "I am beyond exhaustion and am about to collapse right here on the floor in a stupor. I ask that we simply forget all that has passed here tonight and start afresh in the morning."

He stared at her intently for a long moment, his eyes narrowing and probing. After what seemed like forever, a languid smile crossed his face.

"Shall I see you at breakfast then?" he asked.

"Of course."

"Then so be it. Good night, my dear."

He took her hand, pressing a long and lingering kiss on her palm. Then he turned on his heel and walked to the door, slipping out soundlessly and closing the door behind him.

As soon as he was gone, Fiona dropped the poker with a clatter and ran to the bowl of water on the small table. She dunked her hand in it, scrubbing furiously where he had kissed her. Tears coursed down her cheeks and she realized she had never been so frightened in all her life.

Sobbing, she sank to the floor, putting her head in her hands. She had to get control again; she had to calm down. Instinctively, her hands sought Ian's ring around her neck and she gripped it so tightly her knuckles turned white.

"Oh, Ian," she whispered. "I'm so frightened, I don't know if I can do this anymore."

Then she thought of Miles and Faith and how everyone she cared about was risking their lives to bring the two of them back together.

"I can do this," she said, wiping the tears from her cheeks and inhaling several deep, steadying breaths. "I *will* do this." The old, selfish, weak Fiona was gone forever. The new Fiona would be strong.

Fiona rose to her feet, wishing she had some way

to lock or block her door. As it was, she didn't even have a chair to brace against it. In the end, she stripped down to her shift, untied the dagger from her leg, and grabbed the iron poker. She went to bed, gripping one weapon in each hand.

Still frightened and upset, it took her what seemed like an eternity to fall asleep. But when slumber came at last, she dreamt of Ian.

Chapter Sixteen

Dawn was breaking across the sky when Ian and Furlong finally made their way back to camp. Shaun was still awake, guarding the sleeping forms of Faith and Lianna, who lay huddled together, sheltered under a tree and covered head to toe with heavy cloaks. Thankfully the rain had stopped, but Ian was bone weary and soaked to the skin.

The dwarf stood, sword in hand, when he heard them coming.

"How did ye fare?" he asked softly, resheathing his sword.

Ian sank to the damp ground with a groan and Furlong joined him. "We found the entrance to a secret tunnel that leads to the dungeon," Ian said, lying back on the grass and propping his hands behind his head. " 'Twas just where Fiona said it would be, tho' 'twas covered with a layer of dirt and leaves."

"A secret tunnel!" Shaun exclaimed and then low-ered his voice as he looked over at the sleeping women. "What is this all about?"

"Fiona has obviously befriended someone inside the castle who told her about the tunnel," Ian said, stretch-ing his long legs. "Once we found the hidden en-trance, Furlong and I slipped inside and went all the way to what we think is the trapdoor leading to the dungeon. 'Tis a damn maze in there, so we were care-ful to mark our way so we wouldn't get lost. 'Twas no' guarded, tho. I think Fiona was right when she said the English dinna know about it."

"Have ye considered that it might be a trap?" Shaun asked seriously, his eyes wide.

Ian nodded wearily. "Aye, I have, Shaun. But the prisoners' executions are scheduled for tomorrow, which means we dinna have much choice. We must act tonight under the cover o' darkness."

"Did Fiona know how many guards are in the dun-geon?" the dwarf asked.

"Three. It shouldn't be too difficult to take three, especially wi' the element o' surprise on our side. There is one problem: We dinna know exactly where the tunnel comes out in the dungeon."

"What is the condition o' the prisoners?"

" 'Tis mostly unknown. Fiona said she believed Miles was well enough to walk. But fight? I dinna know."

Shaun blew out a breath and then looked over at Furlong, who had fallen asleep where he fell, breathing deeply and evenly, his hat placed over his face. "I envy him that ability," Shaun said with a wry grin.

"As do I," Ian agreed, wondering if he'd ever be

able to fall asleep, given all that was on his mind.

"What about Fiona and Father Michael?" Shaun asked. "How will they get out?"

"They've been instructed to slip out by dusk. We will meet them outside the castle gate, in the forest near the entrance to the village, as planned."

Shaun nodded. " 'Tis a sound strategy."

"There is one problem: Fiona mentioned that she and the Father have been separated. I hope she'll be able to find him to pass on the information about the tunnel."

"She's a steadfast lass, our Fiona," Shaun said with pride. "I don't have any doubts about her."

Ian nodded tiredly. "Aye, and I'm ashamed that I ever did. Now, let's only hope the rest o' the plan goes as smoothly."

"Aye, and may the saints be wi' us," Shaun added emphatically.

Fiona awoke with a gasp as all the memories of the night before came flooding back to her. She sat straight up in bed, noticing that the iron had fallen to the floor and the dagger was tangled beneath the bedsheets. Bloody good thing she hadn't impaled herself on it while she slept.

Sighing, she retrieved the poker and headed for the hearth. The fire had nearly gone out, so she added a log and stabbed at it with the poker until it caught.

Shivering, she walked over to the small table and splashed water on her face, trying to ignore her pounding headache and swollen eyes. God help her, this spy stuff had already taken twenty years off her life. How had Faith managed to do this kind of thing for a living? They might be of the same blood, but they definitely weren't of the same psychology.

She had no idea what time it was, so she lifted a corner of the heavy drape and peeked out into the courtyard. Gold, pink, and orange slivers of dawn streaked across the sky, and Fiona was thankful that it appeared to be quite early. She had a lot of things to accomplish this morning—the first of which was to find Father Michael.

After partaking in the dubious honor of using the chamber pot, she reattached the dagger to her thigh in case she had the misfortune of meeting either of the Bradfords unexpectedly. She brushed her teeth and her hair and dressed herself quickly. She took extra time to pin up her hair, thankful that no one had yet noticed its unusually short length.

After she was dressed, she picked her cloak off the floor where she had left it and fastened it around her neck. It was still damp, and she wished she'd had the strength to lay it out in front of the fire last night before she retired.

There were only a few servants up and about at this hour, and fortunately, no one paid her any attention. Without any fanfare, she slipped out of the castle and headed toward the stable. To her relief, Father Michael was up, washing his hands and face in a bucket of water just outside.

"Father," she said, coming up behind him and placing a hand on his shoulder. "Good morning."

He smiled, patting his face with a rough piece of linen. "A top o' the morning to ye, madame," he said politely, but his eyes twinkled and she knew he felt happy to see her. She felt a tug at her heart and realized that he, like the others, had already become deeply entrenched in her heart.

"Do you have a moment?" she asked, tipping her head away from the stables.

He nodded and threw the linen rag to the ground. "Of course, my child," he said, taking her arm.

They strolled toward the castle garden, not saying a thing until they were certain they were out of earshot of any passersby. Fiona noticed an English soldier was discreetly watching, but he stood far enough away that he could not overhear them. Quickly she briefed the priest on everything she had learned.

Father Michael stopped and stared at her in surprise. "God has truly been wi' ye," he said. " 'Tis as if His hand is guiding ye."

Fiona rubbed her eyes. "Believe me, for that, I am thankful."

"Did ye pass this on to Ian?" the priest asked in a hushed voice.

"I did. He wants us out before dusk. We'll meet at the rendezvous point as planned."

The priest urged her to resume their walk by taking her elbow lightly. "I discovered something as well," he said quietly. "The castle gates close promptly at dusk. We must be out well before then. Do not tarry, child."

"Believe me, I won't. I can't wait to get out of this godforsaken place."

"I think we should go separately," Father Michael said. "I'm being watched. The English don't trust me."

Fiona raised an eyebrow in alarm. "Are you certain?"

He nodded. "Nonetheless, I put in a request to visit the prisoners to perform the last rites. If 'tis true that they are scheduled for execution tomorrow, then I may have a better chance to see them. If ye can delicately bring it up wi' Bradford, mayhap 'twill help my case."

Fiona sighed. "I'll try. Did you know Bradford has a brother here? He's just like Nicholas, except perhaps worse, if that's possible. He has a scar on his face and a horrid black bird tattoo on the back of his hand. Stay away from him if you can. He's dangerous."

Father Michael looked at her worriedly. "Are ye all right, lass? Ye look unwell."

"Just tired. Don't concern yourself with me. I assure you, I'll be counting the minutes until we meet at the rendezvous. Anyway, it's all downhill now for me. I just have to survive breakfast with Bradford and then I intend to spend the rest of the day alone in my chamber. The hard part is now up to you."

The priest patted her arm gently. "Be careful, Fiona. Ian has become terribly fond o' ye, and once this is all o'er, he'll need ye more than ever. I know naught what ye feel for him, but whatever it is, I ask ye to be gentle with his heart."

"I love him, Father," she said simply, amazed at how deeply she felt those words. This was the love Faith had talked about—the completeness she felt when she was with him and the hollow ache she now had without him. The feelings were both terrifying and exhilarating, and she realized that she had never experienced anything even remotely like this before— not even with Edward, the man she had almost married.

" 'Tis a blessed love, then. Go with God, my child," he whispered and slipped away from her.

Fiona watched him go, his black robe flapping in the wind, his thinning reddish-brown hair gleaming in the sun. An ordinary man in appearance, but an extraordinary man within. She felt humbled to know him.

Gathering her cloak and her courage about her, she took a deep breath and returned to the castle. Better to get breakfast over with as soon as possible.

She heard noises coming from the Great Hall and peeked in to see several soldiers eating at the long trestle tables. The hall looked different in the daytime—now she noticed the enormous, gorgeous tapestries hanging on the walls, the huge leaded windows that offered extra light, and the small raised dais where likely the most important guests sat during a real feast.

Nicholas and Andrew were sitting by themselves at the end of one of the trestle tables, deep in discussion. They both rose politely when they saw her enter the room.

"Madame Phillips," Nicholas said, waving her over to the table. His demeanor was as cool and elegant as ever, and she detected none of the annoyance she had seen when she thwarted his seduction plans of the previous evening.

Andrew, on the other hand, shot her an openly lecherous glance, his eyes lingering on her lips and breasts until she flushed and had to look away. For a moment, she stood awkwardly, not certain if Andrew had told his brother about his late-night visit to her room, and what, if anything, to say about it.

"Madame, I would like you to meet my brother Andrew," Nicholas said, stepping sideways and politely dipping his head toward his brother.

"How delightful to meet you," Andrew said smoothly, stepping up and capturing her hand in his.

So, this is how Andrew wanted to play it, Fiona

mused. Well, that was bloody fine with her—so long as everyone stopped trying to touch her.

"My pleasure," she murmured, trying to respectfully extract her hand from his grasp. Instead, he tightened his hold and brushed his cool lips across her fingers. She fought to suppress a shudder and instead gave him a forced smile.

Nicholas ushered her to the table, sitting down beside her. That at least put Andrew across the table, but she didn't know what, if anything, Nicholas might have up his sleeve this morning. It was like swimming in a river of pirahanas.

Nicholas graciously offered her a bowl of warm porridge and several thick slices of bread. There was also a plate of what looked like savory pie and some dates. She glanced about for a spoon but didn't see one; then she noticed the men dipping the bread in the porridge and eating it.

Well, in Rome, do as the Romans do, Fiona thought with a shrug. She dipped a chunk of bread in the porridge and tasted it. The porridge was a bit thick and salty but not bad. She had a few more bites but, not surprisingly, found she had little appetite.

"So, how did you sleep?" Nicholas asked her, lifting a piece of dripping bread to his lips.

Horrified, Fiona noticed that his knuckles were freshly scraped and bruised, and wondered if he had been down to the dungeon before breakfast. She felt the urge to heave, and the remains of any appetite she might have had fled completely.

"I... uh...slept fine," she stammered, glancing over at Andrew.

He smirked, and she felt like smacking him. In just minutes, this had turned into the breakfast from hell.

She looked back at Nicholas, her gaze locking on his bloodied knuckles in morbid distaste.

He saw her staring, and he set down his bread and flexed his hand. "It's just a little scratch," he said, adding, "received in service to the Crown."

"What kind of service?" Fiona asked in a strangled voice, not certain she wanted to hear the answer.

"Not the kind of service a gentleman can speak of in the presence of a lady."

"I was afraid of that," she murmured, looking down at her porridge. She didn't know how much longer breakfast would last. Her stomach was doing flips, and she had to figure out a way to delicately bring up the issue of Father Michael's request to visit the prisoners.

Before she could think of anything, Andrew solved the problem for her.

"By the way, Nicholas, I received a request from that priest of hers," he said, spearing a date with a knife and eating it. "He wishes to visit the prisoners before their execution tomorrow to offer them respite in their final hours."

Fiona looked up, feigning surprise. "He did, did he? I suppose I shouldn't be shocked. Colonel Brooks often let him do so at Enniskillen. Personally, I harbor no affection for the Irish heathen who killed my husband, although I suppose it would be the godly thing to do."

Nicholas looked at her in amusement. "My dear, is that a callus note I hear in your voice?"

She gave an exaggerated sigh. "I hope it doesn't cause you to think badly of me."

"On the contrary, it serves but to fascinate me. As a result, I shall let you decide whether the prisoners shall be permitted to cleanse their souls. What shall it be, my dear?"

Fiona picked up a date and examined it, pretending disinterest. "Being a Christian woman, I am well aware that Our Lord Jesus instructed us to turn the other cheek when wronged. As difficult as it may be, it would be godly of me to transcend my suffering and find forgiveness in my heart, at least on this day. I say, let them have their priest."

Nicholas took a bite of his bread, studying her intently. Fiona held her breath and finally raised her gaze to meet his. After a moment, a smile broke out slowly across his face.

"So it shall be," he said simply.

Chapter Seventeen

Father Michael carefully traversed a second flight of stairs down into the dungeon. Two soldiers accompanied him—one in front and one behind. At the bottom of the first set of stairs, a guard on the other side unlocked the door and then motioned for them to continue.

These stairs were dark, narrow, and slick, difficult for even a healthy man to traverse. He didn't want to think about the difficulty wounded and injured men might have had going this way.

No torches hung on these walls, so the soldier in front of him carried a covered lantern. His own hands were empty, as he had not been permitted to bring anything, not even a Bible. The search of his person by the soldiers had been thorough and humiliating, but he had calmly submitted to it. Anything to have the opportunity to visit the prisoners.

Now he was thankful his hands were empty. He pressed them against the cold stone wall, holding himself steady as he slowly descended. He could feel the moss under his fingertips and hear the faint drip of water. The air was cold and damp. As they got closer to the bottom, he could hear the unmistakable sounds of shuffling feet, sniffling, and an occasional cough. The scent of unwashed bodies and urine hung heavy in the air. His fingers touched the heavy cross around his neck and he silently said a small prayer for courage.

He tripped coming off the last stair and stumbled into the soldier in front of him. The man uttered an oath and shoved him against the wall.

"Don't be touching me, priest," he snarled, and Father Michael nodded, lowering his eyes deferentially.

Two soldiers came out of a room to the right, and Father Michael assumed these were the other two guards on duty. Not counting the two soldiers who accompanied him now, Fiona's information had been correct—three guards regularly on duty. He wondered how often they rotated positions.

He waited patiently as the guards huddled and spoke rapidly in hushed tones. Finally, the one with the lantern approached Father Michael, motioning him wordlessly to follow. He stopped briefly and lifted a ring of keys off a hook on the wall not far from the guardroom. Father Michael made a mental note of the key ring's location, grateful they were not actually on the person of any of the guards. The soldier then continued down a short, dark corridor before stopping abruptly in front of a large cell. Father Michael could hear whispered voices and see the silhouettes of several men spread throughout the cell.

As the guard fumbled with the key ring, finally choosing the one he wanted, the priest carefully observed which key opened the cell. Unaware of the scrutiny, the soldier unlocked the cell and opened the door with a deafening clang.

"You have ten minutes, no more," he said, rudely shoving the priest inside and slamming the iron door closed.

"Please," Father Michael implored, "leave the lantern by the cell."

The soldier grunted in annoyance, but to Father Michael's great relief left the lantern on the ground.

Inhaling a deep breath, Father Michael waited until the soldier's footsteps receded into the darkness. Then he turned around to face the prisoners.

"My name is Father Michael," he said gently. "I have come to offer ye comfort and hear your confessions. Who shall come to me first?"

He heard the sharp intake of breath among some of the men. Finally one man stepped forward. He was short and broad-shouldered, with long, scraggly brown hair and a beard. Squinting in the dim light, he observed Father Michael for nearly a minute before a smile broke out across his face.

"By all the blessed saints," he breathed. " 'Tis really ye."

Father Michael took a step, clasping the man's icy hand between his own. "Quietly now, Finn O'Flahertie," he murmured. "I need to know exactly how many o' ye are here and what condition ye are in."

Father Michael heard the excited rustle of the men in the cell and squeezed Finn's hand warningly. Finn

Julie Moffett

turned to the men, waving his arm and silencing the noise at once.

"There are eleven o' us in all," Finn whispered. "Some o' us are sicker than others, but there are none who canno' at least walk. Thad O'Brien is the worst off—he suffered a cut in his shoulder during the skirmish in Dundrum and 'tis now festering. He's wi' the fever, too, but still has his senses."

"Can he walk alone?"

"Nay, he'll need the help o' at least one man."

"Then see to it that someone stays by his side. Where is Miles?"

Finn tipped his head to the left. "In the next cell o'er—alone. Bradford didn't dare keep us together for fear o' Miles somehow being able to rally us to escape. I don't know how he fares. Bradford has been spending a lot o' time in there lately—the black-hearted bastard."

Father Michael nodded. "We are coming tonight, Finn. Tell the others. We'll bring wi' us what extra weapons we have, but 'tis no' many. Make certain they fall into the hands o' those who are the strongest. There are only a few o' us, so we must all work together. 'Tis a secret tunnel somewhere here in the dungeon and we will come through it—and hopefully surprise the guards."

"We'll be ready, Father," he said in a hushed tone, his beefy hand shooting out and grasping the Father's. "Father, please, spare me a moment. Can ye tell me how my sons fare?"

Father Michael smiled and patted Finn's hand. "They are well and wanting to see ye. Let's make certain they get their wish."

Finn nodded and stepped back. Father Michael be-

242

gan quickly going about to the men, whispering prayers and instructions, and assessing for himself their condition.

In what was surely less than ten minutes, the soldier returned, ordering Father Michael out. The soldier retrieved the lantern and headed back down the dank corridor before Father Michael abruptly stopped.

"I was told there is one more prisoner alone in a cell," he said. "I would like to see him."

"Ain't no one 'cept the commander that gets to see 'im," the soldier said.

"But I was told I could visit all the men," Father Michael persisted. "Those orders came from the commander himself."

The soldier hesitated and then walked the rest of the way down the corridor, leaving Father Michael standing alone in the dark.

"The priest wants to visit the prisoner in the solitary cell," he heard the solider say. "Is that permitted?"

"I dunno," someone answered. "I didn't hear nothing about that."

"Want to go up and ask the commander?"

One of the soldiers snickered. "And bother 'im while he's eating? Hell no. He'll be bloody pissing mad."

"Then let the priest go in," another one said. "No skin off me back. After all, he didn't say the cleric couldn't see 'im. Besides, if we have any luck at all, the prisoner will kill 'im, and we'll be done with the bloody lot of them."

Someone chortled, and Father Michael heard the soldier returning. He walked past without a word and Father Michael silently followed.

The soldier passed the large cell again and then

stopped in front of another. He chose a key and unlocked the door. The darkness was deeper here, and even with the dim light of the lantern, Father Michael couldn't see a thing. When the door swung open, the soldier hastily pushed him inside, closing the door behind him with a clang. Father Michael's heart thudded uncomfortably. He said a silent prayer when the soldier left the lantern without his having to ask again.

"Two minutes," the soldier said, his footsteps receding down the corridor.

For a moment Father Michael stood still, letting his eyes adjust to the ghostly darkness. "Is anyone here?" he whispered.

"Come to save my soul now, have ye?"

Father Michael gasped in surprise. In the shadows at the very back of the cell stood a tall, dark figure. The man stepped forward into the dim rays of the lantern, and the priest saw Miles O'Bruaidar standing erect and proud, his broad shoulders unbent, the long arms bulked with muscle folded casually across his chest.

Father Michael would not have guessed that he'd even been harmed except that his face was battered. One eye was nearly swollen shut and his cheeks and nose were covered with bruises and cuts. His dark hair hung long beyond his shoulders and his jaw was heavily bearded. He had lost a lot of weight, and what garments he had left were little more than rags. Yet he wore those rags with such grace and elegance, it was as if he readied himself for a feast. His eyes glittered in the lantern light with intelligence and awareness. Father Michael felt a surge of pride that this fine son of Ireland had not had his spirit broken by either torture or imprisonment.

"Miles, 'tis God's blessing that ye are yet alive," Father Michael whispered, watching a frown and then recognition flash across his face.

"Father Michael?" Miles murmured. "Is that ye or am I dreaming?"

The priest smiled. "I assure ye, I'm real, 'tis good to see ye, old friend. Altho' no' particularly under such circumstances."

Miles stepped forward, clasping the priest's hand with a surprisingly strong grasp. "How did ye find me?" he asked Father Michael softly.

"Faith's cousin, Fiona. 'Tis a long story. Ian is here, as is Shaun and Furlong. We're going to mount a rescue tonight."

"Just the four o' ye?"

"Well, 'tis more complicated than that. We only just discovered ye were here, and we didn't dare travel in a larger group for fear o' being discovered by the English. Ye are scheduled for execution tomorrow, so we have to act tonight."

Miles stepped back, looking intently at the priest. "Where is Faith?"

Father Michael sighed. "I think ye already know the answer to that. She's here—outside the castle walls. She refused to be left behind."

"Damn stubborn woman. By God, I miss her. Do what ye can to keep her out o' harm's way, will ye, Father?"

"I shall try. But as ye well know, your wife has a mind o' her own. She's a magnificent woman, as is her cousin, Fiona. They've risked a lot for ye, Miles."

"As have ye all. Ye shouldn't have done it. I'm no' worth it."

Father Michael smiled gently. "But ye are, Miles, as

is every man in that adjoining cell. 'Twas by God's hand that we found ye, and wi' God's help we shall save ye magnificent sons o' Ireland. Besides, ye should know that Faith will no' leave here without ye."

For a moment Father Michael saw the hard lines on Miles's face soften. "Faith is the light o' my life, Father. I love her wi' all o' my heart. And I see now that I'll have to live through tonight if for no other reason than to chastise her for risking her life o'er me. What was she thinking?"

"That ye would do the same for her."

Miles sighed. "Aye, as I would. But we have little time left, Father. Tell me what ye have planned for tonight."

Miles knelt down on one knee and Father Michael quickly recounted the rescue plan. He had barely finished when the soldier returned, motioning him to get out.

"May God bless you and keep you, my son," Father Michael said, touching Miles gently on the top of his head.

"Thank you, Father," Miles murmured, keeping his head bowed. "And Godspeed to ye, too."

Fiona paced back and forth in her room, wishing more than anything that time would pass quickly. Just a few more minutes and she would leave her chamber and head out to the gardens, ostensibly for a stroll. Then, when no one was looking, she'd shed her fancy cloak, put a drab-colored shawl around her head and shoulders, grab some firewood, and walk right out of the gate as if she were a village woman returning home. Father Michael would meet up with the others before her, as he intended to ride directly to the village after visiting the prisoners. He was to take both of their horses to the village—purportedly to run them for exercise—and then tie them to a tree near the rendezvous point. Ian and Furlong would be nearby, and when it was safe, they'd spirit both horses away.

Father Michael would then make a show of visiting several of the village folk in case he was being watched and eventually seize a moment to slip into the forest unnoticed and make his way to where the others were hidden. Fiona prayed that he had already made his escape and was now safely with the rest of the rescue party waiting for her.

She lifted a corner of the heavy drape and looked out her window for the umpteenth time. The sun was finally slipping away, hanging just above the treeline and casting orange, pink, and yellow slivers across the sky. It had rained a bit in the afternoon, but thankfully the weather had improved, leaving the air crisp and cool. Just a few more minutes and this castle and the Bradford brothers would be history.

"Not much longer, my love," she whispered, fingering Ian's ring around her neck. "I can do this."

Walking over to the bed, Fiona picked up her cloak and draped it about her shoulders, fastening it at the neck. She was surprised that her hands were so steady. Her insides felt like a jittering tangle of live wires. Taking a deep breath, she stirred the fire one last time and set the poker aside. She stretched out her hands to the flames, taking deep breaths and forcing the muscles in her neck to relax. Sufficiently calmed, she took one last look around the chamber. Her brush and toothbrush were left out and her two other gowns still hung in the wooden wardrobe. No one would sus-

Julie Moffett

pect that she didn't intend to come back from her late afternoon stroll.

"Well, it's been bloody fun, but I'm out of here," she murmured, turning toward the door.

She had taken one step when a sudden knock sounded on the door. Startled, she jumped back a step, her heart thundering in her chest.

"Wh-who is it?" she called out when she finally found her voice.

There was no answer, so she went to the door and opened it a crack. She drew in a sharp breath when she saw the Irish servant Tom O'Connor standing there.

Quickly, she opened the door all the way, a part of her brain registering surprise at the strange, almost frozen expression on his face. But instead of stepping into the room, the servant simply fell forward and landed on the floor with a sickening thud. Fiona gasped when she saw the knife protruding from his back, buried to the hilt.

Fiona tried to scream, but only an odd hissing noise escaped her throat. Just then Andrew and Nicholas Bradford stepped over the body and into her room. Andrew pulled the dead servant across the threshold while Nicholas calmly shut the door. As Fiona backed up, pressing a fist against her mouth in horror, Andrew bent down and yanked the blade from Tom O'Connor's body. The bird tattoo on his hand appeared to be flapping eagerly.

Holding the gory knife out in front of him, Andrew grinned at her while Nicholas looked on, coldly amused. For a moment the two of them simply stared without saying a word.

Then Andrew took a step forward, still holding the knife.

"It seems, madame," he said calmly, "that we have a lot to talk about."

Chapter Eighteen

"She should have been here by now," Ian said, anxiously tapping his fingers against his thigh. He stared out from behind the trees and cursed softly. "Hell and damnation. They are getting ready to close the gate."

"She promised me she'd be here," Father Michael said, putting a hand on Ian's arm. "She must have a reason for no' coming, Ian. Mayhap she felt it wasn't safe to go."

"Perhaps it is something as simple as her falling asleep," Faith said quietly, but something in the way she said it told Ian that she didn't believe it.

Ian glanced up at Furlong and Shaun, who were squinting out from their perches in the trees, looking for anything even remotely resembling a woman trying to slip out of the castle gate. From the expressions on their faces, he knew they were as concerned as he was.

"Father Michael," Ian asked quietly, "did Fiona say anything at all that might explain why she is late? Did she think she was being watched, as ye were?"

Father Michael creased his brow. "No, she didn't think she was being watched. In fact, she didn't think anyone suspected anything o' her at all. But she did say something interesting. She said Nicholas Bradford had a brother here at the garrison in Cavan and that he had some kind of bizarre bird tattoo on his hand." The priest held up his hand and flapped it like a bird.

Ian heard the girl Lianna gasp in horror. He turned sharply to look at her, surprised to see that she quivered while staring at Father Michael's hand in shock.

"What else did Fiona say about Bradford's brother?" Ian asked, his gut twisting with worry. This was not welcome news.

"Naught else, except that I should stay away from him because she felt he was dangerous. She didn't say whether she'd had any contact with him herself."

Ian swore again and began pacing, trying to think. Everything had gone well up until now. Father Michael had successfully visited Miles and the prisoners to warn them of the impending rescue. He'd confirmed the number of guards, the location of the keys to the cells, and the condition of the prisoners. Then he'd rode out of the castle with the two horses, being stopped only once by a soldier. Once the priest had explained that he intended to exercise the beasts in a field outside the village, he had passed through without incident. All in all, it had been easy.

Mayhap too easy.

Ian's mood darkened as he heard the thud of the wooden gate as it slammed shut. Faith stepped up beside him, placing a hand on his arm.

"Ian, it will be all right," she said softly, but he could see the strain of concern around her eyes. "Fiona is resourceful. She'll get out all right. The guards are bound to be distracted after the rescue. No one will pay her any attention at all. We planned for this possibility. She knows where to go if we are separated."

Ian didn't answer, but instead stroked his beard thoughtfully. Faith only vocalized what everyone already knew—the rescue would go on as planned. They had come too far to go back now.

A familiar quiver settled in his stomach, the same feeling he always got before battle. It was time.

"All right," he said crisply, "this is what we do. Father Michael, ye and Lianna will stay together. Put her somewhere safe and then create a diversion by the gate. Set a fire, create a lot o' noise, and then get the hell out o' there. We'll meet up wi' the two o' ye later, as planned."

He paused and looked over at the others. "Shaun and Furlong, ye are wi' me. The three o' us will go in through the tunnel and bring the men out. Our most important task is to keep the guards inside the dungeon from alerting others to our presence. Father Michael says there are three guards—two across from the cells and one at the top o' the stairs. Our priority is to get to that guard at the top o' the stairs before he can call for more help. We'll have to do this as quietly as possible."

He took a breath. "Faith, ye will wait near the exit o' the tunnel wi' the horses. When we come out, if we have the luxury o' time, we'll quickly divvy up the prisoners. The sickliest will ride wi' Shaun, who will lead them toward the first rendezvous point. Furlong, ye will take those who can walk in a different direction, but circle around so ye eventually meet up with Shaun. Faith, ye take Miles alone on a horse and meet up with the others—just tell Miles where we intend to meet. He'll know the way."

Faith looked at him with concern. "What about you, Ian? Which way will you go?"

He exhaled a deep breath. "I'm going back in after Fiona."

Faith drew in her breath sharply, but he was thankful that for once she did not argue with him. Furlong, Shaun, and Father Michael also looked at him gravely but remained silent.

Suddenly Lianna stepped forward and tugged on Ian's arm, her deformed fingers curling awkwardly around his sleeve. Ian looked down, his heart going out to the dirty-faced girl with tangled red hair and round green eyes.

"Worried now, lass, are ye?" he said softly.

"Fiona?" the girl asked, looking anxiously between Faith and Ian.

Ian sighed. "Father Michael, can ye explain to her as simply as possible what has happened and what we intend to do?"

The priest knelt down on one knee in front of Lianna and quickly explained in Gaelic what had happened. Ian started in surprise as he heard the girl ask a halting question. So, she could talk after all.

After a minute, Father Michael stood up, and Lianna walked over to the trunk of a tree and sat down. The girl mournfully pulled her legs up to her chest and wrapped her arms around them, resting her chin on her knees. Ian thought she looked so small and helpless. Just one more lost soul who was counting on him.

"What did she ask ye?" Ian asked curiously.

"She wanted to know about Bradford's brother, the one wi' the bird tattoo on his hand. I got the impression that the two o' them may have crossed paths before."

Ian gave Lianna a sympathetic glance before walking over to Faith. "Come, we need to eat a little something to give us strength and stop the rumbling in our bellies. I dinna know when we'll have the opportunity to eat again."

Faith opened a pouch and pulled out some dried meat and bread. For the last few days they'd had to soak the bread in ale to eat it, it had become so hard. But none of them had much of an appetite tonight.

They ate mostly in silence and after they were done, Ian quietly outlined his plan for opening the dungeon door and freeing the prisoners. Everyone listened intently, and when he was done, a beautiful half-moon had risen high above them.

" 'Tis time," Ian said simply, standing up. "Godspeed to all o' ye."

Father Michael offered a short prayer and Faith hugged everyone tightly, trying not to cry.

Ian went to get his horse but turned back as soon as he heard Shaun call out to him quietly.

"What is it now?" Ian asked.

"We've got a problem," the dwarf said.

"What kind o' problem?"

Shaun looked over his shoulder where Faith, Furlong, and Father Michael stood looking puzzled.

"The girl is missing," he said simply.

"I believe I've been more than generous," Andrew said, cracking his fist against the open palm of his other hand. He strode back and forth in front of the hearth, his black boots thudding against the stone floor. "We've been discussing this for at least two hours, perhaps more. And you, Madame Phillips, have been less than forthcoming."

Fiona wiped the back of her hand across her blood-ied lip and glared at Andrew. She sat perched on the edge of the bed, her cloak long ago discarded. Nich-olas leaned against the stone wall near the window with his arms crossed, watching her impassively.

"It's because I don't know what you're talking about," Fiona said. Damn, but the entire left side of her face had blossomed into one swollen, throbbing ache, her lip had been split, and her eyes kept water-ing. Yet somehow she had gone from being com-pletely terrorized to bloody pissing mad.

Andrew gave an exaggerated sigh, picked up a gob-let from the mantel, and drank deeply. Somewhere along the line, he and Nicholas had gotten hungry and thirsty from interrogating and hitting her, so they had thoughtfully ordered food and drink for themselves. The maidservant who had brought the refreshment shrieked in horror when she saw Tom O'Connor's dead body on the floor and the bruises and cuts on Fiona's face. The two brothers laughed at her fright, and Nicholas dismissed her with a careless wave of his hand. She scurried out without a backward glance, and Fiona felt any hope of a reprieve fade as quickly as the sun had.

She knew the gate had long ago closed and, if all went according to plan, the rescue was likely already underway. Ian, Faith, and the others were probably frantic about her whereabouts, but she knew the show would go on. From their questioning, Fiona realized neither brother knew anything about the secret tunnel, and she fully intended to keep it that way. God bless his soul, Tom O'Connor had apparently taken that secret to the grave, and so would she. She had no idea what would happen to her, but, surprisingly she found that it mattered less and less. What was important now was preserving the integrity of the mission—making certain that neither Nicholas nor Andrew got wind of what was about to happen.

"Now, would you like to tell me where the priest is?" Andrew asked softly.

"What? Do I look like his mum?" Fiona snapped. "Besides, he's not *my* priest. I assure you, he is his own man."

Andrew glanced at his brother. "She is being most uncooperative. Would you like a turn at her? It seems unfair for me to engage in all the pleasantries."

Nicholas sighed, leaving his spot against the wall and approaching her. "Do we need to go over this again? You, madame, have appeared to come out of nowhere. Shortly after your arrival, one of my soldiers went to Enniskillen. He returned this afternoon with the news that no one had ever heard of a soldier named Captain John Phillips. And, not surprisingly, Colonel Brooks had never heard of you. So, what have you to say for yourself?"

Fiona managed a smile, but it hurt. "Who knew that you would be so enterprising?"

His hand shot out so quickly, she didn't have time to flinch. He backhanded her against the bruised side of her face and she cried out as pain exploded behind her eyes.

"Who sent you here?" he asked, taking her by the shoulders and shaking her hard.

Fiona's teeth clattered together. "All I can say is that

your soldier is mistaken. My husband was a loyal subject to the Crown who served at Enniskillen. I accompanied him there from London. I cannot fathom why your soldier would tell falsehoods about my husband and me. Perhaps he never even arrived there. I urge you to send another messenger, or better yet, go yourself to the garrison to get to the truth of this matter."

Nicholas put his face close to hers. "Then tell me, madame, what is the name of the lake at Enniskillen? In what building is the market located? Where do the wives meet every Sunday to sew and have tea?"

Fiona recoiled from his nearness. "I don't know how you can expect me to answer any of these questions after the physical and mental distress you have subjected me to," she retorted haughtily.

Nicholas shot out his hand again, but this time Fiona was prepared. She ducked sideways, but Nicholas tangled a fist in her hair and snapped her head backward. Her wooden hairpins fell to the floor as he dragged her to a standing position.

She saw his cold eyes narrow, and slowly, he released her, fingering a strand of her hair.

"You are indeed a mystery. Odd hair, strange speech, and far too intelligent for a woman. You've asked too many questions since you've been here, and gone missing from your chamber far too many times for it to be mere coincidence." He dropped her hair and walked over to the door where the body of the Irish servant still lay.

Fiona started when he gave the body a vicious kick. "And there is the matter of your conversation with this Irish scum here," Bradford said, his voice chilly. "It cost him his life, you know."

"You are mad," Fiona whispered, wondering just

257

who had been spying on them in the kitchen. Thankfully, it appeared nothing of their actual conversation had been overheard, unless this whole beat-and-torture routine was just some kind of morbid game. Unfortunately, it was something she wouldn't put past the Bradford brothers.

"I was only looking for some wine to help me sleep," she lied. "You killed a man for nothing."

Nicholas stalked back over to her, and Fiona drew herself up and fought to keep from cringing. "I've killed people for a lot less."

"Somehow that doesn't surprise me," Fiona said before she could stop herself.

He hit her across the face again, but this time it didn't hurt as much. Either the nerves in her face were completely shot or there came a point when the brain couldn't effectively register any more pain.

"You are not what you appear, madame," he said coldly. "This much I know. In fact, you remind me of a woman I once knew—a woman who wore her hair in a similar fashion as you and spoke in the same strange manner. I suppose it is no coincidence that she happened to be Miles O'Bruaidar's wife."

Fiona was grateful that her face was so battered Bradford surely couldn't see the look of shock that momentarily flashed across it.

"I don't know what you are talking about," she said, reaching up to touch her nose, not terribly surprised to discover that it was bleeding.

"For a remarkably intelligent woman, you know very little," Nicholas said. "Do you think I don't know that this little game of yours has something to do with the Irish prisoners I hold in the dungeon? That you are likely some kin to O'Bruaidar's wife?" He laughed

258

curtly. "I only regret that I let myself be distracted for far too long by your beauty. But whatever you intend to do, I assure you, it will not work. The prisoners will be executed tomorrow as planned, and all of your efforts will have been in vain. I've posted extra guards in the dungeon and inside the castle perimeter for the night. You, madame, in a word, have failed."

"That's two words, imbecile," she spat out.

Nicholas smiled as he walked to the door. "Goodbye, my dear. This has been a fascinating exchange, but I'm afraid you rather bore me now."

Andrew stepped forward from the hearth where he had been observing the exchange with amusement. "Well, Nicholas?" he asked. "What shall we do with her now?"

Nicholas opened the door, pausing across the threshold. "Do as you like," he said, shrugging. "Then kill her."

Chapter Nineteen

Ian moved steadily through the tunnel darkness, a torch in one hand and his shortsword in the other. Three more daggers and a coil of rope hung on a makeshift belt around his waist, with another small dirk tucked into his boot. Furlong and Shaun were similarly armed, and all would share their weapons with those in the dungeon who could fight. Still, they seemed far too meager for the task ahead.

Nonetheless, Ian pressed forward. Walking was difficult as he had to slouch his shoulders in order to fit his large frame through the narrow space of the tunnel. But his focus was intense and single-minded. Before entering the tunnel he had taken a moment to push all concerns for Fiona to a small corner of his mind. He needed all his concentration on the skirmish ahead so that he would come out of this alive and save her. He did not intend to leave Cavan without her.

His boot caught on a protruding root and he stumbled slightly. He caught himself with an elbow against the wall and continued on. An almost tomblike silence had fallen upon them, broken only by the shuffle of their feet, shallow breathing, and the occasional splashes of their boots in small puddles.

Ian paused for a moment to listen and inhale a deep breath. The air was damp and musty, and he heard Shaun muffle a sneeze behind him. The sooner they got out of here, the better. He moved on ahead, stopping only when the tunnel came to another juncture. Quietly, he instructed Shaun to leave a torch in place to help them expedite their return trip.

" 'Tis no' far now," Ian said in encouragement over his shoulder.

In a few minutes, the three of them stood at a larger juncture with the tunnel branching out in three directions. Ian pointed to the tunnel to the left of him, which corkscrewed up sharply.

"That's it, lads," Ian said softly. "That's our entrance to the dungeon."

Furlong and Shaun nodded as Ian sheathed his sword. Ian squeezed his body through the tunnel, crawling on his elbows and knees, one hand holding the torch alight. Luckily, he didn't have far to go, as the tunnel led up to a large, flat platform. Above his head, Ian saw a heavy iron trapdoor.

Shaun joined him on the platform, and Furlong squeezed in last. Ian held up the torch and examined the door. A ring hung on the upper lefthand side, presumably for easy closure. Ian ran his finger along the rim of the door, blinking as the dirt fell away from it easily.

"The dirt around the door is soft. It means that it

261

shouldn't be too hard to open. That is to our advantage. The less noise we make opening the door, the safer 'twill be for us. When we get through, remember what ye need to do. Furlong, block the guardroom—keep as many soldiers in there as ye can. Shaun, make certain the guard at the top o' the stairs doesn't have time to summon any more reinforcements. I'll do my best to clear the way for both o' ye. Are ye ready?"

Both men nodded, their hands steady and their faces grim but determined. They were good men—loyal, courageous, and trustworthy—and Ian would do his damnedest to see all of them came out of this alive.

Ian propped his torch in a corner. Then he stood, placing both hands above his head on the door. Furlong did the same, and Shaun, who was too short to reach, held a sword in one hand and a dagger in the other in case they had unexpected company waiting for them.

"One...two ... three," Ian said.

He and Furlong shoved at the door with all their strength. The door moved upward slightly with a creak but did not open.

"No' good," Ian said, breathing heavily. "But at least it moved a wee bit. Let's try again."

He and Furlong again pushed hard, the muscles in their arms straining. To Ian's surprise the door groaned and moved considerably more, until Ian felt certain it would open on the next push.

"This is it, lads," he said, sweat starting to trickle down his temples. "Godspeed to ye both."

Ian and Furlong gave a final push and the door suddenly popped open a crack with an abrupt whoosh of air. Ian held the door motionless with both hands, but

Furlong dropped his support and quietly unsheathed his sword.

As the seconds ticked by, Ian realized with great relief that no one appeared to be waiting for them. Another good sign was that the door had opened into total darkness. This meant, at the very least, that they had not exited the tunnel into the guardroom.

Still Ian waited, listening and trying to get his bearings. When several minutes passed and nothing happened, he began to breathe normally again.

"There is noise coming from the dungeon," Ian murmured.

"I think they heard us," Shaun whispered as the noise intensified. "The prisoners are covering for us."

"Can ye tell where we are, Ian?" Furlong asked quietly.

Ian squinted. From his vantage point, it appeared that the noise was coming from the end of a dark corridor on the right side. That was probably the location of the prisoners' cell.

Just then a guard stepped out of a room directly across from the cell and into the corridor. Ian carefully lowered the door.

"Douse the light," he hissed at Shaun, who quickly stamped out the torch.

As they were plunged into darkness, Ian raised the trapdoor again and peeked out. For a minute he let his eyes adjust to the dimness. He could see the soldier at the end of the corridor standing in front of the cell, shouting at the prisoners to be quiet. Then he turned around and disappeared back into the chamber.

"I think the guardroom is down the corridor on the left, just across from the prisoners' cell," Ian whispered. "Luck is on our side, lads. We've come in at

263

the end of a dark corridor, which should protect our advance."

He turned to Furlong. "Hold the door for me. I'm going up."

While Furlong held the door, Ian used both hands to pull himself up and wiggle on his belly into the corridor. Once up, he crouched soundlessly and opened the trapdoor all the way. With a slight tap of his boot, he indicated that Furlong and Shaun should follow him.

When the two men were up and in position, Ian unfastened his cloak, dropping it on the ground; better to fight unencumbered. Furlong and Shaun did the same as Ian began inching down the wall, sword drawn. The two moved just as slowly along the wall opposite him. They hadn't gone far when they suddenly heard the clatter of footsteps coming down the stairs, and a guard tore around the corner and into the guardroom. Ian froze.

"Some bastard set a fire just outside the gate," Ian could hear him shout. "It's a bloody bonfire out there, with someone burning an English flag."

Ian heard the soldiers shout curses, and two of them abruptly left the guardroom and ran up the stairs. Ian could hear the door open and thud closed, and he gave a small prayer that Father Michael's distraction had provided them at least a small respite.

As if sensing something was afoot, the prisoners began hollering and clanging on the iron bars of their cell. Ian again began moving slowly along the wall, the stones so cold, his fingers felt numb. After a few steps he felt the wall turn into bars and realized he had passed a smaller cell. Before he could move another step, an arm snaked around his neck and a hand clamped down over his mouth.

Ian twisted and raised his sword to strike when he heard a voice murmur in his ear. "What took ye so damn long?"

The hand covering his mouth quickly disappeared, and Ian relaxed his sword arm. Without a word, he pulled a dagger off his belt and passed it through the bars.

"Beware, Ian," he heard Miles whisper softly. "Bradford has posted extra guards here for some reason. He may suspect something is afoot."

Ian nodded and continued moving along the wall. Shaun and Furlong were slightly ahead of him and they were all moving closer to the light. Soon they would have to make their move. Ian saw Furlong and Shaun freeze along the wall and realized a guard had stepped into the corridor and was shouting at the prisoners.

"I said stop your complaining in there," he yelled. "You'll all be bloody dead tomorrow."

The prisoners let out a series of protesting howls and clanged angrily against the bars. Three more guards stepped from a room opposite the cell and into the corridor. That meant at least five guards that Ian could account for—one he couldn't see who sat by the door at the top of the stairs and the four here in the corridor. There were still an undetermined number of soldiers in the guardroom, but they'd have to deal with that when they came to it.

Ian's hand gripped the sword tightly. He'd have to take on all four of the men in the corridor himself, while Furlong moved to block the door of the guardroom and Shaun slipped past to remove the guard from the top of the stairs before he could summon more aid.

It seemed bleak, but not impossible. They had the element of surprise on their side and were armed with weapons well suited to fighting in confined spaces. The soldiers, with their long swords, would be at a disadvantage in the narrow corridor. Ian only prayed it would be enough.

He waited another minute to see if any more guards would come into the corridor, but none did. Tension coiled in his gut as he raised his shortsword and saw Furlong and Shaun do the same.

The noise in the dungeon was deafening now. The clanging was intense, the noise ear-splitting in the small area.

Seconds before Ian charged, fortune smiled on them. In the dim light at the bottom of the stairs, Ian saw a guard step down and look around the corner. It was likely the one from the top of the stairs who had come down to see what had happened. Ian paused and glanced at Shaun and Furlong, who had also halted in their tracks. Ian saw Shaun reach for something on his back and nodded approvingly. Returning his gaze to the guard standing at the bottom of the stairs, Ian heard an arrow whistle past his ear and watched the soldier clutch at his neck and stumble forward.

Unnoticed by his fellow compatriots amid the din, the soldier staggered forward and then tumbled head-first to the ground. One soldier turned in disbelief to stare at the man, and Ian took the opportunity to charge. Bellowing a primal battle cry, he cut down one soldier immediately and engaged another who had barely managed to draw his sword.

From the corner of his eye, Ian saw Furlong step

into the doorway of the guardroom and begin fighting with a soldier inside while holding his position and blocking the others from leaving. It was an excellent strategy, as only one soldier could fight him at a time in the narrow doorway. Ian quickly moved to protect Furlong's back.

Clashing furiously with another soldier in the corridor, Shaun managed to put an end to him, leaving Ian only two to duel with. The dwarf abandoned his position next to Ian, instead sliding daggers through the bars to the prisoners and then rushing to retrieve the key ring. Ian used the opportunity to maneuver the two guards back against the cell, where the prisoners could jab at them through the bars.

Shaun disappeared down the corridor, and Ian assumed the dwarf had retrieved the key ring and was headed to unlock Miles's cell. After a moment, Ian heard Miles bellow and thunder down the corridor, attacking one of the soldiers with amazing ferocity.

Ian concentrated on just one of the soldiers now, forcing him away from the cell where Shaun was trying frantically to open the lock. The soldier deftly thrust and parried at Ian with his sword, but he was hampered by the sword's length, and Ian finally finished him off by sliding his shortsword neatly through the man's ribs. With him out of the way, Ian strode to the bottom of the stairs, relieved when he saw the door was still locked tight, with nothing but an empty chair at the top.

Miles had just mortally wounded the solider he had been fighting with, and Furlong was holding his own when Shaun managed to unlock the cell. The prisoners spilled out into the corridor, shouting wildly. Over the din, Ian instructed Shaun to move the prisoners toward the tunnel and get them out.

Rushing over to the door, where Furlong was still fighting, Ian looked over his shoulder and saw one man down, one more engaged with Furlong, and four other English soldiers howling impatiently for action.

"Good work, man," Ian said, tapping Furlong on the shoulder. Furlong obliged by stepping aside, and Ian noticed that the hook-nosed man had taken a bad cut to the left shoulder.

"Bind it up as soon as ye can," Ian ordered as Furlong nodded wordlessly and disappeared down the corridor.

Ian stepped into the guardroom, leaving Miles to block the door, their two huge forms presenting an intimidating presence in the small room.

Miles grinned at Ian. "God's wounds, Ian, I'm going to enjoy this," he said gleefully as one of the soldiers engaged him.

Realizing they were operating on borrowed time, Ian swiftly killed two of the soldiers, while Miles disabled another. The two of them then teamed up to finish off the last guard. Sheathing his sword, Ian stepped over a body on his way out the door.

"Follow me," Ian instructed Miles over his shoulder. The two men quickly moved down to the end of the corridor, where Ian showed Miles the tunnel.

"Faith waits for ye at the end o' the tunnel with a horse," Ian said quietly. "She'll tell ye where we will rendezvous. After ye leave, I'll close the door behind ye, so the English willna be able to follow."

"And just where will ye be going, Ian?" Miles asked, his voice sounding puzzled.

"Inside. After Fiona."

Miles swore softly. "What in God's name is Faith's cousin doing here? Let me help ye, friend."

"And hand Bradford his prize again? I dinna think so. Your safety is the reason we are here, Miles. Ireland needs ye, and so does your wife. Go to Faith now. This is something I need to do for myself."

Miles hesitated before reaching out and clasping Ian's hand firmly. "I don't much like this plan. Be careful, Ian. Bradford is a coldhearted bastard."

"As I am all too aware. Dinna worry. Tell Faith I'll see Fiona to safety."

Ian waited until Miles disappeared down the tunnel before closing the door and brushing dirt back over it. Then he stepped over the bodies littering the corridor and headed up the stairs. He paused at the other side of the door, pressing his ear against the wood and listening. When he heard nothing, he took a deep breath and dropped his sword and its sheath on the stairs. He lifted up his tunic and slid his weapon's belt underneath. He had only two daggers left and a coil of rope, but that would have to be enough to implement his plan. Determinedly, he slid the bolt off the door.

"Hold on, Fiona, love," he murmured as he opened the door. "I'm coming to rescue ye."

"I must confess that I admire your fortitude," Andrew said, striding over to the mantel and taking a drink of wine from a goblet. "I've broken men with the same methods. It seems that I must consider another approach for a woman like you."

Fiona glared at him the best she could, considering one eye had nearly swollen shut. Every bone and muscle in her body ached, and she was pretty certain Andrew had broken her nose and badly bruised her left wrist. He'd been interrogating her for what seemed like days, although a rational part of her brain told her it was likely only a few hours.

For the last half-hour or so, she'd been fairly successful at mentally shutting out his abuse by thinking of Ian and how much she loved him. Now, as she looked across the chamber at Andrew, she realized how insignificant and weak he seemed compared with Ian.

"I'd be willing to spare your life if you'd just tell me who sent you and what you were plotting with this Irish scum," he said.

"And I should tell you this because...?" Fiona spat out, wiping a hand across her bloodied mouth. She tried hard not to look at the body of Tom O'Connor on the floor just inches from her fingers.

"I can make you talk," he said, taking another sip of wine. "I've spared you the worst indignities you could suffer as a woman. I may not continue to be so generous if you refuse to give me some useful information."

"It seems your persuasive powers are rather lacking when it comes to women," Fiona said. "You are nothing more than a pathetic excuse for a man. It's embarrassing that you must use alcohol and intimidation to try to get women to do what you want. And I'll tell you why: because inadequate men like you lack the genuine qualities of a real man, and women know it."

Andrew's face flushed scarlet and he gripped the goblet so tightly in his hand, Fiona could see his knuckles whiten. She knew it hadn't helped matters to bait him, but she couldn't stop herself. And from the way he looked right now, she had just nailed every one of his idiotic male insecurities.

"You know nothing about me," he seethed, throwing the goblet angrily into the fire. "You, madame, will be exceedingly sorry for making such comments. In minutes you will beg for my forgiveness."

"I don't think so," Fiona said calmly. "Actually, you rather embarrass me. As an Englishman, I expected better behavior from you. Frankly speaking, I've been treated more kindly by the Irish and the Scottish since I've been in Ireland than I have by my own countrymen. Doesn't speak well for England, now does it?"

"You, madame, are a disgrace to England." He picked up the wine bottle from the table and drank directly from it. "My patience is at an end."

Fiona took the opportunity to innocuously slide her hand beneath her gown and reach for the dagger Ian had insisted she strap to her thigh. Andrew was nearly drunk enough now that she felt she had a fairly good chance of disabling him if she could catch him unaware. He also seemed poised to resort to rape and perhaps other unspeakable acts, and she bloody well wouldn't permit that without a fight. Still, a part of her wondered if she'd be able to use the dagger with the intent to kill. The way things were going, it seemed highly probable that she was on the verge of finding out.

"I think a slow death would be appropriate for you," Andrew said, stalking over and dragging her to her feet. "I'll keep you alive just long enough for you to wish you were dead."

Fiona's hand curled around the dagger just as Andrew crushed her to him, his mouth descending on hers in a brutal kiss. Recoiling in mock horror, she drew her hand from beneath her skirts and shoved the blade into his stomach with as much force as she could muster.

Andrew screamed in surprise, stepping back and looking down in disbelief. Then, with a firm yank, he pulled out the blade. Fiona realized with sinking dread that it had barely even pierced his skin through the heavy vest and shirt he wore.

"You whore," he hissed between clenched teeth, tossing the dagger aside. Fiona watched her last hope for escape clatter to the floor and slide under the bed. She circled around him warily, backing up against the window.

"You will face my wrath," he said, seizing her by the shoulders and squeezing so hard, she cried out. "You will pleasure me."

Fiona managed a laugh. "You really believe that, don't you? It seems you have a lot to learn about women, Andrew. I must say it is a bit disconcerting to know that time doesn't change everything. There are still brainless twats like you where I come from, men who think they can bully and threaten women into doing what they want. How utterly pitiable."

"You are spouting nonsense," he said.

"No, not at all," Fiona said, with the absolute realization that death was imminent. Suddenly she felt an eerie and almost soothing peace come over her. There was no longer any fear that she would break or give way under torture, only a strange calmness and acceptance.

An exhilarating moment of clarity overtook her. For the first time in her life, she truly understood what it meant to love someone more than life. She was truly willing to die rather than give up information that might lead to the deaths of Ian, Faith, and the others.

God, the irony of it. She, Fiona Sophia Chancellor, perhaps the most self-centered woman in all of England, had just decided to forfeit her life in an act of unselfish love for others. It was remarkable, but more than that, it was liberating.

Fiona threw back her head and laughed again. She finally understood the meaning of true love. It felt so good, so pure, so abso-bloody-lutely wonderful. Who knew it could be such an amazing revelation? And yet how unfortunate that she had to be at death's door before she finally understood it.

"What's wrong with you?" Andrew shouted, snapping Fiona back to reality. He held her in a tight grip, his fingernails digging into the skin on her shoulders.

She looked at him in wonder. "I can't believe it, but I have to thank you, Andrew Bradford. It took a stupid sod like you to finally make me realize that there are so many things in this world that are more important than a perfect cup of coffee, an excellent manicure, or an expensive pair of Italian pumps."

"What are you talking about?"

Fiona grinned, the strange sense of calm remaining with her. "I mean, I never considered myself worthy of love before. So I hid behind my selfishness and indulged in my obsession for perfect fashion and comfort. I cringe now to think of the time I spent surrounding myself with so-called important and influential people. Ian was right—I was pampered and self-centered. But now I realize I could have been so much more had I sought friendship and love in people who liked me for what I really was and not for who I wanted to be."

Andrew stared at her as if she were an alien just

landed from Mars. In a way, maybe she was.

Fiona chuckled. "What? No applause for my incredibly personal revelation?"

"You are quite mad," he whispered.

"Actually quite sane, for the first time in my life. And frankly, I rather like it."

She shrieked as he abruptly kicked her feet out from beneath her and fell on top of her. She managed to claw her fingernails down one side of his face, drawing blood, but he only smiled coldly at her, nearly crushing her right wrist in his fist.

"Your life is at an end, madame. But only when I have finished with you." He reached down with his other hand, gathering her skirts and trying to push them up around her waist.

Fiona struggled, not out of fear, but anger. "You bloody bastard," she yelled. "Keep your disgustingly pathetic willy in your trousers."

Andrew had her skirts tangled around her waist and now fumbled with his breeches. Fiona writhed to the side, managing to pull up her knee and smash it into his groin. Andrew shrieked in pain, collapsing on top of her, his hands circling her neck.

"I'll kill you!" he screamed wildly, increasing the pressure of his hands.

Fiona gasped, the last of the air leaving her lungs. She grabbed his forearms and pulled, but they didn't budge.

"Die!" he screamed again, banging her head against the stone wall.

Summoning the last of her strength, Fiona spit at him, hitting him on the cheek. As she watched the spittle trickle down his cheek, her vision began to swim and edge with blackness. Curiously, she realized that he was still shouting something at her, but she could no longer hear him.

Suddenly, he slumped on top of her, his hands sliding from her neck. Fiona wheezed like a fish out of water, the air trying to push its way into her lungs in an immense, painful rush. She gagged and then coughed, finally managing to draw a few deep breaths. Horrified, she pushed at Bradford, puzzled when he slid off her without protest.

Rolling to the side, she came to her feet, staring at him in shock. He lay facedown on the floor with a dagger stuck in the back of his neck only a half-meter away from the body Tom O'Connor. His arms were splayed above his head, the bizarre bird tattoo on the top of his hand looking grotesquely ready to fly.

"What the hell?" Fiona murmured as she glanced over at the now open doorway. Her mouth slacked wide in astonishment.

"My God," she finally managed to utter. "What on earth are *you* doing here?"

Ian warily climbed the stairs from the dungeon into the kitchen. No one was present on the stairs themselves, but he could hear people in the kitchen above and had no idea how many soldiers might be milling about. He felt naked without his sword, but if his plan was to have any chance of success, he'd have to make do without it. He wasn't completely defenseless; he still had the two daggers and the coil of rope on his belt beneath his tunic, as well as the dirk in his boot. It wasn't much, but he'd have to succeed with what he had. Ian approached the top of the stairs carefully, daring a quick look around the corner and into the kitchen. From his vantage point, he saw several guards standing by a doorway, which appeared to lead out to the courtyard. They were speaking rapidly and pointing out across the courtyard. Ian overheard enough to say a silent prayer of thanks to Father Michael for his clever distraction.

While the guards' backs were turned, Ian slipped from the stairs into a small pantry to the left of the kitchen. The room was empty, and Ian crouched behind a large storage shelf and waited. After only a few minutes a young maidservant entered the room and began searching for something on one of the shelves. Ian stepped out, grabbed her around the waist, and clamped a hand over her mouth so she couldn't scream. He dragged her back behind the shelf, pressing her against the wall.

"Dinna scream," he said softly, seeing her eyes widen with fear. "I dinna intend to hurt ye. We are on the same side. I'm no' working wi' the English and neither is the Englishwoman who recently came to the castle. I need ye to take me to her chamber. Do ye understand?"

She nodded, and Ian looked at her carefully. "If I lift my hand from your mouth, do ye promise no' to scream? If ye do, it will bring the English soldiers down on us at once. I'd tell them ye were helping me. We both know they'd kill ye without trying to determine whether or no' ye are innocent. So, I'd say 'tis in your best interest to help me."

Her eyes widened even farther and began to fill with tears. Ian felt a twinge of guilt for scaring her, but it had to be done. If she helped him, he'd see nothing happened to her. He lifted his hand from her mouth. To his great relief, she didn't scream.

"They k-killed Tom O'Connor," she whispered, her body beginning to tremble. "R-right there in her room."

"Who is Tom O'Connor?"

"His family served the O'Reillys for more than a century. He was a g-good man. He was just lying there in her room."

"Whose room?"

"The Englishwoman's. They were b-beating her, too."

Ian's heart twisted horribly in his chest. "Mary, Mother o' God. Is she all right?"

"She was still alive when I left an hour or more ago.

"Take me there at once," Ian ordered, his hands clenching into fists. "We have to go now." He picked up a small cloth bag and shoved it at her. Then he grabbed a small barrel, tucking it under his arm.

"We'll just be two servants going about our business," he said quietly. "If we are stopped, try to speak for me. I canna hide my Scottish accent and 'twill raise too many suspicions."

"But what about the others who work in the kitchen?"

"Just don't let them see ye are frightened. I think everyone knows something is going on. If they see ye aren't afraid, then they'll suspect I'm working against the English. No one will give us away." He hoped he sounded more confident than he felt. His situation was becoming more perilous by the moment.

The girl thought for a moment and then bit her lower lip. "I hate them," she whispered.

"As do I. Dinna fash yourself, lass. I'll see that the

bastard who killed Tom O'Connor pays for what he has done."

The girl took a deep breath and walked out of the pantry. Ian followed close behind, slouching his shoulders and keeping his eyes lowered deferentially. He could feel the surprised stares of many in the kitchen on his back, but no one said anything. He struggled to keep his expression neutral, but he had never felt so enraged in all his life. Bradford would die for daring to raise his hand against Fiona. He would hurt the man badly before sticking a dirk between the bloody bastard's eyes and turning it with a savage cry of satisfaction. God's wounds, what kind of deranged man beat a woman?

The maidservant straightened her shoulders and led him through the kitchen, down a corridor past the castle's Great Hall, bypassing the large staircase. Instead, she led him to a smaller set of back stairs, apparently those taken by the servants. Ian had taken about six stairs when he heard a heavy tread behind him.

"Hey, you!" he heard a clipped English voice call out.

The girl paused in midstep and turned around slowly. Ian did the same, maintaining his slouched and deferential position.

A young English soldier stood at the bottom of the stairs, staring up at them. He pointed at Ian.

"You," he said coldly. "Come down here at once."

Chapter Twenty

Fiona looked on in stunned amazement as Lianna took a shaky step forward. The girl's gaze was fixated on the dagger in the back of Andrew's neck.

"Lianna," Fiona cried, rushing over to the girl and hugging her tightly. "Oh my God, it was you who saved me. You killed him to protect me."

For a moment Lianna stood rigid and then she collapsed trembling in Fiona's arms. Fiona lifted Lianna's head from her shoulder, tilting her chin up with a finger until the girl looked directly into her eyes.

"Thank you," Fiona whispered, fingering a strand of Lianna's hair. "I don't know how you got in here and where the others are, but I am so grateful. How can I ever thank you for saving my life?" Tears spilled down her cheeks. "What you did was so courageous and so very, very difficult. I'm sorry you had to do it."

Lianna smiled tremulously, her lips quivering. With a small sob, she slid her arms around Fiona's neck, hugging her tightly.

"Oh, sweetheart," Fiona whispered, "what am I going to do with you?"

Lianna buried her face in Fiona's hair. "Mama," she murmured. Fiona pulled Lianna into her chamber and closed the door. "We've got to get out of here," she said, grabbing her cloak from the bed and fastening it around her neck. She knelt on the floor and groped under the bed until her fingers circled around the cold blade of her dagger. "Nicholas Bradford might return at any moment."

After recovering the blade, Fiona strode quickly across the room and grabbed Lianna's hand. She spoke mainly to calm herself and organize her thoughts. Now that death was no longer imminent, her fears had come flooding back. Added to that was the fact that she had just become responsible for saving one more life. Right now her veins were pumping with so much adrenaline, she thought they might burst.

But Lianna refused to move, her face ashen. She was simply unable to take her eyes off the body of Andrew Bradford. Fiona knelt down in front of her, shaking her shoulders gently, trying to snap the girl out of her daze.

"Come on, Lianna, please. We must go now."

The girl took one last look at Bradford and then turned. Before she could take a step, she fell to her knees and began retching on the floor.

"Oh, baby," Fiona murmured, pulling the hair back from Lianna's face and rubbing her back. "Oh, God, what has happened to us?"

After a moment, Fiona stood, taking Lianna by the hand and leading her to the door. "I'm sorry, but we have to go, sweetheart, or else we may end up like them."

She opened the door and peeked out into the dark corridor. Horrified, she heard heavy footfalls coming toward them. Fiona quickly closed the door.

"Quick, behind the door," she whispered to Lianna, pushing her back against the wall and holding the dagger out in her fist. This time, Fiona swore to herself that she would aim for the head and hope for better results.

Slowly the door opened, and a boot-clad foot stepped across the threshold. As soon as the head appeared, Fiona lunged at him. Seconds before the dagger struck the side of his head, his forearm went up and the dagger skimmed across his arm and clattered to the floor.

"Damn!" she shouted as he slammed her against the wall, pressing the cold blade of a dirk against her neck.

"Fiona?"

"Ian?"

For a moment Fiona looked into the stunned eyes of her beloved. Then she threw her arms around his neck, weeping.

"Ian, you're here," she sobbed in relief. "What are you doing here?"

He hugged her tightly. "Fiona, love, are ye all right? What have the bastards done to ye?" He pulled away, cupping her face gently in his hands. When he saw the bruises and cuts, his eyes darkened with anger and his mouth tightened in unspeakable fury.

"Where is Nicholas Bradford?" he asked between clenched teeth.

"He's gone. It's all right, Ian. I didn't tell them anything. Are the prisoners all right? Did Father Michael and Miles make it out safely?"

His eyes softened. "Aye, thanks to ye, lass, they all did."

Fiona kissed him heartily before pulling away suddenly.

"Oh my God," she gasped in horror, a realization just occurring to her. "Did I hurt you?"

Ian looked down at his forearm, which was bleeding slightly. "Just a scratch," he said ruefully, picking up her dagger and returning it to her. "I should be glad ye are no' so proficient wi' a blade."

He glanced around the chamber, his eyes alighting for the first time on Lianna, who stood trembling in the corner, and then on the two dead bodies lying on the floor. His gaze returned to Lianna.

"How did she get here?" he asked.

Fiona lifted her skirts and retied her dagger to her thigh. "I was going to ask the same of you. She saved me, Ian. Andrew Bradford was about to kill me and she threw a dagger at him."

Ian's eyes darkened as he looked at Bradford's body. " 'Tis good for him that he is already dead. Who's that?"

"His name is Tom O'Connor. He helped me and it cost him his life."

Fiona realized then that another young girl stood trembling near the open door. Fiona recognized her as the maidservant who had served the Bradford brothers food and drink during the interrogation.

"What is she doing here?" Fiona asked.

Ian looked over his shoulder at the maidservant. "She brought me to ye. We would have been here sooner, but I had to help move some heavy firewood with about six English soldiers. I'm playing at being a servant, ye see. 'Twas a close call."

Fiona exhaled a deep breath. "I've had far too many of those today. Look, we've got to get out of here. Nicholas Bradford might be back at any moment. Ian, what are we going to do?"

Ian turned to the maidservant. "Do those stairs lead to a servants' exit to the courtyard?"

She nodded wordlessly, and Ian turned to Fiona. "We'll have to go through the courtyard and over the castle wall. I'll help ye up and then toss ye a coil o' rope. Ye can help drag Lianna to safety and I'll pull myself up."

Fiona lifted a hand in protest. "Are you barmy? The courtyard is crawling with guards. Bradford suspected something was up and posted extra guards all about the perimeter. We'll never make it."

"We will make it," he said firmly, taking her hand. "Let's go."

They moved to the door, but Fiona stopped when she realized Lianna wasn't following. The young girl stood trembling in the corner, sucking her thumb as if she were a babe.

Before Fiona could go to her, Ian brushed past, kneeling in front of the girl. He reached out and smoothed her hair back gently from her face and then stroked her cheek with his big hand.

Softly, he whispered something to her, and Lianna wrapped her arms around his neck, burying her tear-stained face in his shoulder.

Fiona felt her heart melt at the sight of them—the

huge Scotsman with the bloodied hands and the fragile little girl holding on to him for dear life. A lump formed in her throat and she thought she had never seen anything so touching or beautiful.

Still holding the girl, Ian stood and walked to the door. "Let's go," he said.

"What did you say to her?" Fiona asked before he stepped out of the door.

"I spoke to her in Scots Gaelic, so I dinna know if she understood me."

"Yes, but what did you say?"

Ian turned and gave her a bone-melting smile. "I said she belongs to us now."

Chapter Twenty-one

The maidservant led them down the back stairs and around a corner to a service door that opened out onto the courtyard. Ian still carried Lianna, and he pressed back against the wall by the door as Fiona peeked around him, surveying their escape route. For the middle of the night, there was an amazing amount of activity going on outside.

Bright torches hung from the walls of the courtyard, casting light and shadows about the area. Soldiers milled around and servants scurried back and forth carrying them food and drink. One young manservant brushed past them in the doorway but gave them little more than a passing glance as he quickly hurried to hand out the steaming hot loaves of bread he carried on a platter.

"Soldiers everywhere," Fiona whispered. "Servants,

too. But it seems no one has yet discovered the missing prisoners."

"Aye, 'tis good. Twill be to our advantage, then, to continue to play at being servants," Ian whispered back.

"At least until we can reach the outer grounds of the castle."

"Me a servant? Do you think I could pass for a servant?" Fiona asked. "What about Lianna?"

"Ye are going to have to trust me, lass."

Just then a middle-aged woman hurried toward them, carrying two tankards of ale and several small cloth-covered baskets on her arm. Ian set Lianna down on her feet and held out a hand, stopping the servant. The woman looked puzzled until the young maidservant hastily interjected, "He'll take care o' it for ye, Kathleen. 'Tis a cold night for ye to be out and about."

The woman looked between Ian and Fiona for some time, but without a word relinquished her items and headed back into the kitchen.

"Do you think she suspects anything?" Fiona asked worriedly.

"If she does, she will no' say anything," the maidservant whispered confidentially. "The English killed her son. She hates them."

"Oh, God, I'm sorry."

Ian turned to the maidservant. "Can ye get me a small barrel o' ale to carry?"

She nodded and disappeared down the corridor to the kitchen. She returned minutes later with a barrel and handed it to Ian.

Ian hoisted it on his shoulder and then handed Fiona and Lianna the baskets. Then he placed a gentle hand on the maidservant's shoulder.

"We have a lot to thank ye for," he said softly. "Ye've helped no' only us, but Ireland. But I have one more favor to ask o' ye. Can I have your cap?"

Puzzled, the young girl reached up, took the cap off her head, and gave it to him. Ian handed it to Fiona.

"Put it on," he ordered.

Fiona grimaced but complied. Ian nodded in approval and then patted the maidservant on the shoulder. "Go on about your work, lass. Ye've done well."

"Yes, thank you," Fiona added as the maidservant slipped away into the kitchen. Fiona thought she saw a new gleam in the girl's eyes—a gleam of satisfaction and accomplishment. She'd certainly have a tale to tell her grandchildren some day, as would all of them, if they lived to have them.

"Ye and the girl go out together," Ian whispered, breaking into her reverie. "Head toward the same place by the castle wall where we had our rendezvous. I'll follow ye shortly. Keep your head down."

Fiona nodded, her palms slick with sweat, her heart fluttering. She took Lianna by the hand. "Come on, sweetheart. Stay close."

Inhaling a deep breath, Fiona strode purposefully into the courtyard, head down and gaze lowered. She walked past several soldiers, but thankfully none of them paid them the slightest bit of attention. She prayed she and Lianna looked like simple maidservants going about their business. If someone stopped them, Fiona didn't know what she'd do. She mustn't speak; her English accent would give her away. She only hoped it wouldn't come to that.

She gave a small sigh of relief when they made it onto the grass and headed for the stables. Soldiers, some carrying torches and others sipping from tankards and eating slabs of bread, seemed to be everywhere. Their manner was relaxed and blessedly calm. Fiona knew that would change the minute they discovered their precious prisoners were in the dungeon no longer.

They had finally passed the stables and were headed toward the outer castle wall when Fiona felt a heavy hand on her shoulder. She bit back a scream, raising her eyes slowly and meeting the gaze of an English soldier. Another one stood nearby, looking at her and Lianna with suspicion.

"Now, just where do you think you are going, missy?" he asked in a thick Yorkshire accent. She had a fleeting memory of a man from York she'd once dated—handsome, elegant, and a complete bastard.

Fiona held up the basket and pointed over his shoulder and into the shadows farther down the castle wall. The soldier looked behind him and snorted.

"Looks like Harry and Daniel couldn't make it the whole night without a little food in their stomachs," he said to the other soldier. "Did they ask for ale, too?"

Fiona shook her head wordlessly. She could feel Lianna tremble beside her, and prayed the girl would remain still.

"All right, be on with you then," the soldier finally said. "Make haste and come back with some food for us, too. And be a good luv, will you, and bring us a spot of ale as well."

Fiona nodded and then hurriedly walked past them, Lianna at her side. She let out her breath, not even realizing she had been holding it.

She and Lianna kept close to the shadow of the castle wall. She nearly screamed when a hand reached out of the shadows and clamped down over her mouth.

" 'Tis just me, lass," she heard Ian murmur in her ear and nearly burst into tears of relief. Lianna gave a small cry and launched herself into his arms.

"We need to make a slight change in our plan," Fiona whispered, tossing her basket and Lianna's into the shrubbery.

"What kind of change?" Ian whispered back.

"There are apparently two soldiers not too far down the wall from here."

Ian swore softly under his breath. "Then we'll need to go o'er the wall, right here."

Fiona nodded. "Let's get on with it, then."

Suddenly Lianna shook her head, taking Fiona's hand and leading her about five steps farther down the wall. Fiona was just about to yank her to a stop when the young girl began feeling along the wall, as if searching for something. After a moment, she gave a small grunt of triumph and placed Fiona's hand against the wall. Fiona felt the rough outline of a tiny ledge on the wall. Then Lianna placed her hand on another one a bit higher, and then another.

"Small outcroppings," Fiona breathed in wonder to Ian. "It's like rock climbing. This is probably how she got in here."

Ian reached past her, feeling the ledges for himself. "These are not big enough to hold the foot o' a man, but they should aid the two o' ye in your climb. I'll pull myself up wi' the rope. Good work, lass," he said, patting Lianna on the head. "'twill make this much easier."

"Thank God for that," Fiona agreed.

"Here we go," Ian said as he lifted Fiona as easily

as if she were a sack of potatoes and placed her sitting on his shoulders. Fiona came to a stand, wobbled a bit unsteadily and then braced herself against the cold stone wall. She searched along the wall with her foot for one of the outcroppings and stepped up, raising her hands above her head until she felt the ledge of the wall.

"I've got it," she whispered down.

Ian squeezed her leg and, with a groan, Fiona began to pull herself up onto the ledge. She ignored the painful scream of her muscles, letting her body operate on sheer adrenaline.

"This is brilliant," she muttered, wishing she was clothed in anything other than mass of skirts. "Remind me why I stopped going to the gym, anyone?"

Finally, she lay belly down on the narrow ledge, breathing heavily and holding on for dear life. Every muscle and bone in her body ached. She wasn't certain she could move.

"Catch this," she heard Ian's voice come out of the darkness.

He threw the rope and she reached for it feebly but missed.

"Sorry," she whispered down.

"Hurry now, lass," she heard him whisper again a bit urgently. This time when he tossed it, she caught it in her fingers.

"Got it," she murmured triumphantly.

"Climb on down," he instructed.

"Ha, easy for you to say," she muttered, grabbing the rope in both hands and slowly rappelling herself down the other side. The small jutting ledges made it almost easy, but when her feet touched the ground, she allowed herself a moment to marvel at what she had done.

"The name is Bond," she murmured, giving the rope a hard yank and digging in her heels against the castle wall. "Fiona Bond."

Moments later, she saw the small, dark form of Lianna appear on the top of the castle wall and then lithely rapel down.

"Not fair," she chided the young girl. "You made that look painless."

She braced as she felt Ian begin to pull himself up. He had barely started when she heard a cry go up within the castle wall.

"Oh, God," she murmured as the shouting became louder. "Hurry up, Ian."

The noise was definitely moving in their direction, and Fiona distinctly heard the word *prisoners*. God help them, but the English must have discovered that the prisoners were missing. Her palms slickened and the rope slipped slightly. Gritting her teeth, she braced her feet harder against the wall and then nearly sobbed in relief as the rope went slack in her hands and she saw Ian's form at the top of the wall.

"Hurry," she hissed.

"Move out o' the way," he whispered down, and Fiona realized that he intended to drop straight down. Quickly, she stepped aside, taking Lianna with her.

He slid his body over the side and hung from his hands for a moment before dropping. She heard him land with a thud and ran over to him.

"Ian, are you all right?" she asked worriedly. "I think they've discovered that the prisoners are missing.

"Aye, they have," he said, standing. " 'Twould be prudent to get out o' here now."

"Halt right there!" came a clipped English voice from the darkness, and Fiona gasped audibly.

Two shrouded figures on horseback emerged from the nearby forest—the man in front holding a torch.

"Nicholas Bradford," she spat, the name dropping from her lips as if it were a curse.

Bradford dismounted, his black cloak billowing about him, making him appear like the devil incarnate. Fiona glanced over at the other figure, realizing he was just an accompanying soldier. Ian stepped in front of Fiona and Lianna, pushing them behind him.

Fiona quickly scoured the treeline but saw no one else emerge. She stepped around Ian and addressed Bradford.

"What in the hell are you doing here?"

He smiled, as if answering an indulgent child. "Do you think me so incapable that I wouldn't add extra guards to patrol the outside of the castle wall as well?"

"Bloody courageous of you to do the patroling yourself," Fiona retorted. "Considering who you might run into."

The shouting on the other side of the wall had reached a crescendo, and Bradford barked for the men to come over the wall. Fiona heard someone shout that a rope was needed, and then the noise diminished.

She saw a deep scowl cover Bradford's face as he turned his attention back to them. "You and your friend have been quite busy, it appears. Just how did you manage to spirit the prisoners out of the dungeon? Where are they?"

"And I'm going to tell you this because... ?" she replied.

"Because I shall make you."

"Like your brother made me talk?"

Nicholas narrowed his eyes. "Where is my brother?"

"Dead. Frankly, I didn't much like his hospitality. He could have used some instruction on how to treat a lady. Something all you Bradfords could use a little more training in."

"Enough," he said, his voice angry. Fiona was gratified to see his control slipping.

"Perchance you would be so kind as to introduce me to your friend here?" he asked, fingering the brooch at his neck.

"I bloody will not," Fiona snapped.

"The name is Ian Maclaren," Ian finally spoke up, his voice deep and calm.

Fiona marveled at how confident, almost nonchalant, he sounded despite their perilous situation. She hoped he'd been using the time she offered engaging Bradford in meaningless conversation to plot some brilliant plan to help them escape from here.

"A Scotsman?" Nicholas exclaimed, clearly surprised.

"Aye. We've actually met before, in a dark alley in London where you were trying to harm another friend o' mine."

She could see Nicholas searching his memory, the torchlight casting an eerie and almost translucent glow on his skin.

"O'Bruaidar's wife," Nicholas finally hissed.

"Aye. I should have killed ye then, when I had the opportunity. Looks like I'll have to do it now."

"My soldiers will be over the wall in minutes," Nicholas answered arrogantly.

Ian drew two daggers from beneath his tunic. "Ye dinna have minutes, Bradford."

Fiona saw the other soldier dismount and draw his sword.

"Fiona," Ian instructed tightly, "take the girl and get out o' here. Ye know where to go."

"This is your plan?" she said incredulously.

"Fiona, dinna argue wi' me."

"B-but—" she stammered before Ian interrupted, this time harshly.

"Now, I said. Damnation, woman, for once do as I say."

He jerked his head slightly toward Lianna and Fiona gasped with sudden realization, her eyes filling with tears. This was no longer about just the two of them—there was a child to consider. A child Ian had declared now belonged to them.

Fiona looked down at Lianna and saw that she understood what was about to happen. Lianna tried to pull away from Fiona's grasp and run to Ian, but Fiona wouldn't let her go.

"Nay," Lianna screamed, struggling furiously. Fiona lifted her into her arms, ignoring the flailing of fists against her chest.

"Go!" Ian shouted as Bradford began to advance on him.

"Ian, I—" Fiona started to say but realized she could not finish. A lump jammed itself in her throat as she realized this would be the last time she would ever see him. How could she leave him when she'd never had the opportunity to tell him how much she loved him and how much she had to thank him for?

"Ian," she said, her voice breaking, "please don't make me do this."

For a moment Ian's face softened as he looked at her and Lianna. "Go, lass," he said simply. "Ye'll be fine. Ye always have been."

Tears streamed down Fiona's face as she began to carry Lianna away. The girl screamed bloody murder and struggled harder.

"Oh, sweetheart, please don't fight me," she begged Lianna.

Fiona glanced over her shoulder at Bradford and saw that he was weighing whether or not to send the other soldier after them. If he did, it meant he would face Ian alone. Despite the fact that Bradford was armed with a sword against Ian's two small daggers, from where she stood Fiona could almost smell the scent of fear on him. She knew Ian was counting on Bradford's cowardice, too, and had seized upon it to give them the opportunity to escape.

Lianna had stopped struggling and simply sobbed uncontrollably on Fiona's shoulder. Fiona set her down and grasped her hand, pulling her toward the shelter of the trees. As expected, neither Bradford nor the other soldier followed.

When they reached the forest, Fiona stopped and turned around. Bradford and the soldier had engaged Ian. She saw Bradford swing his sword at Ian. Ian blocked it with his dagger—the force of it causing him to stagger. The other soldier jabbed at Ian, and Fiona gasped as she saw it slice into his side. He danced out of the way, but Fiona could see he was weakening.

"No!" she screamed. It wasn't fair—two men armed with swords against one man with two small daggers. "No," she whispered again, this time more determinedly. "I'm not going to let this happen."

Quickly, she knelt on one knee and looked at

Lianna. "Go," she said, lifting a hand and pointing into the forest. "Go and hide. I'm going back for Ian."

Lianna stared at her wide-eyed as Fiona yanked the dagger out from beneath her skirts. The girl pressed her lips together and held out her hand, but it was shaking badly.

"No, baby," Fiona said firmly. "This kill is mine. Go on, love. Please, hide."

Lianna seemed to understand what she was saying and, after a long, steady look at Fiona, turned and slipped deeper into the forest.

Seeing Lianna was safe, Fiona ran back toward Ian, shuddering when she heard a loud cry go up from the other side of the wall. She assumed the soldiers had found a rope and would be climbing over shortly.

Fiona stopped about a half-meter from the fighting. She was so close, she could hear muttered curses, grunts, and the horrid clang of steel against steel. Still, she felt thankful that the struggle was so intense that no one noticed her. She took a deep breath, lined up her thumb to the back of Bradford's head, and prayed.

"Practice makes perfect," she murmured as she threw the dagger with all her strength.

Within a split second of throwing the dagger, she realized her aim was completely off and she had cast it too far to the left. But then a miracle happened. Bradford swung at Ian and feinted to the left, directly into the path of the dagger. The blade entered smoothly just below his left shoulder.

She saw Nicholas falter momentarily, and Ian took the opportunity to savagely swipe the dagger across his neck. The other soldier was momentarily stunned by the sudden demise of his commander, and Ian kicked the sword out of his hand with a fierce bellow.

Startled, the soldier lunged for his sword, but Ian dealt him a fatal blow to the back of the head.

Straightening, Ian retrieved his dagger and ran at a full sprint toward Fiona, who still stood in shock, watching the struggle. He ran at her, grabbed her hand, and dragged her into the forest just as the first soldier came over the wall.

"Mary, Mother o' God," he exclaimed. "If we get out o' this alive, I'm going to kill ye myself. What did ye think ye were doing, going back there?"

"Saving you," she retorted through puffs of breath.

"Where's Lianna?" he asked as they crashed through the brush.

A slight form darted out of the brush, grabbing on to Fiona's hand. "Right here," she said with relief. "See, I knew everything would work out all right."

He grunted, leading them twisting and turning until they ducked under the heavily covered tree where Ian's mount was waiting. He pulled himself up and stretched out a hand for Lianna. The girl swung up, but Fiona paused.

"Ian, you're injured," she protested.

"No' now," he said, holding his hand out impatiently. "There is no time."

Reluctantly, she grabbed his hand and got onto the horse. Lianna shivered, and Fiona wrapped her cloak and arms around the girl to keep her warm. With a cluck, Ian rode the horse out from beneath the tree and deeper into the forest.

They moved far too slowly for Fiona's taste, but without a light or path to show them the way, Ian had to guide the horse carefully through the thick brush. Low-hanging branches scratched and yanked at them as it was, and frightening noises seemed to come from

297

everywhere. Fiona could hear the faint shouting of the soldiers, but she doubted they would be able to find them now. Steadily, Ian moved farther and farther away from the castle.

"Ian?" Fiona whispered, finally daring to speak. "Are you feeling all right?"

"I'm fine, lass. But I willna feel safe till we are a bit farther. I'm sorry, but we carina stop yet."

They rode in silence for at least an hour. Thankfully, they had left behind the noise of the soldiers and any pursuit when Ian finally called a halt. He slid from the saddle, helping Lianna and Fiona down. As Fiona landed in his arms, he crushed her to him, pressing his mouth against hers hungrily. After a moment, he pulled away, cupping her face in his bruised and bloody hands.

"I thought I'd never get to do that again," he said softly, and Fiona felt her eyes fill with tears.

"Oh, Ian," she murmured as he kissed her brow, each eye, and the tip of her savaged nose. "I love you."

She wrapped her arms around his waist, pressing her head against his chest and listening to the steady thump of his heart. He was alive—they were alive— by the grace of God. She felt almost giddy as she looked up at him.

"We made it," she said with a smile.

"Aye, we did," he said, and then staggered slightly. Fiona looked at him in alarm, gasping when she realized that her arms were wet and sticky with blood where she had been hugging him.

"I need to get a look at your injury," she exclaimed, seeing that his tunic was stained a dark red. "We've waited too long to treat it."

"I'm fine," he said, kneeling by the creek and lifting

some cool water to his mouth. Fiona knelt beside him.

"Ian, please, let me have a look," she said gently.

" 'Tis naught but a small cut," he said, but from the forced tone of his voice, Fiona knew at once it was much more serious.

"I mean it, Ian. We're not going any farther until I've had a look at it"

He stood, sighing with resignation. She lifted his tunic, horrified to see two jagged gashes—one on his left side near his ribs and the other across his abdomen. His tunic was completely soaked with blood.

Then Fiona did something she had never done in her life. The most fashion-conscious woman in all of England lifted her skirts and, with a hard yank, ripped a long piece of the linen off. She did it again and again until she had several good-sized pieces. Ordering Ian to stand still, she removed his tunic and wound the linen around the wounds, pulling as tightly as she dared. When she was done, she looked up into Ian's face, frightened to see the dazed, sleepy look in his eyes.

Kneeling down to the creek, she cupped some water in her hands and splashed it on his face.

"Let's go," she ordered him briskly. "We've got to reach the others, and soon."

Ian nodded and reached for his tunic, but Fiona unfastened her cloak and gave it to him instead.

"Your shirt is soaking wet," she said. "You'll catch a chill. Drape my cloak around your shoulders instead. Lianna and I will be warm enough."

"Dinna fuss o'er me like a babe," he said irritably, replacing his bloody tunic. "Keep your cloak and I'll be fine."

Fiona swallowed hard but didn't protest. Soon they were all on the horse again, riding on.

Fiona kept up a low chatter to keep Ian awake. After a while, Fiona felt Lianna sag back against her and knew the child had fallen asleep.

"Ian," Fiona said softly, "I didn't have a chance to thank you for coming back for me. You could have got out safely with the others."

He grunted. "Fiona, lass, my life isna worth much. But if I could forfeit it to save ye and the girl, then 'twas worth its weight in gold, wouldn't ye say?"

"Your life is worth something to me," she said, a note of despair creeping into her voice. Ian sounded different now. There was quiet resignation in his tone, and she didn't like it at all.

"You're going to be fine," Fiona whispered fiercely. "We'll soon catch up with the others and you'll get some help."

He surprised her by chuckling. "My sweet Fiona. Did ye know that in Gaelic, *Fiona* means 'fair one'? Who would have known that beneath such a lovely face and body lay a heart as courageous and fierce as a warrior's? I dinna know what I did in my life to deserve someone like ye."

"You did it by being a decent, kind, courageous man, you hardheaded idiot," she snapped. "Can't you see I'm completely, totally, and absolutely over the bloody moon for you? When we get out of this, you are going to marry me and spend the rest of your life with me. I won't take no for an answer."

He laughed outright now, the sound of it deep and baritone. "Are ye asking me to wed ye, lass?"

"No, I think I'm ordering you."

He laughed again. "Do ye have a decent dowry to offer me?"

"A what?"

"What do I get in return for wedding ye?"

She pursed her lips, relieved to hear the teasing note in his voice. "You'll get nights of warm passion, lazy days snuggling in front of the fireplace, and maybe a baby or two to bounce on your knee."

That so surprised him that he pulled the horse to a stop, turning in the saddle to look at her. "Ye want to have wee bairns wi' me?"

She smiled shyly, feeling both elated and nervous by her sudden confession. "And why not?" she said, raising her chin. "Shouldn't Lianna have a little brother or sister to grow up with?"

He reached out and cupped her face. "Fiona, I love ye more than life itself. Ye are a God-sent miracle given to save my miserable life. If ye would be willing to have a man like me wi' nothing more to offer than my hands and my heart, then I would ask ye to be my wife."

She smiled. "I believe I asked first."

His face softened. "Then so be it."

They rode in contented silence until Ian finally spoke again.

"Fiona, I just want ye to know that if something were to happen to me now, I would die a happy man."

Fiona felt a finger of alarm skitter up her spine. "You are not going to die, Ian."

"Mayhap no'. But just in case, I want ye to know that all ye have to do is keep following the creek. 'twill lead ye to the others. Dinna worry; they will find ye."

"Ian, you are going to be fine," she insisted. "In just

a few hours we should be at the rendezvous point, right?"

"Aye."

"Then let's have no more talk of dying. Please?" She knew her voice sounded plaintive and desperate and she hated herself for it. The last thing she wanted to do was to cause him more concern. But her fear for his welfare was growing deeper by the minute. It had been dark, and she hadn't been able to see the depth or severity of his injuries. He had, in all likelihood, lost a lot of blood. What if his wounds were indeed life-threatening?

Swallowing her fears, Fiona, as before, kept up a stream of light chatter to keep Ian awake and alert as they rode. After another hour or so, Ian suddenly slumped forward in the saddle. He would have slipped off the horse completely if Fiona had not managed to grab his arm.

"Ian!" she screamed.

Lianna bolted awake, and Fiona yelled at her to grab onto Ian. She might not have understood Fiona's words, but she quickly assessed what had happened and wrapped her small arms around his waist, holding him steady.

"Oh, God," Fiona said, her breathing coming so fast, she thought she might hyperventilate. "What do I do now?"

She slid her hand down Ian's arm, bringing her fingers to rest on his wrist. She breathed a sigh of relief when she felt his pulse—faint but at least there.

"Thank God, he's still alive," she said aloud, trying frantically to organize her thoughts. "All right, now what do I bloody well do?"

For a moment she lost herself to despair. Here she

was—a woman who couldn't even paint her own nails—suddenly in charge of two lives. And not just any two lives, but the people who meant the most to her in the world.

Her eyes narrowed in determination. She could do this. She *had* to do this.

Ever so carefully, she slipped off the horse. She straightened Ian so he was slumped directly over the horse's mane. Ripping another strip of material from her skirts, she tied his hands together around the horse's neck. With motions and gestures, she instructed Lianna to balance his body the best she could in the saddle. The girl nodded solemnly, and Fiona could feel the girl's trust and faith seep out to her, giving her strength.

Leading the horse by the reins, Fiona began to maneuver her way alongside the creek. The ground was rocky, wet, and rough, and she slipped several times. But she was not confident enough on a horse to ride it while guiding it along such treacherous terrain. This was the only way it could be done.

She walked for what seemed like hours, her legs and feet screaming in pain, her arm feeling like it had been yanked from its socket. She stopped only a few times to lift some cool water to Ian's lips and face and let the horse drink. The sun had started to rise in the sky, offering them the luxury of at least some light by which to tread the unfamiliar and difficult trail. But the light also revealed the ashen face of her beloved slumped over the horse.

Lianna had fared little better; her gaunt face was streaked with dirt and tears, but she determinedly hung on to Ian as if it were her life's mission. Fiona felt so proud of her but dared not engage in even a

Julie Moffett

moment of tenderness for fear her strength would simply dissolve into a sea of hopelessness.

Instead she plodded ahead, keeping her thoughts focused. She had to make it to the rendezvous point. She repeated this over and over again, until she was oblivious to all else. So intent was she on getting them there safely, she didn't even notice the small form that suddenly slipped out from behind a tree with a sword drawn.

"Halt!" the voice said, and Fiona snapped out of her reverie, yelping in surprise.

"Shaun!" she shrieked when she saw the dwarf. He seemed surprised to see her, and she realized she probably looked unrecognizable after the beatings she'd received from the Bradford brothers and the night they had just been through.

Shaun resheathed his sword just as Fiona threw her arms around him, sobbing.

"Please, Shaun, you have to help us," she cried. "Ian has been wounded. He's been unconscious for hours, and he's lost a lot of blood. Where are the others?"

Shaun quickly disentangled himself from her embrace to check on Ian. He raised an eyebrow in surprise when he saw Lianna on the saddle, holding on to Ian for dear life, but said nothing.

"He's still alive," the dwarf said, taking the reins and leading the horse to the left. "Follow me," he said briskly, and Fiona gladly relinquished control.

"Oh, God," she said, her relief to see him so great, it was almost crushing. "I'm so glad you're here, Shaun. I don't know what I would have done if we hadn't found you."

Shaun looked over his shoulder, and Fiona saw a glimmer of pride in his eyes. Pride for her, pride for

304

Ian, pride for the little girl with deformed hands who had somehow defied the English. He said nothing, but he didn't have to. His eyes said it all. It was the most heartfelt compliment Fiona had ever received.

"We're up ahead just a bit," he said quietly. "We knew ye'd make it, lass. We've been waiting for ye."

Chapter Twenty-two

Fiona dipped a cloth in a bowl of cool water, squeezed it, and gently wiped Ian's hot brow. He mumbled something and moved his head but did not awaken. He lay on a cloak beneath a shaded oak tree, fresh binding around his abdomen and a clean tunic warming his body.

Fiona had not left his side since they arrived at the small campsite and had helped Father Michael clean the wounds. As they worked on him in the bright morning sun, she realized with a sinking heart just how grave Ian's injuries were. That he had managed to bring them as far as he had was truly amazing.

"A man of rare strength and courage," she murmured softly, letting her fingers curl around Ian's ring, which still hung around her neck. "My man."

"Fiona?"

She shaded her eyes from the sun and looked up

into the most brilliant pair of emerald eyes she had ever seen.

"You must be Miles O'Bruaidar," she said, coming to her feet. "I'm glad we've finally had the opportunity to meet, although I wish it could have been under different circumstances."

"Aye, as do I," he answered. " 'Tis an honor for me to finally meet ye. Faith speaks o' ye often and wi' great fondness. I want to thank ye."

Fiona nodded, assessing him frankly. Despite having been imprisoned for at least two weeks and certainly subjected to torture at the demented hands of Nicholas Bradford, he stood proud, tall, and strong. His dark hair hung wild about his broad shoulders and a heavy beard covered his ravaged face. Yet he emanated a kind of inner strength that both soothed and inspired confidence. No wonder men followed him willingly into battle, and women… well, she could easily see how Faith fell for him.

He knelt beside Ian. "Don't die on me, old friend," he said softly. "We have a lot to discuss. The first o' which is how ye allowed my wife and her cousin to talk ye into this harebrained scheme o' yours to rescue me.

He stood and took Fiona's hand. It was a big hand, callused and rough. "The women in your family must be made from the stock o' queens," he said. "Beautiful, brave, and incredibly stubborn."

Fiona managed a smile. "More like upper gentry, really."

Miles looked down at Ian and then back at her red-rimmed eyes. "Ye care for Ian, do ye no'?"

"I love him," she said simply, surprising herself by her open declaration to a man she'd just met.

307

He didn't seem surprised by her reply. Compassion and understanding flashed in his eyes. "Aye, then Ian has done well to have found ye. Mayhap 'twas destiny at work after all."

He gently squeezed her hand and walked across the camp to talk with Shaun. Faith came over and pressed a flask and a piece of bread into her hands.

"Eat," she said softly. "You will need your strength."

Fiona took a bite of the bread, but it tasted like sawdust in her mouth. Slowly she sank to the ground beside Ian, and Faith joined her.

Rubbing her weary eyes, Fiona looked about the small campsite. She counted ten people—Faith, Miles, Father Michael, Shaun, Lianna, Ian, herself, and three young Irishmen—all freed from the dungeon at Cavan. Faith had confirmed earlier that Furlong and the rest of the Irish prisoners were traveling by foot and would wait for rescue at a safe location. Lianna, bless her heart, now slept uneasily on a cloak nearby, her small deformed hands curled into tight fists.

Faith arranged her skirts over her legs, plucking at a thread anxiously. "I know this is a most difficult time, but do you have the strength to tell us what happened at the castle, pet?"

Fiona nodded, and Faith motioned for Miles to come and join them. He sat down beside Faith, wrapping an arm possessively around her shoulders. Faith let her hand rest on his muscular thigh. Fiona had noticed their need to continually touch, as if reassuring each other that they were alive and well. Fiona understood the sentiment all too painfully now. As she began to tell them what had happened at O'Reilly Castle, she linked fingers with Ian.

Miles and Faith listened intently to her story. Miles swore under his breath when she told him how Ian had insisted that she and Lianna run to safety while he single-handedly fought Nicholas Bradford and another soldier. When she finished, Miles leapt to his feet and began pacing back and forth, his brow creased in thought.

"So, Bradford is dead, is he?" Miles finally spat out. "I wish the kill had been mine, but good riddance to that pestilence."

"Both Bradford brothers are dead, thank God," Fiona added with emphasis.

"God's wounds, I should have gone back in wi' Ian," Miles suddenly burst out. "I could have insisted. The two o' us would have taken on Bradford and his aide easily."

Fiona set the bread and flask aside and reached for the cloth on Ian's head. "Ian was right not to let you. We are the insignificant players in this game. A loss of one or more of us is acceptable. The loss of the Irish Lion is not. Miles, there are a lot of people in Ireland depending on you."

He stopped and looked directly at her. "I would no' have agreed to risk one life—neither yours nor Faith's nor anyone's—to save mine."

"I know, Miles," Fiona said quietly, "and so does Ian. Your compassion is what makes you a good leader."

"I did this," Faith said, clasping her hands together in her lap. "I put everyone at risk. What have I done?"

"Exactly what I would have done for the man I loved," Fiona replied firmly. "It was my decision to come along, as it was everyone's. We are not children, Faith. We knew the risks. Personally, I don't regret a minute of it. If I hadn't gone, I never would have had the opportunity to know Ian, never realized how wonderful love can be, and"—she paused for a moment, her voice breaking—"never have known my soul mate."

Fiona took a deep breath and plunged on. "Something happened to me on our journey to Cavan and back, Faith. Something magical, terrifying, and profound. Ian helped me understand not only who I am, but why I am. It has changed me for the better, and I think I'm actually beginning to like me for me."

"If only things would have worked out differently," Faith lamented softly.

"We're in this together, pet, for better or worse. We're family, and families stick together. God knows, for far too long all we had in this world was each other. Now look at us—blessed with men we love, people willing to risk their lives for us, and"—she looked over at Lianna's sleeping form—"a child who needs us. We've been blessed in more ways than I can count."

"Faith, Fiona," Miles interrupted gently. "I know ye both are exhausted, but we are going to have to ride now. The English are likely already on their way to Castle Dun na Moor to find us. We need to get there first, collect supplies, and then move on to my uncle's in Omagh, where we will be safe. Do ye think ye can ride more today, lass?"

"I can, but what about Ian?" she asked worriedly.

"He'll have to ride, too. We'll double him up wi' Father Michael. 'Tis dangerous, but 'tis far more risky to stay. We dare no' tarry here any longer."

Fiona nodded and then bent down to kiss Ian's cold lips. Miles and the other men carefully lifted him up onto a horse, and Father Michael climbed on behind him, holding him in place. Fiona was instructed to ride with one of the young men, while Lianna went with Shaun, and Faith with Miles.

Unlike on their journey to Cavan, Miles dared to traverse the main path for long periods of time, occasionally sending Shaun on ahead to scout for English patrols. With Ian near death and the English patrols hot on their heels, they had neither the luxury of time nor stealth. The good news was that this would shave a half-day or more from their journey. The bad news was that riding on the road made them vulnerable to attack. Yet it seemed a risk Miles was willing to take.

The passing countryside soon became a green blur to Fiona. She often sought the comfort of Ian's ring around her neck and kept her eyes focused on his back, as if by sheer will she could keep him alive. The sun rose high in the sky and then set. Darkness fell, bringing a crisp chill to the air and casting eerie moonlight shadows about them. At some point Fiona dozed off, awakening with a start when she realized she had slumped forward against the young man with whom she shared a mount.

"Sorry," she mumbled, straightening her shoulders, having no idea how long she had been asleep but realizing night had already fallen.

"Do you know how Ian fares?" she asked worriedly.

He shook his head. "Nay, but we are no' too much farther from home."

Fiona thought he sounded young—fifteen or sixteen, perhaps. "What's your name?" she asked curiously.

"Paddy Doogan," he answered shyly. "I know who

311

ye are, milady, and what ye risked for all o' us. Ye are surely a gift from the saints."

She felt both surprised and amused to hear the note of awe in his voice. It somewhat shamed her that he considered her some kind of hero when at his tender age, he had probably lived through more than she had in an entire lifetime.

"Ian did the hard part," she replied modestly.

"Oh, aye, but ye've certainly had a difficult time o' it, too, milady," he gushed. "I don't know how to thank ye and Ian and the others for saving my life. I hope Ian will live. I've never met a more stalwart man, except mayhap for Miles. The two o' them have been friends since childhood."

Fiona realized with a start that Miles, too, must be worried sick about Ian. Guilt, anger, helplessness—he surely felt the same emotions. For a moment she experienced a tug of kinship with him—with all of them. Somehow, along the way, she had indeed become part of this family.

She was mulling this over when the horse suddenly picked up its pace, as if sensing something. Moments later they broke through the trees and into a clearing.

There, in the distance, across the moonswept moor, sat the castle. It loomed large atop the small hill, its high stone walls rising steeply. Two formidable towers jutted to the sky.

"Castle Dun na Moor," she breathed in relief.

She saw Miles spur his horse and gallop on ahead. Faith held on tightly to his waist, her hair fluttering out like a banner behind her.

The horses seemed to know respite was just moments away, for they picked up speed as everyone galloped eagerly toward the castle gate. By the time

Fiona and Paddy arrived, a guard had already begun to open it.

In minutes everyone was in the courtyard. Fiona quickly dismounted, ignoring her screaming muscles and rushing over to Ian's side. Lianna quickly joined her, linking fingers and squeezing.

"How is he?" she asked Father Michael worriedly.

"Bless the Lord, he is yet alive," the priest answered wearily, handing Ian down to Miles and another of the men.

Fiona saw Molly, the castle matron, dart out into the courtyard, shrieking with happiness when she saw Miles and then gasping in horror when she saw Ian.

"Bring him up to the north chamber at once," Fiona heard the woman order briskly. As Miles and the other man carried Ian into the castle, Molly turned and quickly instructed a young serving girl to prepare hot water, bandages, and an herbal mixture. Fiona felt relieved that Ian was at last in such capable hands.

With amazing efficiency, a chamber was prepared for Ian. He was laid out on a bed with fresh linens in front of a blazing fire. With Faith's and Fiona's help, Molly carefully unwound the makeshift bandages. Lianna sat huddled by the fire, her legs pulled up to her chest, her chin resting on her knees.

When Ian's wounds were fully exposed, Molly drew in her breath sharply before exchanging a sorrowful, stricken glance with Faith. Then she dipped a cloth into warm water and began carefully wiping his injuries.

"Och, Ian, lad," Molly murmured. "What have the English done to ye?"

Fiona paled considerably when she got a close look at his injuries. Both the wound to his abdomen and the injury to his side had started to fester badly. The skin near the injuries were an angry red, and swollen with pus and blood.

Gasping, Fiona stood, stumbling to the doorway and fighting back tears.

Faith scurried to her side. "Molly is the best nurse around," Faith assured her. "If anyone can save him, it's Molly. She'll take care of him, I promise."

Fiona shook her head, tears beginning to spill onto her cheeks. Lianna sidled up to her, wrapping her arms around Fiona's waist, whimpering softly.

"He's not going to make it," Fiona said softly, holding on to the doorjamb for support. "I don't have to be a doctor to see it. Faith, his wounds are badly infected. His fever is raging. He'll never survive without antibiotics."

"You don't know that."

"I do know it. And so do you. I'm not blind. I can see the truth in your eyes and in Molly's. I saw glimmers of it earlier in both Miles's and Father Michael's expressions. We rushed back here to Castle Dun na Moor not to save Ian, but to give him the dignity to die in comfort. Tell me that isn't the truth."

"Fiona—" Faith started, but she stopped when Fiona held up a hand.

"Just the truth," she whispered, tears sliding down her face. Lianna sobbed mournfully, clutching at Fiona's skirts like a toddler. "Please, don't lie to me, Faith. I couldn't bear it. Just tell me the truth."

Faith stood motionless, her blue eyes filling with tears. "I'm sorry, pet," she finally whispered, her voice breaking. "So very sorry."

Fiona closed her eyes, the force of her own grief and despair slamming into her like a fist to the stomach.

"Oh, God," Faith whispered brokenly. "Ian is my friend, too. He gave his life for me, for Miles."

Fiona couldn't answer, her voice locked in her throat. She felt light-headed and dizzy, a part of her feeling as if she wasn't even present in her own body.

"Fiona? Faith?"

Fiona blinked through the tears and saw Miles, Shaun, and Father Michael standing in the corridor, gazing at them with stricken looks.

"Is Ian... gone?" Miles asked, his voice ragged with sorrow.

"Not yet," Fiona said, her voice sounding oddly detached, as if it belonged to someone else. "But his wounds are mortal and there is nothing I can do to save him."

Miles took a step forward, putting an arm around Faith's shoulder. She wept openly now, her face in her hands.

"Fiona, I don't know what to say," he said, sorrow ravaging his eyes. "Ian has been my closest friend for years. This happened to him because o' me."

Fiona couldn't bear to look at him for long as the agonizing guilt, grief, and torment in his eyes was a painful reflection of her own soul's anguish.

"No, he came back for me," she whispered. "He'll die because of me."

"Nay!" Shaun said suddenly, and everyone turned to look at the dwarf in shock.

"What did you say?" Fiona said, blinking.

Shaun took a deep breath and stepped forward. "I said, nay, we are no' going to let him die," he repeated. "There just might be another way to save him."

Shaun exchanged a long glance with Father Michael,

who stared back at him with questioning eyes. Suddenly, understanding seemed to dawn, and the priest flushed guiltily and looked down at his boots.

"What other way?" Fiona said, a tiny seed of hope beginning to bloom. "Just how do you propose we save him?"

She heard Faith draw a sharp breath, and Miles looked down at her before his mouth gaped open in disbelief.

"Impossible," he murmured.

"What's impossible?" Fiona nearly shouted. "What in God's name is going on here?"

Shaun stepped forward. "Ye are going to be the one to save him, lass," he said firmly. "Because ye are going to take him back wi' ye to your own time."

Everyone started talking at once, so Fiona shrieked like a banshee gone wild until the noise ceased and all eyes looked at her as if she had gone utterly mad. Perhaps she had.

When she finally had everyone's full attention, she turned to Faith. "I thought you said you had tried to go back to our time, but it didn't work."

"It didn't!" Faith exclaimed. "There were stones missing in the configuration that apparently act as some sort of catalyst for opening the portal." She blinked at Shaun and Father Michael in stunned amazement. "How did you know about the secret of the stones?"

"I thought you said no one else except Miles knew," Fiona interrupted.

Faith looked over at Miles accusingly. "So did I."

Miles shook his head in bewilderment. "Don't

blame me, lass. I assure ye, I told no one. I could hardly believe it myself."

Father Michael cleared his voice. "The blame lies wi' no one except myself and Shaun. 'Tis a long and complicated tale. Let it suffice to say that Shaun...ah... overheard Faith and Miles talking about the future once, and how she...um...came from there."

Miles shot an angry glance at Shaun, who flushed and looked away.

"And you simply accepted this tale of traveling between times without explanation?" Fiona asked the priest skeptically.

"We saw it for what it was," Father Michael replied simply. "A gift from God."

Shaun stepped forward. "Mayhap 'twould be better if I explained further. After I overheard the conversation, I had a dream that our Faith was sent through the stones from the future to save Miles. 'Twas the clearest vision I'd ever had, and when 'twas finished, I knew I had seen the truth."

"Aye, and ye know how we all have great faith in Shaun's predictions," Father Michael added hastily.

Miles nodded, crossing his thick arms across his chest, a scowl forming on his lips. "Especially those that are borne by eavesdropping on private conversations."

Shaun coughed and continued. "Aye, well, when I discovered that Faith intended to leave us through the stones, the Father and I decided we couldn't let it happen. We knew we needed her here so that she could help save Miles. And that she did. We didn't mean any harm, and we certainly did no' expect another like her to come through."

Faith gasped in shock. "You and Father Michael

Julie Moffett

took the stones from the configurations to prevent me from returning to my own time?"

Father Michael nodded guiltily. "I'm sorry, Faith. We hid them in the meadow no' far from the circles. It seemed the right course o' action at the time."

"Wait just a bloody minute," Fiona interrupted. "Are you saying that if we put the stones back, I might be able to return home after all?"

Faith held up a hand. "Don't get your hopes up. We don't have any idea whether it will work even if we return the stones to their proper location. And even if it does, we don't know *where* or *when* you might go. For all we know, you could return another three hundred and fifty years further into the past."

"Perhaps, but what about the possibility that the time-travel mechanism is not random, but orderly?" Fiona said excitedly. "I mean, I came back to the same century as you, and the exact same amount of time had passed both here and there. That's not random. Don't you see? We might be able to return to our own time with only a few days having passed since I left."

"But we have no evidence to predict it will be one way or the other," Faith replied evenly. "We've never tried it before. It is completely unknown."

"We have to risk it," Fiona said firmly.

"The experience might kill Ian instantly," Faith warned. "It might kill you both."

Fiona nodded. "Yes, it might. But Ian will die if we do nothing. And if I don't do everything in my power to save him, I will not be able to live with myself. Besides, we can't stay here at the castle much longer. The English are only hours away. Everyone will need to be out by daybreak. Ian can't travel any more, and I'm not leaving him here alone."

318

Faith glanced down at Lianna, who blinked in bewilderment at the heated conversation taking place around her.

"What about Lianna?" Faith asked quietly.

Fiona pressed the girl tighter against her. "She's mine and Ian's. We love her dearly. But I will not risk her life, too. Will you and Miles take care of her for us? She has become our stalwart little girl, our most precious treasure."

Faith looked up questioningly at Miles, who nodded. "We would be honored," she replied softly.

Fiona exhaled a deep breath. "That means a lot to me. Thank you."

"Aye, 'tis settled then," Miles said. "Shaun, Father Michael, dig up the stones and bring them to the circle at once. It's nearing midnight, and that seems to be the most favorable time for this otherworldly portal to open."

Shaun and the priest scurried down the corridor to do his bidding.

Miles leaned down and kissed Faith on the brow. "Have Molly get Ian dressed warmly. I'll see to it that we have torches and cloaks." He strode off down the hall, with Fiona and Faith watching him.

"He's a remarkable man," Fiona said. "You found a diamond among stones."

"As did you," Faith replied softly. "But before we head out to the stone configurations, I need to know something. If you do make it back to our time, and if Ian gets well, will you try to come back here to us?"

Fiona sighed. "I don't know, pet. But my first instinct is to say yes. I mean, Ian doesn't even know I'm from the future yet, and I don't have the slightest idea how this unexpected revelation will go over. If we do

319

survive this, he's going to be in serious shock. I'm not certain a man like Ian could adjust to living in our century."

"I wouldn't underestimate him. Ian is quite self-sufficient and often full of surprises."

Fiona managed a smile. "Yes, that's true."

They were silent for a moment before Faith spoke up again. "Fiona, do you think Father Michael was right when he said my arrival in this century was a gift from God?"

Fiona looked at her cousin closely. Long, pale blond hair tumbled about her shoulders, and her lovely blue eyes shimmered in the dim light. Love had indeed made her beautiful.

"I don't know," Fiona replied softly. "Just as I don't know why I'm here. Maybe it *is* God giving us a second chance. But He certainly isn't making it easy for us. It seems we have to take charge of our own destinies. This is why I have to do this, Faith. I must try and go back home in order to save Ian."

"I know."

Fiona reached out and touched Faith's cheek. "You won't ever come back to our time, will you?"

"No," Faith said softly. "I made peace with my decision to stay here a long time ago. Miles's place is here in Ireland, among the people who need him. My place is at his side. I'll never leave him."

"I understand." Faith looked down at Lianna. "How do you think she'll adjust to being left behind?"

Fiona reached out to stroke Lianna's hair gently. "I don't know. You'll have to step in for me. Do the proper mum thing."

"You're her mum now."

Fiona exhaled a deep breath. "I know. It will be

hard on both of us. But she'll be in the best hands with you and Miles. She's a resilient girl. With a lot of love and nurturing, I'm certain she'll blossom into a remarkable woman."

Faith reached out and took Lianna's hand. For a moment the three of them stood there in silence, linked by flesh and heart, staring at each other.

"Lianna will always be your daughter," Faith finally said. "But I give you my word that I'll do my best to fill your shoes."

Chapter Twenty-three

Ian walked through a tunnel of searing hot flames, searching for Fiona. He could see the slender silhouette of her body moving just ahead and the quick turn of her head as she periodically checked to see if he followed. Yet no matter how quickly he ran to catch up with her, she remained just out of his reach. He realized she would continue to elude him unless he breached the tunnel wall and leapt through the flames to her. Taking a deep breath, he plunged into the inferno, the fire roaring in his ears, flames licking and twisting around his body like a sensuous, devouring snake.

"Fiona," he screamed, stretching out a hand toward the dark silhouette that had now stilled. He saw her reach out to him, and for a brief moment they clasped hands tightly. Then Ian watched in horror as his hand

322

erupted in flames and his body began to melt into nothingness....

"Ian?"

Ian jolted awake, his eyes flying open. "Fiona?" he whispered, seeing her face blur and then come into focus. "Fiona, is that ye, lass?"

"Hush," she whispered softly, and he realized she was stroking his hair back from his face. "You were having a nightmare. Yes, Ian, love, it's me."

He shuddered. "I dreamt that I was burning. I tried to reach ye, but I couldn't."

"You have a fever and that's why you feel hot. But I'm here and you are all right."

"Where are we?"

"Castle Dun na Moor."

"The others found ye safely?"

"Yes, love. I did what you said and followed the creek. Shaun found us just hours later."

"Och, I knew ye could do it." Relief filled him, and he closed his eyes. "My brave Fiona."

She held his hand and squeezed it comfortingly. He tried to squeeze back but was too weary to manage more than a twitch.

"Ian, drink some water."

He could barely lift his head, but she helped him, putting the bowl to his lips. He sucked at the water greedily, the moisture sweet, cool, and soothing. He tried to drink more but began coughing, and she took the bowl away.

He reached for her hand again, needing to touch her and not ever wanting her to leave him. Her long, cool fingers entwined with his, anchoring him to her.

"Kiss me," he whispered hoarsely.

"What?"

"Kiss me," he repeated. "I'm checking to see if I'm dead and ye are my angel."

He heard her laugh softly, glad that he had brought a smile to her face. "You aren't dead, Ian Maclaren," she murmured. Then he felt the softness of her mouth press against his, while strands of her short, dark hair tickled his cheeks.

"Och," he sighed. "Well, then, at least I can die a happy man."

She laid her cool hand on his cheek, stroking away the heat. "Oh, Ian," she said, and he heard the sadness back in her voice. "I'm not going to let you die."

He tried to focus on her face, but it was only a dark blur. "Ye may be the most stubborn lass I've ever met, but even ye canno' challenge Fate."

"Yes, I can," she replied, her voice filled with sadness and regret.

His heart broke for her. "Fiona, lass, dinna be sad."

"Ian, there are so many things about me I never told you. In all truth, I was too afraid to tell you earlier because I feared I might lose you."

He focused on her hand and somehow managed to reach out and grab it. He heard her gasp in surprise as he squeezed.

"Mo *gradhach,* I dinna care about your past and I never did. I knew ye were destined to be mine the moment ye ordered me to kiss ye. Now, if 'tis Fate's will for me to die—than die I shall. But Fate is no' without pity. She sent me an angel so that I'd no' go out o' this world alone—without ever knowing love."

Fiona pressed his hand to her cheek, and Ian could feel the wetness. She had been crying.

"You're not going to die," she answered. "Not if I

have any say in the matter. I know this is going to sound bizarre, but I'm not from this time. Faith and I....we are from the future—more than three hundred years in the future. Somewhere among the stone circles that reside on the O'Bruaidar property is a time portal that catapulted both Faith and me back in time. That's how I knew Miles was in Cavan—I read about the history of the O'Bruaidar family in a book.

He tried to grasp the strange meaning of her words, but the effort was too great. "Fiona," he whispered. "We Scots are great believers in Fate. For whatever reason, ye came to me. Ye are mine for always."

"Yes, for always," he heard her say, "no matter what. But this battle isn't over yet. Ian, listen to me. I'm going to try to take you back to my time. There are medicines, and doctors there who might be able to save you. You've got to hold on just a little bit longer. Please, do it for me."

She spoke between sobs now, but her words ran together so that he no longer understood them. He felt so very tired. "Sweet Fiona," he whispered, his hand sliding from hers.

"Just a little while longer, Ian Maclaren," he heard her whisper fiercely. "You've got to reach down within and find the strength to hold on. Do it, Ian, please. Do it for me."

He heard her say something else, but she sounded so far away now, her voice echoing in his mind as if off the walls of a dark tunnel.

"*Mo gradhach,*" he breathed before the darkness reached up and pulled him into its depths.

They rode in silence through the forest, a light drizzle falling upon them. Faith led the way, holding a covered lantern that lit the path for the others. Miles, holding Ian, came next, and Fiona and Lianna followed them. Fiona wore her jeans, blouse, jacket, and boots. Her car keys were in her pocket and her watch was around her wrist. She was dressed exactly the same way as she had been when she arrived in this time, except somehow she felt different—like an imposter in her own clothes. Had she changed that much in such a short time?

Each thump of the horses' hooves trod a painful rhythm on Fiona's heart. This was truly a leap of faith. She had no idea whether this trip through the stone circles would work and, if it did, whether she and Ian would even survive the journey. She risked a lot to try to return to her own time, and yet she risked even more by staying.

She heard the faint gurgle of a creek, and Miles abruptly pulled back on the reins, halting his horse, as they entered a small clearing. Father Michael and Shaun were digging with shovels next to a small covered lantern. They paused when they saw the small group approach.

"The Beaghmore Stone Circles," Fiona breathed in wonder.

The configurations were the same as in her time, but there was no carpark and no small tourist center nearby. Yet the stones glowed eerily as Miles held the lantern aloft, capturing the strange circles in the dim light.

Fiona dismounted and walked past the six stone circles that were situated in pairs. She headed for the seventh circle, which sat apart from the others, and stood in front of it. There were several fresh piles of dirt around some of the markers.

"This is the 'Dragon's Teeth' configuration," she said aloud. "This is where I came through."

Faith walked up, holding Lianna by the hand. "Yes," she agreed softly, "this is where I came through as well. And now the stones are all here."

Fiona took a deep breath. She walked over to where Shaun and Father Michael stood quietly, still leaning on the shovels.

"I appreciate you coming forward with your knowledge of the stones," she said. "You didn't have to, but in the end you did. I am so grateful for all you've done. All I can say is thank you for being my friends..." She let the sentence trail off and then shook her head, "No, for letting me be a part of your family—an experience that means more than I can adequately say. You accepted me—flaws and all—into your fold. It was a privilege and an honor to be counted among you."

She put her arms around Father Michael and hugged him hard. "Thank you, Father," she whispered in his ear. "You brought back my faith in God and myself. I'll never forget you."

"We'll miss ye, lass. Go with God," she heard the priest whisper.

She turned next to Shaun. "I need to ask a favor of you. Would you please weave one of your fantastic tales about a fey woman named Fiona Chancellor who traveled through time and back again? The legend should go that sometime in the future she will approach a Gogarty and ask for a boon. If this favor is granted, no matter how strange it is, fortune will smile upon the Gogarty family forever. Can you make certain this tale passes down among future generations of Gogartys?"

Shaun looked bewildered but nodded. "Aye, lass, if ye wish it, it shall be so."

"Good," she said, giving him a hug. "Thank you for being my champion."

Fiona straightened, taking a deep breath. Now came the hardest part of all.

Lianna stood trembling next to Faith, clutching her hand fearfully. Back at the castle, Miles had briefly explained to the girl that Fiona and Ian had to leave, but that he and Faith would now take care of her. Lianna had shaken her head in disbelief but had said nothing. Now, as she looked at Fiona, her eyes were far too understanding and sad.

Fiona motioned to Father Michael, who came over and knelt by the girl, translating Fiona's words softly.

"Sweet Lianna," Fiona said gently. "You are my brave, precious little girl. You taught me about what it means to be both a mum and a decent human being. Your childhood was certainly more miserable than mine, yet you rose above it with courage and strength that put me to shame. You are beautiful, both inside and out. Faith and Miles will take care of you, and you will be safe with them. You are part of a family now, a truly wonderful family that will cherish and love you. It is the greatest gift I can give you, sweetheart: a family where you belong. Ian and I will hold you in our hearts until we die, and you'll always be a part of us. Good-bye, my love, but not farewell. Someday, God willing, we'll all be together again. Until then, be a good girl for Faith and Miles. Make us proud."

She threw her arms around Lianna and hugged hard, the tears she had thought long ago exhausted now streaming down her face. "Remember I love you," she whispered in Lianna's ear. "I'll never forget you."

Fiona gathered all her strength and stood, letting go of the girl. Lianna turned and hid her tearstained face in Faith's skirts, sobs wracking her body.

Tears slid from Faith's eyes as she opened her arms for a hug. Fiona embraced her cousin, holding tight.

"Oh, God, Fiona," Faith whispered brokenly. "I just get you back only to lose you again. There was so little time to talk about everything. I never got to thank you for all you have done for me, for all you have meant to me my entire life. You are my sister, my flesh and blood, the one person who knew me as I once was and as I am now. How can I possibly say good-bye?"

"It's never good-bye, Faith," Fiona replied through her tears. "It's only farewell. We'll meet again; I'm certain of it. Perhaps, if all goes well, we'll meet again right here at Castle Dun na Moor in this time, with only a short time gone past. Or if that is not to be, I sincerely believe we will surely meet again in a place where time doesn't matter and where the bonds of friendship and family last for an eternity. I love you, Faith."

Fiona pulled away and held up her hand, palm out. Fiona pressed her palm against Faith's in the simple but solemn childhood gesture they had performed for years. Together they spoke:

> "My sister for always,
> Naught can us part.
> My sister forever,
> One bond to one heart."

"Keep close your double-edged dagger," Fiona said to her cousin, smiling through her tears. "It brought us together once; it may do so again someday."

Faith reached beneath the folds of her skirt and pulled out the dagger. The light from the torch flickered off the double-edged blade, casting the small weapon in a ghostly light.

"It will stay by my side always," Faith promised softly. Dashing the wetness from her cheeks with the back of her hand, Fiona turned to Miles, who still sat astride the horse, holding Ian. The drizzle had abated and a full moon momentarily slid out from behind the clouds, shining brightly above them.

"Let's do it," Fiona said determinedly, glancing at her watch. "It's almost midnight."

Miles nodded, and Father Michael and Shaun rushed to help lower Ian off the horse. The three men carried Ian to the edge of the Dragon's Teeth configuration and paused uncertainly.

"I'll take it from here," Fiona said, stepping up and grabbing Ian beneath his armpits. She dragged him the rest of the way into the circle and sat down. Cradling Ian's head in her lap, she held tight to one of his hands. He moaned, and she kissed him gently on the brow.

"Hang on, love," she murmured. "It's almost showtime."

"Farewell, lass," Miles said softly.

"Take care of my cousin," Fiona ordered him with a brave smile. "And my little girl."

"And ye watch o'er Ian."

"I will."

Fiona glanced down at her watch and saw the second hand rapidly ticking toward twelve. "About fifteen seconds," she said, looking up at Faith. "Oh, God, I hope this works."

She drew in a deep breath, mentally preparing herself for what she hoped would happen, when she heard a faint crackling noise. The hairs on her arms and legs stood straight up.

"It's working!" Fiona exclaimed. "Be careful of the stones; they get hot."

Fiona heard the surprised gasps from the group as they warily stepped back.

The Dragon's Teeth stone markers were now glowing an eerie, haunting red, just as she remembered. A loud buzzing noise hummed about her, growing until it sounded as if a thousand bees were in her ears. The ground trembled and shook beneath her and her stomach lurched wildly.

"This is it, love," she said to Ian, squeezing his hand as he began to thrash about. "Hold on."

She looked up one last time, her gaze capturing Lianna's in the strange red light. "I love you," she mouthed as fire seemed to explode around them.

Lianna's lips quivered, and then with a cry, she suddenly wrenched herself from Faith's arms and threw herself into the circle.

"No!" Fiona shrieked as a clap of thunder sounded and a jagged light abruptly blinded her. The ground seemed to drop out from beneath them, and for a moment Fiona felt her body hanging suspended in space. Before she could draw a breath she began to plummet downward, picking up speed in a whirling, dizzying freefall.

"Lianna," she screamed as the darkness rushed up to greet her and she blacked out.

331

Chapter Twenty-four

Fiona awoke slowly, feeling something wet dripping on her face. Disoriented and dazed, she forced her eyelids open and then gasped in pain at the effort. Ignoring the throbbing ache, she blinked, but water blurred her vision. After a moment she determined that she lay on her back as rain fell softly on her face.

"Ian?" she gasped, bolting upright, memories flooding back in a horrid, painful rush. "Lianna?"

Her head exploded in agony at the sudden motion, and she squeezed her eyes shut in blinding distress. Moaning, she pressed her fingers to her temples, willing the pounding noise to stop. Finally the intense pressure eased, and she cautiously opened her eyes, moving into a sitting position.

It was pitch dark, but she could make out a huddled form lying close by. Her heart thundering, Fiona crawled across the mud on her hands and knees and turned the form over.

"Oh, Lianna," Fiona breathed as she groped for the girl's wrist to see if she could find a pulse. As the blood pumped through the veins beneath her fingers, Fiona let out a sigh of relief.

"Oh, sweetheart," she whispered, reaching up to touch Lianna's face. "What have you done?"

Satisfied Lianna was alive, Fiona left her and groped about in the mud for Ian, still on her hands and knees. The darkness was dense, and she could scarcely see a bloody thing. Even worse, the rain began to pour harder, making her search more difficult. Water ran off her nose and chin as she felt anxiously around the ground. She nearly sobbed in relief when her hands collided with a boot.

"Ian," she cried, her hands following a path up his legs to his torso. She reached his face and then fumbled at his neck, looking for a pulse. The rain made her fingers slick, and she couldn't tell whether he was alive or not. Panic started to grip her around the throat.

"Ian!" she screamed, shaking him, and this time she was rewarded with a deep moan.

"Oh my God," she sobbed, crawling forward and cradling his head in her lap. "Ian, you're alive. But *when* the bloody hell are we?"

She kissed him on the brow and laid his head back on the ground. This time she stood up, holding her hands out in front of her like a blind woman. Her right hand hit against something hard, and she realized it was one of the Dragon's Teeth stone markers.

"Faith?" she shouted into the blackness. "Miles?"

She heard nothing but stillness, and then another faint moan and the soft sound of someone crying. Fiona groped her way back to where she had left Lianna. Thankfully, her eyes were gradually adjusting to the darkness, and she could see that the young girl had curled into a ball and was sobbing softly.

"Hush, baby," Fiona said gently, kneeling down next to her and patting her on the back. "It's me, Fiona. I'm going to get some help. But I need you to be a big girl and wait here with Ian."

She picked up Lianna, carrying her the few steps to where Ian lay. She set Lianna down and placed Ian's cold hand in hers.

"Stay here," she ordered. "Don't go anywhere."

Lianna stopped sobbing and clutched Ian's hand.

"Don't be afraid," Fiona said encouragingly. "I'll be back soon."

Operating on memory alone, Fiona staggered in the direction of what she hoped was the carpark. If they had indeed traveled through time, she only prayed it was to her own time, where her rental auto still waited for her. Whether or not it had been towed or would even start, she didn't dare contemplate at this point.

Thankfully, her sight had become increasingly sharper despite the heavy rain, and she could now see the outline of some of the other stone circles. She was going in the right direction.

"Thank God," she said softly, traversing the slippery ground carefully. As she passed the configurations and reached the edge of the small hill, she looked down the stone stairs that lead directly to a paved carpark.

For a moment she simply stared in stunned amazement. "It worked," Fiona breathed, looking in shock at a single sports car. "It damn well worked."

Uttering a cry of joy, she stumbled down the stairs and rushed across the wet asphalt until she reached the car. A quick glance at the surrounding area revealed a distinct lack of pay phones. Cursing, she fumbled for the keys in her pocket and pulled them out. Her hands were shaking so badly, it took her three tries before she could insert the key into the lock. Once the door was open, she slid inside, resting her head against the steering wheel and saying a small prayer.

"Please God, let it start," she murmured, pushing the key in the ignition and turning it. The engine sputtered once and then roared to life.

"Yes," she shouted, punching a fist in the air and slamming the door shut. She thrust the car into gear and sped out of the parking lot.

"Hold on, my loves," she said under her breath. "I'm coming back with the bloody cavalry."

"Mrs. Chancellor?" a white-coated doctor asked with a deep Irish brogue.

Fiona's eyes snapped open. "Yes?" she said, leaping to her feet in concern. Her face flushed red with mortification that she had fallen asleep in the waiting room while Ian was in surgery and Lianna underwent tests.

"How are they?" she asked. "How is my...ah... husband and little girl?" It seemed odd, calling Ian her husband, but given their unusual circumstances, she didn't see the harm in it right now.

The doctor sighed. "Your husband is in critical condition, but the surgery to repair the damage to his kidneys and spleen went well. Unfortunately, he lost a lot of blood and fluids. His injuries are rather severe and badly infected. We have him on a high dose o' antibiotics, but I'm not certain it will repair all the damage."

Fiona swallowed hard, willing herself to be strong. "I see. And my daughter?"

"She is in stable condition. She became quite distraught upon waking, and I'm afraid we had to both restrain and sedate her. She wouldn't talk but kept saying 'Mama' over and over again."

Fiona felt the tears brim in her eyes. "Can I see her?"

The doctor nodded. "For a few minutes. The constable will be arriving soon to speak with you. I'm sorry that a group o' hooligans with knives robbed ye. 'Tis a shame that no place is safe from violence these days, no' even a sleepy little place like Cookstown."

Fiona rubbed her gritty eyes. How long had it been since she'd had a decent night's sleep?

"Yes, it's been a dreadful experience," she said wearily, "but I assure you, my husband and I still think quite fondly of Ireland."

"I'm glad to hear that. Follow me, please."

Fiona trailed him down a white-walled corridor and into a small room. Lianna lay asleep on a bed, an IV attached to her arm and restraints holding her arms and legs. She looked so small and forlorn. Fiona couldn't even begin to imagine what the poor girl had thought when she awakened and saw all the strange machines and people around her. No wonder she had gone wild.

"My brave little girl," Fiona whispered, stroking Lianna's hair back from her face. "We're going to be all right, you and I." She squeezed her hand and bent down to kiss her brow.

The doctor looked over at her kindly. "If ye don't

mind my saying so, Mrs. Chancellor, I think ye should admit yourself to the hospital for a few hours so we can run some tests and make certain ye are all right as well."

Fiona straightened, smoothing down her hair. "I'm fine really, just a bit tired. Anyway, there is something I have to do first."

She kissed Lianna again and then left the room. "I'll be back in an hour to speak with the constable," she told the doctor. "Please, just keep my husband alive."

Fiona pulled up the rental car in front of the quaint old cottage with blue shutters. She got out of the car and glanced at the small hand-painted wooden sign swinging wildly back and forth on a lamppost.

ANTIQUITIES AND CURIOSITIES, it read.

She stuffed the car keys into her pocket and hurried to the front door. Lifting the heavy brass knocker, she brought it down several times on the weather-beaten wood. When no answer was immediately forthcoming, she put her hand on the doorknob and turned.

The door swung open with a strong gust of wind, and Fiona quickly stepped inside, closing the door behind her.

"Hallo!" she called out, squinting in the dim light.

"So, ye are back," a voice said, and out of the darkness stepped Seamus Gogarty.

He looked the same as when Fiona had last seen him, dressed in a thick wool fisherman's sweater and dark pants. His white hair and matching goatee were neatly combed and his eyes appraised her curiously. For a moment she had the eerie sensation that she looked into the eyes of Shaun, and she felt a bittersweet stab of longing for those she had left behind.

"Mr. Gogarty," she said, stepping forward. "You remember me?"

"Aye, ye are the Englishwoman who came here asking about the legend o' the O'Bruaidar dagger."

"That's right," she said, nodding excitedly. "You *do* remember me. Thank God for that. Do you remember my name?"

He stroked his goatee and looked at her thoughtfully. "Well, actually I do. 'Tis Fiona Chancellor, is it no'?"

"Yes, yes." Her pulse accelerated, her heart thumping nervously.

"Does the name *Fiona Chancellor* mean anything in particular to you?" She gave her name special emphasis and then looked at him carefully, studying every nuance of his expression.

He gazed back at her and then lifted his hands. "Well, of course, 'tis your name, is it no'?"

Her hopes crashed and burned in a single fiery mass. "Oh, hell. It didn't work."

"What didn't work?"

She blew out a deep breath of frustration. "I had hoped my name might mean something special to you. I thought perhaps you might have heard my name in a tale that had been passed down through generations of your family."

Seamus blinked in surprise and then took her gently by the arm, leading her to a small table and chairs.

"Sit down, lass," he said, turning on a small lamp that sat on the table, "and tell me this tale."

Fiona took a deep breath. "Well, it all started when I showed you the O'Bruaidar dagger and told you about my missing cousin," she started, and then stopped when he abruptly held up a hand.

"Nay, lass. 'Twas indeed ye who came to my shop just o'er a week ago. But ye didn't have the dagger wi' ye. Ye simply described it to me, and I found a picture o' it in a book for ye."

Fiona's mouth dropped open in surprise. "What? Y-you mean, I didn't have the dagger?"

"Nay. Ye simply described the dagger in great detail until I knew exactly what ye were talking about. When I showed ye the picture, ye confirmed that this was the dagger ye were seeking."

Fiona realized her mouth still hung open and closed it with a snap. "I... I said I was seeking the dagger?" she repeated dumbly.

"Aye, and I told ye all about the Druid stones at Beaghmore and the legend o' the dagger," he said, leaning forward eagerly. "Did ye visit the spot, lass?"

Fiona nodded, unsure of what to say next. Seamus smiled, leaning back in his chair. "So it has happened and that is why ye have returned."

"What has happened?" Fiona asked, still dazed from the bizarre turn their conversation had taken.

Seamus stood and shuffled across the floor toward the bookshelf. Standing on a stool, he pulled a large volume off the shelf and returned to the table.

He opened the worn leather cover of the book and thumbed through the pages slowly. Fiona watched him with growing curiosity.

"What are you looking for?" she asked.

"This," he said, turning the book for her to see. "The O'Bruaidar dagger."

"Yes," she whispered as she saw the familiar double-edged blade with the jeweled hilt. "That is the dagger and this is the picture you showed me."

"Then ye must be the lass who traveled back in time to set things right for the O'Bruaidars."

This time her mouth dropped open so far it hurt. "H-how did you know?" she stammered.

He turned a page in the book and pushed it toward her. "Read," he said.

Fiona pulled the lamp closer and bent over the yellowed pages. Someone had written carefully by hand, painstakingly crafting every letter. She began to read aloud:

"And so the tale was tolde o' the fey lass named Fiona who went through time to save the O'Bruaidars from ruin. Using the magic o' the O'Bruaidar dagger, she passed through the Druid stones at the mid o' night to rescue the beloved Miles O'Bruaidar, a favorite amonge the fairies. But when she arrived, her magic was gone. Stripped o' her birthright, she had naught except her courage and wits to guide her as she helped bring the fine son home where he belonged. So pleased were the fairies wi' her efforts that they swept her back to her own world, restoring her magic and bestowing lavish gifts and gold upon her. Fiona tolde them she had no need for gifts, but one day would have a single request, a request that could be granted only by a member o' the Gogarty family, an honorable family that had long served the O'Bruaidars. Legend says that she wille bring a lifetime o' good health and fortune to the one who grants her wish. And so, the tale is tolde."

Fiona stopped reading and looked up at Seamus. "God bless you, Shaun," she whispered.

A thousand thoughts whirled through her head, not the least of which was that she had somehow become inextricably tied to the legend of the O'Bruaidar dagger.

"And you believe this?" she asked, more than just a little unsettled. "You believe that I am this Fiona?"

His intelligent eyes appraised her curiously. "I wasn't certain. But just in case, I sent ye to the Druid circles, hoping ye would find what ye sought there. And now ye have returned, so mayhap my luck is changing for the better. Are ye the Fiona o' the legend, lass?"

Fiona smiled, the weight of the world seeming to slide from her shoulders. "That I am."

Seamus stretched out a hand to her, and Fiona reached across the table to grasp it firmly. For a moment they held hands tightly, as if forming a bridge across time and space. Legend and magic.

Finally Fiona spoke. "Well then, Mr. Gogarty, I suggest we test the mettle of the legend. Now, as strange as it may sound, this is what I need you to do for me."

Near Cookstown, Northern Ireland
Eight months later

Fiona rolled down the window of the rental car and let the crisp spring breeze rush inside as she speed along the road. She breathed deeply, marveling at the fresh, clean scent of the Irish countryside.

"Lianna, be a good lass and hand me one o' those brown things, would ye?" Ian asked. He sat in the passenger seat, his long legs wedged up against the dashboard. Lianna, who sat in the back, set aside her handheld electronic game and rustled about in a bag.

"They are called truffles," Fiona said, adjusting her sunglasses on her nose. "And pass one this way, too, please."

Lianna handed over two truffles and Ian popped one in Fiona's mouth before eating one himself.

" 'Tis no contest. These are much better than coffee," he declared, and Fiona smiled.

It had been seven months since they'd last been in Northern Ireland. Shortly after her visit to Seamus Gogarty at the antiques shop, Ian had been transferred to a hospital in Dublin, where he'd stayed for another month before being well enough to travel. Fiona and Lianna had waited for him at a nearby bed-and-breakfast, visiting him every day and trying in hushed tones to explain what had happened to him.

Lianna, drawing on the miracle of childhood acceptance, managed to quickly accept the new time in which she lived and began rapidly picking up the English language.

Ian, on the other hand, was having a much more difficult time of it. Slowly, Fiona brought him around, explaining as much as she could and filling in the gaps of history.

Eventually, they made the journey to England without incident, thanks to the two birth certificates Seamus Gogarty managed to produce for Ian and Lianna. Fiona had paid Seamus an enormous sum of money for the documents, fulfilling at least part of the legend's promise.

Fiona had sequestered Ian and Lianna at her father's estate in the Welsh countryside, where they had spent the past several months using Fiona's sizable inheritance to recuperate and readjust to their new lives. Now they were back in Northern Ireland to visit the Beaghmore Stone Circles and determine whether it was safe to try a return trip to the seventeenth century. They had discussed the possibility at great length and decided that in spite of the danger, they would give it a try. None of them wanted to leave Miles and Faith alone at the mercy of Oliver Cromwell and history. But this time, they fervently agreed, if the return trip went as expected, they would stay in the seventeenth century for good.

Fiona glanced over at Ian, who pulled out his sketchbook and started drawing, his large hands wielding breathtaking skill as he drew across the paper in bold, masterful strokes. She had been amazed to discover this artistic talent, realizing it had been one of the many things about him that she'd never known. For him, it had been a therapy of sorts, his way of coping with the new situation. Fiona knew enough about art to realize that although his efforts were somewhat unrefined, he had enormous potential.

"How can you draw with all these bloody bumps and jars?" she asked him.

"If ye willna let me drive, what else am I supposed to do?" He glanced over at her with a grin that nearly stopped her heart.

She grinned back at him. Despite all that had happened, he had managed well enough. Dressed in a black T-shirt, blue jeans, and, of all things, cowboy boots, he was by far the sexiest man she had ever come across. His dark blond hair had been cut short and his chin and face were cleanly shaven. He looked completely at ease in this century, yet Fiona understood enough of his inner turmoil to know it wasn't that simple.

She knew he missed the physical demands of his century, and in an attempt to compensate, she had introduced him to the sport of rugby. He'd become such a local sensation that there was even talk of him trying to turn pro. But Ian just laughed at all the attention, not wanting to spend a single night away from her and Lianna.

Those nights were magical indeed, spent locked in each other's arms, thankful for the second chance they'd been given. Their lovemaking was passionate and tender, hungry and fulfilling.

Fiona turned her attention back to the road and watched the Irish countryside flash past. Her hands gripped the steering wheel, and a flash of gold caught her eye. She glanced down at her wedding ring—Ian's ring. They had been married on Valentine's Day at a small local parish with only Lianna and the pastor's wife present. It had been the most beautiful day of her life. She had married the man of her dreams. In all truth, it didn't matter any longer whether they lived in the past or the present, as long as they were together.

"The stones are just up ahead," Fiona said, and Ian closed his sketchbook. She heard Lianna set aside her game and lean forward as a palpable tension filled the car.

One kilometer later, Fiona pressed lightly on the brakes and turned right into the small carpark for the Beaghmore Stone Circles. She came to a screeching halt when she saw several police cars parked nearby.

"Oh, no!" she gasped, wrenching open the door and jumping out.

"What is it?" Ian asked, extracting his large frame from the car and looking up at the hill. A perplexed expression creased his handsome face as he studied her. "Fiona, what happened?"

Without answering, she darted up the stone steps. When she reached the top, she stopped in horrified shock. The stone circles had been badly vandalized— many had been knocked over and broken, some spray-painted, and others were missing completely. The Dragon's Teeth configuration had suffered the most damage, with upturned earth and paint every-where. Several constables stood around talking, while one of them took pictures of the carnage. Police tape cordoned off most of the area.

Breathless, Fiona took a wobbly step forward. One of the constables looked over in surprise when he saw her.

"Hey, miss, what are ye doin'?" he called out.

Dazed, she looked at the stone circles. "What happened here?" she asked, but her voice came out as no more than a whisper.

Ian and Lianna joined her at the top of the stairs, both of them looking around in wonder. Ian linked fingers with her and put an arm around Lianna.

"Fiona?" he inquired softly.

Fiona squeezed his hand as the constable strode to-ward them. He had red hair and a beard and looked at them with curious but not unkind eyes. Ian took a step in front of her protectively.

"Sorry, but we've closed the site to tourists," the constable said, eyeing Ian's large frame speculatively. "Can I help ye in some way?"

Fiona swallowed, trying to gather her wits about her. "What happened here?" she asked.

The constable sighed. "The site was vandalized two days ago, and very nearly destroyed. The hooligans knocked o'er the circles, desecrated the cairns, and even carted off a few of the more unusual stone markers."

"No," Fiona whispered, slumping against Ian, who put an arm beneath her elbow to hold her steady.

"Did ye catch who did this?" Ian asked.

"Not yet, but we suspect it was the work of a few local teenagers out after too much drink."

"Can you repair the damage?"

The man shrugged. "I don't see why no'. After all, they can remove the paint and set the stones back up. It will take some time and money, though."

"But what about the stones that are missing?" Fiona piped up.

"Bring in new ones, I suppose. They could bloody well make 'em if they had to. Wi' all the technology today, it shouldn't be too hard to replicate something that looks the same as the old ones."

"But it wouldn't be the same," Fiona said quietly.

"No one would even know the difference," the man replied. "Besides, they are just a bunch o' old stones."

Fiona pressed her lips together tightly, feeling faint. The constable looked at her in concern.

"Is she all right?" he asked Ian. "She looks a wee pale."

"She'll be fine," Ian said, putting an arm firmly around her shoulder. "We'll all be fine."

The constable tipped his head and then turned and walked away. Ian gently led her and Lianna down the stairs. Fiona's heart felt numb. When they reached the car, she turned and pressed her head into Ian's chest. As Ian held her, she began crying. She hadn't realized until that moment how much she had wanted to return. But now, Faith, Shaun, Miles, Father Michael, and the others were gone to her forever. It hadn't seemed so final when they still had the possibility of returning. Now that hope was dashed forever, and the people she loved and left behind were long dead and buried.

"Oh, Ian," she sobbed. "The others are gone to us now. What shall we do?"

"Mayhap we can try it after the site is repaired."

Fiona shook her head through her tears. "Not if some of the stones are missing, and certainly not if the configurations are rearranged. Faith tried it and it didn't work."

Ian exhaled a deep breath. "Well, then, that is it."

He held her close, murmuring soothing words against her hair. She clung to him, her arms wound around his waist. The tears flowed harder.

She had no idea how long she stood there crying, but she finally wiped her eyes and pulled away. Lianna stood huddled near the car, her own eyes filled with tears. Fiona pulled her into an embrace, hugging her fiercely.

"Thank God, I still have you and Ian," she whispered. "We'll get through this somehow, Lianna. I promise."

The girl nodded but looked worriedly at Ian. Fiona glanced over at him. He stood quietly, his hands shoved in the pockets of his jeans, his broad shoulders slumped. She could see the grief ravaging his eyes. Of all of them, this would be the hardest on him. They would get through it together, but the healing would take some time.

>6

Julie Moffett

"Ian," she said softly, touching his cheek, "we'll figure this out."

"Aye, I know. Can ye drive?"

Fiona took a deep breath and nodded. "Let's get out of here."

Once everyone was in the car, Fiona pulled out of the carpark and headed down the road toward Omagh, where they would stay for the night. She'd driven about two kilometers when she suddenly slammed on the brakes and screeched to a stop.

Ian lurched forward, bracing himself against the dashboard with his hands. "Jesus, Joseph, and Mary!" he exclaimed. "What are ye doing?"

"This," Fiona said, checking the rearview mirror and then throwing the car into reverse. She backed up and pulled over until the car sat just beneath a small wooden sign.

Fiona pointed up at the sign. " 'O'Bruaidar Castle, one-point-five kilometers, next right,'" she read aloud, as if she didn't trust her eyes.

"O'Bruaidar Castle?" Ian repeated in wonder. "I thought ye said the castle didna exist in this century."

"It didn't," Fiona breathed.

Ian looked at her and then back at the sign. "Then let's go see what is there."

Fiona shoved the car in gear. At the next right she turned onto a well-kept dirt road. She drove until they reached a clearing and the castle came into view. She heard Lianna give a surprised gasp from the rear seat, and Ian leaned forward, staring out of the car in wonder. Parts of the north wall had crumbled and one of the two towers was in a state of some disrepair, but other than that, the castle stood as majestic and stately as Fiona remembered.

348

"Castle Dun na Moor," Ian and Fiona murmured at the same time.

Fiona slowed down as she drove up a circular driveway that led to the front of the castle. She pulled the car to the side and everyone got out, gazing in awe at the looming structure.

"May I help you?" a voice behind Fiona said.

She turned to see a slender young man of about thirty, wearing gloves and holding a garden shovel. A straw hat sat slightly askew on his dark head and his blue eyes looked at her first in curiosity and then in surprise.

Ian stepped forward. "Sorry. We didna mean to intrude," he said.

"Yes," Fiona quickly interjected. "It's just that we saw the sign for Castle Dun na Moor and thought it might be open to the public."

The young man stared at her oddly for a moment and then smiled. "Well, I haven't heard anyone use the real name o' the castle for years. It's been known around these parts as the O'Bruaidar castle for so long that we simply stopped using the other."

Fiona flushed. "Yes, well, we...ah...have a personal interest in the castle."

He lifted a dark eyebrow and took the hat off his head. "How intriguing. May I introduce myself? My name is Michael O'Bruaidar. I am the owner of the castle."

Fiona's mouth gaped open and she unabashedly stared at him. His eyes were a deep blue, his mouth chiseled and wide. Quite handsome, actually.

"You are an O'Bruaidar?" she asked dumbly.

He grinned. "Aye, but I am."

Fiona stumbled about for words, afraid he would

think her daft if she blurted out something bizarre. "Could you tell us a little about the castle?" she finally asked. "I mean, if it wouldn't be too much of a bother."

He set down the shovel and took off the gloves. "I'd be delighted," he said, motioning her to follow. "We don't have many visitors these days. Please join me for some tea."

"Oh, no, we wouldn't want to impose," Fiona protested.

"I insist," Michael said. "I needed to take a break anyway. Please, do come in."

Fiona glanced at Ian, who shrugged. Turning, they followed him inside the castle and stopped in the entranceway as he spoke with a middle-aged woman with gray hair.

"This is my housekeeper, Lucy," he said. "I don't believe I caught your names."

Fiona flushed when she realized her manners had all but disappeared. "So sorry," she started when Ian smoothly interrupted.

"I'm Ian Maclaren," he said. "This is my wife Fiona, and our daughter Lianna."

Fiona felt a warm glow when Ian introduced her as his wife. She smiled gratefully at him when she suddenly noticed both Michael and Lucy staring at her strangely. Then Lucy dipped her head politely and disappeared down a corridor. Fiona blinked, wondering if she had just imagined their odd expressions.

"Lucy will bring us tea in a moment," Michael said, motioning toward a door. "Please, let's retire to the parlor."

They entered a small chamber cozily decorated with overstuffed, inviting armchairs, throw pillows, and thick throw rugs on the stone floor. A fire blazed in the hearth, and Fiona realized that although it was a warm spring day outside, inside the castle was quite chilly. She crossed the room to the hearth and held out her hands. Ian and Lianna sank into nearby chairs.

Michael joined her at the hearth. "So, ye want to know more about the castle?" he asked in his soft Irish brogue.

"Yes, please," Fiona replied. "If you wouldn't mind."

"I don't mind at all. I rather enjoy talking about my family history." He picked up a poker and stirred the logs as he began speaking.

"Well, the castle was built in the fourteenth century by Douglass O'Bruaidar, and a formidable man was he. It survived many a war, including the invasion o' Oliver Cromwell."

"Do you know what happened to the inhabitants of the castle during Cromwell's campaign?" she asked him. "I mean, in particular, Miles O'Bruaidar and his wife."

Michael looked at her, his eyes curious. "I see ye have, indeed, read about the castle and are familiar wi' the castle's most famous inhabitants."

"Most famous?"

"Aye. Certainly ye've heard that Miles O'Bruaidar was the famous general called the Irish Lion, named after the family's coat of arms. His resistance against the English is legendary in these parts."

"Miles was a general, ye say?" Ian asked, and Fiona turned to see him cocking an eyebrow in amusement.

"Aye. 'Tis said he single-handedly led the resistance at Monaghan in sixteen hundred and fifty-one," Michael continued. "He served in many campaigns before he and his wife fled west to Connemara, where he continued to organize and train more men in the resistance effort against the English. He was one o' the most wanted men in Ireland during the latter part o' the seventeenth century."

"And what of his wife, Faith?" Fiona asked. "Did she also live...ah...a long time?"

" 'Tis most curious, indeed," Michael said, going over to one of the armchairs and sitting down. "Faith O'Bruaidar was English, ye know. Taking such a wife certainly had to have been an enormous risk for a man like Miles, especially at that particular time. Unfortunately, no' many details about their mysterious courtship and marriage exist."

"I'll bet," Fiona murmured under her breath.

Lucy took that moment to enter with tea and delicious-smelling scones. She poured everyone a cup and, after exchanging a quick glance with Michael, exited the room.

Michael picked up his tea and took a sip before continuing. "It is certainly intriguing as to why a lone Englishwoman was in Ireland at that time. Some historical accounts indicate she was thought to be an Irish spy, while others believed she worked for the English all along. Yet, no matter why she came to Ireland, in the end, she proved to be singularly devoted to her husband and to Ireland."

Michael offered the plate of scones to Lianna. The girl eagerly accepted one and bit into the pastry with a look of sheer childish delight on her face. Fiona smiled proudly at her. She looked so pretty in a blue and white dress with dark blue leggings, her red hair cut to her shoulders and tied back neatly in a ponytail.

Michael set down the plate. "Thankfully, both Faith

and Miles lived to a ripe old age," he continued cheer-fully. "In fact, they are buried here on the grounds of the castle in the family crypt."

Fiona swallowed hard, and Ian gave her a compassionate glance. "How did the castle manage to survive Cromwell's occupation?" he asked, leaning forward in his chair. "Didn't the English control the area here for at least some period o' time?"

"Aye, they did. There has been much speculation about that fact. Some historians believe the castle might have been spared because Miles's wife was English. Others believe the castle was simply no' that important to the English, since it is no' in a particularly strategic location. Yet others believe the castle was kept intact in order to lure Miles back and perhaps capture him again."

"Again?" Fiona asked, trying to absorb all he had just said. She sat down in a chair next to Lianna and picked up a teacup.

Michael took a bite of his scone and chewed, dabbing at his mouth with the corner of a napkin. "Miles was captured during a skirmish in Dundrum and taken to the city of Cavan for execution. He was reportedly saved during a daring rescue led by members o' his own family, including his wife Faith, his close friend, a Welshman named Ian, and a mysterious woman who was said to be kin to Miles's wife."

Ian choked on the piece of scone he had just put in his mouth, and Fiona quickly stood, thumping him on the back.

"He wasna a Welshman," Ian said, between coughs. "He was a Scot."

Michael looked at him in surprise, and Fiona quickly intervened. "What my husband means to say

353

is that the name Ian sounds so… Scottish. Since that happens to be his name as well, and he is Scottish… well, you can see the logical extrapolation."

She smiled brightly, hoping Michael would simply think them odd and let it pass. Ian glared at her but wisely remained silent.

Michael looked between the two of them curiously but said nothing. Fiona seized the moment to steer the conversation in another direction.

"So, you say the English occupied the castle for some time," she said, returning to her chair. "Did Miles and Faith ever return here to live?"

"They did, indeed. Nearly twelve years to the day they left, Faith, Miles, and their fifteen children returned to Castle Dun na Moor."

Fiona nearly spewed out the tea she had just put in her mouth. "Sorry, but did you say fifteen children?" she said, after managing to swallow painfully.

"Aye, 'twas one o' their greatest legacies. Miles and Faith were no' only known for their spirited defense o' Ireland—they were also considered great humanitarians. They adopted fifteen Irish children, all o' them orphaned by the ravages o' Cromwell's war."

"F-fifteen children?" Fiona stammered, her mind racing wildly. Adopted children? Could it be that Faith and Miles had not been able to have any children after all? If so, they had not let that stop them. Employing their wisdom and love, these two remarkable people had reached out and gathered orphaned children to their bosom, devoting their lives not only to Ireland but to her children as well.

"Faith was a mother," Fiona whispered in awe. "A mother fifteen times over."

Ian looked over, and she saw the wonder and pride

in his eyes. "They were the greatest o' people," he said simply.

"Yes, they were," Michael said, standing. "Of course, I'm rather prejudiced since I am a direct descendant o' their adopted son Kieran. Would you care to see the family portrait?"

"You have a portrait?" Fiona asked, her eyes widening. "Of the entire family?"

" 'Tis quite a large canvas, and we've placed it o'er the hearth in the Great Hall. I'd be happy to show it to ye, however, if ye are interested."

Fiona stood. "Yes, please," she said eagerly. "We would like that very much."

Silently they followed him down the corridor and into the Great Hall. Fiona heard Lianna gasp in surprise as they approached the hearth, and she gripped the girl's hand tightly. When they were directly beneath the portrait, Fiona slowly lifted her gaze and let it settle on Faith's face.

Faith sat proudly in the center of the portrait with Miles standing behind her, a hand resting lightly on her shoulder. She held an infant in her arms, and children of all ages knelt and sat scattered about her feet. When Fiona saw the peaceful, contented look on her cousin's face as she gazed down at her brood of children, her eyes filled with tears.

"She made her peace," Fiona said softly. "She lived her life as she wanted, surrounded by the people she loved."

Ian stared at the portrait for some time before he approached the hearth's mantel. "What's this?" he asked Michael, pointing to an object encased in a glass box lined with velvet.

" 'Tis the O'Bruaidar double-edged dagger," Michael explained, walking over to Ian. "It has been handed down to the O'Bruaidar women throughout the centuries."

Fiona's eyes widened as she approached the hearth for a look. Indeed, the dagger she had once held in her own hands lay nestled in green velvet. The small flaw near the hilt of the blade still existed, as did the damage to the tip of the blade. The only difference was that the sparkling jewels were still embedded in the handle and the overall condition of the dagger appeared much better.

"Amazing," Fiona breathed.

"There is quite a legend surrounding the dagger," Michael said. " 'Tis said that the dagger was enchanted in honor o' its first owner, Isabel O'Bruaidar. Isabel was believed to have been a fairy lass who had to give up her immortal existence when she fell in love with the handsome Kieran O'Bruaidar. The fey folk felt sorry for the lass and fashioned the dagger complete wi' a wee bit o' enchantment. According to legend, the magic o' the dagger is at its best when used at midnight at a spot considered holy to the Druids."

"Really?" Fiona said with interest, and Ian rolled his eyes at her when Michael looked away.

"There is some mystery surrounding the dagger," Michael continued. "For example, no one has figured out the strange inscription on the blade. It says *sisters* on one side, and *for always* on the other. Some think it had to do with the mysterious woman who was kin to Faith O'Bruaidar and helped rescue Miles from certain death at the hands o' the English. Others say it was simply a message of love written from one O'Bruaidar woman to the other."

Fiona looked at the dagger and then back at the portrait of Faith and her family. "Personally, I'd go with the first theory," she said with a shrug. "Although the second one works for me, too."

Michael looked at her oddly. "Ye know, there is a tale associated with the dagger that says a woman named Fiona used the dagger to go back in time to help save Miles O'Bruaidar from the English."

Fiona exchanged a glance with Ian and then smiled. "Yes, I've heard the tale."

Michael cleared his throat and then paused, as if debating something. "I rather hesitate to mention this because I fear ye might think I've gone 'round the bend, but might ye no' be a descendant o' this Fiona? The reason I ask is because o' this."

He walked across the chamber to a large wooden hutch and opened a drawer. He pulled out something and returned to where they stood.

He held out a small gilded miniature to Fiona. Fiona took it, inhaling sharply as she looked directly into her own eyes.

Her mouth dropped open in surprise. "It's...it's astonishing," she managed to say.

Ian gently took the miniature from her hand and studied it. Michael looked at her apologetically.

"Ye can see why I asked. There is a striking resemblance between ye and the woman in this portrait. I noticed it immediately when I met ye. Then, when ye said your name was Fiona...well, it just piqued my curiosity."

"Shaun," Ian suddenly said. " 'Twas Shaun."

"Shaun?" Michael said in bewilderment. "Who is Shaun?"

"You think Shaun painted this?" Fiona asked in surprise.

Julie Moffett

Michael took the miniature from Ian's hand. "If ye are wondering about the artist, the name on the back o' the canvas is Gogarty. Seamus Gogarty, the owner o' a nearby antiquities shop, says he believes one o' his ancestors painted this portrait."

"Yes, indeed," Fiona murmured.

"So, do ye think ye might be a decendant of this woman?" Michael asked, gazing at her curiously. "After all, ye did say you had a personal interest in the castle."

Fiona looked at the miniature of herself and then back at Ian and Lianna. Slowly, a smile touched her lips.

"Yes, I think I just might be."

Michael smiled broadly. "Well, then, how fortunate for me that I have found ye. Perhaps someday we can exchange information on our family genealogy."

"Perhaps," Fiona agreed. "Anyway, I'd like to thank you. Our visit here has answered a lot of questions about my...ah...past."

"Aye, we thank ye, sir," Ian said, holding out a hand. "Ye were kind to share your time and knowledge wi' us." Michael took it, and the two men shook hands heartily, continuing to speak in low tones.

The two men and Lianna walked from the Great Hall. Fiona paused to take one last look at the portrait above the hearth and the double-edged dagger that sat gleaming just below it. Her heart felt full. Everything had turned out right—both Faith and the dagger were at last where they belonged. And now, so was she.

"Farewell, Faith," Fiona whispered. "I'm glad you found your happiness."

Fiona turned and left the chamber, her footsteps echoing one by one on the stone floor of Castle Dun na Moor until they finally faded into nothingness.

Epilogue

England
One year later

"Push!"

Fiona pushed mightily, sweat trickling down her temples. Pain jackknifed through her as she gritted her teeth to hold back a scream.

"Just a little bit more. Yes, yes, here comes the baby."

Fiona pushed again and then fell back against the pillow, groaning. She glanced up at Ian, who held her hand in a death grip, his face completely ashen. She hadn't ever seen him look so anxious, even when he faced off with Bradford. Clearly, for men, some things were more frightening than certain death.

"It's a girl," she heard the doctor call out, and her

eyes filled with tears. The baby let out a lusty wail and began wiggling its legs.

Ian released her hand and went to look in wonder at the baby as the nurse wrapped her snuggly in a warm blanket.

"A wee lass," Ian murmured as a broad grin split his face. "Fiona, we have a wee lassie," he boomed. "And she's a bonny one, too, fair-headed like me."

Fiona smiled, laughed, and cried at the same time as the nurse placed the baby at her breast. She gently touched the infant on the cheek, marveling at the miracle of her birth. Ian sat beside her, holding out his finger and chuckling as the baby grabbed it in her fist and squeezed.

"She's beautiful," Fiona whispered. Her heart had never felt so full and contented. "So very beautiful."

Ian leaned over and kissed her on the brow. "And so are ye, Fiona. Now I'm surrounded by three beautiful girls. How lucky can a man get?"

How lucky, indeed? Fiona thought. Life hadn't been easy for them. Money, and a lot of it, had helped. Thank God her father had provided at least that comfort in death, if not in life.

Lianna was thriving now; she had started school and was receiving both speech and occupational therapy to help her catch up to her peers. Despite her deformed hands, she had begun making friends who didn't give a whit about her differences. She had started to blossom into a normal, well-adjusted child.

Ian was taking longer, but his participation on the rugby team and his drawing had given him the opportunity to explore parts of his life he had never known before. They hung his masterpieces about the estate, and Fiona had been trying to convince him to show his work to a friend of hers who owned a small gallery in London.

Still, they had found the most comfort in each other, seeking solace and peace. Nonetheless, Fiona had no illusions; they had a long way to go. But love made a big difference, and it was something she and Ian shared in abundance.

"Well, princess, what shall we call the wee one?" Ian asked as he gazed down at his daughter.

The baby let out a high-pitched cry, and Fiona smiled. "Let's call her Faith."

"Perfect," Ian agreed, flashing her a heart-stopping grin. His eyes were filled with happiness and pride as he leaned over and gave her a lingering kiss.

"What was that for?" she asked, her heart brimming with joy as she looked at him.

"That, *mo gradhach,* is a promise for a lifetime o' love," he replied softly. "No matter *what* time we may be in."

AUTHOR'S NOTE

For those of you not familiar with Irish history in the seventeenth century, I thought I might add a few interesting footnotes.

In January 1649, King Charles I of England was beheaded by his own parliament. Oliver Cromwell, among others of the English parliament, signed his death order. The murder of the king set off a war between England and Scotland that lasted little more than a year and resulted in a punishing defeat for the Scots. The Irish by and large supported Scotland in its fight against Cromwell.

Enraged, Cromwell deployed a huge number of soldiers to Ireland to eradicate royalism and bring the fiercely Catholic country under Protestant control. Although the Irish and many citizens loyal to King Charles resisted, Cromwell's campaigns were largely successful. Within three years, he had most of Ireland under his control.

Most Irish-owned land was confiscated and given to English "adventurers" or people who financed Cromwell's invasion in hope of receiving land as a reward. Irish nobility was largely banned to Connemara or west of the Shannon River. By 1652, the Catholic priesthood was officially banned and many priests were hung.

The Beaghmore Stone Circles do indeed exist just a few kilometers from Cookstown in County Tyrone, Northern Ireland. Fortunately, they have not really been destroyed or looted by vandals. For many years the stone configurations were hidden under a thick blanket of peat bog, but were uncovered by archaeologists in the 1940s.

The site boasts of a remarkable group of seven stone configurations—one of that is fondly referred to as the "Dragon's Teeth." Sharp, jagged rocks are arranged in a circle and jut upward to the sky, resembling the mouth of a beast.

The site also has a dozen or more cairns and a number of other stone monuments which together are believed to have once served as an important druid ceremonial spot. It is believed that many more fascinating discoveries await scientists at Beaghmore.

In the small town of Cavan, an O'Reilly castle really did exist in the seventeenth century. Unfortunately, it was completely destroyed during the fierce fighting for control of the town during Cromwell's campaign.

I have many people to thank for their assistance with the manuscript, but for the sake of brevity, I will thank just a few. My mother, Donna Moffett, and my sister and fellow author, Sandra Parks, spent many, many hours reading and offering invaluable advice and suggestions, often under a time crunch. My critique partner, Beth Fedorko—an excellent author in her own right—also provided a wealth of inimitable knowledge and information, as well as friendship and lots of moral support.

Much thanks also go to those of you who wrote and e-mailed me, asking me to write Fiona's story and wondering whether she ever managed to find Faith. I was inundated with letters and was greatly touched by your interest. *Across a Moonswept Moor* is my gift to you, and I sincerely hope you enjoy it.

For those of you who haven't read Miles and Faith's story and would like to, it is told in my novel *A Double-Edged Blade,* also published by Leisure Books. The novel was originally printed in 1996 and reissued in March 2000.

I greatly enjoy hearing from readers, writers and booksellers. If you would like to contact me, you can visit my website: www.tlt.com/authors/jmoffett.htm. If you would like a copy of my newsletter containing information about upcoming releases or some bookmarks, please send a legal-sized self-addressed stamped envelope to: P.O. Box 10001, Alexandria, VA 22310.